Joseph Conrad

THE SECRET SHARER
and other stories

Selected and edited by JOHN LAWTON

PHŒNIX

A PHOENIX PAPERBACK

This edition first published in Great Britain by
Phoenix Paperbacks in 1999
Selection, Introduction and other critical apparatus
© Phoenix Paperbacks 1999

Orion Publishing Group
Orion House
5 Upper Saint Martin's Lane
London WC2H 9EA

Typeset at The Spartan Press Ltd, Lymington, Hants
Printed in Great Britain by
The Guernsey Press Co. Ltd, Guernsey, C.I.

British Library Cataloguing-in-Publication
Data is available on request

ISBN 0 75380 722 X

Contents

Note on the Author v
Note on the Editor vi
Introduction vii

An Outpost of Progress 3
Karain: A Memory 26
Youth: A Narrative 63
Amy Foster 93
Falk: A Reminiscence 121
The Secret Sharer: An Episode from the Coast 191

Note on the Author

JOSEPH CONRAD was born Józef Teodor Konrad Nałęcz, only child of Apollo (essayist, dramatist and translator of Shakespeare) and Evelina Korzienowski in 1857, in the Polish Ukraine – at that time a province of the Russian Empire. Shortly before his fifth birthday his father, an active Polish nationalist, was exiled to Russia – his mother followed, taking the young Conrad with her. Exile was worsened by the death of his mother when he was seven – his was a solitary, literary childhood. The end of exile was followed quickly by the death of his father, and at the age of eleven Conrad was placed in the benign care of his maternal uncle Tadeusz Bobrowski. At fifteen, on a visit to Venice, he saw the sea for the first time and in 1874, supported by an allowance from his uncle, speaking fluent French but little English, left for Marseilles in search of his first berth. His early voyages took him to the West Indies, the Mediterranean and Australia – he did not land in the East Indies (the setting of much of his fiction) until 1883. By this time he had moved to the British Merchant Service. Long before he had need of a pen name the inability of his shipmates to spell or pronounce Korzienowski had led to him becoming "Joseph Conrad". He rose quickly from able seaman to captain – qualifying in 1886 – the same year he became a naturalized British citizen. About this time he began to write – entering a *Tit-Bits* competition with an early version of the story "The Black Mate". Conrad's only command in eighteen years at sea was of the barque *Otago* during 1888–9 – which he captained down the Gulf of Siam to Australia and across the Indian Ocean to Mauritius.

At the end of 1889 Conrad began his first novel *Almayer's Folly*. It took him five years to complete, travelling in manuscript up the Congo, to Australia and on a long-awaited visit to Poland. In 1894 events converged to make him a writer – his uncle died, leaving him a small legacy, the novel was accepted for publication, he met Edward Garnett, who was to become the greatest encouragement to his career – and, try as he might, after leaving his last berth on a transatlantic steamer he could not find another job at sea. Even as late as 1898 with *An Outcast of the Islands* and *Tales of Unrest* also in print, *The Nigger of the Narcissus* in proof, *Heart of Darkness* in progress and a wife and child to support, Conrad still applied for a berth. None was offered.

In 1896 he had married Jessie George, a former typist fifteen years his younger. The marriage bore two sons and lasted Conrad's lifetime, despite the criticism that it was an intellectual and social mismatch, and despite the single-minded dedication to his work that made Conrad a remote and probably difficult man, often utterly oblivious to the domestic life around him. Conrad's health was permanently damaged by his time in the Congo, and Jessie was left a semi-invalid after a fall in 1904.

The critical success of Conrad's early, prolific output was not matched by financial success – but he quickly became part of "literary England", settling in Kent, close to H. G. Wells, Henry James, Ford Madox Ford, Stephen Crane, and W. H. Hudson. His agent J. B. Pinker frequently bailed him out with loans and "advances", and serialization of his work in magazines such as *Blackwood's* became a mainstay of his income. In 1910 he was awarded a Civil List pension. In 1914, nineteen years after the publication of his first novel, *Chance* finally made him a bestseller. Conrad, approaching sixty, now found himself with an international reputation, hugely popular in the USA and translated into most European languages. He declined a knighthood from the 1924 Labour government shortly before his death, from a heart attack, on August 3rd that year.

There is a long Conrad legacy – writers who are aligned with or align themselves with his work in creating the mixture of introspection and action that seems so typical of the best of Conrad – Graham Greene being the most obvious example, and more recently Paul Theroux, Nicolas Freeling and the late Brian Moore.

Note on the Editor

JOHN LAWTON is the author of three novels – *Black Out*, *Old Flames* and *A Little White Death*. He has also edited H. G. Wells's *The Time Machine* and D. H. Lawrence's *Poems* for Everyman.

Introduction

". . . To make you feel . . . before all, to make you *see*."
                    Preface to *The Nigger of the Narcissus*

"And so you make up these tales on your own. How do they ever
come into your head?" . . .
    I explained that one generally got a hint for a tale.
    "What sort of a hint?"   *The Partner*

It may be a far older adage than I think – but I have a recollection
of Beryl Bainbridge recently offering advice to young writers
along the lines of "Don't write an autobiography until you're old
– your life is your capital as a novelist." Joseph Conrad stored up
his capital until the age of thirty-seven and eked it out thereafter
in a large body of fiction, about half of which drew heavily for its
sources upon the life he had led up to that age. The line between
Conrad the merchant sailor and Conrad the writer is clear if
accidental. To invert the words of Arthur Ransome, he *did* mean
to go to sea, but he never meant to settle ashore. That he did so
was not the outcome of any definite decision on Conrad's part,
although the fact that his last commission was on a ship which
never managed to clear the harbour is a symbolism that would
scarcely have been wasted on him (once in print he never sailed
professionally again), any less than the disasters of his first voyage
to the East, which formed the basis of the story "Youth".

It's clear, even at a first reading, that Conrad upholds and
elaborates some strong moral scheme. The Known in Conrad is
human (usually male) – known, that is, by deeds and the morals
that govern them. The rest is nature, the Unknown – hostile, dark
and, as is most often said in Conrad, "obscure". The obscurity of
nature necessitates man's morality – without it we are nothing
and nature will take back all we have gained as a species. The
Conrad hero is male (invariably – his women are snipped from
cardboard), ordinary (arguably), but thrust into extraordinary
circumstances, into that trying, unwanted, treacherous condi-

tion, heroism. The action of an ordinary man in extraordinary circumstances might be said to be "the Conrad plot" – the basis and hence the test of his evolved morality.

So, it surprises me how often this can be misinterpreted. Rather than bash another critic, let me bash film-makers instead – a lot of Conrad's work has been filmed, seems in fact to lend itself to dramatization – *Victory, Nostromo, The Secret Agent* (at least three times), *An Outcast of the Islands, The Secret Sharer,* "Amy Foster" (twice) and *Lord Jim.* The film of *Lord Jim* misconstrues the hero – Jim is played by Peter O'Toole, only a couple of films after *Lawrence of Arabia.* It seems inescapable someone saw a parallel between T. E. Lawrence and Jim, each builders of empires, of sorts – but Lawrence was, above all, an extraordinary man, if not the most extraordinary Englishman of the twentieth century; Jim isn't and nor are any of Conrad's other heroes, and therein lies the point. Conrad's ordinary heroes come from commonality, obscurity – that word again, part of a Conradian vocabulary, a chain of words such as "destiny, toil, craft, fellowship" which, however often or not they occur in these stories, pepper his work as emphatically as that other Conrad word "illusion" on which "Youth" ends. Typhoons, gun-running and burning ships notwithstanding, Conrad pointedly denied heroism or adventure in his own youth – "its colouring wears the sober hue of hard work and exacting calls of duty, things which in themselves are not much charged with a feeling of romance." (Preface to *Within the Tides*) – and in the denial is the reinforcement. This is the world in which the Conrad hero moves – hard toil and exacting duty, forged in the craft of seamanship. Torn from these – the only things that matter – to what does he return? More "obscurity"? Myth? Whatever it is, it isn't peace. The only peace in Conrad's work is to be found in the occasional but very effective framework of Marlow the storyteller recalling in some Thamesside tranquility the illusions ("Youth") and horrors (*Heart of Darkness*) of his youth. Within that frame what Conrad depicts is, unequivocally, a world without peace.

Of the six stories in this collection, three are set at sea – "Youth", "The Secret Sharer" and "Falk", even though "Falk" is set in harbour most of the time – one up an African river – "An Outpost of Progress" – one in the Eastern archipelago – "Karain" – and one in England – "Amy Foster", whose central character is the survivor of a shipwreck – in one way or another ships and sailing underlie every tale – and in every tale is a crisis, a crime or a disaster – individuals, and in "Amy Foster" society, are tested. There's a vital point to be made on the difference between sail and steam. Marlow and the unnamed narrator of "The Secret Sharer" both serve on sailing ships and the fact of them so doing is instrumental in the moral course of the tale – Falk, that most ambiguous of heroes, commands a steam tug. Under sail the morality of fellowship is created out of "exacting duty and obscure toil", as Conrad might have put it, "the wrestling of men with the might of their creator . . . without the amenities and consolations of life" as, in a burst of high flown prose, he did put it in 1912. It isn't in steam, and there is throughout Conrad's sea tales a sense of *fin de siècle*, of the ending of an era made visible in the clash of two technologies – as though sail were knowable, human if you like, and steam isn't. Falk has retreated in his self-denial and self-imposed misanthropy to the most basic form of seamanship, running a tug at exorbitant rates and exploiting fellow sailors. And it's interesting to note that the voyage that changed him for ever, that pushed his morality to breaking point, was on "an iron steamer of most respectable origin . . . the first steamer ever launched there" whose "propeller dropped off". It's too crude, it's missing the point, to say this would not happen under sail – Conrad's sailing ships encounter fire upon calm upon storm – but it's also impossible to ignore the almost mocking simplicity of the statement – " . . . somewhere halfway between Good Hope and New Zealand the tail-shaft broke and the propeller dropped off". The ship drifts "out of men's knowledge" – physically and philosophically, what binds men together now falls apart, the crew are pitted one against the other for survival. Contrast this (and I'm trying not to give away the plot) with, for just one example, the scene aboard the *Judea* in "Youth", where Marlow, at this age recklessly heroic, goes back to the burning ship to find the crew calmly sharing a last meal before the raging inferno that had once been the ship's cargo of coal. Who is the hero? Falk the ruthless? Marlow the bold? Or an unnamed crew of worn-out sailors eating bread and cheese and swilling stout? The Conrad hero is a hero only by dint of belonging – in belonging is the only freedom.

"Amy Foster" is about the failure of belonging. It's a portrait of the English at their most miserable, nor is it wholly unrealistic. It's starkly tragic – so poignant that it seems impossible not to wonder how much of Conrad's own feelings of loss in exile he put into this tale of a Mitteleuropean peasant stranded on his adoptive Kent coast. "Amy Foster" is Conrad's English world rejecting the refugee he surely felt himself to be. It's a necessary reminder that Conrad is not Marlow, Marlow is not Conrad, and that beneath Conrad there was always Korzienowski, the name with which he continued to sign any letter to family or friends on the Continent. Conrad, according to his first biographer, G. Jean-Aubry, always spoke English with a French accent – and his mentor, Edward Garnett, recalled listening to Conrad reading aloud, to a man who had learnt his English as much off the page as by the ear, who knew the precise use of every word better than most Englishmen but, on occasion, had no idea how to pronounce them. "Amy Foster" is a story about tensions – the attraction and fear of the unknown – the weight of earth, the lightness of being – about not quite being English, about being Polish, and at that without Poland even getting a mention.

Note

"An Outpost of Progress" and "Karain" appeared in volume form in *Tales of Unrest* (1898), "Youth" in *Youth: a Narrative*; and *Two Other Stories* (1902), "Amy Foster" and "Falk" in *Typhoon and Other Stories* (1903) and "The Secret Sharer" in *'Twixt Land and Sea* (1912). The dates at the end of each story represent the year of composition and the year of first publication, which, in every case but "Falk" means a magazine. I am indebted to the work of Jocelyn Baines and Samuel Hynes in dating these stories.

JOHN LAWTON

THE SECRET SHARER
and other stories

An Outpost of Progress

I

There were two white men in charge of the trading station. Kayerts, the chief, was short and fat; Carlier, the assistant, was tall, with a large head and a very broad trunk perched upon a long pair of thin legs. The third man on the staff was a Sierra Leone nigger, who maintained that his name was Henry Price. However, for some reason or other, the natives down the river had given him the name of Makola, and it stuck to him through all his wanderings about the country. He spoke English and French with a warbling accent, wrote a beautiful hand, understood bookkeeping, and cherished in his innermost heart the worship of evil spirits. His wife was a negress from Loanda, very large and very noisy. Three children rolled about in sunshine before the door of his low, shed-like dwelling. Makola, taciturn and impenetrable, despised the two white men. He had charge of a small clay storehouse with a dried-grass roof, and pretended to keep a correct account of beads, cotton cloth, red kerchiefs, brass wire, and other trade goods it contained. Besides the storehouse and Makola's hut, there was only one large building in the cleared ground of the station. It was built neatly of reeds, with a verandah on all the four sides. There were three rooms in it. The one in the middle was the living-room, and had two rough tables and a few stools in it. The other two were the bedrooms for the white men. Each had a bedstead and a mosquito net for all furniture. The plank floor was littered with the belongings of the white men; open half-empty boxes, torn wearing apparel, old boots; all the things dirty, and all the things broken, that accumulate mysteriously round untidy men. There was also another dwelling-place some distance away from the buildings. In it, under a tall cross much out of the perpendicular, slept the man who had seen the beginning of all this; who had planned and had watched the construction of this outpost of progress. He had been, at home, an unsuccessful painter who, weary of pursuing fame on an empty stomach, had gone out there through high protections. He had been the first chief of that station. Makola had watched the energetic artist die of fever in the just finished house with his usual kind of "I told you so" indifference. Then, for a time, he dwelt alone with his family, his account books, and the Evil Spirit that rules the lands under the equator. He got on very well with his god. Perhaps he had propitiated him by a promise of more white men to play with, by and by. At any rate the director of the Great Trading Company, coming up in a steamer that resembled an enormous sardine box with a flat-roofed shed erected on it, found the station in good order, and Makola as usual quietly diligent. The director had the cross put up over the first agent's grave, and appointed Kayerts to the post. Carlier was told off as second in charge. The director was a man ruthless and efficient, who at times, but very imperceptibly, indulged in grim humour. He made a speech to Kayerts and Carlier, pointing out to them the promising aspect of their station. The nearest trading-post was about three hundred miles away. It was an exceptional opportunity for them to distinguish themselves and to earn percentages on the trade. This appointment was a favour done to beginners. Kayerts was moved almost to tears by his director's kindness. He would, he said, by doing his best, try to justify the flattering confidence, &c., &c. Kayerts had been in the Administration of the Telegraphs, and knew how to express himself correctly. Carlier, an ex-non-commissioned officer of cavalry in an army guaranteed from harm by several European Powers, was less impressed If there were commissions to get, so much the better; and, trailing a sulky glance over the river, the forests, the impenetrable bush that seemed to cut off the station from the rest of the world, he muttered between his teeth, "We shall see, very soon."

Next day, some bales of cotton goods and a few cases of provisions having been thrown on shore, the sardine-box steamer went off, not to return for another six months. On the deck the director touched his cap to the two agents, who stood on the bank waving their hats, and turning to an old servant of the Company on his passage to headquarters, said, "Look at those two imbeciles. They must be mad at home to send me such specimens. I told those fellows to plant a vegetable garden, build new storehouses and fences, and construct a landing-stage. I bet nothing will be done! They won't know how to begin. I always thought the station on this river useless, and they just fit the station!"

"They will form themselves there," said the old stager with a quiet smile.

"At any rate, I am rid of them for six months," retorted the director.

The two men watched the steamer round the bend, then, ascending arm in arm the slope of the bank, returned to the station. They had been in this vast and dark country only a very short time, and as yet always in the midst of other white men, under the eye and guidance of their superiors. And now, dull as they were to the subtle influences of surroundings, they felt themselves very much alone, when suddenly left unassisted to face the wilderness; a wilderness rendered more strange, more incomprehensible by the mysterious glimpses of the vigorous life it contained. They were two perfectly insignificant and incapable individuals, whose existence is only rendered possible through the high organization of civilized crowds. Few men realize that their life, the very essence of their character, their capabilities and their audacities, are only the expression of their belief in the safety of their surroundings. The courage, the composure, the confidence; the emotions and principles; every great and every insignificant thought belongs not to the individual but to the crowd: to the crowd that believes blindly in the irresistible force of its institutions and of its morals, in the power of its police and of its opinion. But the contact with pure unmitigated savagery, with primitive nature and primitive man, brings sudden and profound trouble into the heart. To the sentiment of being alone of one's kind, to the clear perception of the loneliness of one's thoughts, of one's sensations – to the negation of the habitual, which is safe, there is added the affirmation of the unusual, which is dangerous; a suggestion of things vague, uncontrollable, and repulsive, whose discomposing intrusion excites the imagination and tries the civilized nerves of the foolish and the wise alike.

Kayerts and Carlier walked arm in arm, drawing close to one another as children do in the dark; and they had the same, not altogether unpleasant, sense of danger which one half suspects to be imaginary. They chatted persistently in familiar tones. "Our station is prettily situated," said one. The other assented with enthusiasm, enlarging volubly on the beauties of the situation.

Then they passed near the grave. "Poor devil!" said Kayerts. "He died of fever, didn't he?" muttered Carlier, stopping short. "Why," retorted Kayerts, with indignation, "I've been told that the fellow exposed himself recklessly to the sun. The climate here, everybody says, is not at all worse than at home, as long as you keep out of the sun. Do you hear that, Carlier? I am chief here, and my orders are that you should not expose yourself to the sun!" He assumed his superiority jocularly, but his meaning was serious. The idea that he would, perhaps, have to bury Carlier and remain alone, gave him an inward shiver. He felt suddenly that this Carlier was more precious to him here, in the centre of Africa, than a brother could be anywhere else. Carlier, entering into the spirit of the thing, made a military salute and answered in a brisk tone, "Your orders shall be attended to, chief!" Then he burst out laughing, slapped Kayerts on the back and shouted, "We shall let life run easily here! Just sit still and gather in the ivory those savages will bring. This country has its good points, after all!" They both laughed loudly while Carlier thought: That poor Kayerts; he is so fat and unhealthy. It would be awful if I had to bury him here. He is a man I respect . . . Before they reached the verandah of their house they called one another "my dear fellow".

The first day they were very active, pottering about with hammers and nails and red calico, to put up curtains, make their house habitable and pretty; resolved to settle down comfortably to their new life. For them an impossible task. To grapple effectually with even purely material problems requires more serenity of mind and more lofty courage than people generally imagine. No two beings could have been more unfitted for such a struggle. Society, not from any tenderness, but because of its strange needs, had taken care of those two men, forbidding them all independent thought, all initiative, all departure from routine; and forbidding it under pain of death. They could only live on condition of being machines. And now, released from the fostering care of men with pens behind the ears, or of men with gold lace on the sleeves, they were like those lifelong prisoners who, liberated after many years, do not know what use to make of their freedom. They did not know what use to make of their faculties, being both, through want of practice, incapable of independent thought.

At the end of two months Kayerts often would say, "If it was not for my Melie, you wouldn't catch me here." Melie was his daughter. He had thrown up his post in the Administration of the Telegraphs, though he had been for seventeen years perfectly happy there, to earn a dowry for his girl. His wife was dead, and the child was being brought up by his sisters. He regretted the streets, the pavements, the cafés, his friends of many years; all the things he used to see, day after day; all the thoughts suggested by familiar things – the thoughts effortless, monotonous, and soothing of a Government clerk; he regretted all the gossip, the small enmities, the mild venom, and the little jokes of Government offices. "If I had had a decent brother-in-law," Carlier would remark, "a fellow with a heart, I would not be here." He had left the army and had made himself so obnoxious to his family by his laziness and impudence, that an exasperated brother-in-law had made superhuman efforts to procure him an appointment in the Company as a second-class agent. Having not a penny in the world he was compelled to accept this means of livelihood as soon as it became quite clear to him that there was nothing more to squeeze out of his relations. He, like Kayerts, regretted his old life. He regretted the clink of sabre and spurs on a fine afternoon, the barrack-room witticisms, the girls of garrison towns; but, besides, he had also a sense of grievance. He was evidently a much ill-used man. This made him moody, at times. But the two men got on well together in the fellowship of their stupidity and laziness. Together they did nothing, absolutely nothing, and enjoyed the sense of the idleness for which they were paid. And in time they came to feel something resembling affection for one another.

They lived like blind men in a large room, aware only of what came in contact with them (and of that only imperfectly), but unable to see the general aspect of things. The river, the forest, all the great land throbbing with life, were like a great emptiness. Even the brilliant sunshine disclosed nothing intelligible. Things appeared and disappeared before their eyes in an unconnected and aimless kind of way. The river seemed to come from nowhere and flow nowhither. It flowed through a void. Out of that void, at times, came canoes, and men with spears in their hands would suddenly crowd the yard of the station. They were naked, glossy black, ornamented with snowy shells and glistening brass wire, perfect of limb. They made an uncouth babbling noise when they spoke, moved in a stately manner, and sent quick, wild glances out of their startled, never-resting eyes. Those warriors would squat in long rows, four or more deep, before the verandah, while their chiefs bargained for hours with Makola over an elephant tusk. Kayerts sat on his chair and looked down on the proceedings, understanding nothing. He stared at them with his round blue eyes, called out to Carlier, "Here, look! look at that fellow there – and that other one, to the left. Did you ever see such a face? Oh, the funny brute!"

Carlier, smoking native tobacco in a short wooden pipe, would swagger up twirling his moustaches, and surveying the warriors with haughty indulgence, would say—

"Fine animals. Brought any bone? Yes? It's not any too soon. Look at the muscles of that fellow – third from the end. I wouldn't care to get a punch on the nose from him. Fine arms, but legs no good below the knee. Couldn't make cavalry men of them." And after glancing down complacently at his own shanks, he always concluded: "Pah! Don't they stink! You, Makola! Take that herd over to the fetish" (the storehouse was in every station called the fetish, perhaps because of the spirit of civilization it contained) "and give them up some of the rubbish you keep there. I'd rather see it full of bone than full of rags."

Kayerts approved.

"Yes, yes! Go and finish that palaver over there, Mr Makola. I will come round when you are ready, to weigh the tusk. We must be careful." Then turning to his companion: "This is the tribe that lives down the river; they are rather aromatic. I remember, they had been once before here. D'ye hear that row? What a fellow has got to put up with in this dog of a country! My head is split."

Such profitable visits were rare. For days the two pioneers of trade and progress would look on their empty courtyard in the vibrating brilliance of vertical sunshine. Below the high bank, the silent river flowed on glittering and steady. On the sands in the middle of the stream, hippos and alligators sunned themselves side by side. And stretching away in all directions, surrounding the insignificant cleared spot of the trading post, immense forests, hiding fateful complications of fantastic life, lay in the eloquent silence of mute greatness. The two men understood nothing, cared for nothing but for the passage of days that separated them from the steamer's return. Their predecessor had left some torn books. They took up these wrecks of novels, and, as they had never read anything of the kind before, they were surprised and amused. Then during long days there were interminable and silly discussions about plots and personages. In the centre of Africa they made acquaintance of Richelieu and d'Artagnan, of Hawk's Eye and of Father Goriot, and of many other people. All these imaginary personages became subjects for gossip as if they had been living friends. They discounted their virtues, suspected their motives, decried their successes; were scandalized at their duplicity or were doubtful about their courage. The accounts of crimes filled them with indignation, while tender or pathetic passages moved them deeply. Carlier cleared his throat and said in a soldierly voice, "What nonsense!" Kayerts, his round eyes suffused with tears, his fat cheeks quivering, rubbed his bald head, and declared, "This is a splendid book. I had no idea there were such clever fellows in the world." They also found some old copies of a home paper. That print discussed what it was pleased to call "Our Colonial Expansion" in high-flown language. It spoke much of the rights and duties of civilization, of the sacredness of the civilizing work, and extolled the merits of those who went about bringing light, and faith and commerce to the dark places of the earth. Carlier and Kayerts read, wondered, and began to think better of themselves. Carlier said one evening, waving his hand about, "In a hundred years, there will be perhaps a town here. Quays, and warehouses, and barracks, and – and – billiard-rooms. Civilization, my boy, and virtue – and all. And then, chaps will read that two good fellows, Kayerts and Carlier, were the first civilized men to live in this very spot!" Kayerts nodded, "Yes, it is a consolation to think of that." They seemed to forget their dead predecessor; but, early one day, Carlier went out and replanted the cross firmly. "It used to make me squint whenever I walked that way," he explained to Kayerts over the morning coffee. "It made me squint, leaning over so much. So I just planted it upright. And solid, I promise you! I suspended myself with both hands to the cross-piece. Not a move. Oh, I did that properly."

At times Gobila came to see them. Gobila was the chief of the neighbouring villages. He was a grey-headed savage, thin and black, with a white cloth round his loins and a mangy panther skin hanging over his back. He came up with long strides of his skeleton legs, swinging a staff as tall as himself, and, entering the common room of the station, would squat on his heels to the left of the door. There he sat, watching Kayerts, and now and then making a speech which the other did not understand. Kayerts, without interrupting his occupation, would from time to time say in a friendly manner: "How goes it, you old image?" and they would smile at one another. The two whites had a liking for that old and incomprehensible creature, and called him Father Gobila. Gobila's manner was paternal, and he seemed really to love all white men. They all appeared to him very young, indistinguishably alike (except for stature), and he knew that they were all brothers, and also immortal. The death of the artist, who was the first white man whom he knew intimately, did not disturb this belief, because he was firmly convinced that the white stranger had pretended to die and got himself buried for some mysterious purpose of his own, into which it was useless to inquire. Perhaps it was his way of going home to his own country? At any rate, these were his brothers, and he transferred his absurd affection to them. They returned it in a way. Carlier slapped him on the back, and recklessly struck off matches for his amusement. Kayerts was always ready to let him have a sniff at the ammonia bottle. In short, they behaved just like that other white creature that had hidden itself in a hole in the ground. Gobila considered them attentively. Perhaps they were the same being with the other – or one of them was. He couldn't decide – clear up that mystery; but he remained always very friendly. In consequence of that friendship the women of Gobila's village walked in single file through the reedy grass, bringing every morning to the station, fowls, and sweet potatoes, and palm wine, and sometimes a goat. The Company never provisions the stations fully, and the agents required those local supplies to live. They had them through the good-will of Gobila, and lived well. Now and then one of them had a bout of fever, and the other nursed him with gentle devotion. They did not think much of it. It left them weaker, and their appearance changed for the worse. Carlier was hollow-eyed and irritable. Kayerts showed a drawn, flabby face above the rotundity of his stomach, which gave him a weird aspect. But being constantly together, they did not notice the change that took place gradually in their appearance, and also in their dispositions.

Five months passed in that way.

Then, one morning, as Kayerts and Carlier, lounging in their chairs under the verandah, talked about the approaching visit of the steamer, a knot of armed men came out of the forest and advanced towards the station. They were strangers to that part of the country. They were tall, slight, draped classically from neck to heel in blue fringed cloths, and carried percussion muskets over their bare right shoulders. Makola showed signs of excitement, and ran out of the storehouse (where he spent all his days) to meet these visitors. They came into the court-yard and looked about them with steady, scornful glances. Their leader, a powerful and determined-looking negro with bloodshot eyes, stood in front of the verandah and made a long speech. He gesticulated much, and ceased very suddenly.

There was something in his intonation, in the sounds of the long sentences he used, that startled the two whites. It was like a reminiscence of something not exactly familiar, and yet resembling the speech of civilized men. It sounded like one of those impossible languages which sometimes we hear in our dreams.

"What lingo is that?" said the amazed Carlier. "In the first moment I fancied the fellow was going to speak French. Anyway, it is a different kind of gibberish to what we ever heard."

"Yes," replied Kayerts. "Hey, Makola, what does he say? Where do they come from? Who are they?"

But Makola, who seemed to be standing on hot bricks, answered hurriedly, "I don't know. They come from very far. Perhaps Mrs Price will understand. They are perhaps bad men."

The leader, after waiting for a while, said something sharply to Makola, who shook his head. Then the man, after looking round, noticed Makola's hut and walked over there. The next moment Mrs Makola was heard speaking with great volubility. The other strangers – they were six in all – strolled about with an air of ease, put their heads through the door of the store-room, congregated round the grave, pointed understandingly at the cross, and generally made themselves at home.

"I don't like those chaps – and, I say, Kayerts, they must be from the coast; they've got firearms," observed the sagacious Carlier.

Kayerts also did not like those chaps. They both, for the first time, became aware that they lived in conditions where the unusual may be dangerous, and that there was no power on earth outside of themselves to stand between them and the unusual. They became uneasy, went in and loaded their revolvers. Kayerts said, "We must order Makola to tell them to go away before dark."

The strangers left in the afternoon, after eating a meal prepared for them by Mrs Makola. The immense woman was excited, and talked much with the visitors. She rattled away shrilly, pointing here and there at the forests and at the river. Makola sat apart and watched. At times he got up and whispered to his wife. He accompanied the strangers across the ravine at the back of the station-ground, and returned slowly looking very thoughtful. When questioned by the white men he was very strange, seemed not to understand, seemed to have forgotten French – seemed to have forgotten how to speak altogether. Kayerts and Carlier agreed that the nigger had had too much palm wine.

There was some talk about keeping a watch in turn, but in the evening everything seemed so quite and peaceful that they retired as usual. All night they were disturbed by a lot of drumming in the villages. A deep, rapid roll near by would be followed by another far off – then all ceased. Soon short appeals would rattle out here and there, then all mingle together, increase, become vigorous and sustained, would spread out over the forest, roll through the night, unbroken and ceaseless, near and far, as if the whole land had been one immense drum booming out steadily an appeal to heaven. And through the deep and tremendous noise sudden yells that resembled snatches of songs from a madhouse darted shrill and high in discordant jets of sound which seemed to rush far above the earth and drive all peace from under the stars.

Carlier and Kayerts slept badly. They both thought they had heard shots fired during the night – but they could not agree as to the direction. In the morning Makola was gone somewhere. He returned about noon with one of yesterday's strangers, and eluded all Kayerts' attempts to close with him: had become deaf apparently. Kayerts wondered. Carlier, who had been fishing off the bank, came back and remarked while he showed his catch, "The niggers seem to be in a deuce of a stir; I wonder what's up. I saw about fifteen canoes cross the river during the two hours I was there fishing." Kayerts, worried, said, "Isn't this Makola very queer to-day?" Carlier advised, "Keep all our men together in case of some trouble."

II

There were ten station men who had been left by the Director. Those fellows, having engaged themselves to the Company for six months (without having any idea of a month in particular and only a very faint notion of time in general), had been serving the cause of progress for upwards of two years. Belonging to a tribe from a very distant part of the land of darkness and sorrow, they did not run away, naturally supposing that as wandering strangers they would be killed by the inhabitants of the country; in which they were right. They lived in straw huts on the slope of a ravine overgrown with reedy grass, just behind the station buildings. They were not happy, regretting the festive incantations, the sorceries, the human sacrifices of their own land; where they also had parents, brothers, sisters, admired chiefs, respected magicians, loved friends, and other ties supposed generally to be human. Besides, the rice rations served out by the Company did not agree with them, being a food unknown to their land, and to which they could not get used. Consequently they were unhealthy and miserable. Had they been of any other tribe they would have made up their minds to die – for nothing is easier to certain savages than suicide – and so have escaped from the puzzling difficulties of existence. But belonging, as they did, to a warlike tribe with filed teeth, they had more grit, and went on stupidly living through disease and sorrow. They did very little work, and had lost their splendid physique. Carlier and Kayerts doctored them assiduously without being able to bring them back into condition again. They were mustered every morning and told off to different tasks – grass-cutting, fence-building, tree-felling, &c., &c., which no power on earth could induce them to execute efficiently. The two whites had practically very little control over them.

In the afternoon Makola came over to the big house and found Kayerts watching three heavy columns of smoke rising above the forests. "What is that?" asked Kayerts. "Some villages burn," answered Makola, who seemed to have regained his wits. Then he said abruptly: "We have got very little ivory; bad six months' trading. Do you like get a little more ivory?"

"Yes," said Kayerts, eagerly. He thought of percentages which were low.

"Those men who came yesterday are traders from Loanda who have got more ivory than they can carry home. Shall I buy? I know their camp."

"Certainly," said Kayerts. "What are those traders?"

"Bad fellows," said Makola, indifferently. "They fight with people, and catch women and children. They are bad men, and got guns. There is a great disturbance in the country. Do you want ivory?"

"Yes," said Kayerts. Makola said nothing for a while. Then: "Those workmen of ours are no good at all," he muttered, looking round. "Station in very bad order, sir. Director will growl. Better get a fine lot of ivory, then he say nothing."

"I can't help it; the men won't work," said Kayerts. "When will you get that ivory?"

"Very soon," said Makola. "Perhaps to-night. You leave it to me, and keep indoors, sir. I think you had better give some palm wine to our men to make a dance this evening. Enjoy themselves. Work better tomorrow. There's plenty palm wine – gone a little sour."

Kayerts said "yes," and Makola, with his own hands carried big calabashes to the door of his hut. They stood there till the evening, and Mrs Makola looked into every one. The men got them at sunset. When Kayerts and Carlier retired, a big bonfire was flaring before the men's huts. They could hear their shouts and drumming. Some men from Gobila's village had joined the station hands, and the entertainment was a great success.

In the middle of the night, Carlier waking suddenly, heard a man shout loudly; then a shot was fired. Only one. Carlier ran out and met Kayerts on the verandah. They were both startled. As they went across the yard to call Makola, they saw shadows moving in the night. One of them cried, "Don't shoot! It's me, Price." Then Makola appeared close to them. "Go back, go back, please," he urged, "you spoil all." "There are strange men about," said Carlier. "Never mind; I know," said Makola. Then he whispered, "All right. Bring ivory. Say nothing! I know my business." The two white men reluctantly went back to the house, but did not sleep. They heard footsteps, whispers, some groans. It seemed as if a lot of men came in, dumped heavy things on the ground, squabbled a long time, then went away. They lay on their hard beds and thought: "This Makola is invaluable." In the morning Carlier came out, very sleepy, and pulled at the cord of the big bell. The station hands mustered every morning to the sound of the bell. That morning nobody came. Kayerts turned out also, yawning. Across the yard they saw Makola come out of his hut, a tin basin of soapy water in his hand. Makola, a civilized nigger, was very neat in his person. He threw the soapsuds skilfully over a wretched little yellow cur he had, then turning his face to the agent's house, he shouted from the distance, "All the men gone last night!"

They heard him plainly, but in their surprise they both yelled out together: "What?" Then they stared at one another. "We are in a proper fix now," growled Carlier. "It's incredible!" muttered Kayerts. "I will go to the huts and see," said Carlier, striding off. Makola coming up found Kayerts standing alone.

"I can hardly believe it," said Kayerts, tearfully. "We took care of them as if they had been our children."

"They went with the coast people," said Makola after a moment of hesitation.

"What do I care with whom they went – the ungrateful brutes!" exclaimed the other. Then with sudden suspicion, and looking hard at Makola, he added: "What do you know about it?"

Makola moved his shoulders, looking down on the ground. "What do I know? I think only. Will you come and look at the ivory I've got there? It is a fine lot. You never saw such."

He moved towards the store. Kayerts followed him mechanically, thinking about the incredible desertion of the men. On the ground before the door of the fetish lay six splendid tusks.

"What did you give for it?" asked Kayerts, after surveying the lot with satisfaction.

"No regular trade," said Makola. "They brought the ivory and gave it to me. I told them to take what they most wanted in the station. It is a beautiful lot. No station can show such tusks. Those traders wanted carriers badly, and our men were no good here. No trade, no entry in books; all correct."

Kayerts nearly burst with indignation. "Why!" he shouted, "I believe you have sold our men for these tusks!" Makola stood impassive and silent. "I–I–will–I," stuttered Kayerts. "You fiend!" he yelled out.

"I did the best for you and the Company," said Makola, imperturbably. "Why you shout so much? Look at this tusk."

"I dismiss you! I will report you – I won't look at the tusk. I forbid you to touch them. I order you to throw them into the river. You – you!"

"You very red, Mr Kayerts. If you are so irritable in the sun, you will get fever and die – like the first chief!" pronounced Makola impressively.

They stood still, contemplating one another with intense eyes, as if they had been looking with effort across immense distances. Kayerts shivered. Makola had meant no more than he said, but his words seemed to Kayerts full of ominous menace! He turned sharply and went away to the house. Makola retired into the bosom of his family; and the tusks, left lying before the store, looked very large and valuable in the sunshine.

Carlier came back on the verandah. "They're all gone, hey?" asked Kayerts from the far end of the common room in a muffled voice. "You did not find anybody?"

"Oh, yes," said Carlier, "I found one of Gobila's people lying dead before the huts – shot through the body. We heard that shot last night."

Kayerts came out quickly. He found his companion staring grimly over the yard at the tusks, away by the store. They both sat in silence for a while. Then Kayerts related his conversation with Makola. Carlier said nothing. At the midday meal they ate very little. They hardly exchanged a word that day. A great silence seemed to lie heavily over the station and press on their lips. Makola did not open the store; he spent the day playing with his children. He lay full-length on a mat outside his door, and the youngsters sat on his chest and clambered all over him. It was a touching picture. Mrs Makola was busy cooking all day as usual. The white men made a somewhat better meal in the evening. Afterwards, Carlier smoking his pipe strolled over to the store; he stood for a long time over the tusks, touched one or two with his foot, even tried to lift the largest one by its small end. He came back to his chief, who had not stirred from the verandah, threw himself in the chair and said—

"I can see it! They were pounced upon while they slept heavily after drinking all that palm wine you've allowed Makola to give them. A put-up job! See? The worst is, some of Gobila's people were there, and got carried off too, no doubt. The least drunk woke up, and got shot for his sobriety. This is a funny country. What will you do now?"

"We can't touch it, of course," said Kayerts.

"Of course not," assented Carlier.

"Slavery is an awful thing," stammered out Kayerts in an unsteady voice.

"Frightful – the sufferings," grunted Carlier with conviction.

They believed their words. Everybody shows a respectful deference to certain sounds that he and his fellows can make. But about feelings people really know nothing. We talk with indignation or enthusiasm; we talk about oppression, cruelty, crime, devotion, self-sacrifice, virtue, and we know nothing real beyond the words. Nobody knows what suffering or sacrifice mean – except, perhaps the victims of the mysterious purpose of these illusions.

Next morning they saw Makola very busy setting up in the yard the big scales used for weighing ivory. By and by Carlier said: "What's that filthy scoundrel up to?" and lounged out into the yard. Kayerts followed. They stood watching. Makola took no notice. When the balance was swung true, he tried to lift a tusk into the scale. It was too heavy. He looked up helplessly without a word, and for a minute they stood round that balance as mute and still as three statues. Suddenly Carlier said: "Catch hold of the other end, Makola – you beast!" and together they swung the tusk up. Kayerts trembled in every limb. He muttered, "I say! O! I say!" and putting his hand in his pocket found there a dirty bit of paper and the stump of a pencil. He turned his back on the others, as if about to do something tricky, and noted stealthily the weights which Carlier shouted out to him with unnecessary loudness. When all was over Makola whispered to himself: "The sun's very strong here for the tusks." Carlier said to Kayerts in a careless tone: "I say, chief, I might just as well give him a lift with this lot into the store."

As they were going back to the house Kayerts observed with a sigh: "It had to be done." And Carlier said: "It's deplorable, but, the men being Company's men the ivory is Company's ivory. We must look after it." "I will report to the Director, of course," said Kayerts. "Of course; let him decide," approved Carlier.

At midday they made a hearty meal. Kayerts sighed from time to time. Whenever they mentioned Makola's name they always added to it an opprobrious epithet. It eased their conscience. Makola gave himself a half-holiday, and bathed his children in the river. No one from Gobila's villages came near the station that day. No one came the next day, and the next, nor for a whole week. Gobila's people might have been dead and buried for any sign of life they gave. But they were only mourning for those they had lost by the witchcraft of white men, who had brought wicked people into their country. The wicked people were gone, but fear remained. Fear always remains. A man may destroy everything within himself, love and hate and belief, and even doubt; but as long as he clings to life he cannot destroy fear: the fear, subtle, indestructible, and terrible, that pervades his being; that tinges his thoughts; that lurks in his heart; that watches on his lips the struggle of his last breath. In his fear, the mild old Gobila offered extra human sacrifices to all the Evil Spirits that had taken possession of his white friends. His heart was heavy. Some warriors spoke about burning and killing, but the cautious old savage dissuaded them. Who could foresee the woe those mysterious creatures, if irritated, might bring? They should be left alone. Perhaps in time they would disappear into the earth as the first one had disappeared. His people must keep away from them, and hope for the best.

Kayerts and Carlier did not disappear, but remained above on this earth, that, somehow, they fancied had become bigger and very empty. It was not the absolute and dumb solitude of the post that impressed them so much as an inarticulate feeling that something from within them was gone, something that worked for their safety, and had kept the wilderness from interfering with their hearts. The images of home; the memory of people like them, of men that thought and felt as they used to think and feel, receded into distances made indistinct by the glare of unclouded sunshine. And out of the great silence of the surrounding wilderness, its very hopelessness and savagery seemed to approach them nearer, to draw them gently, to look upon them, to envelop them with a solicitude irresistible, familiar, and disgusting.

Days lengthened into weeks, then into months. Gobila's people drummed and yelled to every new moon, as of yore, but kept away from the station. Makola and Carlier tried once in a canoe to open communications, but were received with a shower of arrows, and had to fly back to the station for dear life. That attempt set the country up and down the river into an uproar that could be very distinctly heard for days. The steamer was late. At first they spoke of delay jauntily, then anxiously, then gloomily. The matter was becoming serious. Stores were running short. Carlier cast his lines off the bank, but the river was low, and the fish kept out in the stream. They dared not stroll far away from the station to shoot. Moreover, there was no game in the impenetrable forest. Once Carlier shot a hippo in the river. They had no boat to secure it, and it sank. When it floated up it drifted away, and Gobila's people secured the carcase. It was the occasion for a national holiday, but Carlier had a fit of rage over it and talked about the necessity of exterminating all the niggers before the country could be made habitable. Kayerts mooned about silently; spent hours looking at the portrait of his Melie. It represented a little girl with long bleached tresses and a rather sour face. His legs were much swollen, and he could hardly walk. Carlier, undermined by fever, could not swagger any more, but kept tottering about, still with a devil-may-care air, as became a man who remembered his crack regiment. He had become hoarse, sarcastic, and inclined to say unpleasant things. He called it, "being frank with you". They had long ago reckoned their percentages on trade, including in them that last deal of "this infamous Makola". They had also concluded not to say anything about it. Kayerts hesitated at first – was afraid of the Director.

"He has seen worse things done on the quiet," maintained Carlier, with a hoarse laugh. "Trust him! He won't thank you if you blab. He is no better than you or me. Who will talk if we hold our tongues? There is nobody here."

That was the root of the trouble! There was nobody there; and being left there alone with their weakness, they became daily more like a pair of accomplices than like a couple of devoted friends. They had heard nothing from home for eight months. Every evening they said, "To-morrow we shall see the steamer." But one of the Company's steamers had been wrecked, and the Director was busy with the other, relieving very distant and important stations on the main river. He thought that the useless station, and the useless men, could wait. Meantime Kayerts and Carlier lived on rice boiled without salt, and cursed the Company, all Africa, and the day they were born. One must have lived on such diet to discover what ghastly trouble the necessity of swallowing one's food may become. There was literally nothing else in the station but rice and coffee; they drank the coffee without sugar. The last fifteen lumps Kayerts had solemnly locked away in his box, together with a half-bottle of Cognâc, "in case of sickness", he explained. Carlier approved. "When one is sick," he said, "any little extra like that is cheering."

They waited. Rank grass began to sprout over the courtyard. The bell never rang now. Days passed, silent, exasperating, and slow. When the two men spoke, they snarled; and their silences were bitter, as if tinged by the bitterness of their thoughts.

One day after a lunch of boiled rice, Carlier put down his cup untasted, and said: "Hang it all! Let's have a decent cup of coffee for once. Bring out that sugar, Kayerts!"

"For the sick," muttered Kayerts, without looking up.

"For the sick," mocked Carlier. "Bosh! . . . Well! I am sick."

"You are no more sick than I am, and I go without," said Kayerts in a peaceful tone.

"Come! out with that sugar, you stingy old slave-dealer."

Kayerts looked up quickly. Carlier was smiling with marked insolence. And suddenly it seemed to Kayerts that he had never seen that man before. Who was he? He knew nothing about him. What was he capable of? There was a surprising flash of violent emotion within him, as if in the presence of something undreamt-of, dangerous, and final. But he managed to pronounce with composure—

"That joke is in very bad taste. Don't repeat it."

"Joke!" said Carlier, hitching himself forward on his seat. "I am hungry – I am sick – I don't joke! I hate hypocrites. You are a hypocrite. You are a slave-dealer. I am a slave-dealer. There's nothing but slave-dealers in this cursed country. I mean to have sugar in my coffee to-day, anyhow!"

"I forbid you to speak to me in that way," said Kayerts with a fair show of resolution.

"You! – What?" shouted Carlier, jumping up.

Kayerts stood up also. "I am your chief," he began, trying to master the shakiness of his voce.

"What?" yelled the other. "Who's chief? There's no chief here. There's nothing here: there's nothing but you and I. Fetch the sugar – you pot-bellied ass."

"Hold your tongue. Go out of this room," screamed Kayerts. "I dismiss you – you scoundrel!"

Carlier swung a stool. All at once he looked dangerously in earnest. "You flabby, good-for-nothing civilian – take that!" he howled.

Kayerts dropped under the table, and the stool struck the grass inner wall of the room. Then, as Carlier was trying to upset the table, Kayerts in desperation made a blind rush, head low, like a cornered pig would do, and over-turning his friend, bolted along the verandah, and into his room. He locked the door, snatched his revolver, and stood panting. In less than a minute Carlier was kicking at the door furiously, howling, "If you don't bring out that sugar, I will shoot you at sight, like a dog. Now then – one – two – three. You won't? I will show you who's the master."

Kayerts thought the door would fall in, and scrambled through the square hole that served for a window in his room. There was then the whole breadth of the house between them. But the other was apparently not strong enough to break in the door, and Kayerts heard him running round. Then he also began to run laboriously on his swollen legs. He ran as quickly as he could, grasping the revolver, and unable yet to understand what was happening to him. He saw in succession Makola's house, the store, the river, the ravine, and the low bushes; and he saw all those things again as he ran for the second time round the house. Then again they flashed past him. That morning he could not have walked a yard without a groan.

And now he ran. He ran fast enough to keep out of sight of the other man.

Then as, weak and desperate, he thought, "Before I finish the next round I shall die," he heard the other man stumble heavily, then stop. He stopped also. He had the back and Carlier the front of the house, as before. He heard him drop into a chair cursing, and suddenly his own legs gave way, and he slid down into a sitting posture with his back to the wall. His mouth was as dry as a cinder, and his face was wet with perspiration – and tears. What was it all about? He thought it must be a horrible illusion; he thought he was dreaming; he thought he was going mad! After a while he collected his senses. What did they quarrel about? That sugar! How absurd! He would give it to him – didn't want it himself. And he began scrambling to his feet with a sudden feeling of security. But before he had fairly stood upright, a common-sense reflection occurred to him and drove him back into despair. He thought: "If I give way now to that brute of a soldier, he will begin this horror again to-morrow – and the day after – every day – raise other pretensions, trample on me, torture me, make me his slave – and I will be lost! Lost! The steamer may not come for days – may never come." He shook so that he had to sit down on the floor again. He shivered forlornly. He felt he could not, would not move any more. He was completely distracted by the sudden perception that the position was without issue – that death and life had in a moment become equally difficult and terrible.

All at once he heard the other push his chair back; and he leaped to his feet with extreme facility. He listened and got confused. Must run again! Right or left? He heard footsteps. He darted to the left, grasping his revolver, and at the very same instant, as it seemed to him, they came into violent collision. Both shouted with surprise. A loud explosion took place between them; a roar of red fire, thick smoke; and Kayerts, deafened and blinded, rushed back thinking: "I am hit – it's all over." He expected the other to come round – to gloat over his agony. He caught hold of an upright of the roof – "All over!" Then he heard a crashing fall on the other side of the house, as if somebody had tumbled headlong over a chair – then silence. Nothing more happened. He did not die. Only his shoulder felt as if it had been badly wrenched, and he had lost his revolver. He was disarmed and helpless! He waited for his fate. The other man made no sound. It was a stratagem. He was stalking him now! Along what side? Perhaps he was taking aim this very minute!

After a few moments of an agony frightful and absurd, he decided to go and meet his doom. He was prepared for every surrender. He turned the corner, steadying himself with one hand on the wall; made a few paces, and nearly swooned. He had seen on the floor, protruding past the other corner, a pair of turned-up feet. A pair of white naked feet in red slippers. He felt deadly sick, and stood for a time in profound darkness. Then Makola appeared before him, saying quietly: "Come along, Mr Kayerts. He is dead." He burst into tears of gratitude; a loud, sobbing fit of crying. After a time he found himself sitting in a chair and looking at Carlier, who lay stretched on his back. Makola was kneeling over the body.

"Is this your revolver?" asked Makola, getting up.

"Yes," said Kayerts; then he added very quickly, "He ran after me to shoot me – you saw!"

"Yes, I saw," said Makola. "There is only one revolver; where's his?"

"Don't know," whispered Kayerts in a voice that had become suddenly very faint.

"I will go and look for it," said the other, gently. He made the round along the verandah, while Kayerts sat still and looked at the corpse. Makola came back empty-handed, stood in deep thought, then stepped quietly into the dead man's room, and came out directly with a revolver, which he held up before Kayerts. Kayerts shut his eyes. Everything was going round. He found life more terrible and difficult than death. He had shot an unarmed man.

After meditating for a while, Makola said softly, pointing at the dead man who lay there with his right eye blown out—

"He died of fever." Kayerts looked at him with a stony stare. "Yes," repeated Makola, thoughtfully, stepping over the corpse, "I think he died of fever. Bury him to-morrow."

And he went away slowly to his expectant wife, leaving the two white men alone on the verandah.

Night came, and Kayerts sat unmoving on his chair. He sat quiet as if he had taken a dose of opium. The violence of the emotions he had passed through produced a feeling of exhausted serenity. He had plumbed in one short afternoon the depths of horror and despair, and now found repose in the conviction that life had no more secrets for him: neither had death! He sat by the corpse thinking; thinking very actively, thinking very new thoughts. He seemed to have broken loose from himself altogether. His old thoughts, convictions, likes and dislikes, things he respected and things he abhorred, appeared in their true light at last! Appeared contemptible and childish, false and ridiculous. He revelled in his new wisdom while he sat by the man he had killed. He argued with himself about all things under heaven with that kind of wrong-headed lucidity which may be observed in some lunatics. Incidentally he reflected that the fellow dead there had been a noxious beast anyway; that men died every day in thousands; perhaps in hundreds of thousands – who could tell? – and that in the number, that one death could not possibly make any difference; couldn't have any importance, at least to a thinking creature. He, Kayerts, was a thinking creature. He had been all his life, till that moment, a believer in a lot of nonsense like the rest of mankind – who are fools; but now he thought! He knew! He was at peace; he was familiar with the highest wisdom! Then he tried to imagine himself dead, and Carlier sitting in his chair watching him; and his attempt met with such unexpected success, that in a very few moments he became not at all sure who was dead and who was alive. This extraordinary achievement of his fancy startled him, however, and by a clever and timely effort of mind he saved himself just in time from becoming Carlier. His heart thumped, and he felt hot all over at the thought of that danger. Carlier! What a beastly thing! To compose his now disturbed nerves – and no wonder! – he tried to whistle a little. Then, suddenly, he fell asleep, or thought he had slept; but at any rate there was a fog, and somebody had whistled in the fog.

He stood up. The day had come, and a heavy mist had descended upon the land: the mist penetrating, enveloping, and silent; the morning mist of tropical lands; the mist that clings and kills; the mist white and deadly, immaculate and poisonous. He stood up, saw the body, and threw his arms above his head with a cry like that of a man who, waking from a trance, finds himself immured forever in a tomb. *"Help! . . . My God!"*

A shriek inhuman, vibrating and sudden, pierced like a sharp dart the white shroud of that land of sorrow. Three short, impatient screeches followed, and then, for a time, the fog-wreaths rolled on, undisturbed, through a formidable silence. Then many more shrieks, rapid and piercing, like the yells of some exasperated and ruthless creature, rent the air. Progress was calling to Kayerts from the river. Progress and civilization and all the virtues. Society was calling to its accomplished child to come, to be taken care of, to be instructed, to be judged, to be condemned; it called him to return to that rubbish heap from which he had wandered away, so that justice could be done.

Kayerts heard and understood. He stumbled out of the verandah, leaving the other man quite alone for the first time since they had been thrown there together. He groped his way through the fog, calling in his ignorance upon the invisible heaven to undo its work. Makola flitted by in the mist, shouting as he ran—

"Steamer! Steamer! They can't see. They whistle for the station. I go ring the bell. Go down to the landing, sir. I ring."

He disappeared. Kayerts stood still. He looked upwards; the fog rolled low over his head. He looked round like a man who has lost his way; and he saw a dark smudge, a cross-shaped stain, upon the shifting purity of the mist. As he began to stumble towards it, the station bell rang in a tumultuous peal its answer to the impatient clamour of the steamer.

The Managing Director of the Great Civilizing Company (since we know that civilization follows trade) landed first, and incontinently lost sight of the steamer. The fog down by the river was exceedingly dense; above, at the station, the bell rang unceasing and brazen.

The Director shouted loudly to the steamer:

"There is nobody down to meet us; there may be something wrong, though they are ringing. You had better come, too!"

And he began to toil up the steep bank. The captain and the engine-driver of the boat followed behind. As they scrambled up the fog thinned, and they could see their Director a good way ahead. Suddenly they saw him start forward, calling to them over his shoulder:— "Run! Run to the house! I've found one of them. Run, look for the other!"

He had found one of them! And even he, the man of varied and startling experience, was somewhat discomposed by the manner of this finding. He stood and fumbled in his pockets (for a knife) while he faced Kayerts, who was hanging by a leather strap from the cross. He had evidently climbed the grave, which was high and narrow, and after tying the end of the strap to the arm, had swung himself off. His toes were only a couple of inches above the ground; his arms hung stiffly down; he seemed to be standing rigidly at attention, but with one purple cheek playfully posed on the shoulder. And, irreverently, he was putting out a swollen tongue at his Managing Director.

1896/1897

Karain: A Memory

We knew him in those unprotected days when we were content to hold in our hands our lives and our property. None of us, I believe, has any property now, and I hear that many, negligently, have lost their lives; but I am sure that the few who survive are not yet so dim-eyed as to miss in the befogged respectability of their newspapers the intelligence of various native risings in the Eastern Archipelago. Sunshine gleams between the lines of those short paragraphs – sunshine and the glitter of the sea. A strange name wakes up memories; the printed words scent the smoky atmosphere of to-day faintly, with the subtle and penetrating perfume as of land breezes breathing through the starlight of bygone nights; a signal fire gleams like a jewel on the high brow of a sombre cliff; great trees, the advanced sentries of immense forests, stand watchful and still over sleeping stretches of open water; a line of white surf thunders on an empty beach, the shallow water foams on the reefs; and green islets scattered through the calm of noonday lie upon the level of a polished sea, like a handful of emeralds on a buckler of steel.

There are faces too – faces dark, truculent, and smiling; the frank audacious faces of men barefooted, well armed and noiseless. They thronged the narrow length of our schooner's decks with their ornamented and barbarous crowd, with the variegated colours of checkered sarongs, red turbans, white jackets, embroideries; with the gleam of scabbards, gold rings, charms, armlets, lance blades, and jewelled handles of their weapons. They had an independent bearing, resolute eyes, a restrained manner; and we seem yet to hear their soft voices speaking of battles, travels, and escapes; boasting with composure, joking quietly; sometimes in well-bred murmurs extolling their own valour, our generosity; or celebrating with loyal enthusiasm the virtues of their ruler. We remember the faces, the eyes, the voices, we see again the gleam of silk and metal; the murmuring stir of that crowd, brilliant, festive, and martial; and we seem to feel the touch of friendly brown hands that, after one short grasp, return to rest on a chased hilt. They were Karain's people – a devoted following. Their movements hung on his lips; they read their thoughts in his eyes; he murmured to them nonchalantly of life and death, and they accepted his words humbly, like gifts of fate. They were all free men, and when speaking to him said, "Your slave." On his passage voices died out as though he had walked guarded by silence; awed whispers followed him. They called him their war-chief. He was the ruler of three villages on a narrow plain; the master of an insignificant foothold on the earth – of a conquered foothold that, shaped like a young moon, lay ignored between the hills and the sea.

From the deck of our schooner, anchored in the middle of the bay, he indicated by a theatrical sweep of his arm along the jagged outline of the hills the whole of his domain; and the ample movement seemed to drive back its limits, augmenting it suddenly into something so immense and vague that for a moment it appeared to be bounded only by the sky. And really, looking at that place, landlocked from the sea and shut off from the land by the precipitous slopes of mountains, it was difficult to believe in the existence of any neighbourhood. It was still, complete, unknown, and full of a life that went on stealthily with a troubling effect of solitude; of a life that seemed unaccountably empty of anything that would stir the thought, touch the heart, give a hint of the ominous sequence of days. It appeared to us a land without memories, regrets, and hopes; a land where nothing could survive the coming of the night, and where each sunrise, like a dazzling act of special creation, was disconnected from the eve and the morrow.

Karain swept his hand over it. "All mine!" He struck the deck with his long staff; the gold head flashed like a falling star; very close behind him a silent old fellow in a richly embroidered black jacket alone of all the Malays around did not follow the masterful gesture with a look. He did not even lift his eyelids. He bowed his head behind his master, and without stirring held hilt up over his right shoulder a long blade in a silver scabbard. He was there on duty, but without curiosity, and seemed weary, not with age, but with the possession of a burdensome secret of existence. Karain,

heavy and proud, had a lofty pose and breathed calmly. It was our
first visit, and we looked about curiously.

The bay was like a bottomless pit of intense light. The circular
sheet of water reflected a luminous sky, and the shores enclosing
it made an opaque ring of earth floating in an emptiness of
transparent blue. The hills, purple and arid, stood out heavily on
the sky: their summits seemed to fade into a coloured tremble as of
ascending vapour; their steep sides were streaked with the green
of narrow ravines; at their foot lay rice-fields, plantain-patches,
yellow sands. A torrent wound about like a dropped thread.
Clumps of fruit-trees marked the villages; slim palms put their
nodding heads together above the low houses; dried palm-leaf
roofs shone afar, like roofs of gold, behind the dark colonnades of
tree-trunks; figures passed vivid and vanishing; the smoke of fires
stood upright above the masses of flowering bushes; bamboo
fences glittered, running away in broken lines between the fields.
A sudden cry on the shore sounded plaintive in the distance, and
ceased abruptly, as if stifled in the downpour of sunshine. A puff of
breeze made a flash of darkness on the smooth water, touched our
faces, and became forgotten. Nothing moved. The sun blazed
down into a shadowless hollow of colours and stillness.

It was the stage where, dressed splendidly for his part, he
strutted, incomparably dignified, made important by the power he
had to awaken an absurd expectation of something heroic going
to take place – a burst of action or song – upon the vibrating tone
of a wonderful sunshine. He was ornate and disturbing, for one
could not imagine what depth of horrible void such an elaborate
front could be worthy to hide. He was not masked – there was too
much life in him, and a mask is only a lifeless thing; but he
presented himself essentially as an actor, as a human being
aggressively disguised. His smallest acts were prepared and
unexpected, his speeches grave, his sentences ominous like hints
and complicated like arabesques. He was treated with a solemn
respect accorded in the irreverent West only to the monarchs of
the stage, and he accepted the profound homage with a sustained
dignity seen nowhere else but behind the footlights and in the
condensed falseness of some grossly tragic situation. It was almost
impossible to remember who he was – only a petty chief of a
conveniently isolated corner of Mindanao, where we could in
comparative safety break the law against the traffic in firearms

and ammunition with the natives. What would happen should one of the moribund Spanish gun-boats be suddenly galvanized into a flicker of active life did not trouble us, once we were inside the bay – so completely did it appear out of the reach of a meddling world; and besides, in those days we were imaginative enough to look with a kind of joyous equanimity on any chance there was of being quietly hanged somewhere out of the way of diplomatic remonstrance. As to Karain, nothing could happen to him unless what happens to all – failure and death; but his quality was to appear clothed in the illusion of unavoidable success. He seemed too effective, too necessary there, too much of an essential condition for the existence of his land and his people, to be destroyed by anything short of an earthquake. He summed up his race, his country, the elemental force of ardent life, of tropical nature. He had its luxuriant strength, its fascination; and, like it, he carried the seed of peril within.

In many successive visits we came to know his stage well – the purple semicircle of hills, the slim trees leaning over houses, the yellow sands, the streaming green of ravines. All that had the crude and blended colouring, the appropriateness almost excessive, the suspicious immobility of a painted scene; and it enclosed so perfectly the accomplished acting of his amazing pretences that the rest of the world seemed shut out forever from the gorgeous spectacle. There could be nothing outside. It was as if the earth had gone on spinning, and had left that crumb of its surface alone in space. He appeared utterly cut off from everything but the sunshine, and that even seemed to be made for him alone. Once when asked what was on the other side of the hills, he said, with a meaning smile, "Friends and enemies – many enemies; else why should I buy your rifles and powder?" He was always like this – word-perfect in his part, playing up faithfully to the mysteries and certitudes of his surroundings. "Friends and enemies" – nothing else. It was impalpable and vast. The earth had indeed rolled away from under his land, and he, with his handful of people, stood surrounded by a silent tumult as of contending shades. Certainly no sound came from outside. "Friends and enemies!" He might have added, "and memories", at least as far as he himself was concerned; but he neglected to make that point then. It made itself later on, though; but it was after the daily performance – in the wings, so to speak, and with the lights out. Meantime he filled the stage with barbarous dignity. Some ten years ago he had led his people – a scratch lot of wandering Bugis – to the conquest of the bay, and now in his august care they had forgotten all the past, and had lost all concern for the future. He gave them wisdom, advice, reward, punishment, life or death, with the same serenity of attitude and voice. He understood irrigation and the art of war – the qualities of weapons and the craft of boat-building. He could conceal his heart; had more endurance; he could swim longer, and steer a canoe better than any of his people; he could shoot straighter, and negotiate more tortuously than any man of his race I knew. He was an adventurer of the sea, an outcast, a ruler – and my very good friend. I wish him a quick death in a stand-up fight, a death in sunshine; for he had known remorse and power, and no man can demand more from life. Day after day he appeared before us, incomparably faithful to the illusions of the stage, and at sunset the night descended upon him quickly, like a falling curtain. The seamed hills became black shadows towering high upon a clear sky; above them the glittering confusion of stars resembled a mad turmoil stilled by a gesture; sounds ceased, men slept, forms vanished – and the reality of the universe alone remained – a marvellous thing of darkness and glimmers.

II

But it was at night that he talked openly, forgetting the exactions of his stage. In the daytime there were affairs to be discussed in state. There were at first between him and me his own splendour, my shabby suspicions, and the scenic landscape that intruded upon the reality of our lives by its motionless fantasy of outline and colour. His followers thronged round him; above his head the broad blades of their spears made a spiked halo of iron points, and they hedged him from humanity by the shimmer of silks, the gleam of weapons, the excited and respectful hum of eager voices. Before sunset he would take leave with ceremony, and go off sitting under a red umbrella, and escorted by a score of boats. All the paddles flashed and struck together with a mighty splash that reverberated loudly in the monumental amphitheatre of hills. A broad stream of dazzling foam trailed behind the flotilla. The canoes appeared very black on the white hiss of water; turbaned heads swayed back and forth; a multitude of arms in crimson and

yellow rose and fell with one movement; the spearmen upright in
the bows of canoes had variegated sarongs and gleaming
shoulders like bronze statues; the muttered strophes of the
paddlers' song ended periodically in a plaintive shout. They
diminished in the distance; the song ceased; they swarmed on
the beach in the long shadows of the western hills. The sunlight
lingered on the purple crests, and we could see him leading the
way to his stockade, a burly bareheaded figure walking far in
advance of a straggling *cortège*, and swinging regularly an ebony
staff taller than himself. The darkness deepened fast; torches
gleamed fitfully, passing behind bushes; a long hail or two trailed
in the silence of the evening; and at last the night stretched its
smooth veil over the shore, the lights, and the voices.

Then, just as we were thinking of repose, the watch-men of the
schooner would hail a splash of paddles away in the starlit gloom
of the bay; a voice would respond in cautious tones, and our
serang, putting is head down the open skylight, would inform us
without surprise, "That Rajah, he coming. He here now." Karain
appeared noiselessly in the doorway of the little cabin. He was
simplicity itself then; all in white; muffled about his head; for arms
only a kriss with a plain buffalo-horn handle, which he would
politely conceal within a fold of his sarong before stepping over
the threshold. The old sword-bearer's face, the worn-out and
mournful face so covered with wrinkles that it seemed to look out
through the meshes of a fine dark net, could be seen close above
his shoulders. Karain never moved without that attendant, who
stood or squatted close at his back. He had a dislike of an open
space behind him. It was more than a dislike – it resembled fear, a
nervous preoccupation of what went on where he could not see.
This, in view of the evident and fierce loyalty that surrounded
him, was inexplicable. He was there alone in the midst of devoted
men; he was safe from neighbourly ambushes, from fraternal
ambitions; and yet more than one of our visitors had assured us
that their ruler could not bear to be alone. They said, "Even when
he eats and sleeps there is always one on the watch near him who
has strength and weapons." There was indeed always one near
him, though our informants had no conception of that watcher's
strength and weapons, which were both shadowy and terrible.
We knew, but only later on, when we had heard the story.
Meantime we noticed that, even during the most important

interviews, Karain would often give a start, and interrupting his discourse, would sweep his arm back with a sudden movement, to feel whether the old fellow was there. The old fellow, impenetrable and weary, was always there. He shared his food, his repose, and his thoughts; he knew his plans, guarded his secrets; and, impassive behind his master's agitation, without stirring the least bit, murmured above his head in a soothing tone some words difficult to catch.

It was only on board the schooner, when surrounded by white faces, by unfamiliar sights and sounds, that Karain seemed to forget the strange obsession that wound like a black thread through the gorgeous pomp of his public life. At night we treated him in a free and easy manner, which just stopped short of slapping him on the back, for there are liberties one must not take with a Malay. He said himself that on such occasions he was only a private gentleman coming to see other gentlemen whom he supposed as well born as himself. I fancy that to the last he believed us to be emissaries of Government, darkly official persons furthering by our illegal traffic some dark scheme of high state-craft. Our denials and protestations were unavailing. He only smiled with discreet politeness and inquired about the Queen. Every visit began with that inquiry; he was insatiable of details; he was fascinated by the holder of a sceptre the shadow of which, stretching from the westward over the earth and over the seas, passed far beyond his own hand's-breadth of conquered land. He multiplied questions; he could never know enough of the Monarch of whom he spoke with wonder and chivalrous respect – with a kind of affectionate awe! Afterwards, when we had learned that he was the son of a woman who had many years ago ruled a small Bugis state, we came to suspect that the memory of his mother (of whom he spoke with enthusiasm) mingled some-how in his mind with the image he tried to form for himself of the far-off Queen whom he called Great, Invincible, Pious, and Fortunate. We had to invent details at last to satisfy his craving curiosity; and our loyalty must be pardoned, for we tried to make them fit for his august and resplendent ideal. We talked. The night slipped over us, over the still schooner, over the sleeping land, and over the sleepless sea that thundered amongst the reefs outside the bay. His paddlers, two trustworthy men, slept in the canoe at the foot of our side-ladder. The old confidant, relieved from duty, dozed on his heels, with his back against the companion-door-way; and Karain sat squarely in the ship's wooden armchair, under the slight sway of the cabin lamp, a cheroot between his dark fingers, and a glass of lemonade before him. He was amused by the fizz of the thing, but after a sip or two would let it get flat, and with a courteous wave of his hand ask for a fresh bottle. He decimated our slender stock; but we did not begrudge it to him, for, when he began, he talked well. He must have been a great Bugis dandy in his time, for even then (and when we knew him he was no longer young) his splendour was spotlessly neat, and he dyed his hair a light shade of brown. The quiet dignity of his bearing transformed the dim-lit cuddy of the schooner into an audience-hall. He talked of inter-island politics with an ironic and melancholy shrewdness. He had travelled much, suffered not a little, intrigued, fought. He knew native Courts, European Settlements, the forests, the sea, and, as he said himself, had spoken in his time to many great men. He liked to talk with me because I had known some of these men: he seemed to think that I could understand him, and, with a fine confidence, assumed that I, at least, could appreciate how much greater he was himself. But he preferred to talk of his native country – a small Bugis state on the island of Celebes. I had visited it some time before, and he asked eagerly for news. As men's names came up in conversation he would say, "We swam against one another when we were boys"; or, "We hunted the deer together – he could use the noose and the spear as well as I." Now and then his big dreamy eyes would roll restlessly; he frowned or smiled, or he would become pensive, and, staring in silence, would not slightly for a time at some regretted vision of the past.

His mother had been the ruler of a small semi-independent state on the sea-coast at the head of the Gulf of Boni. He spoke of her with pride. She had been a woman resolute in affairs of state and of her own heart. After the death of her first husband, undismayed by the turbulent opposition of the chiefs, she married a rich trader, a Korinchi man of no family. Karain was her son by that second marriage, but his unfortunate descent had apparently nothing to do with his exile. He said nothing as to its cause, though once he let slip with a sigh, "Ha! my land will not feel any more the weight of my body." But he related willingly the story of his wanderings, and told us all about the conquest of the bay.

Alluding to the people beyond the hills, he would murmur gently,
with a careless wave of the hand, "They came over the hills once
to fight us, but those who got away never came again." He
thought for a while, smiling to himself. "Very few got away," he
added, with proud serenity. He cherished the recollections of his
successes; he had an exulting eagerness for endeavour; when he
talked, his aspect was warlike, chivalrous, and uplifting. No
wonder his people admired him. We saw him once walking in
daylight amongst the houses of the settlement. At the doors of
huts groups of women turned to look after him, warbling softly,
and with gleaming eyes; armed men stood out of the way,
submissive and erect; others approached from the side, bending
their backs to address him humbly; an old woman stretched out a
draped lean arm – "Blessings on thy head!" she cried from a dark
doorway; a fiery-eyed man showed above the low fence of a
plantain-patch a streaming face, a bare breast scarred in two
places, and bellowed out pantingly after him, "God give victory to
our master!" Karain walked fast, and with firm long strides; he
answered greetings right and left by quick piercing glances.
Children ran forward between the houses, peeped fearfully round
corners; young boys kept up with him, gliding between bushes;
their eyes gleamed through the dark leaves. The old sword-bearer,
shouldering the silver scabbard, shuffled hastily at his heels with
bowed head, and his eyes on the ground. And in the midst of a
great stir they passed swift and absorbed, like two men hurrying
through a great solitude.

In his council hall he was surrounded by the gravity of armed
chiefs, while two long rows of old headmen dressed in cotton stuffs
squatted on their heels, with idle arms hanging over their knees.
Under the thatch roof supported by smooth columns, of which
each one had cost the life of a straight-stemmed young palm, the
scent of flowering hedges drifted in warm waves. The sun was
sinking. In the open court-yard suppliants walked through the
gate, raising, when yet far off, their joined hands above bowed
heads, and bending low in the bright stream of sunlight. Young
girls, with flowers in their laps, sat under the wide-spreading
boughs of a big tree. The blue smoke of wood fires spread in a thin
mist above the high-pitched roofs of houses that had glistening
walls of woven reeds, and all round them rough wooden pillars
under the sloping eaves. He dispensed justice in the shade; from a

high seat he gave orders, advice, reproof. Now and then the hum of approbation rose louder, and idle spearmen that lounged listlessly against the posts, looking at the girls, would turn their heads slowly. To no man had been given the shelter of so much respect, confidence, and awe. Yet at times he would lean forward and appear to listen as for a far-off note of discord, as if expecting to hear some faint voice, the sound of light footsteps; or he would start half up in his seat, as though he had been familiarly touched on the shoulder. He glanced back with apprehension; his aged follower whispered inaudibly at his ear; the chiefs turned their eyes away in silence, for the old wizard, the man who could command ghosts and send evil spirits against enemies, was speaking low to their ruler. Around the short stillness of the open place the trees rustled faintly, the soft laughter of girls playing with the flowers rose in clear bursts of joyous sound. At the end of upright spear-shafts the long tufts of dyed horse-hair waved crimson and filmy in the gust of wind; and beyond the blaze of hedges the brook of limpid quick water ran invisible and loud under the drooping grass of the bank, with a great murmur, passionate and gentle.

After sunset, far across the fields and over the bay, clusters of torches could be seen burning under the high roofs of the council shed. Smoky red flames swayed on high poles, and the fiery blaze flickered over faces, clung to the smooth trunks of palm-trees, kindled bright sparks on the rims of metal dishes standing on fine floor-mats. That obscure adventurer feasted like a king. Small groups of men crouched in tight circles round the wooden platters; brown hands hovered over snowy heaps of rice. Sitting upon a rough couch apart from the others, he leaned on his elbow with inclined head; and near him a youth improvised in a high tone a song that celebrated his valour and wisdom. The singer rocked himself to and fro, rolling frenzied eyes; old women hobbled about with dishes, and men, squatting low, lifted their heads to listen gravely without ceasing to eat. The song of triumph vibrated in the night, and the stanzas rolled out mournful and fiery like the thoughts of a hermit. He silenced it with a sign, "Enough!" An owl hooted far away, exulting in the delight of deep gloom in dense foliage; overhead lizards ran in the attap thatch, calling softly; the dry leaves of the roof rustled; the rumour of mingled voices grew louder suddenly. After a circular and startled glance, as of a man waking up abruptly to the sense of danger, he would throw himself back, and under the downward gaze of the old sorcerer take up, wide-eyed, the slender thread of his dream. They watched his moods; the swelling rumour of animated talk subsided like a wave on a sloping beach. The chief is pensive. And above the spreading whisper of lowered voices only a light rattle of weapons would be heard, a single louder word distinct and alone, or the grave ring of a big brass tray.

III

For two years at short intervals we visited him. We came to like him, to trust him, almost to admire him. He was plotting and preparing a war with patience, with foresight – with a fidelity to his purpose and with a steadfastness of which I would have thought him racially incapable. He seemed fearless of the future, and in his plans displayed a sagacity that was only limited by his profound ignorance of the rest of the world. We tried to enlighten him, but our attempts to make clear the irresistible nature of the forces which he desired to arrest failed to discourage his eagerness to strike a blow for his own primitive ideas. He did not understand us, and replied by arguments that almost drove one to desperation by their childish shrewdness. He was absurd and unanswerable. Sometimes we caught glimpses of a sombre, glowing fury within him – a brooding and vague sense of wrong, and a concentrated lust of violence which is dangerous in a native. He raved like one inspired. On one occasion, after we had been talking to him late in his campong, he jumped up. A great, clear fire blazed in the grove; lights and shadows danced together between the trees; in the still night bats flitted in and out of the boughs like fluttering flakes of denser darkness. He snatched the sword from the old man, whizzed it out of the scabbard, and thrust the point into the earth. Upon the thin, upright blade the silver hilt, released, swayed before him like something alive. He stepped back a pace, and in a deadened tone spoke fiercely to the vibrating steel: "If there is virtue in the fire, in the iron, in the hand that forged thee, in the words spoken over thee, in the desire of my heart, and in the wisdom of thy makers,—then we shall be victorious together!" He drew it out, looked along the edge. "Take," he said over his shoulder to the old sword-bearer. The other, unmoved on his hams, wiped the point with a corner of his sarong, and returning the weapon to its scabbard, sat nursing it on his knees without a single look upwards. Karain, suddenly very calm, reseated himself with dignity. We gave up remonstrating after this, and let him go his way to an honourable disaster. All we could do for him was to see to it that the powder was good for the money and the rifles serviceable, if old.

But the game was becoming at last too dangerous; and if we, who had faced it pretty often, thought little of the danger, it was decided for us by some very respectable people sitting safely in counting-houses that the risks were too great, and that only one more trip could be made. After giving in the usual way many misleading hints as to our destination, we slipped away quietly, and after a very quick passage entered the bay. It was early morning, and even before the anchor went to the bottom the schooner was surrounded by boats.

The first thing we heard was that Karain's mysterious sword-bearer had died a few days ago. We did not attach much importance to the news. It was certainly difficult to imagine Karain without his inseparable follower; but the fellow was old, he had never spoken to one of us, we hardly ever had heard the sound of his voice; and we had come to look upon him as upon something inanimate, as a part of our friend's trappings of state – like that sword he had carried, or the fringed red umbrella displayed during an official progress. Karain did not visit us in the afternoon as usual. A message of greeting and a present of fruit and vegetables came off for us before sunset. Our friend paid us like a banker, but treated us like a prince. We sat up for him till midnight. Under the stern awning bearded Jackson jingled an old guitar and sang, with an execrable accent, Spanish love-songs; while young Hollis and I, sprawling on the deck, had a game of chess by the light of a cargo lantern. Karain did not appear. Next day we were busy unloading, and heard that the Rajah was unwell. The expected invitation to visit him ashore did not come. We sent friendly messages, but, fearing to intrude upon some secret council, remained on board. Early on the third day we had landed all the powder and rifles, and also a six-pounder brass gun with its carriage which we had subscribed together for a present for our friend. The afternoon was sultry.

Ragged edges of black clouds peeped over the hills, and invisible thunderstorms circled outside, growling like wild beasts. We got the schooner ready for sea, intending to leave next morning at day-light. All day a merciless sun blazed down into the bay, fierce and pale, as if at white heat. Nothing moved on the land. The beach was empty, the villages seemed deserted; the trees far off stood in unstirring clumps, as if painted; the white smoke of some invisible bush-fire spread itself low over the shores of the bay like a settling fog. Late in the day three of Karain's chief men, dressed in their best and armed to the teeth, came off in a canoe, bringing a case of dollars. They were gloomy and languid, and told us they had not seen their Rajah for five days. No one had seen him! We settled all accounts, and after shaking hands in turn and in profound silence, they descended one after another into their boat, and were paddled to the shore, sitting close together, clad in vivid colours, with hanging heads: the gold embroideries of their jackets flashed dazzlingly as they went away gliding on the smooth water, and not one of them looked back once. Before sunset the growling clouds carried with a rush the ridge of hills, and came tumbling down the inner slopes. Everything disappeared; black whirling vapours filled the bay, and in the midst of them the schooner swung here and there in the shifting gusts of wind. A single clap of thunder detonated in the hollow with a violence that seemed capable of bursting into small pieces the ring of high land, and a warm deluge descended. The wind died out. We panted in the close cabin; our faces streamed; the bay outside hissed as if boiling; the water fell in perpendicular shafts as heavy as lead; it swished about the deck, poured off the spars, gurgled, sobbed, splashed, murmured in the blind night. Our lamp burned low. Hollis, stripped to the waist, lay stretched out on the lockers, with closed eyes and motionless like a despoiled corpse; at his head Jackson twanged the guitar, and gasped out in sighs a mournful dirge about hopeless love and eyes like stars. Then we heard startled voices on deck crying in the rain, hurried footsteps overhead, and suddenly Karain appeared in the doorway of the cabin. His bare breast and his face glistened in the light; his sarong, soaked, clung about his legs; he had his sheathed kriss in his left hand; and wisps of wet hair, escaping from under his red kerchief, stuck over his eyes and down his cheeks. He stepped in with a headlong stride and looking over his shoulder like a man pursued. Hollis turned on his side quickly and opened his eyes. Jackson clapped his big hand over the strings and the jingling vibration died suddenly. I stood up.

"We did not hear your boat's hail!" I exclaimed.

"Boat! The man's swum off," drawled out Hollis from the locker. "Look at him!"

He breathed heavily, wild-eyed, while we looked at him in silence. Water dripped from him, made a dark pool, and ran crookedly across the cabin floor. We could hear Jackson, who had gone out to drive away our Malay seamen from the doorway of the companion; he swore menacingly in the patter of a heavy shower, and there was a great commotion on deck. The watchmen, scared out of their wits by the glimpse of a shadowy figure leaping over the rail, straight out of the night as it were, had alarmed all hands.

Then Jackson, with glittering drops of water on his hair and beard, came back looking angry, and Hollis, who, being the youngest of us, assumed an indolent superiority, said without stirring, "Give him a dry sarong – give him mine; it's hanging up in the bathroom." Karain laid the kriss on the table, hilt inwards, and murmured a few words in a strangled voice.

"What's that?" asked Hollis, who had not heard.

"He apologizes for coming in with a weapon in his hand," I said, dazedly.

"Ceremonious beggar. Tell him we forgive a friend . . . on such a night," drawled out Hollis. "What's wrong?"

Karain slipped the dry sarong over his head, dropped the wet one at his feet, and stepped out of it. I pointed to the wooden armchair – his armchair. He sat down very straight, said "Ha!" in a strong voice; a short shiver shook his broad frame. He looked over his shoulder uneasily, turned as if to speak to us, but only stared in a curious blind manner, and again looked back. Jackson bellowed out, "Watch well on deck there!" heard a faint answer from above, and reaching out with his foot slammed-to the cabin door.

"All right now," he said.

Karain's lips moved slightly. A vivid flash of lightning made the two round sternports facing him glimmer like a pair of cruel and phosphorescent eyes. The flame of the lamp seemed to wither into

brown dust for an instant, and the looking-glass over the little
sideboard leaped out behind his back in a smooth sheet of livid
light. The roll of thunder came near, crashed over us; the
schooner trembled, and the great voice went on, threatening
terribly, into the distance. For less than a minute a furious shower
rattled on the decks. Karain looked slowly from face to face, and
then the silence became so profound that we all could hear
distinctly the two chronometers in my cabin ticking along with
unflagging speed against one another.

And we three, strangely moved, could not take our eyes from
him. He had become enigmatical and touching, in virtue of that
mysterious cause that had driven him through the night and
through the thunderstorm to the shelter of the schooner's cuddy.
Not one of us doubted that we were looking at a fugitive,
incredible as it appeared to us. He was haggard, as though he
had not slept for weeks; he had become lean, as though he had
not eaten for days. His cheeks were hollow, his eyes sunk, the
muscles of his chest and arms twitched slightly as if after an
exhausting contest. Of course it had been a long swim off to the
schooner; but his face showed another kind of fatigue, the
tormented weariness, the anger and the fear of a struggle against
a thought, an idea – against something that cannot be grappled,
that never rests – a shadow, a nothing, unconquerable and
immortal, that preys upon life. We knew it as though he had
shouted it at us. His chest expanded time after time, as if it could
not contain the beating of his heart. For a moment he had the
power of the possessed – the power to awaken in the beholders
wonder, pain, pity, and a fearful near sense of things invisible, of
things dark and mute, that surround the loneliness of mankind.
His eyes roamed about aimlessly for a moment, then became still.
He said with effort—

"I came here . . . I leaped out of my stockade as after a defeat. I
ran in the night. The water was black. I left him calling on the
edge of black water . . . I left him standing alone on the beach. I
swam . . . he called out after me . . . I swam . . ."

He trembled from head to foot, sitting very upright and gazing
straight before him. Left whom? Who called? We did not know.
We could not understand. I said at all hazards—

"Be firm."

The sound of my voice seemed to steady him into a sudden

rigidity, but otherwise he took no notice. He seemed to listen, to expect something for a moment, then went on—

"He cannot come here – therefore I sought you. You men with white faces who despise the invisible voices. He cannot abide your unbelief and your strength."

He was silent for a while, then exclaimed softly—

"Oh! the strength of unbelievers!"

"There's no one here but you – and we three," said Hollis, quietly. He reclined with his head supported on elbow and did not budge.

"I know," said Karain. "He has never followed me here. Was not the wise man ever by my side? But since the old wise man, who knew of my trouble, has died, I have heard the voice every night. I shut myself up – for many days – in the dark. I can hear the sorrowful murmurs of women, the whisper of the wind, of the running waters; the clash of weapons in the hands of faithful men, their footsteps – and his voice! . . . Near . . . So! In my ear! I felt him near . . . His breath passed over my neck. I leaped out without a cry. All about me men slept quietly. I ran to the sea. He ran by my side without footsteps, whispering, whispering old words – whispering into my ear in his old voice. I ran into the sea; I swam off to you, with my kriss between my teeth. I, armed, I fled before a breath – to you. Take me away to your land. The wise old man has died, and with him is gone the power of his words and charms. And I can tell no one. No one. There is no one here faithful enough and wise enough to know. It is only near you, unbelievers, that my trouble fades like a mist under the eye of day."

He turned to me.

"With you I go!" he cried in a contained voice. "With you, who know so many of us. I want to leave this land – my people . . . and him – there!"

He pointed a shaking finger at random over his shoulder. It was hard for us to bear the intensity of that undisclosed distress. Hollis stared at him hard. I asked gently—

"Where is the danger?"

"Everywhere outside this place," he answered, mournfully. "In every place where I am. He waits for me on the paths, under the trees, in the place where I sleep – everywhere but here."

He looked round the little cabin, at the painted beams, at the tarnished varnish of bulkheads; he looked round as if appealing to all its shabby strangeness, to the disorderly jumble of unfamiliar things that belong to an inconceivable life of stress, of power, of endeavour, of unbelief – to the strong life of white men, which rolls on irresistible and hard on the edge of outer darkness. He stretched out his arms as if to embrace it and us. We waited. The wind and rain had ceased, and the stillness of the night round the schooner was as dumb and complete as if a dead world had been laid to rest in a grave of clouds. We expected him to speak. The necessity within him tore at his lips. There are those who say that a native will not speak to a white man. Error. No man will speak to his master; but to a wanderer and a friend, to him who does not come to teach or to rule, to him who asks for nothing and accepts all things, words are spoken by the camp-fires, in the shared solitude of the sea, in riverside villages, in resting-places surrounded by forests – words are spoken that take no account of race or colour. One heart speaks – another one listens; and the earth, the sea, the sky, the passing wind and the stirring leaf, hear also the futile tale of the burden of life.

He spoke at last. It is impossible to convey the effect of his story. It is undying, it is but a memory, and its vividness cannot be made clear to another mind, any more than the vivid emotions of a dream. One must have seen his innate splendour, one must have known him before – looked at him then. The wavering gloom of the little cabin; the breathless stillness outside, through which only the lapping of water against the schooner's sides could be heard; Hollis's pale face, with steady dark eyes; the energetic head of Jackson held up between two big palms, and with the long yellow hair of his beard flowing over the strings of the guitar lying on the table; Karain's upright and motionless pose, his tone – all this made an impression that cannot be forgotten. He faced us across the table. His dark head and bronze torso appeared above the tarnished slab of wood, gleaming and still as if cast in metal. Only his lips moved, and his eyes glowed, went out, blazed again, or stared mournfully. His expressions came straight from his tormented heart. His words sounded low, in a sad murmur as of running water; at times they rang loud like the clash of a war-gong – or trailed slowly like weary travellers – or rushed forward with the speed of fear.

IV

This is, imperfectly, what he said—

"It was after the great trouble that broke the alliance of the four states of Wajo. We fought amongst ourselves, and the Dutch watched from afar till we were weary. Then the smoke of their fire-ships was seen at the mouth of our rivers, and their great men came in boats full of soldiers to talk to us of protection and peace. We answered with caution and wisdom, for our villages were burnt, our stockades weak, the people weary, and the weapons blunt. They came and went; there had been much talk, but after they went away everything seemed to be as before, only their ships remained in sight from our coast, and very soon their traders came amongst us under a promise of safety. My brother was a Ruler, and one of those who had given the promise. I was young then, and had fought in the war, and Pata Matara had fought by my side. We had shared hunger, danger, fatigue, and victory. His eyes saw my danger quickly, and twice my arm had preserved his life. It was his destiny. He was my friend. And he was great amongst us – one of those who were near my brother, the Ruler. He spoke in council, his courage was great, he was the chief of many villages round the great lake that is in the middle of our country as the heart is in the middle of a man's body. When his sword was carried into a campong in advance of his coming, the maidens whispered wonderingly under the fruit-trees, the rich men consulted together in the shade, and a feast was made ready with rejoicing and songs. He had the favour of the Ruler and the affection of the poor. He loved war, deer hunts, and the charms of women. He was the possessor of jewels, of lucky weapons, and of men's devotion. He was a fierce man; and I had no other friend.

"I was the chief of a stockade at the mouth of the river, and collected tolls for my brother from the passing boats. One day I saw a Dutch trader go up the river. He went up with three boats, and no toll was demanded from him, because the smoke of Dutch war-ships stood out from the open sea, and we were too weak to forget treaties. He went up under the promise of safety, and my brother gave him protection. He said he came to trade. He listened to our voices, for we are men who speak openly and without fear; he counted the number of our spears, he examined the trees, the running waters, the grasses of the bank, the slopes of our hills. He went up to Matara's country and obtained permission to build a house. He traded and planted. He despised our joys, our thoughts, and our sorrows. His face was red, his hair like flame, and his eyes pale, like a river mist; he moved heavily, and spoke with a deep voice; he laughed aloud like a fool, and knew no courtesy in his speech. He was a big, scornful man, who looked into women's faces and put his hand on the shoulders of free men as though he had been a noble-born chief. We bore with him. Time passed.

"Then Pata Matara's sister fled from the campong and went to live in the Dutchman's house. She was a great and wilful lady: I had seen her once carried high on slaves' shoulders amongst the people, with uncovered face, and I had heard all men say that her beauty was extreme, silencing the reason and ravishing the heart of the beholders. The people were dismayed; Matara's face was blackened with that disgrace, for she knew she had been promised to another man. Matara went to the Dutchman's house, and said, 'Give her up to die – she is the daughter of chiefs.' The white man refused and shut himself up, while his servants kept guard night and day with loaded guns. Matara raged. My brother called a council. But the Dutch ships were near, and watched our coast greedily. My brother said, 'If he dies now our land will pay for his blood. Leave him alone till we grow stronger and the ships are gone.' Matara was wise; he waited and watched. But the white man feared for her life and went away.

"He left his house, his plantations, and his goods! He departed, armed and menacing, and left all – for her! She had ravished his heart! From my stockade I saw him put out to sea in a big boat. Matara and I watched him from the fighting platform behind the pointed stakes. He sat cross-legged, with his gun in his hands, on the roof at the stern of his prau. The barrel of his rifle glinted aslant before his big red face. The broad river was stretched under him – level, smooth, shining, like a plain of silver; and his prau, looking very short and black from the shore, glided along the silver plain and over into the blue of the sea.

"Thrice Matara, standing by my side, called aloud her name with grief and imprecations. He stirred my heart. It leaped three times; and three times with the eye of my mind I saw in the gloom within the enclosed space of the prau a woman with streaming hair going away from her land and her people. I was angry – and sorry. Why? And then I also cried out insults and threats. Matara said, 'Now they have left our land their lives are mine. I shall follow and strike – and, alone, pay the price of blood.' A great wind was sweeping towards the setting sun over the empty river. I cried, 'By your side I will go!' He lowered his head in sign of assent. It was his destiny. The sun had set, and the trees swayed their boughs with a great noise above our heads.

"On the third night we two left our land together in a trading prau.

"The sea met us – the sea, wide, pathless, and without voice. A sailing prau leaves no track. We went south. The moon was full; and, looking up, we said to one another, 'When the next moon shines as this one, we shall return and they will be dead.' It was fifteen years ago. Many moons have grown full and withered and I have not seen my land since. We sailed south; we overtook many praus; we examined the creeks and the bays; we saw the end of our coast, of our island – a steep cape over a disturbed strait, where drift the shadows of shipwrecked praus and drowned men clamour in the night. The wide sea was all round us now. We saw a great mountain burning in the midst of water; we saw thousands of islets scattered like bits of iron fired from a big gun; we saw a long coast of mountain and low-lands stretching away in sunshine from west to east. It was Java. We said, 'They are there; their time is near, and we shall return or die cleansed from dishonour.'

"We landed. Is there anything good in that country? The paths run straight and hard and dusty. Stone campongs, full of white faces, are surrounded by fertile fields, but every man you meet is a slave. The rulers live under the edge of a foreign sword. We ascended mountains, we traversed valleys; at sunset we entered villages. We asked everyone, 'Have you seen such a white man?' Some stared; others laughed; women gave us food, sometimes, with fear and respect, as though we had been distracted by the visitation of God; but some did not understand our language, and some cursed us, or, yawning, asked with contempt the reason of our quest. Once, as we were going away, an old man called after us, 'Desist!'

"We went on. Concealing our weapons, we stood humbly aside before the horsemen on the road; we bowed low in the courtyards of chiefs who were no better than slaves. We lost ourselves in the fields, in the jungle; and one night, in a tangled forest, we came upon a place where crumbling old walls had fallen amongst the trees, and where strange stone idols – carved images of devils with many arms and legs, with snakes twined round their bodies, with twenty heads and holding a hundred swords – seemed to live and threaten in the light of our camp fire. Nothing dismayed us. And on the road, by every fire, in resting-places, we always talked of her and of him. Their time was near. We spoke of nothing else. No! not of hunger, thirst, weariness, and faltering hearts. No! we spoke of him and her! Of her! And we thought of them – of her! Matara brooded by the fire. I sat and thought and thought, till suddenly I could see again the image of a woman, beautiful, and young, and great and proud, and tender, going away from her land and her people. Matara said, 'When we find them we shall kill her first to cleanse the dishonour – then the man must die.' I would say, 'It shall be so; it is your vengeance.' He stared long at me with his big sunken eyes.

"We came back to the coast. Our feet were bleeding, our bodies thin. We slept in rags under the shadow of stone enclosures; we prowled, soiled and lean, about the gateways of white men's court-yards. Their hairy dogs barked at us, and their servants shouted from afar, 'Begone!' Low-born wretches, that keep watch over the streets of stone campongs, asked us who we were. We lied, we cringed, we smiled with hate in our hearts, and we kept looking here, looking there for them – for the white man with hair like flame, and for her, for the woman who had broken faith, and therefore must die. We looked. At last in every woman's face I thought I could see hers. We ran swiftly. No! Sometimes Matara would whisper, 'Here is the man,' and we waited, crouching. He came near. It was not the man – those Dutchmen are all alike. We suffered the anguish of deception. In my sleep I saw her face, and was both joyful and sorry . . . Why? . . . I seemed to hear a whisper near me. I turned swiftly. She was not there! And as we trudged wearily from stone city to stone city I seemed to hear a light footstep near me. A time came when I heard it always, and I was glad. I thought, walking dizzy and weary in sunshine on the hard paths of white men – I thought, She is there – with us! . . . Matara was sombre. We were often hungry.

"We sold the carved sheaths of our krisses – the ivory sheaths with golden ferules. We sold the jewelled hilts. But we kept the blades – for them. The blades that never touch but kill – we kept the blades for her . . . Why? She was always by our side . . . We starved. We begged. We left Java at last.

"We went West, we went East. We saw many lands, crowds of strange faces, men that live in trees and men who eat their old people. We cut rattans in the forest for a handful of rice, and for a living swept the decks of big ships and heard curses heaped upon our heads. We toiled in villages; we wandered upon the seas with the Bajow people, who have no country. We fought for pay; we hired ourselves to work for Goram men, and were cheated; and under the orders of rough white faces we dived for pearls in barren bays, dotted with black rocks, upon a coast of sand and desolation. And everywhere we watched, we listened, we asked. We asked traders, robbers, white men. We heard jeers, mockery, threats – words of wonder and words of contempt. We never knew rest; we never thought of home, for our work was not done. A year passed, then another. I ceased to count the number of nights, of moons, of years. I watched over Matara. He had my last handful of rice; if there was water enough for one he drank it; I covered him up when he shivered with cold; and when the hot sickness came upon him I sat sleepless through many nights and fanned his face. He was a fierce man, and my friend. He spoke of her with fury in the daytime, with sorrow in the dark; he remembered her in health, in sickness. I said nothing; but I saw her every day – always! At first I saw only her head, as of a woman walking in the low mist on a river bank. Then she sat by our fire. I saw her! I looked at her! She had tender eyes and a ravishing face. I murmured to her in the night. Matara said sleepily sometimes, 'To whom are you talking? Who is there?' I answered quickly, 'No one' . . . It was a lie! She never left me. She shared the warmth of our fire, she sat on my couch of leaves, she swam on the sea to follow me . . . I saw her! . . . I tell you I saw her long black hair spread behind her upon the moonlit water as she struck out with bare arms by the side of a swift prau. She was beautiful, she was faithful, and in the silence of foreign countries she spoke to me very low in the language of my people. No one saw her; no one heard her; she was mine only! In daylight she moved with a swaying walk before me upon the weary paths; her figure was straight and flexible like the stem of a slender tree; the heels of her feet were round and polished like shells of eggs; with her round arm she made signs. At night she looked into my face.

And she was sad! Her eyes were tender and frightened; her voice soft and pleading. Once I murmured to her, 'You shall not die,' and she smiled . . . ever after she smiled! . . . She gave me courage to bear weariness and hardships. Those were times of pain, and she soothed me. We wandered patient in our search. We knew deception, false hopes; we knew captivity, sickness, thirst, misery, despair . . . Enough! We found them! . . ."

He cried out the last words and paused. His face was impassive, and he kept still like a man in a trance. Hollis sat up quickly, and spread his elbows on the table. Jackson made a brusque movement, and accidentally touched the guitar. A plaintive resonance filled the cabin with confused vibrations and died out slowly. Then Karain began to speak again. The restrained fierceness of his tone seemed to rise like a voice from outside, like a thing unspoken but heard; it filled the cabin and enveloped in its intense and deadened murmur the motionless figure in the chair.

"We were on our way to Atjeh, where there was war; but the vessel ran on a sandbank, and we had to land in Delli. We had earned a little money, and had bought a gun from some Selangore traders; only one gun, which was fired by the spark of a stone: Matara carried it. We landed. Many white men lived there, planting tobacco on conquered plains, and Matara . . . But no matter. He saw him! . . . The Dutchman! . . . At last! . . . We crept and watched. Two nights and a day we watched. He had a house – a big house in a clearing in the midst of his fields; flowers and bushes grew around; there were narrow paths of yellow earth between the cut grass, and thick hedges to keep people out. The third night we came armed, and lay behind a hedge.

"A heavy dew seemed to soak through our flesh and made our very entrails cold. The grass, the twigs, the leaves, covered with drops of water, were grey in the moonlight. Matara, curled up in the grass, shivered in his sleep. My teeth rattled in my head so loud that I was afraid the noise would wake up all the land. Afar, the watchmen of white men's houses struck wooden clappers and hooted in the darkness. And, as every night, I saw her by my side. She smiled no more! . . . The fire of anguish burned in my breast, and she whispered to me with compassion, with pity, softly – as women will; she soothed the pain of my mind; she bent her face over me – the face of a woman who ravishes the hearts and silences the reason of men. She was all mine, and no one could see her – no one of living mankind! Stars shone through her bosom, through her floating hair. I was overcome with regret, with tenderness, with sorrow. Matara slept . . . Had I slept? Matara was shaking me by the shoulder, and the fire of the sun was drying the grass, the bushes, the leaves. It was day. Shreds of white mist hung between the branches of trees.

"Was it night or day? I saw nothing again till I heard Matara breathe quickly where he lay, and then outside the house I saw her. I saw them both. They had come out. She sat on a bench under the wall, and twigs laden with flowers crept high above her head, hung over her hair. She had a box on her lap, and gazed into it, counting the increase of her pearls. The Dutchman stood by looking on; he smiled down at her; his white teeth flashed; the hair on his lip was like two twisted flames. He was big and fat, and joyous, and without fear. Matara tipped fresh priming from the hollow of his palm, scraped the flint with his thumb-nail, and gave the gun to me. To me! I took it . . . O fate!

"He whispered into my ear, lying on his stomach, 'I shall creep close and then amok . . . let her die by my hand. You take aim at the fat swine there. Let him see me strike my shame off the face of the earth – and then . . . you are my friend – kill with a sure shot.' I said nothing; there was no air in my chest – there was no air in the world. Matara had gone suddenly from my side. The grass nodded. Then a bush rustled. She lifted her head.

"I saw her! The consoler of sleepless nights, of weary days; the companion of troubled years! I saw her! She looked straight at the place where I crouched. She was there as I had seen her for years – a faithful wanderer by my side. She looked with sad eyes and had smiling lips; she looked at me . . . Smiling lips! Had I not promised that she should not die!

"She was far off and I felt her near. Her touch caressed me, and her voice murmured, whispered above me, around me, 'Who shall be thy companion, who shall console thee if I die?' I saw a flowering thicket to the left of her stir a little . . . Matara was ready . . . I cried aloud— 'Return!'

"She leaped up; the box fell; the pearls streamed at her feet. The big Dutchman by her side rolled menacing eyes through the still sunshine. The gun went up to my shoulder. I was kneeling and I was firm – firmer than the trees, the rocks, the mountains. But in front of the steady long barrel the fields, the house, the earth, the sky swayed to and fro like shadows in a forest on a windy day. Matara burst out of the thicket; before him the petals of torn flowers whirled high as if driven by a tempest. I heard her cry; I saw her spring with open arms in front of the white man. She was a woman of my country and of noble blood. They are so! I heard her shriek of anguish and fear – and all stood still! The fields, the house, the earth, the sky stood still – while Matara leaped at her with uplifted arm. I pulled the trigger, saw a spark, heard nothing; the smoke drove back into my face, and then I could see Matara roll over head first and lie with stretched arms at her feet. Ha! A sure shot! The sunshine fell on my back colder than the running water. A sure shot! I flung the gun after the shot. Those two stood over the dead man as though they had been bewitched by a charm. I shouted at her, 'Live and remember!' Then for a time I stumbled about in a cold darkness.

"Behind me there were great shouts, the running of many feet; strange men surrounded me, cried meaningless words into my face, pushed me, dragged me, supported me . . . I stood before the big Dutchman: he stared as if bereft of his reason. He wanted to know, he talked fast, he spoke of gratitude, he offered me food, shelter, gold – he asked many questions. I laughed in his face. I said, 'I am a Korinchi traveller from Perak over there, and know nothing of that dead man. I was passing along the path when I heard a shot, and your senseless people rushed out and dragged me here.' He lifted his arms, he wondered, he could not believe, he could not understand, he clamoured in his own tongue! She had her arms clasped round his neck, and over her shoulder stared back at me with wide eyes. I smiled and looked at her; I smiled and waited to hear the sound of her voice. The white man asked her suddenly, 'Do you know him?' I listened – my life was in my ears! She looked at me long, she looked at me with unflinching eyes, and said aloud, 'No! I never saw him before.' . . . What! Never before? Had she forgotten already? Was it possible? Forgotten already – after so many years – so many years of wandering, of companionship, of trouble, of tender words! Forgotten already! . . . I tore myself out from the hands that held me and went away without a word . . . They let me go.

"I was weary. Did I sleep? I do not know. I remember walking upon a broad path under a clear starlight; and that strange country seemed so big, the rice-fields so vast, that, as I looked around, my head swam with the fear of space. Then I saw a forest. The joyous starlight was heavy upon me. I turned off the path and entered the forest, which was very sombre and very sad."

V

Karain's tone had been getting lower and lower, as though he had been going away from us, till the last words sounded faint but clear, as if shouted on a calm day from a very great distance. He moved not. He stared fixedly past the motionless head of Hollis, who faced him, as still as himself. Jackson had turned sideways, and with elbow on the table shaded his eyes with the palm of his hand. And I looked on, surprised and moved; I looked at that man, loyal to a vision, betrayed by his dream, spurned by his illusion, and coming to us unbelievers for help – against a thought. The silence was profound; but it seemed full of noiseless phantoms, of things sorrowful, shadowy, and mute, in whose invisible presence the firm, pulsating beat of the two ship's chronometers ticking off steadily the seconds of Greenwich Time seemed to me a protection and a relief. Karain stared stonily; and looking at his rigid figure, I thought of his wanderings, of that obscure Odyssey of revenge, of all the men that wander amongst illusions; of the illusions as restless as men; of the illusions faithful, faithless; of the illusions that give joy, that give sorrow, that give pain, that give peace; of the invincible illusions that can make life and death appear serene, inspiring, tormented, or ignoble.

A murmur was heard; that voice from outside seemed to flow out of a dreaming world into the lamp-light of the cabin. Karain was speaking.

"I lived in the forest.

"She came no more. Never! Never once! I lived alone. She had forgotten. It was well. I did not want her; I wanted no one. I found an abandoned house in an old clearing. Nobody came near. Sometimes I heard in the distance the voices of people going along a path. I slept; I rested; there was wild rice, water from a running stream – and peace! Every night I sat alone by my small fire before the hut. Many nights passed over my head.

"Then, one evening, as I sat by my fire after having eaten, I looked down on the ground and began to remember my wanderings. I lifted my head. I had heard no sound, no rustle, no footsteps – but I lifted my head. A man was coming towards me across the small clearing. I waited. He came up without a greeting and squatted down into the firelight. Then he turned his face to me. It was Matara. He stared at me fiercely with his big sunken eyes. The night was cold; the heat died suddenly out of the fire, and he stared at me. I rose and went away from there, leaving him by the fire that had no heat.

"I walked all that night, all next day, and in the evening made up a big blaze and sat down – to wait for him. He had not come into the light. I heard him in the bushes here and there, whispering, whispering. I understood at last – I had heard the words before, 'You are my friend – kill with a sure shot.'

"I bore it as long as I could – then leaped away, as on this very night I leaped from my stockade and swam to you. I ran – I ran crying like a child left alone and far from the houses. He ran by my side, without footsteps, whispering, whispering – invisible and heard. I sought people – I wanted men around me! Men who had not died! And again we two wandered. I sought danger, violence, and death. I fought in the Atjeh war, and a brave people wondered at the valiance of a stranger. But we were two; he warded off the blows . . . Why? I wanted peace, not life. And no one could see him; no one knew – I dared tell no one. At times he would leave me, but not for long; then he would return and whisper or stare. My heart was torn with a strange fear, but could not die. Then I met an old man.

"You all knew him. People here called him my sorcerer, my servant and sword-bearer; but to me he was father, mother, protection, refuge and peace. When I met him he was returning from a pilgrimage, and I heard him intoning the prayer of sunset. He had gone to the holy place with his son, his son's wife, and a little child; and on their return, by the favour of the Most High, they all died: the strong man, the young mother, the little child – they died; and the old man reached his country alone. He was a pilgrim serene and pious, very wise and very lonely. I told him all. For a time we lived together. He said over me words of compassion, of wisdom, of prayer. He warded from me the shade of the dead. I begged him for a charm that would make me safe. For a long time he refused; but at last, with a sigh and a smile, he gave me one. Doubtless he could command a spirit stronger than the unrest of my dead friend, and again I had peace; but I had become restless, and a lover of turmoil and danger. The old man never left me. We travelled together. We were welcomed by the great; his wisdom and my courage are remembered where your strength, O white men, is forgotten! We served the Sultan of Sula. We fought the Spaniards. There were victories, hopes, defeats, sorrow, blood, women's tears . . . What for? . . . We fled. We collected wanderers of a warlike race and came here to fight again. The rest you know. I am the ruler of a conquered land, a lover of war and danger, a fighter and a plotter. But the old man has died, and I am again the slave of the dead. He is not here now to drive away the reproachful shade – to silence the lifeless voice! The power of his charm has died with him. And I know fear; and I hear the whisper, 'Kill! kill! kill!' . . . Have I not killed enough? . . ."

For the first time that night a sudden convulsion of madness and rage passed over his face. His wavering glances darted here and there like scared birds in a thunderstorm. He jumped up, shouting—

"By the spirits that drink blood: by the spirits that cry in the night: by all the spirits of fury, misfortune, and death, I swear – some day I will strike into every heart I meet – I . . ."

He looked so dangerous that we all three leaped to our feet, and Hollis, with the back of his hand, sent the kriss flying off the table. I believe we shouted together. It was a short scare, and the next moment he was again composed in his chair, with three white men standing over him in rather foolish attitudes. We felt a little ashamed of ourselves. Jackson picked up the kriss, and, after an inquiring glance at me, gave it to him. He received it with a stately inclination of the head and stuck it in the twist of his sarong, with punctilious care to give his weapon a pacific position. Then he looked up at us with an austere smile. We were abashed and reproved. Hollis sat sideways on the table and, holding his chin in his hand, scrutinized him in pensive silence. I said—

"You must abide with your people. They need you. And there is forgetfulness in life. Even the dead cease to speak in time."

"Am I a woman, to forget long years before an eyelid has had the time to beat twice?" he exclaimed, with bitter resentment. He startled me. It was amazing. To him his life – that cruel mirage of love and peace – seemed as real, as undeniable, as theirs would be to any saint, philosopher, or fool of us all. Hollis muttered—

"You won't soothe him with your platitudes."

Karain spoke to me.

"You know us. You have lived with us. Why? – we cannot know; but you understand our sorrows and our thoughts. You have lived with my people, and you understand our desires and our fears. With you I will go. To your land – to your people. To your people, who live in unbelief; to whom day is day, and night is night – nothing more, because you understand all things seen, and despise all else! To your land of unbelief, where the dead do not speak, where every man is wise, and alone – and at peace!"

"Capital description," murmured Hollis, with the flicker of a smile.

Karain hung his head.

"I can toil, and fight – and be faithful," he whispered, in a weary tone, "but I cannot go back to him who waits for me on the shore. No! Take me with you . . . Or else give me some of your strength – of your unbelief . . . A charm! . . ."

He seemed utterly exhausted.

"Yes, take him home," said Hollis, very low, as if debating with himself. "That would be one way. The ghosts there are in society, and talk affably to ladies and gentlemen, but would scorn a naked human being – like our princely friend . . . Naked . . . Flayed! I should say. I am sorry for him. Impossible – of course. The end of all this shall be," he went on, looking up at us – "the end of this shall be, that some day he will run amuck amongst his faithful subjects and send *ad patres* ever so many of them before they make up their minds to the disloyalty of knocking him on the head."

I nodded. I thought it more than probable that such would be the end of Karain. It was evident that he had been hunted by his thought along the very limit of human endurance, and very little more pressing was needed to make him swerve over into the form of madness peculiar to his race. The respite he had during the old man's life made the return of the torment unbearable. That much was clear.

He lifted his head suddenly; we had imagined for a moment that he had been dozing.

"Give me your protection – or your strength!" he cried. "A charm . . . a weapon!"

Again his chin fell on his breast. We looked at him, then looked at one another with suspicious awe in our eyes, like men who come unexpectedly upon the scene of some mysterious disaster.

He had given himself up to us; he had thrust into our hands his errors and his torment, his life and his peace; and we did not know what to do with that problem from the outer darkness. We three white men, looking at the Malay, could not find one word to the purpose amongst us – if indeed there existed a word that could solve that problem. We pondered, and our hearts sank. We felt as though we three had been called to the very gate of Infernal Regions to judge, to decide the fate of a wanderer coming suddenly from a world of sunshine and illusions.

"By Jove, he seems to have a great idea of our power," whispered Hollis, hopelessly. And then again there was a silence, the feeble plash of water, the steady tick of chronometers. Jackson, with bare arms crossed, leaned his shoulders against the bulkhead of the cabin. He was bending his head under the deck beam; his fair beard spread out magnificently over his chest; he looked colossal, ineffectual, and mild. There was something lugubrious in the aspect of the cabin; the air in it seemed to become slowly charged with the cruel chill of helplessness, with the pitiless anger of egoism against the incomprehensible form of an intruding pain. We had no idea what to do; we began to resent bitterly the hard necessity to get rid of him.

Hollis mused, muttered suddenly with a short laugh, "Strength . . . Protection . . . Charm." He slipped off the table and left the cuddy without a look at us. It seemed a base desertion. Jackson and I exchanged indignant glances. We could hear him rummaging in his pigeon-hole of a cabin. Was the fellow actually going to bed? Karain sighed. It was intolerable!

Then Hollis reappeared, holding in both hands a small leather box. He put it down gently on the table and looked at us with a queer gasp, we thought, as though he had from some cause become speechless for a moment, or were ethically uncertain about producing that box. But in an instant the insolent and unerring wisdom of his youth gave him the needed courage. He said, as he unlocked the box with a very small key, "Look as solemn as you can, you fellows."

Probably we looked only surprised and stupid, for he glanced over his shoulder, and said angrily—

"This is no play; I am going to do something for him. Look serious. Confound it! . . . Can't you lie a little . . . for a friend!"

Karain seemed to take no notice of us, but when Hollis threw open the lid of the box his eyes flew to it – and so did ours. The quilted crimson satin of the inside put a violent patch of colour into the sombre atmosphere; it was something positive to look at – it was fascinating.

VI

Hollis looked smiling into the box. He had lately made a dash home through the Canal. He had been away six months, and only joined us again just in time for this last trip. We had never seen the box before. His hands hovered above it; and he talked to us ironically, but his face became as grave as though he were pronouncing a powerful incantation over the things inside.

"Every one of us," he said, with pauses that somehow were more offensive then his words— "every one of us, you'll admit, has been haunted by some woman . . . And . . . as to fiends . . . dropped by the way . . . Well! . . . ask yourselves . . ."

He paused. Karain stared. A deep rumble was heard high up under the deck. Jackson spoke seriously—

"Don't be so beastly cynical."

"Ah! You are without guile," said Hollis, sadly. "You will learn . . . Meantime this Malay has been our friend . . ."

He repeated several times thoughtfully, "Friend . . . Malay. Friend, Malay," as though weighing the words against one another, then went on more briskly—

"A good fellow – a gentleman in his way. We can't, so to speak, turn our backs on his confidence and belief in us. Those Malays are easily impressed – all nerves, you know – therefore . . ."

He turned to me sharply.

"You know him best," he said, in a practical tone. "Do you think he is fanatical – I mean very strict in his faith?"

I stammered in profound amazement that "I did not think so."

"It's on account of its being a likeness – an engraved image," muttered Hollis, enigmatically, turning to the box. He plunged his fingers into it. Karain's lips were parted and his eyes shone. We looked into the box.

There were there a couple of reels of cotton, a packet of needles, a bit of silk ribbon, dark blue; a cabinet photograph, at which Hollis stole a glance before laying it on the table face downwards. A girl's portrait, I could see. There were, amongst a lot of various small objects, a bunch of flowers, a narrow white glove with many buttons, a slim packet of letters carefully tied up. Amulets of white men! Charms and talismans! Charms that keep them straight, that drive them crooked, that have the power to make a young man sigh, an old man smile. Potent things that procure dreams of joy, thoughts of regret; that soften hard hearts, and can temper a soft one to the hardness of steel. Gifts of heaven – things of earth . . .

Hollis rummaged in the box.

And it seemed to me, during that moment of waiting, that the cabin of the schooner was becoming filled with a stir invisible and living as of subtle breaths. All the ghosts driven out of the unbelieving West by men who pretend to be wise and alone and at peace – all the homeless ghosts of an unbelieving world – appeared suddenly round the figure of Hollis bending over the box; all the exiled and charming shades of loved women; all the beautiful and tender ghosts of ideals, remembered, forgotten, cherished, execrated; all the cast-out and reproachful ghosts of friends admired, trusted, traduced, betrayed, left dead by the way – they all seemed to come from the inhospitable regions of the earth to crowd into the gloomy cabin, as though it had been a refuge and, in all the unbelieving world, the only place of avenging belief . . . It lasted a second – all disappeared. Hollis was facing us alone with something small that glittered between his fingers. It looked like a coin.

"Ah! here it is," he said.

He held it up. It was a sixpence – a Jubilee sixpence. It was gilt; it had a hole punched near the rim. Hollis looked towards Karain.

"A charm for our friend," he said to us. "The thing itself is of great power – money, you know – and his imagination is struck. A loyal vagabond; if only his puritanism doesn't shy at a likeness . . ."

We said nothing. We did not know whether to be scandalized, amused, or relieved. Hollis advanced towards Karain, who stood up as if startled, and then, holding the coin up, spoke in Malay.

"This is the image of the Great Queen, and the most powerful thing the white men know," he said, solemnly.

Karain covered the handle of his kriss in sign of respect, and stared at the crowned head.

"The Invincible, the Pious," he muttered.

"She is more powerful than Suleiman the Wise, who commanded the genii, as you know," said Hollis, gravely. "I shall give this to you."

He held the sixpence in the palm of his hand, and looking at it thoughtfully, spoke to us in English.

"She commands a spirit, too – the spirit of her nation; a masterful, conscientious, unscrupulous, unconquerable devil . . . that does a lot of good – incidentally . . . a lot of good . . . at times – and wouldn't stand any fuss from the best ghost out for such a little thing as our friend's shot. Don't look thunderstruck, you fellows. Help me to make him believe – everything's in that."

"His people will be shocked," I murmured.

Hollis looked fixedly at Karain, who was the incarnation of the very essence of still excitement. He stood rigid, with head thrown back; his eyes rolled wildly, flashing; the dilated nostrils quivered.

"Hang it all!" said Hollis at last, "he is a good fellow. I'll give him something that I shall really miss."

He took the ribbon out of the box, smiled at it scornfully, then with a pair of scissors cut out a piece from the palm of the glove.

"I shall make him a thing like those Italian peasants wear, you know."

He sewed the coin in the delicate leather, sewed the leather to the ribbon, tied the ends together. He worked with haste. Karain watched his fingers all the time.

"Now then," he said – then stepped up to Karain. They looked close into one another's eyes. Those of Karain stared in a lost glance, but Hollis's seemed to grow darker and looked out masterful and compelling. They were in violent contrast together – one motionless and the colour of bronze, the other dazzling white and lifting his arms, where the powerful muscles rolled slightly under a skin that gleamed like satin. Jackson moved near with the air of a man closing up to a chum in a tight place. I said impressively, pointing to Hollis—

"He is young, but he is wise. Believe him!"

Karain bent his head: Hollis threw lightly over it the dark-blue ribbon and stepped back.

"Forget, and be at peace!" I cried.

Karain seemed to wake up from a dream. He said, "Ha!" shook himself as if throwing off a burden. He looked round with assurance. Someone on deck dragged off the skylight cover, and a flood of light fell into the cabin. It was morning already.

"Time to go on deck," said Jackson.

Hollis put on a coat, and we went up, Karain leading.

The sun had risen beyond the hills, and their long shadows stretched far over the bay in the pearly light. The air was clear, stainless, and cool. I pointed at the curved line of yellow sands.

"He is not there," I said, emphatically, to Karain. "He waits no more. He has departed forever."

A shaft of bright hot rays darted into the bay between the summits of two hills, and the water all round broke out as if by magic into a dazzling sparkle.

"No! He is not there waiting," said Karain, after a long look over the beach. "I do not hear him," he went on, slowly. "No!"

He turned to us.

"He has departed again – forever!" he cried.

We assented vigorously, repeatedly, and without compunction. The great thing was to impress him powerfully; to suggest absolute safety – the end of all trouble. We did our best; and I hope we affirmed our faith in the power of Hollis's charm efficiently enough to put the matter beyond the shadow of a doubt. Our voices rang around him joyously in the still air, and above his head the sky, pellucid, pure, stainless, arched its tender blue from shore to shore and over the bay, as if to envelop the water, the earth, and the man in the caress of its light.

The anchor was up, the sails hung still, and half-a-dozen big boats were seen sweeping over the bay to give us a tow out. The paddlers in the first one that came alongside lifted their heads and saw their ruler standing amongst us. A low murmur of surprise arose – then a shout of greeting.

He left us, and seemed straightaway to step into the glorious splendour of his stage, to wrap himself in the illusion of unavoidable success. For a moment he stood erect, one foot over the gangway, one hand on the hilt of his kriss, in a martial pose; and, relieved from the fear of outer darkness, he held his head high, he swept a serene look over his conquered foothold on the earth. The boats far off took up the cry of greeting; a great clamour rolled on the water; the hills echoed it, and seemed to toss back at him the words invoking long life and victories.

He descended into a canoe, and as soon as he was clear of the

side we gave him three cheers. They sounded faint and orderly
after the wild tumult of his loyal subjects, but it was the best we
could do. He stood up in the boat, lifted up both his arms, then
pointed to the infallible charm. We cheered again; and the Malays
in the boats stared – very much puzzled and impressed. I
wondered what they thought; what he thought; . . . what the
reader thinks?

We towed out slowly. We saw him land and watch us from the
beach. A figure approached him humbly but openly – not at all
like a ghost with a grievance. We could see other men running
towards him. Perhaps he had been missed? At any rate there was
a great stir. A group formed itself rapidly near him, and he walked
along the sands, followed by a growing *cortège* and kept nearly
abreast of the schooner. With our glasses we could see the blue
ribbon on his neck and a patch of white on his brown chest. The
bay was waking up. The smokes of morning fires stood in faint
spirals higher than the heads of palms; people moved between the
houses; a herd of buffaloes galloped clumsily across a green slope;
the slender figures of boys brandishing sticks appeared black and
leaping in the long grass; a coloured line of women, with water
bamboos on their heads, moved swaying through a thin grove of
fruit-trees. Karain stopped in the midst of his men and waved his
hand; then, detaching himself from the splendid group, walked
alone to the water's edge and waved his hand again. The
schooner passed out to sea between the steep headlands that shut
in the bay, and at the same instant Karain passed out of our life
forever.

But the memory remains. Some years afterwards I met Jackson,
in the Strand. He was magnificent as ever. His head was high
above the crowd. His beard was gold, his face red, his eyes blue; he
had a wide-brimmed grey hat and no collar or waistcoat; he was
inspiring; he had just come home – had landed that very day! Our
meeting caused an eddy in the current of humanity. Hurried
people would run against us, then walk round us, and turn back
to look at that giant. We tried to compress seven years of life into
seven exclamations; then, suddenly appeased, walked sedately
along, giving one another the news of yesterday. Jackson gazed
about him, like a man who looks for landmarks, then stopped
before Bland's window. He always had a passion for firearms; so
he stopped short and contemplated the row of weapons, perfect

and severe, drawn up in a line behind the black-framed panes. I
stood by his side. Suddenly he said—

"Do you remember Karain?"

I nodded.

"The sight of all this made me think of him," he went on, with
his face near the glass . . . and I could see another man, powerful
and bearded, peering at him intently from amongst the dark and
polished tubes that can cure so many illusions. "Yes; it made me
think of him," he continued, slowly. "I saw a paper this morning;
they are fighting over there again. He's sure to be in it. He will
make it hot for the cabelleros. Well, good luck to him, poor devil!
He was perfectly stunning."

We walked on.

"I wonder whether the charm worked – you remember Hollis's
charm, of course. If it did . . . never was a sixpence wasted to
better advantage! Poor devil! I wonder whether he got rid of that
friend of his. Hope so . . . Do you know, I sometimes think that—"

I stood still and looked at him.

"Yes . . . I mean, whether the thing was so, you know . . .
whether it really happened to him . . . What do you think?"

"My dear chap," I cried, "you have been too long away from
home. What a question to ask! Only look at all this."

A watery gleam of sunshine flashed from the west and went out
between two long lines of walls; and then the broken confusion of
roofs, the chimney-stacks, the gold letters sprawling over the
fronts of houses, the sombre polish of windows, stood resigned
and sullen under the falling gloom. The whole length of the street,
deep as a well and narrow like a corridor, was full of a sombre and
ceaseless stir. Our ears were filled by a headlong shuffle and beat
of rapid footsteps and an underlying rumour – a rumour vast,
faint, pulsating, as of panting breaths, of beating hearts, of
gasping voices. Innumerable eyes stared straight in front, feet
moved hurriedly, blank faces flowed, arms swung. Over all, a
narrow ragged strip of smoky sky wound about between the high
roofs, extended and motionless, like a soiled streamer flying above
the rout of a mob.

"Ye-e-e-s," said Jackson, meditatively.

The big wheels of hansoms turned slowly along the edge of side-
walks, a pale-faced youth strolled, overcome by weariness, by the
side of his stick and with the tails of his overcoat flapping gently

near his heels; horses stepped gingerly on the greasy pavement, tossing their heads; two young girls passed by, talking vivaciously and with shining eyes; a fine old fellow strutted, red-faced, stroking a white moustache; and a line of yellow boards with blue letters on them approached us slowly, tossing on high behind one another like some queer wreckage adrift upon a river of hats.

"Ye-e-es," repeated Jackson. His clear blue eyes looked about, contemptuous, amused and hard, like the eyes of a boy. A clumsy string of red, yellow, and green omnibuses rolled swaying, monstrous and gaudy; two shabby children ran across the road; a knot of dirty men with red neckerchiefs round their bare throats lurched along, discussing filthily; a ragged old man with a face of despair yelled horribly in the mud the name of a paper; while far off, amongst the tossing heads of horses, the dull flash of harnesses, the jumble of lustrous panels and roofs of carriages, we could see a policeman, helmeted and dark, stretching out a rigid arm at the crossing of the streets.

"Yes; I see it," said Jackson, slowly. "It is there; it pants, it runs, it rolls; it is strong and alive; it would smash you if you didn't look out; but I'll be hanged if it is yet as real to me as . . . as the other thing . . . say, Karain's story."

I think that, decidedly, he had been too long away from home.

1897/1897

Youth: A Narrative

This could have occurred nowhere but in England, where men and sea interpenetrate, so to speak – the sea entering into the life of most men, and the men knowing something or everything about the sea, in the way of amusement, of travel, or of bread-winning.

We were sitting round a mahogany table that reflected the bottle, the claret-glasses, and our faces as we leaned on our elbows. There was a director of companies, an accountant, a lawyer, Marlow, and myself. The director had been a *Conway* boy, the accountant had served four years at sea, the lawyer – a fine crusted Tory, High Churchman, the best of old fellows, the soul of honour – had been chief officer in the P. & O. service in the good old days when mail-boats were square-rigged at least on two masts, and used to come down the China Sea before a fair monsoon with stun'-sails set alow and aloft. We all began life in the merchant service. Between the five of us there was the strong bond of the sea, and also the fellowship of the craft, which no amount of enthusiasm for yachting, cruising, and so on can give, since one is only the amusement of life and the other is life itself.

Marlow (at least I think that is how he spelt his name) told the story, or rather the chronicle, of a voyage:—

"Yes, I have seen a little of the Eastern seas; but what I remember best is my first voyage there. You fellows know there are those voyages that seem ordered for the illustration of life, that might stand for a symbol of existence. You fight, work, sweat, nearly kill yourself, sometimes do kill yourself, trying to accomplish something – and you can't. Not from any fault of yours. You simply can do nothing, neither great nor little – not a thing in the world – not even marry an old maid, or get a wretched 600-ton cargo of coal to its port of destination.

"It was altogether a memorable affair. It was my first voyage to the East, and my first voyage as second mate; it was also my skipper's first command. You'll admit it was time. He was sixty if a day; a little man, with a broad, not very straight back, with bowed

shoulders and one leg more bandy than the other, he had that
queer twisted-about appearance you see so often in men who
work in the fields. He had a nut-cracker face – chin and nose
trying to come together over a sunken mouth – and it was framed
in iron-grey fluffy hair, that looked like a chin-strap of cotton-
wool sprinkled with coal-dust. And he had blue eyes in that old
face of his, which were amazingly like a boy's, with that candid
expression some quite common men preserve to the end of their
days by a rare internal gift of simplicity of heart and rectitude of
soul. What induced him to accept me was a wonder. I had come
out of a crack Australian clipper, where I had been third officer,
and he seemed to have a prejudice against crack clippers as
aristocratic and high-toned. He said to me, 'You know, in this ship
you will have to work.' I said I had to work in every ship I had
ever been in. 'Ah, but this is different, and you gentlemen out of
them big ships; . . . but there! I dare say you will do. Join to-
morrow.'

"I joined to-morrow. It was twenty-two years ago; and I was
just twenty. How time passes! It was one of the happiest days of
my life. Fancy! Second mate for the first time – a really responsible
officer! I wouldn't have thrown up my new billet for a fortune.
The mate looked me over carefully. He was also an old chap, but
of another stamp. He had a Roman nose, a snow-white, long
beard, and his name was Mahon, but he insisted that it should be
pronounced Mann. He was well connected; yet there was something wrong with his luck, and he had never got on.

"As to the captain, he had been for years in coasters, then in
the Mediterranean, and last in the West Indian trade. He had
never been round the Capes. He could just write a kind of sketchy
hand, and didn't care for writing at all. Both were thorough good
seamen of course, and between those two old chaps I felt like a
small boy between two grandfathers.

"The ship also was old. Her name was the *Judea*. Queer name,
isn't it? She belonged to a man Wilmer, Wilcox – some name like
that; but he has been bankrupt and dead these twenty years or
more, and his name don't matter. She had been laid up in
Shadwell basin for ever so long. You may imagine her state. She
was all rust, dust, grime – soot aloft, dirt on deck. To me it was like
coming out of a palace into a ruined cottage. She was about 400
tons, had a primitive windlass, wooden latches to the doors, not a

bit of brass about her, and a big square stern. There was on it, below her name in big letters, a lot of scrollwork, with the gilt off, and some sort of coat of arms, with the motto 'Do or Die' underneath. I remember it took my fancy immensely. There was a touch of romance in it, something that made me love the old thing – something that appealed to my youth!

"We left London in ballast – sand ballast – to load a cargo of coal in a northern port for Bankok. Bankok! I thrilled. I had been six years at sea, but had only seen Melbourne and Sydney, very good places, charming places in their way – but Bankok!

"We worked out of the Thames under canvas, with a North Sea pilot on board. His name was Jermyn, and he dodged all day long about the galley drying his handkerchief before the stove. Apparently he never slept. He was a dismal man, with a perpetual tear sparkling at the end of his nose, who either had been in trouble, or was in trouble, or expected to be in trouble – couldn't be happy unless something went wrong. He mistrusted my youth, my common-sense, and my seamanship, and made a point of showing it in a hundred little ways. I dare say he was right. It seems to me I knew very little then, and I know not much more now; but I cherish a hate for that Jermyn to this day.

"We were a week working up as far as Yarmouth Roads, and then we got into a gale – the famous October gale of twenty-two years ago. It was wind, lightning, sleet, snow, and a terrific sea. We were flying light, and you may imagine how bad it was when I tell you we had smashed bulwarks and a flooded deck. On the second night she shifted her ballast into the lee bow, and by that time we had been blown off somewhere on the Dogger Bank. There was nothing for it but go below with shovels and try to right her, and there we were in that vast hold, gloomy like a cavern, the tallow dips stuck and flickering on the beams, the gale howling above, the ship tossing about like mad on her side; there we all were, Jermyn, the captain, every one, hardly able to keep our feet, engaged on that gravedigger's work, and trying to toss shovelfuls of wet sand up to windward. At every tumble of the ship you could see vaguely in the dim light men falling down with a great flourish of shovels. One of the ship's boys (we had two), impressed by the weirdness of the scene, wept as if his heart would break. We could hear him blubbering somewhere in the shadows.

"On the third day the gale died out, and by and by a north-country tug picked us up. We took sixteen days in all to get from London to the Tyne! When we got into dock we had lost our turn for loading, and they hauled us off to a tier where we remained for a month. Mrs Beard (the captain's name was Beard) came from Colchester to see the old man. She lived on board. The crew of runners had left, and there remained only the officers, one boy and the steward, a mulatto who answered to the name of Abraham. Mrs Beard was an old woman, with a face all wrinkled and ruddy like a winter apple, and the figure of a young girl. She caught sight of me once, sewing on a button, and insisted on having my shirts to repair. This was something different from the captains' wives I had known on board crack clippers. When I brought her the shirts, she said: 'And the socks? They want mending, I am sure, and John's – Captain Beard's – things are all in order now. I would be glad of something to do.' Bless the old woman. She overhauled my outfit for me, and meantime I read for the first time *Sartor Resartus* and Burnaby's *Ride to Khiva*. I didn't understand much of the first then; but I remember I preferred the soldier to the philosopher at the time; a preference which life has only confirmed. One was a man, and the other was either more – or less. However, they are both dead and Mrs Beard is dead, and youth, strength, genius, thoughts, achievements, simple hearts – all die . . . No matter.

"They loaded us at last. We shipped a crew. Eight able seamen and two boys. We hauled off one evening to the buoys at the dock-gates, ready to go out and with a fair prospect of beginning the voyage next day. Mrs Beard was to start for home by a late train. When the ship was fast we went to tea. We sat rather silent through the meal – Mahon, the old couple, and I. I finished first, and slipped away for a smoke, my cabin being a deck-house just against the poop. It was high water, blowing fresh with a drizzle; the double dock-gates were opened, and the steam-colliers were going in and out in the darkness with their lights burning bright, a great splashing of propellers, rattling of winches, and a lot of hailing on the pier-heads. I watched the procession of head-lights gliding high and of green lights gliding low in the night, when suddenly a red gleam flashed at me, vanished, came into view again, and remained. The fore-end of a steamer loomed up close. I shouted down the cabin, 'Come up, quick!' and then heard a startled voice saying afar in the dark, 'Stop her, sir.' A bell jingled.

Another voice cried warningly, 'We are going right into that barque, sir.' The answer to this was a gruff 'All right,' and the next thing was a heavy crash as the steamer struck a glancing blow with the bluff of her bow about our fore-rigging. There was a moment of confusion, yelling, and running about. Steam roared. Then somebody was heard saying, 'All clear, sir.' . . . 'Are you all right?' asked the gruff voice. I had jumped forward to see the damage and hailed back, 'I think so.' 'Easy astern,' said the gruff voice. A bell jingled. 'What steamer is that?' screamed Mahon. By that time she was no more to us than a bulky shadow manoeuvring a little way off. They shouted at us some name – a woman's name, Miranda or Melissa – or some such thing. 'This means another month in this beastly hole,' said Mahon to me, as we peered with lamps about the splintered bulwarks and broken braces. 'But where's the captain?'

"We had not heard or seen anything of him all that time. We went aft to look. A doleful voice arose hailing somewhere in the middle of the dock, '*Judea* ahoy!' . . . How the devil did he get there? . . . 'Hallo!' we shouted. 'I am adrift in our boat without oars,' he cried. A belated water-man offered his services, and Mahon struck a bargain with him for half-a-crown to tow our skipper alongside; but it was Mrs Beard that came up the ladder first. They had been floating about the dock in that mizzly cold rain for nearly an hour. I was never so surprised in my life.

"It appears that when he heard my shout 'Come up' he understood at once what was the matter, caught up his wife, ran on deck, and across, and down into our boat, which was fast to the ladder. Not bad for a sixty-year-old. Just imagine that old fellow saving heroically in his arms that old woman – the woman of his life. He set her down on a thwart, and was ready to climb back on board when the painter came adrift somehow, and away they went together. Of course in the confusion we did not hear him shouting. He looked abashed. She said cheerfully, 'I suppose it does not matter my losing the train now?' 'No, Jenny – you go below and get warm,' he growled. Then to us: 'A sailor has no business with a wife – I say. There I was, out of the ship. Well, no harm done this time. Let's go and look at what that fool of a steamer smashed.'

"It wasn't much, but it delayed us three weeks. At the end of that time, the captain being engaged with his agents, I carried

Mrs Beard's bag to the railway-station and put her all comfy into a third-class carriage. She lowered the window to say, 'You are a good young man. If you see John – Captain Beard – without his muffler at night, just remind him from me to keep his throat well wrapped up.' 'Certainly, Mrs Beard,' I said. 'You are a good young man; I noticed how attentive you are to John – to Captain—' The train pulled out suddenly; I took my cap off to the old woman: I never saw her again . . . Pass the bottle.

"We went to sea next day. When we made that start for Bankok we had been already three months out of London. We had expected to be a fortnight or so – at the outside.

"It was January, and the weather was beautiful – the beautiful sunny winter weather that has more charm than in the summer-time, because it is unexpected, and crisp, and you know it won't, it can't, last long. It's like a windfall, like a godsend, like an unexpected piece of luck.

"It lasted all down the North Sea, all down Channel; and it lasted till we were three hundred miles or so to the westward of the Lizards: then the wind went round to the sou'west and began to pipe up. In two days it blew a gale. The *Judea*, hove to, wallowed on the Atlantic like an old candle-box. It blew day after day: it blew with spite, without interval, without mercy, without rest. The world was nothing but an immensity of great foaming waves rushing at us, under a sky low enough to touch with the hand and dirty like a smoked ceiling. In the stormy space surrounding us there was as much flying spray as air. Day after day and night after night there was nothing round the ship but the howl of the wind, the tumult of the sea, the noise of water pouring over her deck. There was no rest for her and no rest for us. She tossed, she pitched, she stood on her head, she sat on her tail, she rolled, she groaned, and we had to hold on while on deck and cling to our bunks when below, in a constant effort of body and worry of mind.

"One night Mahon spoke through the small window of my berth. It opened right into my very bed, and I was lying there sleepless, in my boots, feeling as though I had not slept for years, and could not if I tried. He said excitedly—

"'You got the sounding-rod in here, Marlow? I can't get the pumps to suck. By God! it's no child's play.'

"I gave him the sounding-rod and lay down again, trying to

think of various things – but I thought only of the pumps. When I came on deck they were still at it, and my watch relieved at the pumps. By the light of the lantern brought on deck to examine the sounding-rod I caught a glimpse of their weary, serious faces. We pumped all the four hours. We pumped all night, all day, all the week – watch and watch. She was working herself loose, and leaked badly – not enough to drown us at once, but enough to kill us with the work at the pumps. And while we pumped the ship was going from us piecemeal: the bulwarks went, the stanchions were torn out, the ventilators smashed, the cabin-door burst in. There was not a dry spot in the ship. She was being gutted bit by bit. The long-boat changed, as if by magic, into matchwood where she stood in her gripes. I had lashed her myself, and was rather proud of my handiwork, which had withstood so long the malice of the sea. And we pumped. And there was no break in the weather. The sea was white like a sheet of foam, like a caldron of boiling milk; there was not a break in the clouds, no – not the size of a man's hand – no, not for so much as ten seconds. There was for us no sky, there were for us no stars, no sun, no universe – nothing but angry clouds and an infuriated sea. We pumped watch and watch, for dear life; and it seemed to last for months, for years, for all eternity, as though we had been dead and gone to a hell for sailors. We forgot the day of the week, the name of the month, what year it was, and whether we had ever been ashore. The sails blew away, she lay broadside on under a weather-cloth, the ocean poured over her, and we did not care. We turned those handles, and had the eyes of idiots. As soon as we had crawled on deck I used to take a round turn with a rope about the men, the pumps, and the mainmast, and we turned, we turned incessantly, with the water to our waists, to our necks, over our heads. It was all one. We had forgotten how it felt to be dry.

"And there was somewhere in me the thought: By Jove! this is the deuce of an adventure – something you read about; and it is my first voyage as second mate – and I am only twenty – and here I am lasting it out as well as any of these men, and keeping my chaps up to the mark. I was pleased. I would not have given up the experience for worlds. I had moments of exultation. Whenever the old dismantled craft pitched heavily with her counter high in the air, she seemed to me to throw up, like an appeal, like a defiance, like a cry to the clouds without mercy, the words written on her stern: '*Judea*, London. Do or Die.'

"O, youth! The strength of it, the faith of it, the imagination of it! To me she was not an old rattle-trap carting about the world a lot of coal for a freight – to me she was the endeavour, the test, the trial of life. I think of her with pleasure, with affection, with regret – as you would think of someone dead you have loved. I shall never forget her . . . Pass the bottle.

"One night when tied to the mast, as I explained, we were pumping on, deafened with the wind, and without spirit enough in us to wish ourselves dead, a heavy sea crashed aboard and swept clean over us. As soon as I got my breath I shouted, as in duty bound, 'Keep on, boys!' when suddenly I felt something hard floating on deck strike the calf of my leg. I made a grab at it and missed. It was so dark we could not see each other's faces within a foot – you understand.

"After that thump the ship kept quiet for a while, and the thing, whatever it was, struck my leg again. This time I caught it – and it was a saucepan. At first, being stupid with fatigue and thinking of nothing but the pumps, I did not understand what I had in my hand. Suddenly it dawned upon me, and I shouted, 'Boys, the house on deck is gone. Leave this, and let's look for the cook.'

"There was a deck-house forward, which contained the galley, the cook's berth, and the quarters of the crew. As we had expected for days to see it swept away, the hands had been ordered to sleep in the cabin – the only safe place in the ship. The steward, Abraham, however, persisted in clinging to his berth, stupidly, like a mule – from sheer fright I believe, like an animal that won't leave a stable falling in an earthquake. So we went to look for him. It was chancing death, since once out of our lashings we were as exposed as if on a raft. But we went. The house was shattered as if a shell had exploded inside. Most of it had gone overboard – stove, men's quarters, and their property, all was gone; but two posts, holding a portion of the bulkhead to which Abraham's bunk was attached, remained as if by a miracle. We groped in the ruins and came upon this, and there he was, sitting in his bunk, surrounded by foam and wreckage, jabbering cheerfully to himself. He was out of his mind; completely and for ever mad, with this sudden shock coming upon the fag-end of his endurance. We snatched him up, lugged him aft, and pitched him head-first down the cabin companion. You understand there was no time to carry him down with infinite precautions and wait to see how he got on. Those below would pick him up at the bottom of the stairs all right. We were in a hurry to go back to the pumps. That business could not wait. A bad leak is an inhuman thing.

"One would think that the sole purpose of that fiendish gale had been to make a lunatic of that poor devil of a mulatto. It eased before morning, and next day the sky cleared, and as the sea went down the leak took up. When it came to bending a fresh set of sails the crew demanded to put back – and really there was nothing else to do. Boats gone, decks swept clean, cabin gutted, men without a stitch but what they stood in, stores spoiled, ship strained. We put her head for home, and – would you believe it? The wind came east right in our teeth. It blew fresh, it blew continuously. We had to beat up every inch of the way, but she did not leak so badly, the water keeping comparatively smooth. Two hours' pumping in every four is no joke – but it kept her afloat as far as Falmouth.

"The good people there live on casualties of the sea, and no doubt were glad to see us. A hungry crowd of shipwrights sharpened their chisels at the sight of that carcass of a ship. And, by Jove! they had pretty pickings off us before they were done. I fancy the owner was already in a tight place. There were delays. Then it was decided to take part of the cargo out and caulk her topsides. This was done, the repairs finished, cargo reshipped; a new crew came on board, and we went out – for Bankok. At the end of a week we were back again. The crew said they weren't going to Bankok – a hundred and fifty days' passage – in a something hooker that wanted pumping eight hours out of the twenty-four; and the nautical papers inserted again the little paragraph: '*Judea*. Barque. Tyne to Bankok; coals; put back to Falmouth leaky and with crew refusing duty.'

"There were more delays – more tinkering. The owner came down for a day, and said she was as right as a little fiddle. Poor old Captain Beard looked like the ghost of a Geordie skipper – through the worry and humiliation of it. Remember he was sixty, and it was his first command. Mahon said it was foolish business, and would end badly. I loved the ship more than ever, and wanted awfully to get to Bankok. To Bankok! Magic name, blessed name.

Mesopotamia wasn't a patch on it. Remember I was twenty, and it was my first second-mate's billet, and the East was waiting for me.

"We went out and anchored in the outer roads with a fresh crew – the third. She leaked worse than ever. It was as if those confounded shipwrights had actually made a hole in her. This time we did not even go outside. The crew simply refused to man the windlass.

"They towed us back to the inner harbour, and we became a fixture, a feature, an institution of the place. People pointed us out to visitors as 'That 'ere barque that's going to Bankok – has been here six months – put back three times.' On holidays the small boys pulling about in boats would hail, '*Judea*, ahoy!' and if a head showed above the rail shouted, 'Where you bound to? – Bankok?' and jeered. We were only three on board. The poor old skipper mooned in the cabin. Mahon undertook the cooking, and unexpectedly developed all a Frenchman's genius for preparing nice little messes. I looked languidly after the rigging. We became citizens of Falmouth. Every shopkeeper knew us. At the barber's or tobacconist's they asked familiarly, 'Do you think you will ever get to Bankok?' Meantime the owner, the underwriters, and the charterers squabbled amongst themselves in London, and our pay went on . . . Pass the bottle.

"It was horrid. Morally it was worse than pumping for life. It seemed as though we had been forgotten by the world, belonged to nobody, would get nowhere; it seemed that, as if bewitched, we would have to live for ever and ever in that inner harbour, a derision and a by-word to generations of long-shore loafers and dishonest boatmen. I obtained three months' pay and a five days' leave, and made a rush for London. It took me a day to get there and pretty well another to come back – but three months' pay went all the same. I don't know what I did with it. I went to a music-hall, I believe, lunched, dined, and supped in a swell place in Regent Street, and was back to time, with nothing but a complete set of Byron's works and a new railway rug to show for three months' work. The boat-man who pulled me off to the ship said: 'Hallo! I thought you had left the old thing. *She* will never get to Bankok.' 'That's all *you* know about it,' I said scornfully – but I didn't like that prophecy at all.

"Suddenly a man, some kind of agent to somebody, appeared with full powers. He had grog-blossoms all over his face, an indomitable energy, and was a jolly soul. We leaped into life again. A hulk came alongside, took our cargo, and then we went into dry dock to get our copper stripped. No wonder she leaked. The poor thing, strained beyond endurance by the gale, had, as if in disgust, spat out all the oakum of her lower seams. She was recaulked, new coppered, and made as tight as a bottle. We went back to the hulk and re-shipped our cargo.

"Then, on a fine moonlight night, all the rats left the ship.

"We had been infested with them. They had destroyed our sails, consumed more stores than the crew, affably shared our beds and our dangers, and now, when the ship was made seaworthy, concluded to clear out. I called Mahon to enjoy the spectacle. Rat after rat appeared on our rail, took a last look over his shoulder, and leaped with a hollow thud into the empty hulk. We tried to count them, but soon lost the tale. Mahon said: 'Well, well! don't talk to me about the intelligence of rats. They ought to have left before, when we had that narrow squeak from foundering. There you have the proof how silly is the superstition about them. They leave a good ship for an old rotten hulk, where there is nothing to eat, too, the fools! . . . I don't believe they know what is safe or what is good for them, any more than you or I.'

"And after some more talk we agreed that the wisdom of rats had been grossly overrated, being in fact no greater than that of men.

"The story of the ship was known, by this, all up the Channel from Land's End to the Forelands, and we could get no crew on the south coast. Then sent us one all complete from Liverpool, and we left once more – for Bankok.

"We had fair breezes, smooth water right into the tropics, and the old *Judea* lumbered along in the sunshine. When she went eight knots everything cracked aloft, and we tied our caps to our heads; but mostly she strolled on at the rate of three miles an hour. What could you expect? She was tired – that old ship. Her youth was where mine is – where yours is – you fellows who listen to this yarn; and what friend would throw your years and your weariness in your face? We didn't grumble at her. To us aft, at least, it seemed as though we had been born in her, reared in her, had lived in her for ages, had never known any other ship. I would just as soon have abused the old village church at home for not being a cathedral.

"And for me there was also my youth to make me patient. There was all the East before me, and all life, and the thought that I had been tried in that ship and had come out pretty well. And I thought of men of old who, centuries ago, went that road in ships that sailed no better, to the land of palms, and spices, and yellow sands, and of brown nations ruled by kings more cruel than Nero the Roman, and more splendid that Solomon the Jew. The old barque lumbered on, heavy with her age and the burden of her cargo, while I lived the life of youth in ignorance and hope. She lumbered on through an interminable procession of days; and the fresh gilding flashed back at the setting sun, seemed to cry out over the darkening sea the words painted on her stern, '*Judea*, London. Do or Die.'

"Then we entered the Indian Ocean and steered northerly for Java Head. The winds were light. Weeks slipped by. She crawled on, do or die, and people at home began to think of posting us as overdue.

"One Saturday evening, I being off duty, the men asked me to give them an extra bucket of water or so – for washing clothes. As I did not wish to screw on the fresh-water pump so late, I went forward whistling, and with a key in my hand to unlock the forepeak scuttle, intending to serve the water out of a spare tank we kept there.

"The smell down below was as unexpected as it was frightful. One would have thought hundreds of paraffin-lamps had been flaring and smoking in that hole for days. I was glad to get out. The man with me coughed and said, 'Funny smell, sir.' I answered negligently, 'It's good for the health they say,' and walked aft.

"The first thing I did was to put my head down the square of the midship ventilator. As I lifted the lid a visible breath, something like a thin fog, a puff of faint haze, rose from the opening. The ascending air was hot, and had a heavy, sooty, paraffiny smell. I gave one sniff, and put down the lid gently. It was no use choking myself. The cargo was on fire.

"Next day she began to smoke in earnest. You see it was to be expected, for though the coal was of a safe kind, that cargo had been so handled, so broken up with handling, that it looked more like smithy coal than anything else. Then it had been wetted – more than once. It rained all the time we were taking it back from the hulk, and now with this long passage it got heated, and there was another case of spontaneous combustion.

"The captain called us into the cabin. He had a chart spread on the table, and looked unhappy. He said, 'The coast of West Australia is near, but I mean to proceed to our destination. It is the hurricane month, too; but we will just keep her head for Bankok, and fight the fire. No more putting back anywhere, if we all get roasted. We will try first to stifle this 'ere damned combustion by want of air.'

"We tried. We battened down everything, and still she smoked. The smoke kept coming out through imperceptible crevices; it forced itself through bulkheads and covers; it oozed here and there and everywhere in slender threads, in an invisible film, in an incomprehensible manner. It made its way into the cabin, into the forecastle; it poisoned the sheltered places on the deck, it could be sniffed as high as the main-yard. It was clear that if the smoke came out the air came in. This was disheartening. This combustion refused to be stifled.

"We resolved to try water, and took the hatches off. Enormous volumes of smoke, whitish, yellowish, thick, greasy, misty, choking, ascended as high as the trucks. All hands cleared out aft. Then the poisonous cloud blew away, and we went back to work in a smoke that was no thicker now than that of an ordinary factory chimney.

"We rigged the force-pump, got the hose along, and by and by it burst. Well, it was as old as the ship – a prehistoric hose, and past repair. Then we pumped with the feeble head-pump, drew water with buckets, and in this way managed in time to pour lots of Indian Ocean into the main hatch. The bright stream flashed in sunshine, fell into a layer of white crawling smoke, and vanished on the black surface of coal. Steam ascended mingling with the smoke. We poured salt water as into a barrel without a bottom. It was our fate to pump in that ship, to pump out of her, to pump into her; and after keeping water out of her to save ourselves from being drowned, we frantically poured water into her to save ourselves from being burnt.

"And she crawled on, do or die, in the serene weather. The sky was a miracle of purity, a miracle of azure. The sea was polished, was blue, was pellucid, was sparkling like a precious stone, extending on all sides, all round to the horizon – as if the whole terrestrial globe had been one jewel, one colossal sapphire, a single gem fashioned into a planet. And on the lustre of the great calm waters the *Judea* glided imperceptibly, enveloped in languid and unclean vapours, in a lazy cloud that drifted to leeward, light and slow; a pestiferous cloud defiling the splendour of sea and sky.

"All this time of course we saw no fire. The cargo smouldered at the bottom somewhere. Once Mahon, as we were working side by side, said to me with a queer smile: 'Now, if she only would spring a tidy leak – like that time when we first left the Channel – it would put a stopper on this fire. Wouldn't it?' I remarked irrelevantly, 'Do you remember the rats?'

"We fought the fire and sailed the ship too as carefully as though nothing had been the matter. The steward cooked and attended on us. Of the other twelve men, eight worked while four rested. Everyone took his turn, captain included. There was equality, and if not exactly fraternity, then a deal of good feeling. Sometimes a man, as he dashed a bucketful of water down the hatchway, would yell out, 'Hurrah for Bankok!' and the rest laughed. But generally we were taciturn and serious – and thirsty. Oh! how thirsty! And we had to be careful with the water. Strict allowance. The ship smoked, the sun blazed . . . Pass the bottle.

"We tried everything. We even made an attempt to dig down to the fire. No good, of course. No man could remain more than a minute below. Mahon, who went first, fainted there, and the man who went to fetch him out did likewise. We lugged them out on deck. Then I leaped down to show how easily it could be done. They had learned wisdom by that time, and contented themselves by fishing for me with a chain-hook tied to a broom-handle, I believe. I did not offer to go and fetch up my shovel, which was left down below.

"Things began to look bad. We put the long-boat into the water. The second boat was ready to swing out. We had also another, a 14-foot thing, on davits aft, where it was quite safe.

"Then, behold, the smoke suddenly decreased. We redoubled our efforts to flood the bottom of the ship. In two days there was no smoke at all. Everybody was on the broad grin. This was on a Friday. On Saturday no work, but sailing the ship of course, was done. The men washed their clothes and their faces for the first time in a fortnight, and had a special dinner given them. They spoke of spontaneous combustion with contempt, and implied *they* were the boys to put out combustions. Somehow we all felt as though we each had inherited a large fortune. But a beastly smell of burning hung about the ship. Captain Beard had hollow eyes and sunken cheeks. I had never noticed so much before how twisted and bowed he was. He and Mahon prowled soberly about hatches and ventilators, sniffing. It struck me suddenly poor Mahon was a very, very old chap. As to me, I was as pleased and proud as though I had helped to win a great naval battle. O! Youth!

"The night was fine. In the morning a homeward-bound ship passed us hull down – the first we had seen for months; but we were nearing the land at last, Java Head being about 190 miles off, and nearly due north.

"Next day it was my watch on deck from eight to twelve. At breakfast the captain observed, 'It's wonderful how that smell hangs about the cabin.' About ten, the mate being on the poop, I stepped down on the main-deck for a moment. The carpenter's bench stood abaft the mainmast: I leaned against it sucking at my pipe, and the carpenter, a young chap, came to talk to me. He remarked, 'I think we have done very well, haven't we?' and then I perceived with annoyance the fool was trying to tilt the bench. I said curtly, 'Don't, Chips,' and immediately became aware of a queer sensation, of an absurd delusion – I seemed somehow to be in the air. I heard all round me like a pent-up breath released – as if a thousand giants simultaneously had said Phoo! – and felt a dull concussion which made my ribs ache suddenly. No doubt about it – I was in the air, and my body was describing a short parabola. But short as it was, I had the time to think several thoughts in, as far as I can remember, the following order: 'This can't be the carpenter – What is it? – Some accident – Submarine volcano? – Coals, gas! – By Jove! we are being blown up – Everybody's dead – I am falling into the after-hatch – I see fire in it.'

"The coal-dust suspended in the air of the hold had glowed dull-red at the moment of the explosion. In the twinkling of an eye, in an infinitesimal fraction of a second since the first tilt of the bench, I was sprawling full length on the cargo. I picked myself up and scrambled out. It was quick like a rebound. The deck was a wilderness of smashed timber, lying crosswise like trees in a wood after a hurricane; an immense curtain of soiled rags waved gently before me – it was the main-sail blown to strips. I thought, The masts will be toppling over directly; and to get out of the way bolted on all-fours towards the poop-ladder. The first person I saw was Mahon, with eyes like saucers, his mouth open, and the long white hair standing straight on end round his head like a silver halo. He was just about to go down when the sight of the main-deck stirring, heaving up, and changing into splinters before his eyes, petrified him on the top step. I stared at him in unbelief, and he stared at me with a queer kind of shocked curiosity. I did not know that I had no hair, no eyebrows, no eyelashes, that my young moustache was burnt off, that my face was black, one cheek laid open, my nose cut, and my chin bleeding. I had lost my cap, one of my slippers, and my shirt was torn to rags. Of all this I was not aware. I was amazed to see the ship still afloat, the poop-deck whole – and, most of all, to see anybody alive. Also the peace of the sky and the serenity of the sea were distinctly surprising. I suppose I expected to see them convulsed with horror . . . Pass the bottle.

"There was a voice hailing the ship from somewhere – in the air, in the sky – I couldn't tell. Presently I saw the captain – and he was mad. He asked me eagerly, 'Where's the cabin-table?' and to hear such a question was a frightful shock. I had just been blown up, you understand, and vibrated with that experience – I wasn't quite sure whether I was alive. Mahon began to stamp with both feet and yelled at him, 'Good God! don't you see the deck's blown out of her?' I found my voice, and stammered out as if conscious of some gross neglect of duty, 'I don't know where the cabin-table is.' It was like an absurd dream.

"Do you know what he wanted next? Well, he wanted to trim the yards. Very placidly, and as if lost in thought, he insisted on having the foreyard squared. 'I don't know if there's anybody alive,' said Mahon, almost tearfully. 'Surely,' he said, gently, 'there will be enough left to square the foreyard.'

"The old chap, it seems, was in his own berth winding up the chronometers, when the shock sent him spinning. Immediately it occurred to him – as he said afterwards – that the ship had struck something, and he ran out into the cabin. There, he saw, the cabin-table had vanished somewhere. The deck being blown up, it had fallen down into the lazarette of course. Where we had our breakfast that morning he saw only a great hole in the floor. This appeared to him so awfully mysterious, and impressed him so immensely, that what he saw and heard after he got on deck were mere trifles in comparison. And, mark, he noticed directly the wheel deserted and his barque off her course – and his only thought was to get that miserable, stripped, undecked, smouldering shell of a ship back again with her head pointing at her port of destination. Bankok! That's what he was after. I tell you this quiet, bowed, bandy-legged, almost deformed little man was immense in the singleness of his idea and in his placid ignorance of our agitation. He motioned us forward with a commanding gesture, and went to take the wheel himself.

"Yes; that was the first thing we did – trim the yards of that wreck! No one was killed, or even disabled, but everyone was more or less hurt. You should have seen them! Some were in rags, with black faces, like coal-heavers, like sweeps, and had bullet heads that seemed closely cropped, but were in fact singed to the skin. Others, of the watch below, awakened by being shot out from their collapsing bunks, shivered incessantly, and kept on groaning even as we went about our work. But they all worked. That crew of Liverpool hard cases had in them the right stuff. It's my experience they always have. It is the sea that gives it – the vastness, the loneliness surrounding their dark stolid souls. Ah! Well! we stumbled, we crept, we fell, we barked our shins on the wreckage, we hauled. The masts stood, but we did not know how much they might be charred down below. It was nearly calm, but a long swell ran from the west and made her roll. They might go at any moment. We looked at them with apprehension. One could not foresee which way they would fall.

"Then we retreated aft and looked about us. The deck was a tangle of planks on edge, of planks on end, of splinters, of ruined woodwork. The masts rose from that chaos like big trees above a matted undergrowth. The interstices of that mass of wreckage were full of something whitish, sluggish, stirring – of something that was like a greasy fog. The smoke of the invisible fire was coming up again, was trailing, like a poisonous thick mist in some valley choked with dead wood. Already lazy wisps were beginning to curl upwards amongst the mass of splinters. Here and there a piece of timber, stuck upright, resembled a post. Half of a fife-rail had been shot through the foresail, and the sky made a patch of glorious blue in the ignobly soiled canvas. A portion of several boards holding together had fallen across the rail, and one end protruded overboard, like a gangway leading upon nothing, like a gangway leading over the deep sea, leading to death – as if inviting us to walk the plank at once and be done with our ridiculous troubles. And still the air, the sky – a ghost, something invisible was hailing the ship.

"Someone had the sense to look over, and there was the helmsman, who had impulsively jumped overboard, anxious to come back. He yelled and swam lustily like a merman, keeping up with the ship. We threw him a rope, and presently he stood amongst us streaming with water and very crestfallen. The captain had surrendered the wheel, and apart, elbow on rail and chin in hand, gazed at the sea wistfully. We asked ourselves, What next? I thought, Now, this is something like. This is great. I wonder what will happen. O youth!

"Suddenly Mahon sighted a steamer far astern. Captain Beard said, 'We may do something with her yet.' We hoisted two flags, which said in the international language of the sea, 'On fire. Want immediate assistance.' The steamer grew bigger rapidly, and by and by spoke with two flags on her foremast, 'I am coming to your assistance.'

"In half an hour she was abreast, to windward, within hail, and rolling slightly, with her engines stopped. We lost our composure, and yelled all together with excitement, 'We've been blown up.' A man in a white helmet, on the bridge, cried, 'Yes! All right! all right!' and he nodded his head, and smiled, and made soothing motions with his hand as though at a lot of frightened children. One of the boats dropped in the water, and walked towards us upon the sea with her long oars. Four Calashes pulled a swinging stroke. This was my first sight of Malay seamen. I've known them since, but what struck me then was their unconcern: they came alongside, and even the bowman standing up and holding to our main chains with the boat-hook did not deign to lift his head for a glance. I thought people who had been blown up deserved more attention.

"A little man, dry like a chip and agile like a monkey, clambered up. It was the mate of the steamer. He gave one look, and cried, 'O boys – you had better quit.'

"We were silent. He talked apart with the captain for a time –

seemed to argue with him. Then they went away together to the steamer.

"When our skipper came back we learned that the steamer was the *Somerville*, Captain Nash, from West Australia to Singapore *via* Batavia with mails, and that the agreement was she should tow us to Anjer or Batavia, if possible, where we could extinguish the fire by scuttling, and then proceed on our voyage – to Bankok! The old man seemed excited. 'We will do it yet,' he said to Mahon, fiercely. He shook his fist at the sky. Nobody else said a word.

"At noon the steamer began to tow. She went ahead slim and high, and what was left of the *Judea* followed at the end of seventy fathom of tow-rope – followed her swiftly like a cloud of smoke with mastheads protruding above. We went aloft to furl the sails. We coughed on the yards, and were careful about the bunts. Do you see the lot of us there, putting a neat furl on the sails of that ship doomed to arrive nowhere? There was not a man who didn't think that at any moment the masts would topple over. From aloft we could not see the ship for smoke, and they worked carefully, passing the gaskets with even turns. 'Harbour furl – aloft there!' cried Mahon from below.

"You understand this? I don't think one of those chaps expected to get down in the usual way. When we did I heard them saying to each other, 'Well, I thought we would come down overboard, in a lump – sticks and all – blame me if I didn't.' 'That's what I was thinking to myself,' would answer wearily another battered and bandaged scarecrow. And, mind, these were men without the drilled-in habit of obedience. To an onlooker they would be a lot of profane scallywags without a redeeming point. What made them do it – what made them obey me when I, thinking consciously how fine it was, made them drop the bunt of the foresail twice to try and do it better? What? They had no professional reputation – no examples, no praise. It wasn't a sense of duty; they all knew well enough how to shirk, and laze, and dodge – when they had a mind to it – and mostly they had. Was it the two pounds ten a-month that sent them there? They didn't think their pay half good enough. No; it was something in them, something inborn and subtle and everlasting. I don't say positively that the crew of a French or German merchantman wouldn't have done it, but I doubt whether it would have been done in the same way. There was a completeness in it, something solid like a principle, and masterful like an instinct – a disclosure of something secret – of that hidden something, that gift of good or evil that makes racial difference, that shapes the fate of nations.

"It was that night at ten that, for the first time since we had been fighting it, we saw the fire. The speed of the towing had fanned the smouldering destruction. A blue gleam appeared forward, shining below the wreck of the deck. It wavered in patches, it seemed to stir and creep like the light of a glowworm. I saw it first, and told Mahon. 'Then the game's up,' he said. 'We had better stop this towing, or she will burst out suddenly fore and aft before we can clear out.' We set up a yell; rang bells to attract their attention; they towed on. At last Mahon and I had to crawl forward and cut the rope with an axe. There was no time to cast off the lashings. Red tongues could be seen licking the wilderness of splinters under our feet as we made our way back to the poop.

"Of course they very soon found out in the steamer that the rope was gone. She gave a loud blast of her whistle, her lights were seen sweeping in a wide circle, she came up ranging close along-side, and stopped. We were all in a tight group on the poop looking at her. Every man had saved a little bundle or a bag. Suddenly a conical flame with a twisted top shot up forward and threw upon the black sea a circle of light, with the two vessels side by side and heaving gently in its centre. Captain Beard had been sitting on the gratings still and mute for hours, but now he rose slowly and advanced in front of us, to the mizzen-shrouds. Captain Nash hailed: 'Come along! Look sharp. I have mail-bags on board. I will take you and your boats to Singapore.'

" 'Thank you! No!' said our skipper. 'We must see the last of the ship.'

" 'I can't stand by any longer,' shouted the other. 'Mails – you know.'

" 'Ay! ay! We are all right.'

" 'Very well! I'll report you in Singapore . . . Good-bye!'

"He waved his hand. Our men dropped their bundles quietly. The steamer moved ahead, and passing out of the circle of light, vanished at once from our sight, dazzled by the fire which burned fiercely. And then I knew that I would see the East first as commander of a small boat. I thought it fine; and the fidelity to the old ship was fine. We should see the last of her. Oh, the glamour of youth! Oh, the fire of it, more dazzling than the flames of the burning ship, throwing a magic light on the wide earth, leaping audaciously to the sky, presently to be quenched by time, more cruel, more pitiless, more bitter than the sea – and like the flames of the burning ship surrounded by an impenetrable night.

"The old man warned us in his gentle and inflexible way that it was part of our duty to save for the underwriters as much as we could of the ship's gear. Accordingly we went to work aft, while she blazed forward to give us plenty of light. We lugged out a lot of rubbish. What didn't we save? An old barometer fixed with an absurd quantity of screws nearly cost me my life: a sudden rush of smoke came upon me, and I just got away in time. There were various stores, bolts of canvas, coils of rope; the poop looked like a marine bazaar, and the boats were lumbered to the gunwales. One would have thought the old man wanted to take as much as he could of his first command with him. He was very, very quiet, but off his balance evidently. Would you believe it? He wanted to take a length of old stream-cable and a kedge-anchor with him in the long-boat. We said, 'Ay, ay, sir,' deferentially, and on the quiet let the things slip overboard. The heavy medicine-chest went that way, two bags of green coffee, tins of paint – fancy, paint! – a whole lot of things. Then I was ordered with two hands into the boats to make a stowage and get them ready against the time it would be proper for us to leave the ship.

"We put everything straight, stepped the long-boat's mast for our skipper, who was to take charge of her, and I was not sorry to sit down for a moment. My face felt raw, every limb ached as if broken, I was aware of all my ribs, and would have sworn to a twist in the back-bone. The boats, fast astern, lay in a deep shadow, and all around I could see the circle of the sea lighted by the fire. A gigantic flame arose forward straight and clear. It flared fierce, with noises like the whirr of wings, with rumbles as of thunder. There were cracks, detonations, and from the cone of flame the sparks flew upwards, as man is born to trouble, to leaky ships, and to ships that burn.

"What bothered me was that the ship, lying broadside to the swell and to such wind as there was – a mere breath – the boats would not keep astern where they were safe, but persisted, in a pig-headed way boats have, in getting under the counter and then swinging alongside. They were knocking about dangerously and coming near the flame, while the ship rolled on them, and, of course, there was always the danger of the masts going over the side at any moment. I and my two boat-keepers kept them off as best we could, with oars and boat-hooks; but to be constantly at it became exasperating, since there was no reason why we should not leave at once. We could not see those on board, nor could we imagine what caused the delay. The boat-keepers were swearing feebly, and I had not only my share of the work but also had to keep at it two men who showed a constant inclination to lay themselves down and let things slide.

"At last I hailed, 'On deck there,' and someone looked over. 'We're ready here,' I said. The head disappeared, and very soon popped up again. 'The captain says, All right, sir, and to keep the boats well clear of the ship.'

"Half an hour passed. Suddenly there was a frightful racket, rattle, clanking of chain, hiss of water, and millions of sparks flew up into the shivering column of smoke that stood leaning slightly above the ship. The cat-heads had burned away, and the two red-hot anchors had gone to the bottom, tearing out after them two hundred fathom of red-hot chain. The ship trembled, the mass of flame swayed as if ready to collapse, and the fore top-gallant-mast fell. It darted down like an arrow of fire, shot under, and instantly leaping up within an oar's-length of the boats, floated quietly, very black on the luminous sea. I hailed the deck again. After some time a man in an unexpectedly cheerful but also muffled tone, as though he had been trying to speak with his mouth shut, informed me, 'Coming directly, sir,' and vanished. For a long time I heard nothing but the whirr and roar of the fire. There were also whistling sounds. The boats jumped, tugged at the painters, ran at each other playfully, knocked their sides together, or, do what we would, swung in a bunch against the ship's side. I couldn't stand it any longer, and swarming up a rope, clambered aboard over the stern.

"It was as bright as day. Coming up like this, the sheet of fire facing me was a terrifying sight, and the heat seemed hardly bearable at first. On a settee cushion dragged out of the cabin Captain Beard, his legs drawn up and one arm under his head, slept with the light playing on him. Do you know what the rest were busy about? They were sitting on deck right aft, round an open case, eating bread and cheese and drinking bottled stout.

"On the background of flames twisting in fierce tongues above their heads they seemed at home like salamanders, and looked like a band of desperate pirates. The fire sparkled in the whites of their eyes, gleamed on patches of white skin seen through the torn shirts. Each had the marks as of a battle about him – bandaged heads, tied-up arms, a strip of dirty rag round a knee – and each man had a bottle between his legs and a chunk of cheese in his hand. Mahon got up. With his handsome and disreputable head, his hooked profile, his long white beard, and with an uncorked bottle in his hand, he resembled one of those reckless sea-robbers of old making merry amidst violence and disaster. 'The last meal on board,' he explained solemnly. 'We had nothing to eat all day, and it was no use leaving all this.' He flourished the bottle and indicated the sleeping skipper. 'He said he couldn't swallow anything, so I got him to lie down,' he went on; and as I stared, 'I don't know whether you are aware, young fellow, the man had no sleep to speak of for days – and there will be dam' little sleep in the boats.' 'There will be no boats by-and-by if you fool about much longer,' I said, indignantly. I walked up to the skipper and shook him by the shoulder. At last he opened his eyes, but did not move. 'Time to leave her, sir,' I said quietly.

"He got up painfully, looked at the flames, at the sea sparkling round the ship, and black, black as ink farther away; he looked at the stars shining dim through a thin veil of smoke in a sky black, black as Erebus.

" 'Youngest first,' he said.

"And the ordinary seaman, wiping his mouth with the back of his hand, got up, clambered over the taffrail, and vanished. Others followed. One, on the point of going over, stopped short to drain his bottle, and with a great swing of his arm flung it at the fire. 'Take this!' he cried.

"The skipper lingered disconsolately, and we left him to commune alone for a while with his first command. Then I went up again and brought him away at last. It was time. The ironwork on the poop was hot to the touch.

"Then the painter of the long-boat was cut, and the three boats, tied together, drifted clear of the ship. It was just sixteen hours after the explosion when we abandoned her. Mahon had charge of the second boat, and I had the smallest – the 14-foot thing. The long-boat would have taken the lot of us; but the skipper said we must save as much property as we could – for the underwriters – and so I got my first command. I had two men with me, a bag of biscuits, a few tins of meat, and a beaker of water. I was ordered to keep close to the long-boat, that in case of bad weather we might be taken into her.

"And do you know what I thought? I thought I would part company as soon as I could. I wanted to have my first command all to myself. I wasn't going to sail in a squadron if there were a chance for independent cruising. I would make land by myself. I would beat the other boats. Youth! All youth! The silly, charming, beautiful youth.

"But we did not make a start at once. We must see the last of the ship. And so the boats drifted about that night, heaving and setting on the swell. The men dozed, waked, sighed, groaned. I looked at the burning ship.

"Between the darkness of earth and heaven she was burning fiercely upon a disc of purple sea shot by the blood-red play of gleams; upon a disc of water glittering and sinister. A high, clear flame, an immense and lonely flame, ascended from the ocean, and from its summit the black smoke poured continuously at the sky. She burned furiously; mournful and imposing like a funeral pile kindled in the night, surrounded by the sea, watched over by the stars. A magnificent death had come like a grace, like a gift, like a reward to that old ship at the end of her laborious days. The surrender of her weary ghost to the keeping of stars and sea was stirring like the sight of a glorious triumph. The masts fell just before daybreak, and for a moment there was a burst and turmoil of sparks that seemed to fill with flying fire the night patient and watchful, the vast night lying silent upon the sea. At daylight she was only a charred shell, floating still under a cloud of smoke and bearing a glowing mass of coal within.

"Then the oars were got out, and the boats forming in a line moved round her remains as if in procession – the long-boat leading. As we pulled across her stern a slim dart of fire shot out viciously at us, and suddenly she went down, head first, in a great hiss of steam. The unconsumed stern was the last to sink; but the paint had gone, had cracked, had peeled off, and there were no letters, there was no word, no stubborn device that was like her soul, to flash at the rising sun her creed and her name.

"We made our way north. A breeze sprang up, and about noon

all the boats came together for the last time. I had no mast or sail in mine, but I made a mast out of a spare oar and hoisted a boat-awning for a sail, with a boat-hook for a yard. She was certainly over-masted, but I had the satisfaction of knowing that with the wind aft I could beat the other two. I had to wait for them. Then we all had a look at the captain's chart, and, after a sociable meal of hard bread and water, got our last instructions. These were simple: steer north, and keep together as much as possible. 'Be careful with that jury-rig, Marlow,' said the captain; and Mahon, as I sailed proudly past his boat, wrinkled his curved nose and hailed, 'You will sail that ship of yours under water, if you don't look out, young fellow.' He was a malicious old man – and may the deep sea where he sleeps now rock him gently, rock him tenderly to the end of time!

"Before sunset a thick rain-squall passed over the two boats, which were far astern, and that was the last I saw of them for a time. Next day I sat steering my cockle-shell – my first command – with nothing but water and sky around me. I did sight in the afternoon the upper sails of a ship far away, but said nothing, and my men did not notice her. You see I was afraid she might be homeward bound, and I had no mind to turn back from the portals of the East. I was steering for Java – another blessed name – like Bankok, you know. I steered many days.

"I need not tell you what it is to be knocking about in an open boat. I remember nights and days of calm, when we pulled, we pulled, and the boat seemed to stand still, as if bewitched within the circle of the sea horizon. I remember the heat, the deluge of rain-squalls that kept us baling for dear life (but filled our water-cask), and I remember sixteen hours on end with a mouth dry as a cinder and a steering-oar over the stern to keep my first command head on to a breaking sea. I did not know how good a man I was till then. I remember the drawn faces, the dejected figures of my two men, and I remember my youth and the feeling that will never come back any more – the feeling that I could last for ever, outlast the sea, the earth, and all men; the deceitful feeling that lures us on to joys, to perils, to love, to vain effort – to death; the triumphant conviction of strength, the heat of life in the handful of dust, the glow in the heart that with every year grows dim, grows cold, grows small, and expires – and expires, too soon, too soon – before life itself.

"And this is how I see the East. I have seen its secret places and have looked into its very soul; but now I see it always from a small boat, a high outline of mountains, blue and afar in the morning; like faint mist at noon; a jagged wall of purple at sunset. I have the feel of the oar in my hand, the vision of a scorching blue sea in my eyes. And I see a bay, a wide bay, smooth as glass and polished like ice, shimmering in the dark. A red light burns far off upon the gloom of the land, and the night is soft and warm. We drag at the oars with aching arms, and suddenly a puff of wind, a puff faint and tepid and laden with strange odours of blossoms, of aromatic wood, comes out of the still night – the first sigh of the East on my face. That I can never forget. It was impalpable and enslaving, like a charm, like a whispered promise of mysterious delight.

"We had been pulling this finishing spell for eleven hours. Two pulled, and he whose turn it was to rest sat at the tiller. We had made out the red light in that bay and steered for it, guessing it must mark some small coasting port. We passed two vessels, outlandish and high-sterned, sleeping at anchor, and, approaching the light, now very dim, ran the boat's nose against the end of a jutting wharf. We were blind with fatigue. My men dropped the oars and fell off the thwarts as if dead. I made fast to a pile. A current rippled softly. The scented obscurity of the shore was grouped into vast masses, a density of colossal clumps of vegetation, probably – mute and fantastic shapes. And at their foot the semicircle of a beach gleamed faintly, like an illusion. There was not a light, not a stir, not a sound. The mysterious East faced me, perfumed like a flower, silent like death, dark like a grave.

"And I sat weary beyond expression, exulting like a conqueror, sleepless and entranced as if before a profound, a fateful enigma.

"A splashing of oars, a measured dip reverberating on the level of water, intensified by the silence of the shore into loud claps, made me jump up. A boat, a European boat, was coming in. I invoked the name of the dead; I hailed: *Judea* ahoy! A thin shout answered.

"It was the captain. I had beaten the flagship by three hours, and I was glad to hear the old man's voice again, tremulous and tired. 'Is it you, Marlow?' 'Mind the end of that jetty, sir,' I cried.

"He approached cautiously, and brought up with the deep-sea lead-line which he had saved – for the underwriters. I eased my

painter and fell alongside. He sat, a broken figure at the stern, wet
with dew, his hands clasped in his lap. His men were asleep
already. 'I had a terrible time of it,' he murmured. 'Mahon is
behind – not very far.' We conversed in whispers, in low whispers,
as if afraid to wake up the land. Guns, thunder, earthquakes
would not have awakened the men just then.

"Looking round as we talked, I saw away at sea a bright light
travelling in the night. 'There's a steamer passing the bay,' I said.
She was not passing, she was entering, and she even came close
and anchored. 'I wish,' said the old man, 'you would find out
whether she is English. Perhaps they could give us a passage
somewhere.' He seemed nervously anxious. So by dint of punch-
ing and kicking I started one of my men into a state of
somnambulism, and giving him an oar, took another and pulled
towards the lights of the steamer.

"There was a murmur of voices in her, metallic hollow clangs
of the engine-room, footsteps on the deck. Her ports shone, round
like dilated eyes. Shapes moved about, and there was a shadowy
man high up on the bridge. He heard my oars.

"And then, before I could open my lips, the East spoke to me,
but it was in a Western voice. A torrent of words was poured into
the enigmatical, the fateful silence; outlandish, angry words,
mixed with words and even whole sentences of good English, less
strange but even more surprising. The voice swore and cursed
violently; it riddled the solemn peace of the bay by a volley of
abuse. It began by calling me Pig, and from that went crescendo
into unmentionable adjectives – in English. The man up there
raged aloud in two languages, and with a sincerity in his fury that
almost convinced me I had, in some way, sinned against the
harmony of the universe. I could hardly see him, but began to
think he would work himself into a fit.

"Suddenly he ceased, and I could hear him snorting and
blowing like a porpoise. I said—

" 'What steamer is this, pray?'

" 'Eh? What's this? And who are you?'

" 'Castaway crew of an English barque burnt at sea. We came
here to-night. I am the second mate. The captain is in the long-
boat, and wishes to know if you would give us a passage
somewhere.'

" 'Oh, my goodness! I say . . . This is the *Celestial* from

Singapore on her return trip. I'll arrange with your captain in the morning . . . and . . . I say . . . did you hear me just now?'

" 'I should think the whole bay heard you.'

" 'I thought you were a shore-boat. Now, look here – this infernal lazy scoundrel of a caretaker has gone to sleep again – curse him. The light is out, and I nearly ran foul of the end of this damned jetty. This is the third time he plays me this trick. Now, I ask you, can anybody stand this kind of thing? It's enough to drive a man out of his mind. I'll report him . . . I'll get the Assistant Resident to give him the sack, by . . . ! See – there's no light. It's out, isn't it? I take you to witness the light's out. There should be a light, you know. A red light on the—'

" 'There was a light,' I said, mildly.

" 'But it's out, man! What's the use of talking like this? You can see for yourself it's out – don't you? If you had to take a valuable steamer along this God-forsaken coast you would want a light, too. I'll kick him from end to end of his miserable wharf. You'll see if I don't. I will—'

" 'So I may tell my captain you'll take us?' I broke in.

" 'Yes, I'll take you. Good-night,' he said, brusquely.

"I pulled back, made fast again to the jetty, and then went to sleep at last. I had faced the silence of the East. I had heard some of its language. But when I opened my eyes again the silence was as complete as though it had never been broken. I was lying in a flood of light, and the sky had never looked so far, so high, before. I opened my eyes and lay without moving.

"And then I saw the men of the East – they were looking at me. The whole length of the jetty was full of people. I saw brown, bronze, yellow faces, the black eyes, the glitter, the colour of an Eastern crowd. And all these beings stared without a murmur, without a sigh, without a movement. They stared down at the boats, at the sleeping men who at night had come to them from the sea. Nothing moved. The fronds of palms stood still against the sky. Not a branch stirred along the shore, and the brown roofs of hidden houses peeped through the green foliage, through the big leaves that hung shining and still like leaves forged of heavy metal. This was the East of the ancient navigators, so old, so mysterious, resplendent and sombre, living and unchanged, full of danger and promise. And these were the men. I sat up suddenly. A wave of movement passed through the crowd from end to end,

passed along the heads, swayed the bodies, ran along the jetty like
a ripple on the water, like a breath of wind on a field – and all was
still again. I see it now – the wide sweep of the bay, the glittering
sands, the wealth of green infinite and varied, the sea blue like the
sea of a dream, the crowd of attentive faces, the blaze of vivid
colour – the water reflecting it all, the curve of the shore, the jetty,
the high-sterned outlandish craft floating still, and the three boats
with the tired men from the West sleeping, unconscious of the
land and the people and of the violence of sunshine. They slept
thrown across the thwarts, curled on bottom-boards, in the
careless attitudes of death. The head of the old skipper, leaning
back in the stern of the long-boat, had fallen on his breast, and he
looked as though he would never wake. Farther out old Mahon's
face was upturned to the sky, with the long white beard spread
out on his breast, as though he had been shot where he sat at the
tiller; and a man, all in a heap in the bows of the boat, slept with
both arms embracing the stem-head and with his cheek laid on
the gunwale. The East looked at them without a sound.

"I have known its fascination since; I have seen the mysterious
shores, the still water, the lands of brown nations, where a
stealthy Nemesis lies in wait, pursues, overtakes so many of the
conquering race, who are proud of their wisdom, of their knowledge, of their strength. But for me all the East is contained in that
vision of my youth. It is all in that moment when I opened my
young eyes on it. I came upon it from a tussle with the sea – and I
was young – and I saw it looking at me. And this is all that is left
of it! Only a moment; a moment of strength, of romance, of
glamour – of youth! . . . A flick of sunshine upon a strange shore,
the time to remember, the time for a sigh, and – good-bye! – Night
– Good-bye . . . !"

He drank.

"Ah! The good old time – the good old time. Youth and the sea.
Glamour and the sea! The good, strong sea, the salt, bitter sea,
that could whisper to you and roar at you and knock your breath
out of you."

He drank again.

"By all that's wonderful it is the sea, I believe, the sea itself – or
is it youth alone? Who can tell? But you here – you all had
something out of life: money, love – whatever one gets on shore –
and, tell me, wasn't that the best time, that time when we were

young at sea; young and had nothing, on the sea that gives nothing, except hard knocks – and sometimes a chance to feel your strength – that only – what you all regret?"

And we all nodded at him: the man of finance, the man of accounts, the man of law, we all nodded at him over the polished table that like a still sheet of brown water reflected our faces, lined, wrinkled; our faces marked by toil, by deceptions, by success, by love; our weary eyes looking still, looking always, looking anxiously for something out of life, that while it is expected is already gone – has passed unseen, in a sigh, in a flash – together with the youth, with the strength, with the romance of illusions.

1898/1898

Amy Foster

Kennedy is a country doctor, and lives in Colebrook, on the shores of Eastbay. The high ground rising abruptly behind the red roofs of the little town crowds the quaint High Street against the wall which defends it from the sea. Beyond the sea-wall there curves for miles in a vast and regular sweep the barren beach of shingle, with the village of Brenzett standing out darkly across the water, a spire in a clump of trees; and still further out the perpendicular column of a lighthouse, looking in the distance no bigger than a lead-pencil, marks the vanishing-point of the land. The country at the back of Brenzett is low and flat; but the bay is fairly well sheltered from the seas, and occasionally a big ship, windbound or through stress of weather, makes use of the anchoring ground a mile and a half due north from you as you stand at the back door of the "Ship Inn" in Brenzett. A dilapidated wind-mill near by, lifting its shattered arms from a mound no loftier than a rubbish-heap, and a Martello tower squatting at the water's edge half a mile to the south of the Coastguard cottages, are familiar to the skippers of small craft. These are the official sea-marks for the patch of trustworthy bottom represented on the Admiralty charts by an irregular oval of dots enclosing several figures six, with a tiny anchor engraved among them, and the legend "mud and shells" over all.

The brow of the upland overtops the square tower of the Colebrook Church. The slope is green and looped by a white road. Ascending along this road, you open a valley broad and shallow, a wide green trough of pastures and hedges merging inland into a vista of purple tints and flowing lines closing the view.

In this valley down to Brenzett and Colebrook and up to Darnford, the market town fourteen miles away, lies the practice of my friend Kennedy. He had begun life as surgeon in the Navy, and afterwards had been the companion of a famous traveller, in the days when there were continents with unexplored interiors. His papers on the fauna and flora made him known to scientific societies. And now he had come to a country practice – from choice. The penetrating power of his mind, acting like a corrosive fluid, had destroyed his ambition, I fancy. His intelligence is of a scientific order, of an investigating habit, and of that unappeasable curiosity which believes that there is a particle of a general truth in every mystery.

A good many years ago now, on my return from abroad, he invited me to stay with him. I came readily enough, and as he could not neglect his patients to keep me company, he took me on his rounds – thirty miles or so of an afternoon, sometimes. I waited for him on the roads; the horse reached after the leafy twigs, and, sitting high in the dogcart, I could hear Kennedy's laugh through the half-open door of some cottage. He had a big, hearty laugh that would have fitted a man twice his size, a brisk manner, a bronzed face, and a pair of grey, profoundly attentive eyes. He had the talent of making people talk to him freely, and an inexhaustible patience in listening to their tales.

One day, as we trotted out of a large village into a shady bit of road, I saw on our left hand a low, black cottage, with diamond panes in the windows, a creeper on the end wall, a roof of shingle, and some roses climbing on the rickety trellis-work of the tiny porch. Kennedy pulled up to a walk. A woman, in full sunlight, was throwing a dripping blanket over a line stretched between two old apple-trees. And as the bobtailed, long-necked chestnut, trying to get his head, jerked the left hand, covered by a thick dogskin glove, the doctor raised his voice over the hedge: "How's your child, Amy?"

I had the time to see her dull face, red, not with a mantling blush, but as if her flat cheeks had been vigorously slapped, and to take in the squat figure, the scanty, dusty brown hair drawn into a tight knot at the back of the head. She looked quite young. With a distinct catch in her breath, her voice sounded low and timid.

"He's well, thank you."

We trotted again. "A young patient of yours," I said; and the doctor, flicking the chestnut absently, muttered, "Her husband used to be."

"She seems a dull creature," I remarked, listlessly.

"Precisely," said Kennedy. "She is very passive. It's enough to look at the red hands hanging at the end of those short arms, at those slow, prominent brown eyes, to know the inertness of her mind – an inertness that one would think made it everlastingly safe from all the surprises of imagination. And yet which of us is safe? At any rate, such as you see her, she had enough imagination to fall in love. She's the daughter of one Isaac Foster, who from a small farmer has sunk into a shepherd; the beginning of his misfortunes dating from his runaway marriage with the cook of his widowed father – a well-to-do, apoplectic grazier, who passionately struck his name off his will, and had been heard to utter threats against his life. But this old affair, scandalous enough to serve as a motive for a Greek tragedy, arose from the similarity of their characters. There are other tragedies, less scandalous and of a subtler poignancy, arising from irreconcilable differences and from that fear of the Incomprehensible that hangs over all our heads – over all our heads . . ."

The tired chestnut dropped into a walk; and the rim of the sun, all red in a speckless sky, touched familiarly the smooth top of a ploughed rise near the road as I had seen it times innumerable touch the distant horizon of the sea. The uniform brownness of the harrowed field glowed with a rose tinge, as though the powdered clods had sweated out in minute pearls of blood the toil of uncounted ploughmen. From the edge of a copse a wagon with two horses was rolling gently along the ridge. Raised above our heads upon the sky-line, it loomed up against the red sun, triumphantly big, enormous, like a chariot of giants drawn by two slow-stepping steeds of legendary proportions. And the clumsy figure of the man plodding at the head of the leading horse projected itself on the background of the Infinite with a heroic uncouthness. The end of his carter's whip quivered high up in the blue. Kennedy discoursed.

"She's the eldest of a large family. At the age of fifteen they put her out to service at the New Barns Farm. I attended Mrs Smith, the tenant's wife, and saw that girl there for the first time. Mrs Smith, a genteel person with a sharp nose, made her put on a black dress every afternoon. I don't know what induced me to notice her at all. There are faces that call your attention by a curious want of definiteness in their whole aspect, as, walking in a mist, you peer attentively at a vague shape which, after all, may be nothing more curious or strange than a signpost. The only peculiarity I perceived in her was a slight hesitation in her utterance, a sort of preliminary stammer which passes away with the first word. When sharply spoken to, she was apt to lose her head at once; but her heart was of the kindest. She had never been heard to express a dislike for a single human being, and she was tender to every living creature. She was devoted to Mrs Smith, to Mr Smith, to their dogs, cats, canaries; and as to Mrs Smith's grey parrot, its peculiarities exercised upon her a positive fascination. Nevertheless, when that outlandish bird, attacked by the cat, shrieked for help in human accents, she ran out into the yard stopping her ears, and did not prevent the crime. For Mrs Smith this was another evidence of her stupidity; on the other hand, her want of charm, in view of Smith's well-known frivolousness, was a great recommendation. Her short-sighted eyes would swim with pity for a poor mouse in a trap, and she had been seen once by some boys on her knees in the wet grass helping a toad in difficulties. If it's true, as some German fellow has said, that without phosphorus there is no thought, it is still more true that there is no kindness of heart without a certain amount of imagination. She had some. She had even more than is necessary to understand suffering and to be moved by pity. She fell in love under circumstances that leave no room for doubt in the matter; for you need imagination to form a notion of beauty at all, and still more to discover your ideal in an unfamiliar shape.

"How this aptitude came to her, what it did feed upon, is an inscrutable mystery. She was born in the village, and had never been further away from it than Colebrook or perhaps Darnford. She lived for four years with the Smiths. New Barns is an isolated farm-house a mile away from the road, and she was content to look day after day at the same fields, hollows, rises; at the trees and the hedgerows; at the faces of the four men about the farm, always the same – day after day, month after month, year after year. She never showed a desire for conversation, and, as it seemed to me, she did not know how to smile. Sometimes of a fine Sunday afternoon she would put on her best dress, a pair of stout boots, a large grey hat trimmed with a black feather (I've seen her in that finery), seize an absurdly slender parasol, climb over two stiles, tramp over three fields and along two hundred yards of road – never further. There stood Foster's cottage. She would help her mother to give their tea to the younger children, wash up the crockery, kiss the little ones, and go back to the farm. That was all. All the rest, all the change, all the relaxation. She never seemed to wish for anything more. And then she fell in love. She fell in love silently, obstinately – perhaps helplessly. It came slowly, but when it came it worked like a powerful spell; it was love as the Ancients understood it: an irresistible and fateful impulse – a possession! Yes, it was in her to become haunted and possessed by a face, by a presence, fatally, as though she had been a pagan worshipper of form under a joyous sky – and to be awakened at last from that mysterious forgetfulness of self, from that enchantment, from that transport, by a fear resembling the unaccountable terror of a brute . . ."

With the sun hanging low on its western limit, the expanse of the grass-lands framed in the counter-scarps of the rising ground took on a gorgeous and sombre aspect. A sense of penetrating sadness, like that inspired by a grave strain of music, disengaged itself from the silence of the fields. The men we met walked past, slow, unsmiling, with downcast eyes, as if the melancholy of an over-burdened earth had weighted their feet, bowed their shoulders, borne down their glances.

"Yes," said the doctor to my remark, "one would think the earth is under a curse, since of all her children these that cling to her the closest are uncouth in body and as leaden of gait as if their very hearts were loaded with chains. But here on this same road you might have seen amongst these heavy men a being lithe, supple and long-limbed, straight like a pine, with something striving upwards in his appearance as though the heart within him had been buoyant. Perhaps it was only the force of the contrast, but when he was passing one of these villagers here, the soles of his feet did not seem to me to touch the dust of the road. He vaulted over the stiles, paced these slopes with a long elastic stride that made him noticeable at a great distance, and had lustrous black eyes. He was so different from the mankind around that, with his freedom of movement, his soft – a little startled – glance, his olive complexion and graceful bearing, his humanity suggested to me the nature of a woodland creature. He came from there."

The doctor pointed with his whip, and from the summit of the descent seen over the rolling tops of the trees in a park by the side of the road, appeared the level sea far below us, like the floor of an immense edifice inlaid with bands of dark ripple, with still trails of glitter, ending in a belt of glassy water at the foot of the sky. The light blur of smoke, from an invisible steamer, faded on the great clearness of the horizon like the mist of a breath on a mirror; and, inshore, the white sails of a coaster, with the appearance of disentangling themselves slowly from under the branches, floated clear of the foliage of the trees.

"Shipwrecked in the bay?" I said.

"Yes; he was a castaway. A poor emigrant from Central Europe bound to America and washed ashore here in a storm. And for him, who knew nothing of the earth, England was an undiscovered country. It was some time before he learned its name; and for all I know he might have expected to find wild beasts or wild men here, when, crawling in the dark over the sea-wall, he rolled down the other side into a dyke, where it was another miracle he didn't get drowned. But he struggled instinctively like an animal under a net, and this blind struggle threw him out into a field. He must have been, indeed, of a tougher fibre than he looked to withstand without expiring such buffetings, the violence of his exertions, and so much fear. Later on, in his broken English that resembled curiously the speech of a young child, he told me himself that he put his trust in God, believing he was no longer in this world. And truly – he would add – how was he to know? He fought his way against the rain and the gale on all fours, and crawled at last among some sheep huddled close under the lee of a hedge. They ran off in all directions, bleating in the darkness, and he welcomed the first familiar sound he heard on these shores. It must have been two in the morning then. And this is all we know of the manner of his landing, though he did not arrive unattended by any means. Only his grisly company did not begin to come ashore till much later in the day . . ."

The doctor gathered the reins, clicked his tongue; we trotted down the hill. Then turning, almost directly, a sharp corner into High Street, we rattled over the stones and were home.

Late in the evening Kennedy, breaking a spell of moodiness that had come over him, returned to the story. Smoking his pipe, he paced the long room from end to end. A reading-lamp concentrated all its light upon the papers on his desk; and, sitting by the open window, I saw, after the windless, scorching day, the frigid splendour of a hazy sea lying motionless under the moon. Not a whisper, not a splash, not a stir of the shingle, not a footstep, not a sigh came up from the earth below – never a sign of life but the scent of climbing jasmine: and Kennedy's voice, speaking behind me, passed through the wide casement, to vanish outside in a chill and sumptuous stillness.

". . . The relations of shipwrecks in the olden time tell us of much suffering. Often the castaways were only saved from drowning to die miserably from starvation on a barren coast; others suffered violent death or else slavery, passing through years of precarious existence with people to whom their strangeness was an object of suspicion, dislike or fear. We read about these things, and they are very pitiful. It is indeed hard upon a man to find himself a lost stranger, helpless, incomprehensible, and of a mysterious origin, in some obscure corner of the earth. Yet amongst all the adventurers shipwrecked in all the wild parts of the world, there is not one, it seems to me, that ever had to suffer a fate so simply tragic as the man I am speaking of, the most innocent of adventurers cast out, by the sea in the bight of this bay, almost within sight from this very window.

"He did not know the name of his ship. Indeed, in the course of time we discovered he did not even know that ships had names – 'like Christian people'; and when, one day, from the top of Talfourd Hill, he beheld the sea lying open to his view, his eyes roamed afar, lost in an air of wild surprise, as though he had never seen such a sight before. And probably he had not. As far as I could make out, he had been hustled together with many others on board an emigrant ship at the mouth of the Elbe, too bewildered to take note of his surroundings, too weary to see anything, too anxious to care. They were driven below into the 'tween-deck and battened down from the very start. It was a low timber dwelling – he would say – with wooden beams overhead, like the houses in his country, but you went into it down a ladder. It was very large, very cold, damp and sombre, with places in the manner of wooden boxes where people had to sleep one above another, and it kept on rocking all ways at once all the time. He crept into one of these boxes and lay down there in the clothes in which he had left his home many days before, keeping his bundle and his stick by his side. People groaned, children cried, water dripped, the lights went out, the walls of the place creaked, and everything was being shaken so that in one's little box one dared not lift one's head. He had lost touch with his only companion (a young man from the same valley, he said), and all the time a great noise of wind went on outside and heavy blows fell – boom! boom!

An awful sickness overcame him, even to the point of making him neglect his prayers. Besides, one could not tell whether it was morning or evening. It seemed always to be night in that place.

"Before that he had been travelling a long, long time on the iron track. He looked out of the window, which had a wonderfully clear glass in it, and the trees, the houses, the fields, and the long roads seemed to fly round and round about him till his head swam. He gave me to understand that he had on his passage beheld uncounted multitudes of people – whole nations – all dressed in such clothes as the rich wear. Once he was made to get out of the carriage, and slept through a night on a bench in a house of bricks with his bundle under his head; and once for many hours he had to sit on a floor of flat stones, dozing, with his knees up and with his bundle between his feet. There was a roof over him, which seemed made of glass, and was so high that the tallest mountain-pine he had ever seen would have had room to grow under it. Steam-machines rolled in at one end and out at the other. People swarmed more than you can see on a feast-day round the miraculous Holy Image in the yard of the Carmelite Convent down in the plains where, before he left his home, he drove his mother in a wooden cart:— a pious old woman who wanted to offer prayers and make a vow for his safety. He could not give me an idea of how large and lofty and full of noise and smoke and gloom, and clang of iron, the place was, but someone had told him it was called Berlin. Then they rang a bell, and another steam-machine came in, and again he was taken on and on through a land that wearied his eyes by its flatness without a single bit of a hill to be seen anywhere. One more night he spent shut up in a building like a good stable with a litter of straw on the floor, guarding his bundle amongst a lot of men, of whom not one could understand a single word he said. In the morning they were all led down to the stony shores of an extremely broad muddy river, flowing not between hills but between houses that seemed immense. There was a steam-machine that went on the water, and they all stood upon it packed tight, only now there were with them many women and children who made much noise. A cold rain fell, the wind blew in his face; he was wet through, and his teeth chattered. He and the young man from the same valley took each other by the hand.

"They thought they were being taken to America straight

away, but suddenly the steam-machine bumped against the side of a thing like a great house on the water. The walls were smooth and black, and there uprose, growing from the roof as it were, bare trees in the shape of crosses, extremely high. That's how it appeared to him then, for he had never seen a ship before. This was the ship that was going to swim all the way to America. Voices shouted, everything swayed; there was a ladder dipping up and down. He went up on his hands and knees in mortal fear of falling into the water below, which made a great splashing. He got separated from his companion, and when he descended into the bottom of that ship his heart seemed to melt suddenly within him.

"It was then also, as he told me, that he lost contact for good and all with one of those three men who the summer before had been going about through all the little towns in the foothills of his country. They would arrive on market-days driving in a peasant's cart, and would set up an office in an inn or some other Jew's house. There were three of them, of whom one with a long beard looked venerable; and they had red cloth collars round their necks and gold lace on their sleeves like Government officials. They sat proudly behind a long table; and in the next room, so that the common people shouldn't hear, they kept a cunning telegraph machine, through which they could talk to the Emperor of America. The fathers hung about the door, but the young men of the mountains would crowd up to the table asking many questions, for there was work to be got all the year round at three dollars a day in America, and no military service to do.

"But the American Kaiser would not take everybody. Oh, no! He himself had a great difficulty in getting accepted, and the venerable man in uniform had to go out of the room several times to work the telegraph on his behalf. The American Kaiser engaged him at last at three dollars, he being young and strong. However, many able young men backed out, afraid of the great distance; besides, those only who had some money could be taken. There were some who sold their huts and their land because it cost a lot of money to get to America; but then, once there, you had three dollars a day, and if you were clever you could find places where true gold could be picked up on the ground. His father's house was getting over full. Two of his brothers were married and had children. He promised to send money home from America by post twice a year. His father sold an old cow, a pair of piebald mountain ponies of his own raising, and a cleared plot of fair pasture land on the sunny slope of a pine-clad pass to a Jew inn-keeper, in order to pay the people of the ship that took men to America to get rich in a short time.

"He must have been a real adventurer at heart, for how many of the greatest enterprises in the conquest of the earth had for their beginning just such a bargaining away of the paternal cow for the mirage of true gold far away! I have been telling you more or less in my own words what I learned fragmentarily in the course of two or three years, during which I seldom missed an opportunity of a friendly chat with him. He told me this story of his adventure with many flashes of white teeth and lively glances of black eyes, at first in a sort of anxious baby-talk, then, as he acquired the language, with great fluency, but always with that singing, soft, and at the same time vibrating intonation that instilled a strangely penetrating power into the sound of the most familiar English words, as if they had been the words of an unearthly language. And he always would come to an end, with many emphatic shakes of his head, upon that awful sensation of his heart melting within him directly he set foot on board that ship. Afterwards there seemed to come for him a period of blank ignorance, at any rate as to facts. No doubt he must have been abominably seasick and abominably unhappy – this soft and passionate adventurer, taken thus out of his knowledge, and feeling bitterly as he lay in his emigrant bunk his utter loneliness; for his was a highly sensitive nature. The next thing we know of him for certain is that he had been hiding in Hammond's pig pound by the side of the road to Norton, six miles, as the crow flies, from the sea. Of these experiences he was unwilling to speak: they seemed to have seared into his soul a sombre sort of wonder and indignation. Through the rumours of the country-side, which lasted for a good many days after his arrival, we know that the fishermen of West Colebrook had been disturbed and startled by heavy knocks against the walls of weatherboard cottages, and by a voice crying piercingly strange words in the night. Several of them turned out even, but, no doubt, he had fled in sudden alarm at their rough angry tones hailing each other in the darkness. A sort of frenzy must have helped him up the steep Norton hill. It was he, no doubt, who early the following morning had been seen lying (in a swoon, I should say) on the roadside grass by the

Brenzett carrier, who actually got down to have a nearer look, but drew back, intimidated by the perfect immobility, and by something queer in the aspect of that tramp, sleeping so still under the showers. As the day advanced, some children came dashing into school at Norton in such a fright that the schoolmistress went out and spoke indignantly to a 'horrid-looking man' on the road. He edged away, hanging his head, for a few steps, and then suddenly ran off with extraordinary fleetness. The driver of Mr Bradley's milk-cart made no secret of it that he had lashed with his whip at a hairy sort of gypsy fellow who, jumping up at a turn of the road by the Vents, made a snatch at the pony's bridle. And he caught him a good one, too, right over the face, he said, that made him drop down in the mud a jolly sight quicker than he had jumped up; but it was a good half a mile before he could stop the pony. Maybe that in his desperate endeavours to get help, and in his need to get in touch with someone, the poor devil had tried to stop the cart. Also three boys confessed afterwards to throwing stones at a funny tramp, knocking about all wet and muddy, and, it seemed, very drunk, in the narrow deep lane by the limekilns. All this was the talk of three villages for days; but we have Mrs Finn's (the wife of Smith's waggoner) unimpeachable testimony that she saw him get over the low wall of Hammond's pig-pound and lurch straight at her, babbling aloud in a voice that was enough to make one die of fright. Having the baby with her in a perambulator, Mrs Finn called out to him to go away, and as he persisted in coming nearer, she hit him courageously with her umbrella over the head, and, without once looking back, ran like the wind with the perambulator as far as the first house in the village. She stopped then, out of breath, and spoke to old Lewis, hammering there at a heap of stones; and the old chap, taking off his immense black wire goggles, got up on his shaky legs to look where she pointed. Together they followed with their eyes the figure of the man running over a field; they saw him fall down, pick himself up, and run on again, staggering and waving his long arms above his head, in the direction of the New Barns Farm. From that moment he is plainly in the toils of his obscure and touching destiny. There is no doubt after this of what happened to him. All is certain now: Mrs Smith's intense terror; Amy Foster's stolid conviction held against the other's nervous attack, that the man 'meant no harm'; Smith's exasperation (on his return from Darnford Market) at finding the dog barking himself into a fit, the back-door locked, his wife in hysterics; and all for an unfortunate dirty tramp, supposed to be even then lurking in his stackyard, Was he? He would teach him to frighten women.

"Smith is notoriously hot-tempered, but the sight of some nondescript and miry creature sitting cross-legged amongst a lot of loose straw, and swinging itself to and fro like a bear in a cage, made him pause. Then this tramp stood up silently before him, one mass of mud and filth from head to foot. Smith, alone amongst his stacks with this apparition, in the stormy twilight ringing with the infuriated barking of the dog, felt the dread of an inexplicable strangeness. But when that being, parting with his black hands the long matted locks that hung before his face, as you part the two halves of a curtain, looked out at him with glistening, wild, back-and-white eyes, the weirdness of this silent encounter fairly staggered him. He has admitted since (for the story has been a legitimate subject of conversation about here for years) that he made more than one step backwards. Then a sudden burst of rapid, senseless speech persuaded him at once that he had to do with an escaped lunatic. In fact, that impression never wore off completely. Smith has not in his heart given up his secret conviction of the man's essential insanity to this very day.

"As the creature approached him, jabbering in a most discomposing manner, Smith (unaware that he was being addressed as 'gracious lord', and adjured in God's name to afford food and shelter) kept on speaking firmly but gently to it, and retreating all the time into the other yard. At last, watching his chance, by a sudden charge he bundled him headlong into the wood-lodge, and instantly shot the bolt. Thereupon he wiped his brow, though the day was cold. He had done his duty to the community by shutting up a wandering and probably dangerous maniac. Smith isn't a hard man at all, but he had room in his brain only for that one idea of lunacy. He was not imaginative enough to ask himself whether the man might not be perishing with cold and hunger. Meantime, at first, the maniac made a great deal of noise in the lodge. Mrs Smith was screaming upstairs, where she had locked herself in her bedroom; but Amy Foster sobbed piteously at the kitchen-door, wringing her hands and muttering, 'Don't! don't!' I daresay Smith had a rough time of it that evening with one noise and another, and this insane, disturbing voice crying obstinately through the door only added to his irritation. He couldn't possibly have connected this troublesome lunatic with the sinking of a ship in Eastbay, of which there had been a rumour in the Darnford market place. And I daresay the man inside had been very near to insanity on that night. Before his excitement collapsed and he became unconscious he was throwing himself violently about in the dark, rolling on some dirty sacks, and biting his fists with rage, cold, hunger, amazement, and despair.

"He was a mountaineer of the eastern range of the Carpathians, and the vessel sunk the night before in Eastbay was the Hamburg emigrant-ship *Herzogin Sophia-Dorothea*, of appalling memory.

"A few months later we could read in the papers the accounts of the bogus 'Emigration Agencies' among the Sclavonian peasantry in the more remote provinces of Austria. The object of these scoundrels was to get hold of the poor ignorant people's homesteads, and they were in league with the local usurers. They exported their victims through Hamburg mostly. As to the ship, I had watched her out of this very window, reaching close-hauled under short canvas into the bay on a dark, threatening afternoon. She came to an anchor, correctly by the chart, off the Brenzett Coastguard station. I remember before the night fell looking out again at the outlines of her spars and rigging that stood out dark and pointed on a background of ragged, slaty clouds like another and a slighter spire to the left of the Brenzett church-tower. In the evening the wind rose. At midnight I could hear in my bed the terrific gusts and the sounds of a driving deluge.

"About that time the Coastguardmen thought they saw the lights of a steamer over the anchoring-ground. In a moment they vanished; but it is clear that another vessel of some sort had tried for shelter in the bay on that awful, blind night, had rammed the German ship amidships (a breach – as one of the divers told me afterwards – 'that you could sail a Thames barge through'), and then had gone out either scathless or damaged, who shall say; but had gone out, unknown, unseen, and fatal, to perish mysteriously at sea. Of her nothing ever came to light, and yet the hue and cry that was raised all over the world would have found her out if she had been in existence anywhere on the face of the waters.

"A completeness without a clue, and stealthy silence as of a neatly executed crime, characterize this murderous disaster, which, as you may remember, had its gruesome celebrity. The wind would have prevented the loudest outcries from reaching the shore; there had been evidently no time for signals of distress. It was death without any sort of fuss. The Hamburg ship, filling all at once, capsized as she sank, and at daylight there was not even the end of a spar to be seen above water. She was missed, of course, and at first the Coastguardmen surmised that she had either dragged her anchor or parted her cable some time during the night, and had been blown out to sea. Then, after the tide turned, the wreck must have shifted a little and released some of the bodies, because a child – a little fair-headed child in a red frock – came ashore abreast of the Martello tower. By the afternoon you could see along three miles of beach dark figures with bare legs dashing in and out of the tumbling foam, and rough-looking men, women with hard faces, children, mostly fair-haired, were being carried, stiff and dripping, on stretchers, on wattles, on ladders, in a long procession past the door of the "Ship Inn", to be laid out in a row under the north wall of the Brenzett Church.

"Officially, the body of the little girl in the red frock is the first thing that came ashore from that ship. But I have patients amongst the seafaring population of West Colebrook, and, unofficially, I am informed that very early that morning two brothers, who went down to look after their cobble hauled up on the beach, found, a good way from Brenzett, an ordinary ship's hencoop, lying high and dry on the shore, with eleven drowned ducks inside. Their families ate the birds, and the hencoop was split into firewood with a hatchet. It is possible that a man (supposing he happened to be on deck at the time of the accident) might have floated ashore on that hencoop. He might. I admit it is improbable, but there was the man – and for days, nay, for weeks – it didn't enter our heads that we had amongst us the only living soul that had escaped from that disaster. The man himself, even when he learned to speak intelligibly, could tell us very little. He remembered he had felt better (after the ship had anchored, I suppose), and that the darkness, the wind, and the rain took his breath away. This looks as if he had been on deck some time during that night. But we mustn't forget he had been taken out of his knowledge, that he had been sea-sick and battened down below for four days, that he had no general notion of a ship or of the sea, and therefore could have no definite idea of what was happening to him. The rain, the wind, the darkness he knew; he understood the bleating of the sheep, and he remembered the pain of his wretchedness and misery, his heartbroken astonishment that it was neither seen nor understood, his dismay at finding all the men angry and all the women fierce. He had approached them as a beggar, it is true, he said; but in his country, even if they gave nothing, they spoke gently to beggars. The children in his country were not taught to throw stones at those who asked for compassion. Smith's strategy overcame him completely. The wood-lodge presented the horrible aspect of a dungeon. What would be done to him next? . . . No wonder that Amy Foster appeared to his eyes with the aureole of an angel of light. The girl had not been able to sleep for thinking of the poor man, and in the morning, before the Smiths were up, she slipped out across the back yard. Holding the door of the wood-lodge ajar, she looked in and extended to him half a loaf of white bread – 'such bread as the rich eat in my country,' he used to say.

"At this he got up slowly from amongst all sorts of rubbish, stiff, hungry, trembling, miserable, and doubtful. 'Can you eat this?' she asked in her soft and timid voice. He must have taken her for a 'gracious lady.' He devoured ferociously, and tears were falling on the crust. Suddenly he dropped the bread, seized her wrist, and imprinted a kiss on her hand. She was not frightened. Through his forlorn condition she had observed that he was good-looking. She shut the door and walked back slowly to the kitchen. Much later on, she told Mrs Smith, who shuddered at the bare idea of being touched by that creature.

"Through this act of impulsive pity he was brought back again within the pale of human relations with his new surroundings. He never forgot it – never.

"That very same morning old Mr Swaffer (Smith's nearest neighbour) came over to give his advice, and ended by carrying him off. He stood, unsteady on his legs, meek, and caked over in half-dried mud, while the two men talked around him in an incomprehensible tongue. Mrs Smith had refused to come down-stairs till the mad-man was off the premises; Amy Foster, far from within the dark kitchen, watched through the open back-door; and he obeyed the signs that were made to him to the best of his ability. But Smith was full of mistrust. 'Mind, sir! It may be all his cunning,' he cried repeatedly in a tone of warning. When Mr

Swaffer started the mare, the deplorable being sitting humbly by his side, through weakness, nearly fell out over the back of the high two-wheeled cart. Swaffer took him straight home. And it is then that I come upon the scene.

"I was called in by the simple process of the old man beckoning to me with his forefinger over the gate of his house as I happened to be driving past. I got down, of course.

" 'I've got something here,' he mumbled, leading the way to an outhouse at a little distance from his other farm-buildings.

"It was there that I saw him first, in a long, low room taken upon the space of that sort of coach-house. It was bare and whitewashed, with a small square aperture glazed with one cracked, dusty pane at its further end. He was lying on his back upon a straw pallet; they had given him a couple of horse-blankets, and he seemed to have spent the remainder of his strength in the exertion of cleaning himself. He was almost speechless; his quick breathing under the blankets pulled up to his chin, his glittering, restless black eyes reminded me of a wild bird caught in a snare. While I was examining him, old Swaffer stood silently by the door, passing the tips of his fingers along his shaven upper lip. I gave some directions, promised to send a bottle of medicine, and naturally made some inquiries.

" 'Smith caught him in the stackyard at New Barns,' said the old chap in his deliberate, unmoved manner, and as if the other had been indeed a sort of wild animal. 'That's how I came by him. Quite a curiosity, isn't he? Now tell me, doctor – you've been all over the world – don't you think that's a bit of a Hindoo we've got hold of here?'

"I was greatly surprised. His long black hair scattered over the straw bolster contrasted with the olive pallor of his face. It occurred to me he might be a Basque. It didn't necessarily follow that he should understand Spanish; but I tried him with the few words I know, and also with some French. The whispered sounds I caught by bending my ear to his lips puzzled me utterly. That afternoon the young ladies from the Rectory (one of them read Goethe with a dictionary, and the other had struggled with Dante for years), coming to see Miss Swaffer, tried their German and Italian on him from the doorway. They retreated, just the least bit scared by the flood of passionate speech which, turning on his pallet, he let out at them. They admitted that the sound was pleasant, soft, musical – but, in conjunction with his looks perhaps, it was startling – so excitable, so utterly unlike anything one had ever heard. The village boys climbed up the bank to have a peep through the little square aperture. Everybody was wondering what Mr Swaffer would do with him.

"He simply kept him.

"Swaffer would be called eccentric were he not so much respected. They will tell you that Mr Swaffer sits up as late as ten o'clock at night to read books, and they will tell you also that he can write a cheque for two hundred pounds without thinking twice about it. He himself would tell you that the Swaffers had owned land between this and Darnford for these three hundred years. He must be eighty-five to-day, but he does not look a bit older than when I first came here. He is a great breeder of sheep, and deals extensively in cattle. He attends market days for miles around in every sort of weather, and drives sitting bowed low over the reins, his lank grey hair curling over the collar of his warm coat, and with a green plaid rug round his legs. The calmness of advanced age gives a solemnity to his manner. He is clean-shaved; his lips are thin and sensitive; something rigid and monachal in the set of his features lends a certain elevation to the character of his face. He has been known to drive miles in the rain to see a new kind of rose in somebody's garden, or a monstrous cabbage grown by a cottager. He loves to hear tell of or to be shown something what he calls 'outlandish'. Perhaps it was just that outlandishness of the man which influenced old Swaffer. Perhaps it was only an inexplicable caprice. All I know is that at the end of three weeks I caught sight of Smith's lunatic digging in Swaffer's kitchen garden. They had found out he could use a spade. He dug barefooted.

"His black hair flowed over his shoulders. I suppose it was Swaffer who had given him the striped old cotton shirt; but he wore still the national brown cloth trousers (in which he had been washed ashore) fitting to the leg almost like tights; was belted with a broad leathern belt studded with little brass discs; and had never yet ventured into the village. The land he looked upon seemed to him kept neatly, like the grounds round a landowner's house; the size of the cart-horses struck him with astonishment; the roads resembled garden walks, and the aspect of the people, especially on Sundays, spoke of opulence. He wondered what

made them so hardhearted and their children so bold. He got his
food at the back-door, carried it in both hands, carefully, to his
outhouse, and, sitting alone on his pallet, would make the sign of
the cross before he began. Beside the same pallet, kneeling in the
early darkness of the short days, he recited aloud the Lord's
Prayer before he slept. Whenever he saw old Swaffer he would
bow with veneration from the waist, and stand erect while the old
man, with his fingers over his upper lip, surveyed him silently. He
bowed also to Miss Swaffer, who kept house frugally for her father
– a broad-shouldered, big-boned woman of forty-five, with the
pocket of her dress full of keys, and a grey, steady eye. She was
Church – as people said (while her father was one of the trustees
of the Baptist Chapel) – and wore a little steel cross at her waist.
She dressed severely in black, in memory of one of the innumerable Bradleys of the neighbourhood, to whom she had been
engaged some twenty-five years ago – a young farmer who broke
his neck out hunting on the eve of the wedding-day. She had the
unmoved countenance of the deaf, spoke very seldom, and her
lips, thin like her father's, astonished one sometimes by a
mysteriously ironic curl.

"These were the people to whom he owed allegiance, and an
overwhelming loneliness seemed to fall from the leaden sky of that
winter without sunshine. All the faces were sad. He could talk to
no one, and had no hope of ever understanding anybody. It was
as if these had been the faces of people from the other world – dead
people – he used to tell me years afterwards. Upon my word, I
wonder he did not go mad. He didn't know where he was.
Somewhere very far from his mountains – somewhere over the
water. Was this America, he wondered?

"If it hadn't been for the steel cross at Miss Swaffer's belt he
would not, he confessed, have known whether he was in a
Christian country at all. He used to cast stealthy glances at it, and
feel comforted. There was nothing here the same as in his
country! The earth and the water were different; there were no
images of the Redeemer by the roadside. The very grass was
different, and the trees. All the trees but the three old Norway
pines on the bit of lawn before Swaffer's house, and these
reminded him of his country. He had been detected once, after
dusk, with his forehead against the trunk of one of them, sobbing,
and talking to himself. They had been like brothers to him at that

time, he affirmed. Everything else was strange. Conceive you the kind of an existence over-shadowed, oppressed, by the everyday material appearances, as if by the visions of a nightmare. At night, when he could not sleep, he kept on thinking of the girl who gave him the first piece of bread he had eaten in this foreign land. She had been neither fierce nor angry, nor frightened. Her face he remembered as the only comprehensible face amongst all these faces that were as closed, as mysterious, and as mute as the faces of the dead who are possessed of a knowledge beyond the comprehension of the living. I wondered whether the memory of her compassion prevented him from cutting his throat. But there! I suppose I am an old sentimentalist, and forget the instinctive love of life which it takes all the strength of an uncommon despair to overcome.

"He did the work which was given him with an intelligence which surprised old Swaffer. By-and-by it was discovered that he could help at the ploughing, could milk the cows, feed the bullocks in the cattle-yard, and was of some use with the sheep. He began to pick up words, too, very fast; and suddenly, one fine morning in spring, he rescued from an untimely death a grand-child of old Swaffer.

"Swaffer's younger daughter is married to Wilcox, a solicitor and the Town Clerk of Colebrook. Regularly twice a year they come to stay with the old man for a few days. Their only child, a little girl not three years old at the time, ran out of the house alone in her little white pinafore, and, toddling across the grass of a terraced garden, pitched herself over a low wall head first into the horsepond in the yard below.

"Our man was out with the waggoner and the plough in the field nearest to the house, and as he was leading the team round to begin a fresh furrow, he saw, through the gap of a gate, what for anybody else would have been a mere flutter of something white. But he had straight-glancing, quick, far-reaching eyes, that only seemed to flinch and lose their amazing power before the immensity of the sea. He was barefooted, and looking as out-landish as the heart of Swaffer could desire. Leaving the horses on the turn, to the inexpressible disgust of the waggoner he bounded off, going over the ploughed ground in long leaps, and suddenly appeared before the mother, thrust the child into her arms, and strode away.

"The pond was not very deep; but still, if he had not had such good eyes, the child would have perished – miserably suffocated in the foot or so of sticky mud at the bottom. Old Swaffer walked out slowly into the field, waited till the plough came over to his side, had a good look at him, and without saying a word went back to the house. But from that time they laid out his meals on the kitchen table; and at first, Miss Swaffer, all in black and with an inscrutable face, would come and stand in the doorway of the living-room to see him make a big sign of the cross before he fell to. I believe that from that day, too, Swaffer began to pay him regular wages.

"I can't follow step by step his development. He cut his hair short, was seen in the village and along the road going to and fro to his work like any other man. Children ceased to shout after him. He became aware of social differences, but remained for a long time surprised at the bare poverty of the churches among so much wealth. He couldn't understand either why they were kept shut up on week-days. There was nothing to steal in them. Was it to keep people from praying too often? The rectory took much notice of him about that time, and I believe the young ladies attempted to prepare the ground for his conversion. They could not, however, break him of his habit of crossing himself, but he went so far as to take off the string with a couple of brass medals the size of a sixpence, a tiny metal cross, and a square sort of scapulary which he wore round his neck. He hung them on the wall by the side of his bed, and he was still to be heard every evening reciting the Lord's Prayer, in incomprehensible words and in a slow, fervent tone, as he had heard his old father do at the head of all the kneeling family, big and little, on every evening of his life. And though he wore corduroys at work, and a slop-made pepper-and-salt suit on Sundays, strangers would turn round to look after him on the road. His foreignness had a peculiar and indelible stamp. At last people became used to seeing him. But they never because used to him. His rapid, skimming walk; his swarthy complexion; his hat cocked on the left ear; his habit, on warm evenings, of wearing his coat over one shoulder, like a hussar's dolman; his manner of leaping over the stiles, not as a feat of agility, but in the ordinary course of progression – all these peculiarities were, as one may say, so many causes of scorn and offence to the inhabitants of the village. *They* wouldn't in their dinner hour lie flat on their backs on the grass to stare at the sky. Neither did they go about the fields screaming dismal tunes. Many times have I heard his high-pitched voice from behind the ridge of some sloping sheep-walk, a voice light and soaring, like a lark's, but with a melancholy human note, over our fields that hear only the song of birds. And I would be startled myself. Ah! He was different; innocent of heart, and full of good will, which nobody wanted, this castaway, that, like a man transplanted into another planet, was separated by an immense space from his past and by an immense ignorance from his future. His quick, fervent utterance positively shocked everybody. 'An excitable devil', they called him. One evening, in the tap-room of the Coach and Horses, (having drunk some whisky), he upset them all by singing a love-song of his country. They hooted him down, and he was pained; but Preble, the lame wheelwright, and Vincent, the fat black-smith, and the other notables, too, wanted to drink their evening beer in peace. On another occasion he tried to show them how to dance. The dust rose in clouds from the sanded floor; he leaped straight up amongst the deal tables, struck his heels together, squatted on one heel in front of old Preble, shooting out the other leg, uttered wild and exulting cries, jumped up to whirl on one foot, snapping his fingers above his head – and a strange carter who was having a drink in there began to swear, and cleared out with his half-pint in his hand into the bar. But when suddenly he sprang upon a table and continued to dance among the glasses, the landlord interfered. He didn't want any 'acrobat tricks in the tap-room'. They laid their hands on him. Having had a glass or two, Mr Swaffer's foreigner tried to expostulate: was ejected forcibly: got a black eye.

"I believe he felt the hostility of his human surroundings. But he was tough – tough in spirit, too, as well as in body. Only the memory of the sea frightened him, with that vague terror that is left by a bad dream. His home was far away; and he did not want now to go to America. I had often explained to him that there is no place on earth where true gold can be found lying ready and to be got for the trouble of the picking up. How, then, he asked, could he ever return home with empty hands when there had been sold a cow, two ponies, and a bit of land to pay for his going? His eyes would fill with tears, and, averting them from the immense shimmer of the sea, he would throw himself face down on the grass. But sometimes, cocking his hat with a little conquering air, he would defy my wisdom. He had found his bit of true gold. That was Amy Foster's heart; which was 'a golden heart, and soft to people's misery', he would say in the accents of overwhelming conviction.

"He was called Yanko. He had explained that this meant Little John; but as he would also repeat very often that he was a mountaineer (some word sounding in the dialect of his country like Goorall) he got it for his surname. And this is the only trace of him that the succeeding ages may find in the marriage register of the parish. There it stands – Yanko Goorall – in the rector's handwriting. The crooked cross made by the castaway, a cross whose tracing no doubt seemed to him the most solemn part of the whole ceremony, is all that remains now to perpetuate the memory of his name.

"His courtship had lasted some time – ever since he got his precarious footing in the community. It began by his buying for Amy Foster a green satin ribbon in Darnford. This was what you did in his country. You bought a ribbon at a Jew's stall on a fair-day. I don't suppose the girl knew what to do with it, but he seemed to think that his honourable intentions could not be mistaken.

"It was only when he declared his purpose to get married that I fully understood how, for a hundred futile and inappreciable reasons, how – shall I say odious? – he was to all the countryside. Every old woman in the village was up in arms. Smith, coming upon him near the farm, promised to break his head for him if he found him about again. But he twisted his little black moustache with such a bellicose air and rolled such big, black fierce eyes at Smith that this promise came to nothing. Smith, however, told the girl that she must be mad to take up with a man who was surely wrong in his head. All the same, when she heard him in the gloaming whistle from beyond the orchard a couple of bars of a weird and mournful tune, she would drop whatever she had in her hand – she would leave Mrs Smith in the middle of a sentence – and she would run out to his call. Mrs Smith called her a shameless hussy. She answered nothing. She said nothing at all to anybody, and went on her way as if she had been deaf. She and I alone in all the land, I fancy, could see his very real beauty. He was very good-looking, and most graceful in his bearing, with that something wild as of a woodland creature in his aspect. Her mother moaned over her dismally whenever the girl came to see her on her day out. The father was surly, but pretended not to know; and Mrs Finn once told her plainly that 'this man, my dear, will do you some harm some day yet'. And so it went on. They could be seen on the roads, she tramping stolidly in her finery – grey dress, black feather, stout boots, prominent white cotton gloves that caught your eye a hundred yards away; and he, his coat slung picturesquely over one shoulder, pacing by her side, gallant of bearing and casting tender glances upon the girl with the golden heart. I wonder whether he saw how plain she was. Perhaps among types so different from what he had ever seen, he had not the power to judge; or perhaps he was seduced by the divine quality of her pity.

"Yanko was in great trouble meantime. In his country you get an old man for an ambassador in marriage affairs. He did not know how to proceed. However, one day in the midst of sheep in a field (he was now Swaffer's under-shepherd with Foster) he took off his hat to the father and declared himself humbly. 'I daresay she's fool enough to marry you,' was all Foster said. 'And then,' he used to relate, 'he puts his hat on his head, looks black at me as if he wanted to cut my throat, whistles the dog, and off he goes, leaving me to do the work.' The Fosters, of course, didn't like to lose the wages the girl earned: Amy used to give all her money to her mother. But there was in Foster a very genuine aversion to that match. He contended that the fellow was very good with sheep, but was not fit for any girl to marry. For one thing, he used to go along the hedges muttering to himself like a dam' fool; and then, these foreigners behave very queerly to women sometimes. And perhaps he would want to carry her off somewhere – or run off himself. It was not safe. He preached it to his daughter that the fellow might ill-use her in some way. She made no answer. It was, they said in the village, as if the man had done something to her. People discussed the matter. It was quite an excitement, and the two went on 'walking out' together in the face of opposition. Then something unexpected happened.

"I don't know whether old Swaffer ever understood how much he was regarded in the light of a father by his foreign retainer. Anyway the relation was curiously feudal. So when Yanko asked formally for an interview – 'and the Miss, too' (he called the severe, deaf Miss Swaffer simply *Miss*) – it was to obtain their permission to marry. Swaffer heard him unmoved, dismissed him by a nod, and then shouted the intelligence into Miss Swaffer's best ear. She showed no surprise, and only remarked grimly, in a veiled blank voice, 'He certainly won't get any other girl to marry him.'

"It is Miss Swaffer who has all the credit of the munificence: but in a very few days it came out that Mr Swaffer had presented Yanko with a cottage (the cottage you've seen this morning) and something like an acre of ground – had made it over to him in absolute property. Wilcox expedited the deed, and I remember him telling me he had a great pleasure in making it ready. It recited: 'In consideration of saving the life of my beloved grand-child, Bertha Wilcox.'

"Of course, after that no power on earth could prevent them from getting married.

"Her infatuation endured. People saw her going out to meet him in the evening. She stared with unblinking, fascinated eyes up the road where he was expected to appear, walking freely, with a swing from the hip, and humming one of the love-tunes of his country. When the boy was born, he got elevated at the 'Coach and Horses,' essayed again a song and a dance, and was again ejected. People expressed ther commiseration for a woman married to that Jack-in-the-box. He didn't care. There was a man now (he told me boastfully) to whom he could sing and talk in the language of his country, and show how to dance by-and-by.

"But I don't know. To me he appeared to have grown less springy of step, heavier in body, less keen of eye. Imagination, no doubt; but it seems to me now as if the net of fate had been drawn closer round him already.

"One day I met him on the footpath over the Talfourd Hill. He told me that 'women were funny'. I had heard already of domestic differences. People were saying that Amy Foster was beginning to find out what sort of man she had married. He looked upon the sea with indifferent, unseeing eyes. His wife had snatched the child out of his arms one day as he sat on the door-step crooning to it a song such as the mothers sing to babies in his mountains. She seemed to think he was doing it some harm. Women are funny. And she had objected to him praying aloud in the evening. Why? He expected the boy to repeat the prayer aloud after him by-

and-by, as he used to do after his old father when he was a child –
in his own country. And I discovered he longed for their boy to
grow up so that he could have a man to talk with in that language
that to our ears sounded so disturbing, so passionate, and so
bizarre. Why his wife should dislike the idea he couldn't tell. But
that would pass, he said. And tilting his head knowingly, he
tapped his breastbone to indicate that she had a good heart: not
hard, not fierce, open to compassion, charitable to the poor!

"I walked away thoughtfully; I wondered whether his difference, his strangeness, were not penetrating with repulsion that
dull nature they had begun by irresistibly attracting. I wondered . . ."

The Doctor came to the window and looked out at the frigid
splendour of the sea, immense in the haze, as if enclosing all the
earth with all the hearts lost among the passions of love and fear.

"Physiologically, now," he said, turning away abruptly, "it
was possible. It was possible."

He remained silent. Then went on—

"At all events, the next time I saw him he was ill – lung trouble.
He was tough, but I daresay he was not acclimatized as well as I
had supposed. It was a bad winter; and, of course, these
mountaineers do get fits of home-sickness; and a state of
depression would make him vulnerable. He was lying half dressed
on a couch downstairs.

"A table covered with a dark oilcloth took up all the middle of
the little room. There was a wicker cradle on the floor, a kettle
spouting steam on the hob, and some child's linen lay drying on
the fender. The room was warm, but the door opens right into the
garden, as you noticed perhaps.

"He was very feverish, and kept on muttering to himself. She
sat on a chair and looked at him fixedly across the table with her
brown, blurred eyes. 'Why don't you have him upstairs?' I asked.
With a start and a confused stammer she said, 'Oh! ah! I couldn't
sit with him upstairs sir.'

"I gave her certain directions; and going outside, I said again
that he ought to be in bed upstairs. She wrung her hands. 'I
couldn't. I couldn't. He keeps on saying something – I don't know
what.' With the memory of all the talk against the man that had
been dinned into her ears, I looked at her narrowly. I looked into
her short-sighted eyes, at her dumb eyes that once in her life had

seen an enticing shape, but seemed, staring at me, to see nothing at all now. But I saw she was uneasy.

" 'What's the matter with him?' she asked in a sort of vacant trepidation. 'He doesn't look very ill. I never did see anybody look like this before . . .'

" 'Do you think,' I asked indignantly, 'he is shamming?'

" 'I can't help it, sir,' she said, stolidly. And suddenly she clapped her hands and looked right and left. 'And there's the baby. I am so frightened. He wanted me just now to give him the baby. I can't understand what he says to it.'

" 'Can't you ask a neighbour to come in to-night?' I asked.

" 'Please, sir, nobody seems to care to come,' she muttered, dully resigned all at once.

"I impressed upon her the necessity of the greatest care, and then had to go. There was a good deal of sickness that winter. 'Oh, I hope he won't talk!' she exclaimed softly just as I was going away.

"I don't know how it is I did not see – but I didn't. And yet, turning in my trap, I saw her lingering before the door, very still, and as if meditating a flight up the miry road.

"Towards the night his fever increased.

"He tossed, moaned, and now and then muttered a complaint. And she sat with the table between her and the couch, watching every movement and every sound, with the terror, the unreasonable terror, of that man she could not understand creeping over her. She had drawn the wicker cradle close to her feet. There was nothing in her now but the maternal instinct and that unaccountable fear.

"Suddenly coming to himself, parched, he demanded a drink of water. She did not move. She had not understood, though he may have thought he was speaking in English. He waited, looking at her, burning with fever, amazed at her silence and immobility, and then he shouted impatiently, 'Water! Give me water!'

"She jumped to her feet, snatched up the child, and stood still. He spoke to her, and his passionate remonstrances only increased her fear of that strange man. I believe he spoke to her for a long time, entreating, wondering, pleading, ordering, I suppose. She says she bore it as long as she could. And then a gust of rage came over him.

"He sat up and called out terribly one word – some word. Then he got up as though he hadn't been ill at all, she says. And as in fevered dismay, indignation, and wonder he tried to get to her round the table, she simply opened the door and ran out with the child in her arms. She heard him call twice after her down the road in a terrible voice – and fled . . . Ah! but you should have seen stirring behind the dull, blurred glance of those eyes the spectre of the fear which had hunted her on that night three miles and a half to the door of Foster's cottage! I did the next day.

"And it was I who found him lying face down and his body in a puddle, just outside the little wicket-gate.

"I had been called out that night to an urgent case in the village, and on my way home at daybreak passed by the cottage. The door stood open. My man helped me to carry him in. We laid him on the couch. The lamp smoked, the fire was out, the chill of the stormy night oozed from the cheerless yellow paper on the wall. 'Amy!' I called aloud, and my voice seemed to lose itself in the emptiness of this tiny house as if I had cried in a desert. He opened his eyes. 'Gone!' he said, distinctly. 'I had only asked for water – only for a little water . . .'

"He was muddy. I covered him up and stood waiting in silence, catching a painfully gasped word now and then. They were no longer in his own language. The fever had left him, taking with it the heat of life. And with his panting breast and lustrous eyes he reminded me again of a wild creature under the net; of a bird caught in a snare. She had left him. She had left him – sick – helpless – thirsty. The spear of the hunter had entered his very soul. 'Why?' he cried, in the penetrating and indignant voice of a man calling to a responsible Maker. A gust of wind and a swish of rain answered.

"And as I turned away to shut the door he pronounced the word 'Merciful!' and expired.

"Eventually I certified heart-failure as the immediate cause of death. His heart must have indeed failed him, or else he might have stood this night of storm and exposure, too. I closed his eyes and drove away. Not very far from the cottage I met Foster walking sturdily between the dripping hedges with his collie at his heels.

" 'Do you know where your daughter is?' I asked.

" 'Don't I!' he cried. 'I am going to talk to him a bit. Frightening a poor woman like this.'

" 'He won't frighten her any more,' I said. 'He is dead.'

"He struck with his stick at the mud.

" 'And there's the child.'

"Then, after thinking deeply for a while—

" 'I don't know that it isn't for the best.'

"That's what he said. And she says nothing at all now. Not a word of him. Never. Is his image as utterly gone from her mind as his lithe and striding figure, his carolling voice are gone from our fields? He is no longer before her eyes to excite her imagination into a passion of love or fear; and his memory seems to have vanished from her dull brain as a shadow passes away upon a white screen. She lives in the cottage and works for Miss Swaffer. She is Amy Foster for everybody, and the child is 'Amy Foster's boy'. She calls him Johnny – which means Little John.

"It is impossible to say whether this name recalls anything to her. Does she ever think of the past? I have seen her hanging over the boy's cot in a very passion of maternal tenderness. The little fellow was lying on his back, a little frightened at me, but very still, with his big black eyes, with his fluttered air of a bird in a snare. And looking at him I seemed to see again the other one – the father, cast out mysteriously by the sea to perish in the supreme disaster of loneliness and despair."

1901/1901

Falk: A Reminiscence

Several of us, all more or less connected with the sea, were dining in a small river-hostelry not more than thirty miles from London and less than twenty from that shallow and dangerous puddle to which our coasting men give the grandiose name of "German Ocean". And through the wide windows we had a view of the Thames; an enfilading view down the Lower Hope Reach. But the dinner was execrable, and all the feast was for the eyes.

That flavour of salt-water which for so many of us had been the very water of life permeated our talk. He who hath known the bitterness of the Ocean shall have its taste for ever in his mouth. But one or two of us, pampered by the life of the land, complained of hunger. It was impossible to swallow any of that stuff. And indeed there was a strange mustiness in everything. The wooden dining-room stuck out over the mud of the shore like a lacustrine dwelling; the planks of the floor seemed rotten; a decrepid old waiter tottered pathetically to and fro before an antediluvian and worm-eaten sideboard; the chipped plates might have been disinterred from some kitchen midden near an inhabited lake; and the chops recalled times more ancient still. They brought forcibly to one's mind the night of ages when the primeval man, evolving the first rudiments of cookery from his dim consciousness, scorched lumps of flesh at a fire of sticks in the company of other good fellows; then, gorged and happy, sat him back among the gnawed bones to tell his artless tales of experience – the tales of hunger and hunt – and of women, perhaps!

But luckily the wine happened to be as old as the waiter. So, comparatively empty, but upon the whole fairly happy, we sat back and told our artless tales. We talked of the sea and all its works. The sea never changes, and its works, for all the talk of men, are wrapped in mystery. But we agreed that the times were changed. And we talked of old ships, of sea-accidents, of break-downs, dismastings; and of a man who brought his ship safe to Liverpool all the way from the River Plate under a jury rudder. We talked of wrecks, of short rations and of heroism – or at least of what the newspapers would have called heroism at sea – a manifestation of virtues quite different from the heroism of primitive times. And now and then falling silent all together we gazed at the sights of the river.

A P. & O. boat passed bound down. "One gets jolly good dinners on board these ships," remarked one of our band. A man with sharp eyes read out the name on her bows: *Arcadia*. "What a beautiful model of a ship!" murmured some of us. She was followed by a small cargo-steamer, and the flag they hauled down aboard while we were looking showed her to be a Norwegian. She made an awful lot of smoke, and before it had quite blown away, a high-sided, short, wooden barque, in ballast and towed by a paddle-tug, appeared in front of the windows. All her hands were forward busy setting up the headgear; and aft a woman in a red hood, quite alone with the man at the wheel, paced the length of the poop back and forth, with the grey wool of some knitting work in her hands.

"German I should think," muttered one. "The skipper has his wife on board," remarked another; and the light of the crimson sunset all ablaze behind the London smoke, throwing a glow of Bengal light upon the barque's spars, faded away from the Hope Reach.

Then one of us, who had not spoken before, a man of more than fifty, that had commanded ships for a quarter of a century, looking after the barque now gliding far away, all black on the lustre of the river, said:

This reminds me of an absurd episode in my life, now many years ago, when I got first the command of an iron barque, loading then in a certain Eastern sea-port. It was also the capital of an Eastern kingdom, lying up a river as might be London lies up this old Thames of ours. No more need be said of the place; for this sort of thing might have happened anywhere where there are ships, skippers, tugboats, and orphan nieces of indescribable splendour. And the absurdity of the episode concerns only me, my enemy Falk, and my friend Hermann.

There seemed to be something like peculiar emphasis on the words "My friend Hermann," which caused one of us (for we had just been speaking of heroism at sea) to say idly and nonchalantly:

"And was this Hermann a hero?"

Not at all, said our grizzled friend. No hero at all. He was a Schiff-führer: Ship-conductor. That's how they call a Master Mariner in Germany. I prefer our way. The alliteration is good, and there is something in the nomenclature that gives to us as a body the sense of corporate existence: Apprentice, Mate, Master, in the ancient and honourable craft of the sea. As to my friend Hermann, he might have been a consummate master of the honourable craft, but he was called officially Schiff-führer, and had the simple, heavy appearance of a well-to-do farmer, combined with the good-natured shrewdness of a small shop-keeper. With his shaven chin, round limbs, and heavy eyelids he did not look like a toiler, and even less like an adventurer of the sea. Still, he toiled upon the seas, in his own way, much as a shopkeeper works behind his counter. And his ship was the means by which he maintained his growing family.

She was a heavy, strong, blunt-bowed affair, awakening the ideas of primitive solidity, like the wooden plough of our forefathers. And there were, about her, other suggestions of a rustic and homely nature. The extraordinary timber projections which I have seen in no other vessel made her square stern resemble the tail end of a miller's waggon. But the four stern ports of her cabin, glazed with six little greenish panes each, and framed in wooden sashes painted brown, might have been the windows of a cottage in the country. The tiny white curtains and the greenery of flower-pots behind the glass completed the resemblance. On one or two occasions when passing under her stern I had detected from my boat a round arm in the act of tilting a watering-pot, and the bowed sleek head of a maiden whom I shall always call Hermann's niece, because as a matter of fact I've never heard her name, for all my intimacy with the family.

This, however, sprang up later on. Meantime in common with the rest of the shipping in that Eastern port, I was left in no doubt as to Hermann's notions of hygienic clothing. Evidently he believed in wearing good stout flannel next his skin. On most days little frocks and pinafores could be seen drying in the mizzen rigging of his ship, or a tiny row of socks fluttering on the signal halyards; but once a fortnight the family washing was exhibited in force. It covered the poop entirely. The afternoon breeze would incite to a weird and flabby activity all that crowded mass of clothing, with its vague suggestions of drowned, mutilated and flattened humanity. Trunks without heads waved at you arms without hands; legs without feet kicked fantastically with collapsible flourishes; and there were long white garments, that taking the wind fairly through their neck openings edged with lace, became for a moment violently distended as by the passage of obese and invisible bodies. On these days you could make out that ship at a great distance by the multi-coloured grotesque riot going on abaft her mizzen-mast.

She had her berth just ahead of me, and her name was *Diana* – Diana not of Ephesus but of Bremen. This was proclaimed in white letters a foot long spaced widely across the stern (somewhat like the lettering of a shop-sign) under the cottage windows. This ridiculously unsuitable name struck one as an impertinence towards the memory of the most charming of goddesses; for, apart from the fact that the old craft was physically incapable of engaging in any sort of chase, there was a gang of four children belonging to her. They peeped over the rail at passing boats and occasionally dropped various objects into them. Thus, sometime before I knew Hermann to speak to, I received on my hat a horrid rag-doll belonging to Hermann's eldest daughter. However, these youngsters were upon the whole well behaved. They had fair heads, round eyes, round little knobby noses, and they resembled their father a good deal.

This *Diana* of Bremen was a most innocent old ship, and seemed to know nothing of the wicked sea, as there are on shore households that know nothing of the corrupt world. And the sentiments she suggested were unexceptionable and mainly of a domestic order. She was a home. All these dear children had learned to walk on her roomy quarter-deck. In such thoughts there is something pretty, even touching. Their teeth, I should judge, they cut on the ends of her running gear. I have many times observed the baby Hermann (Nicholas) engaged in gnawing the whipping of the fore-royal brace. Nicholas' favourite place of residence was under the main fife-rail. Directly he was let loose he would crawl off there, and the first seaman who came along would bring him, carefully held aloft in tarry hands, back to the cabin door. I fancy there must have been a standing order to that effect. In the course of these transportations the baby, who was the only peppery person in the ship, tried to smite these stalwart young German sailors on the face.

Mrs Hermann, an engaging, stout housewife, wore on board baggy blue dresses with white dots. When, as happened once or twice, I caught her at an elegant little wash-tub rubbing hard on white collars, baby's socks, and Hermann's summer neck-ties, she would blush in girlish confusion, and raising her wet hands greet me from afar with many friendly nods. Her sleeves would be rolled up to the elbows, and the gold hoop of her wedding ring glittered among the soapsuds. Her voice was pleasant, she had a serene brow, smooth bands of very fair hair, and a good-humoured expression of the eyes. She was motherly and moderately talkative. When this simple matron smiled, youthful dimples broke out on her fresh broad cheeks. Hermann's niece, on the other hand, an orphan and very silent, I never saw attempt a smile. This, however, was not gloom on her part but the restraint of youthful gravity.

They had carried her about with them for the last three years, to help with the children and be company for Mrs Hermann, as Hermann mentioned once to me. It had been very necessary while they were all little, he had added in a vexed manner. It was her arm and her sleek head that I had glimpsed one morning, through the stern-windows of the cabin, hovering over the pots of fuchsias and mignonette; but the first time I beheld her full length I surrendered to her proportions. They fix her in my mind, as great beauty, great intelligence, quickness of wit or kindness of heart might have made some other woman memorable.

With her it was form and size. It was her physical personality that had this imposing charm. She might have been witty, intelligent, and kind to an exceptional degree. I don't know, and this is not to the point. All I know is that she was built on a magnificent scale. Built is the only word. She was constructed, she was erected, as it were, with regal lavishness. It staggered you to see this reckless expenditure of material upon a chit of a girl. She was youthful and also perfectly mature, as though she had been some fortunate immortal. She was heavy, too, perhaps, but that's nothing. It only added to that notion of permanence. She was barely nineteen. But such shoulders! Such round arms! Such a shadowing forth of mighty limbs when with three long strides she pounced across the deck upon the overturned Nicholas – it's perfectly indescribable! She seemed a good, quiet girl, vigilant as to Lena's needs, Gustav's tumbles, the state of Karl's dear little nose – conscientious, hardworking, and all that. But what magnificent hair she had! Abundant, long, thick, of a tawny colour. It had the sheen of precious metals. She wore it plaited tightly into one single tress hanging girlishly down her back; and its end reached down to her waist. The massiveness of it surprised you. On my word it reminded one of a club. Her face was big, comely, of an unruffled expression. She had a good complexion, and her blue eyes were so pale that she appeared to look at the world with the empty white candour of a statue. You could not call her good-looking. It was something much more impressive. The simplicity of her apparel, the opulence of her form, her imposing stature, and the extraordinary sense of vigorous life that seemed to emanate from her like a perfume exhaled by a flower, made her beautiful with a beauty of a rustic and olympian order. To watch her reaching up to the clothes-line with both arms raised high above her head, caused you to fall a-musing in a strain of pagan piety. Excellent Mrs Hermann's baggy cotton gowns had some sort of rudimentary frills at neck and bottom, but this girl's print frocks hadn't even a wrinkle; nothing but a few straight folds in the skirt falling to her feet, and these, when she stood still, had a severe and statuesque quality. She was inclined naturally to be still whether sitting or standing. However, I don't mean to say she was statuesque. She was too generously alive; but she could have stood for an allergoric statue of the Earth. I don't mean the worn-out earth of our possession, but a young Earth, a virginal planet undisturbed by the vision of a future teeming with the monstrous forms of life, clamorous with the cruel battles of hunger and thought.

The worthy Hermann himself was not very entertaining, though his English was fairly comprehensible. Mrs Hermann, who always let off one speech at least at me in an hospitable, cordial tone (and in Platt-Deutsch I suppose) I could not understand. As to their niece, however satisfactory to look upon (and she inspired you somehow with a hopeful view as to the prospects of mankind) she was a modest and silent presence, mostly engaged in sewing, only now and then, as I observed, falling over that work into a state of maidenly meditation. Her aunt sat opposite her, sewing also, with her feet propped on a wooden foot-stool. On the other side of the deck Hermann and I would get a couple of chairs out of the cabin and settle down to a smoking match, accompanied at long intervals by the pacific exchange of a few words. I came nearly every evening. Hermann I would find in his shirt-sleeves. As soon as he returned from the shore on board his ship he commenced operations by taking off his coat; then he put on his head an embroidered round cap with a tassel, and changed his boots for a pair of cloth slippers. Afterwards he smoked at the cabin-door, looking at his children with an air of civic virtue, till they got caught one after another and put to bed in various staterooms. Lastly, we would drink some beer in the cabin, which was furnished with a wooden table on cross legs, and with black straight-backed chairs – more like a farm kitchen than a ship's cuddy. The sea and all nautical affairs seemed very far removed from the hospitality of this exemplary family.

And I liked this because I had a rather worrying time on board my own ship. I had been appointed ex officio by the British Consul to take charge of her after a man who had died suddenly, leaving for the guidance of his successor some suspiciously unreceipted bills, a few dry-dock estimates hinting at bribery, and a quantity of vouchers for three years' extravagant expenditure; all these mixed up together in a dusty old violin-case lined with ruby velvet. I found besides a large account-book, which, when opened, hopefully turned out to my infinite consternation to be filled with verses – page after page of rhymed doggerel of a jovial and improper character, written in the neatest minute hand I ever did see. In the same fiddle-case a photograph of my predecessor, taken lately in Saigon, represented in front of a garden view, and in company of a female in strange draperies, an elderly, squat, rugged man of stern aspect in a clumsy suit of black broadcloth, and with the hair brushed forward above the temples in a manner reminding one of a boar's tusks. Of a fiddle, however, the only trace on board was the case, its empty husk as it were; but of the two last freights the ship had indubitably earned of late, there were not even the husks left. It was impossible to say where all that money had gone to. It wasn't on board. It had not been remitted home; for a letter from the owners, preserved in a desk evidently by the merest accident, complained mildly enough that they had not been favoured by a scratch of the pen for the last eighteen months. There were next to no stores on board, not an inch of spare rope or a yard of canvas. The ship had been run bare, and I foresaw no end of difficulties before I could get her ready for sea.

As I was young then – not thirty yet – I took myself and my troubles very seriously. The old mate, who had acted as chief mourner at the captain's funeral, was not particularly pleased at my coming. But the fact is the fellow was not legally qualified for command, and the Consul was bound, if at all possible, to put a properly certificated man on board. As to the second mate, all I can say is his name was Tottersen, or something like that. His practice was to wear on his head, in that tropical climate, a mangy fur cap. He was, without exception, the stupidest man I had ever seen on board ship. And he looked it, too. He looked so confoundedly stupid that it was a matter of surprise for me when he answered to his name.

I drew no great comfort from their company, to say the least of it; while the prospect of making a long sea passage with those two fellows was depressing. And my other thoughts in solitude could not be of a gay complexion. The crew was sickly, the cargo was coming very slow; I foresaw I would have lots of trouble with the charterers, and doubted whether they would advance me enough money for the ship's expenses. Their attitude towards me was unfriendly. Altogether I was not getting on. I would discover at odd times (generally about midnight) that I was totally inexperienced, greatly ignorant of business, and hopelessly unfit for any sort of command; and when the steward had to be taken to the hospital ill with choleraic symptoms I felt bereaved of the only decent person at the after end of the ship. He was fully expected to recover, but in the meantime had to be replaced by some sort of servant. And on the recommendation of a certain Schomberg, the proprietor of the smaller of the two hotels in the place, I engaged a Chinaman. Schomberg, a brawny, hairy Alsatian, and an awful gossip, assured me that it was all right. "First-class boy that. Came in the *suite* of his Excellency Tseng the Commissioner – you know. His Excellency Tseng lodged with me here for three weeks."

He mouthed the Chinese Excellency at me with great unction, though the specimen of the "*suite*" did not seem very promising. At the time, however, I did not know what an untrustworthy humbug Schomberg was. The "boy" might have been forty or a hundred and forty for all you could tell – one of those Chinamen of the death's-head type of face and completely inscrutable. Before the end of the third day he had revealed himself as a confirmed opium-smoker, a gambler, a most audacious thief, and a first-class sprinter. When he departed at the top of his speed with thirty-two golden sovereigns of my own hard-earned savings it was the last straw. I had reserved that money in case my difficulties came to the worst. Now it was gone I felt as poor and naked as a fakir. I clung to my ship, for all the bother she caused me, but what I could not bear were the long lonely evenings in her cuddy, where the atmosphere, made smelly by a leaky lamp, was agitated by the snoring of the mate. That fellow shut himself up in his stuffy cabin punctually at eight, and made gross and revolting noises like a water-logged trombone. It was odious not to be able to worry oneself in comfort on board one's own ship. Everything in this world, I reflected, even the command of a nice little barque, may be made a delusion and a snare for the unwary spirit of pride in man.

From such reflections I was glad to make my escape on board that Bremen *Diana*. There apparently no whisper of the world's iniquities had ever penetrated. And yet she lived upon the wide sea: and the sea tragic and comic, the sea with its horrors and its peculiar scandals, the sea peopled by men and ruled by iron necessity is indubitably a part of the world. But that patriarchal old tub, like some saintly retreat, echoed nothing of it. She was world proof. Her venerable innocence apparently put a restraint on the roaring lusts of the sea. And yet I have known the sea too long to believe in its respect for decency. An elemental force is ruthlessly frank. It may, of course, have been Hermann's skilful seamanship, but to me it looked as if the allied oceans had refrained from smashing these high bulwarks, unshipping the lumpy rudder, frightening the children, and generally opening this family's eyes out of sheer reticence. It looked like reticence. The ruthless disclosure was, in the end, left for a man to make; a man strong and elemental enough and driven to unveil some secrets of the sea by the power of a simple and elemental desire.

This, however, occurred much later, and meantime I took sanctuary in that serene old ship early every evening. The only person on board that seemed to be in trouble was little Lena, and in due course I perceived that the health of the rag-doll was more than delicate. This object led a sort of in extremis existence in a wooden box placed against the starboard mooring-bitts tended and nursed with the greatest sympathy and care by all the children, who greatly enjoyed pulling long faces and moving with hushed footsteps. Only the baby – Nicholas – looked on with a cold, ruffianly leer, as if he had belonged to another tribe altogether. Lena perpetually sorrowed over the box, and all of them were in deadly earnest. It was wonderful the way these children would work up their compassion for that bedraggled thing I wouldn't have touched with a pair of tongs. I suppose they were exercising and developing their racial sentimentalism by the means of that dummy. I was only surprised that Mrs Hermann let Lena cherish and hug that bundle of rags to that extent, it was so disreputably and completely unclean. But Mrs Hermann would raise her fine womanly eyes from her needlework to look on with amused sympathy, and did not seem to see it, somehow, that this object of affection was a disgrace to the ship's purity. Purity, not cleanliness, is the word. It was pushed so far that I seemed to detect in this, too, a sentimental excess, as if dirt had been removed in very love. It is impossible to give you an idea of such a meticulous neatness. It was as if every morning that ship had been arduously explored with – with toothbrushes. Her very bowsprit three times a week had its toilette made with a cake of soap and a piece of soft flannel. Arrayed – I *must* say arrayed – arrayed artlessly in dazzling white paint as to wood and dark green as to ironwork, the simple-minded distribution of these colours evoked the images of guileless peace, of arcadian felicity; and the childish comedy of disease and sorrow struck me sometimes as an abominably real blot upon that ideal state.

I enjoyed it greatly, and on my part I brought a little mild excitement into it. Our intimacy arose from the pursuit of that thief. It was in the evening, and Hermann, who, contrary to his habits, had stayed on shore late that day, was extricating himself backwards out of a little gharry on the river bank, opposite his ship, when the hunt passed. Realizing the situation as though he had eyes in his shoulder-blades, he joined us with a leap and took the lead. The Chinaman fled silent like a rapid shadow on the dust of an extremely oriental road. I followed. A long way in the rear my mate whooped like a savage. A young moon threw a bashful light on a plain like a monstrous waste ground: the architectural mass of a Buddhist temple far away projected itself in dead black on the sky. We lost the thief of course; but in my disappointment I had to admire Hermann's presence of mind. The velocity that stodgy man developed in the interests of a complete stranger earned my warm gratitude – there was something truly cordial in his exertions.

He seemed as vexed as myself at our failure, and would hardly listen to my thanks. He said it was "nothings", and invited me on the spot to come on board his ship and drink a glass of beer with him. We poked sceptically for a while amongst the bushes, peered without conviction into a ditch or two. There was not a sound: patches of slime glimmered feebly amongst the reeds. Slowly we trudged back, drooping under the thin sickle of the moon, and I heard him mutter to himself, "Himmel! Zwei und dreissig Pfund!" He was impressed by the figure of my loss. For a long time we had ceased to hear the mate's whoops and yells.

Then he said to me, "Everybody has his troubles," and as we went on remarked that he would never have known anything of mine hadn't he by an extraordinary chance been detained on shore by Captain Falk. He didn't like to stay late ashore – he added with a sigh. The something doleful in his tone I put to his sympathy with my misfortune, of course.

On board the *Diana* Mrs Hermann's fine eyes expressed much interest and commiseration. We had found the two women sewing face to face under the open skylight in the strong glare of the lamp. Hermann walked in first, starting in the very doorway to pull off his coat, and encouraging me with loud, hospitable ejaculations: "Come in! This way! Come in, captain!" At once, coat in hand, he began to tell his wife all about it. Mrs Hermann put the palms of her plump hands together; I smiled and bowed with a heavy heart: the niece got up from her sewing to bring Hermann's slippers and his embroidered calotte, which he assumed pontifically, talking (about me) all the time. Billows of white stuff lay between the chairs on the cabin floor; I caught the words "Zwei und dreissig Pfund" repeated several times, and presently came the beer, which seemed delicious to my throat, parched with running and the emotions of the chase.

I didn't get away till well past midnight, long after the women had retired. Hermann had been trading in the East for three years or more, carrying freights of rice and timber mostly. His ship was well known in all the ports from Vladivostok to Singapore. She was his own property. The profits had been moderate, but the trade answered well enough while the children were small yet. In another year or so he hoped he would be able to sell the old *Diana* to a firm in Japan for a fair price. He intended to return home, to Bremen, by mail boat, second class, with Mrs Hermann and the children. He told me all this stolidly, with slow puffs at his pipe. I was sorry when knocking the ashes out he began to rub his eyes. I would have sat with him till morning. What had I to hurry on board my own ship for? To face the broken rifled drawer in my stateroom. Ugh! The very thought made me feel unwell.

I became their daily guest, as you know. I think that Mrs Hermann from the first looked upon me as a romantic person. I did not, of course, tear my hair *coram populo* over my loss, and she took it for lordly indifference. Afterwards, I daresay, I did tell them some of my adventures – such as they were – and they marvelled greatly at the extent of my experience. Hermann would translate what he thought the most striking passages. Getting upon his legs, and as if delivering a lecture on a phenomenon, he addressed himself, with gestures, to the two women, who would let their sewing sink slowly on their laps. Meantime I sat before a glass of Hermann's beer, trying to look modest. Mrs Hermann would glance at me quickly, emit slight "Ach's!" The girl never made a sound. Never. But she, too, would sometimes raise her pale eyes to look at me in her unseeing, gentle way. Her glance was by no means stupid; it beamed out soft and diffuse as the moon beams upon a landscape – quite differently from the scrutinizing inspection of the stars. You were drowned in it, and imagined yourself to appear blurred. And yet this same glance when turned upon Christian Falk must have been as efficient as the searchlight of a battle-ship.

Falk was the other assiduous visitor on board, but from his behaviour he might have been coming to see the quarter-deck capstan. He certainly used to stare at it a good deal when keeping us company outside the cabin door, with one muscular arm thrown over the back of the chair, and his big shapely legs, in very tight white trousers, extended far out and ending in a pair of black shoes as roomy as punts. On arrival he would shake Hermann's hand with a mutter, bow to the women, and take up his careless and misanthropic attitude by our side. He departed abruptly, with a jump, going through the performance of grunts, hand-shakes, bow, as if in a panic. Sometimes, with a sort of discreet and convulsive effort, he approached the women and exchanged a few low words with them, half a dozen at most. On these occasions Hermann's usual stare became positively glassy and Mrs Hermann's kind countenance would colour up. The girl herself never turned a hair.

Falk was a Dane or perhaps a Norwegian, I can't tell now. At all events he was a Scandinavian of some sort, and a bloated monopolist to boot. It is possible he was unacquainted with the word, but he had a clear perception of the thing itself. His tariff of charges for towing ships in and out was the most brutally inconsiderate document of the sort I had ever seen. He was the commander and owner of the only tug-boat on the river, a very trim white craft of 150 tons or more, as elegantly neat as a yacht, with a round wheelhouse rising like a glazed turret high above her sharp bows, and with one slender varnished pole mast forward. I daresay there are yet a few shipmasters afloat who remember Falk and his tug very well. He extracted his pound and a half of flesh from each of us merchant-skippers with an inflexible sort of indifference which made him detested and even feared. Schomberg used to remark: "I won't talk about the fellow. I don't think he has six drinks from year's end to year's end in my place. But my advice is, gentlemen, don't you have anything to do with him, if you can help it."

This advice, apart from unavoidable business relations, was easy to follow because Falk intruded upon no one. It seems absurd to compare a tug-boat skipper to a centaur: but he reminded me somehow of an engraving in a little book I had as a boy, which represented centaurs at a stream, and there was one especially, in the foreground, prancing bow and arrows in hand, with regular severe features and an immense curled wavy beard, flowing down his breast. Falk's face reminded me of that centaur. Besides, he was a composite creature. Not a man-horse, it is true, but a man-boat. He lived on board his tug, which was always dashing up and down the river from early morn till dewy eve. In the last rays of the setting sun you could pick out, far away down the reach, his beard borne high up on the white structure, foaming up stream to anchor for the night. There was the white-clad man's body, and the rich brown patch of the hair, and nothing below the waist but the 'thwart-ship white lines of the bridge-screens, that led the eye to the sharp white lines of the bows cleaving the muddy water of the river.

Separated from his boat, to me at least he seemed incomplete. The tug herself without his head and torso on the bridge looked mutilated as it were. But he left her very seldom. All the time I remained in harbour I saw him only twice on shore. On the first occasion it was at my charterers, where he came in misanthropically to get paid for towing out a French barque the day before. The second time I could hardly believe my eyes, for I beheld him reclining under his beard in a cane-bottomed chair in the billiard-room of Schomberg's hotel.

It was very funny to see Schomberg ignoring him pointedly. The artificiality of it contrasted strongly with Falk's natural unconcern. The big Alsatian talked loudly with his other customers, going from one little table to the other, and passing Falk's place of repose with his eyes fixed straight ahead. Falk sat there with an untouched glass at his elbow. He must have known by sight and name every white man in the room, but he never addressed a word to anybody. He acknowledged my presence by a drop of his eyelids, and that was all. Sprawling there in the chair, he would, now and again, draw the palms of both his hands down his face, giving at the same time a slight, almost imperceptible, shudder.

It was a habit he had, and of course I was perfectly familiar with it, since you could not remain an hour in his company without being made to wonder at such a passionate and inexplicable gesture breaking some long period of stillness. He used to make it at all sorts of times; as likely as not after he had been listening to little Lena's chatter about the suffering doll, for instance. The Hermann children always besieged him about his legs closely, though, in a gentle way, he shrank from them a little. He seemed, however, to feel a great affection for the whole family. For Hermann himself especially. He sought his company. In this case, for instance, he must have been waiting for him, because as soon as he appeared Falk rose hastily, and they went out together. Then Schomberg expounded in my hearing to three or four people his theory that Falk was after Captain Hermann's niece, and asserted confidently that nothing would come of it. It was the same last year when Captain Hermann was loading here, he said.

Naturally, I did not believe Schomberg, but I own that for a time I observed closely what went on. All I discovered was some impatience on Hermann's part. At the sight of Falk, stepping over the gangway, the excellent man would begin to mumble and chew between his teeth something that sounded like German swear-words. However, as I've said, I'm not familiar with the language, and Hermann's soft, round-eyed countenance remained unchanged. Staring stolidly ahead he greeted him with, "Wie geht's?" or in English, "How are you?" with a throaty enunciation. The girl would look up for an instant and move her lips slightly: Mrs Hermann let her hands rest on her lap to talk volubly to him for a minute or so in her pleasant voice before she went on with her sewing again. Falk would throw himself into a chair, stretch his big legs, as like as not draw his hands down his face passionately. As to myself, he was not pointedly impertinent: it was rather as though he could not be bothered with such trifles as my existence; and the truth is that being a monopolist he was under no necessity to be amiable. He was sure to get his own extortionate terms out of me for towage whether he frowned or smiled. As a matter of fact, he did neither: but before many days went by he managed to astonish me not a little and to set Schomberg's tongue clacking more than ever.

It came about in this way. There was a shallow bar at the mouth of the river which ought to have been kept down, but the authorities of the State were piously busy gilding afresh the great Buddhist Pagoda just then, and had no money to spare for dredging operations. I don't know how it may be now, but at the time I speak of that sandbank was a great nuisance to the shipping. One of its consequences was that vessels of a certain draught of water, like Hermann's or mine, could not complete their loading in the river. After taking in as much as possible of their cargo, they had to go outside to fill up. The whole procedure was an unmitigated bore. When you thought you had as much on board as your ship could carry safely over the bar, you went and gave notice to your agents. They, in their turn, notified Falk that so-and-so was ready to go out. Then Falk (ostensibly when it fitted in with his other work, but, if the truth were known, simply when his arbitrary spirit moved him), after ascertaining carefully in the office that there was enough money to meet his bill, would come along unsympathetically, glaring at you with his yellow eyes from the bridge, and would drag you out dishevelled as to rigging, lumbered as to the decks, with unfeeling haste, as if to execution. And he would force you, too, to take the end of his own wire hawser, for the use of which there was of course an extra charge. To your shouted remonstrances against this extortion this towering trunk with one hand on the engine-room telegraph only shook its bearded head above the splash, the racket and the clouds of smoke, in which the tug, backing and filling in the smother of churning paddle-wheels, behaved like a ferocious and impatient creature. He had her manned by the cheekiest gang of lascars I ever did see, whom he allowed to bawl at you insolently, and, once fast, he plucked you out of your berth as if he did not care what he smashed. Eighteen miles down the river you had to go behind him, and then three more along the coast to where a group of uninhabited rocky islets enclosed a sheltered anchorage. There you would have to lie at single anchor with your naked spars showing to seaward over these barren fragments of land scattered upon a very intensely blue sea. There was nothing to look at besides but a bare coast, the muddy edge of the brown plain with the sinuosities of the river you had left, traced in dull green, and the Great Pagoda uprising lonely and massive with shining curves and pinnacles like the gorgeous and stony efflorescence of tropical rocks. You had nothing to do but to wait fretfully for the balance of your cargo, which was sent out of the river with the greatest irregularity. And it was open to you to console yourself with the thought that, after all, this stage of bother meant that your departure from these shores was indeed approaching at last.

We both had to go through that stage, Hermann and I, and there was a sort of tacit emulation between the ships as to which should be ready first. We kept on neck and neck almost to the finish, when I won the race by going personally to give notice in the forenoon; whereas Hermann, who was very slow in making up his mind to go ashore, did not get to the agents' office till late in the day. They told him there that my ship was first on turn for next morning, and I believe he told them he was in no hurry. It suited him better to go the day after.

That evening, on board the *Diana*, he sat staring with his plump knees well apart and puffing at the curved mouthpiece of his pipe. Presently he spoke with some impatience to his niece about putting the children to bed. Mrs Hermann, who was talking to Falk, stopped short and looked at her husband uneasily, but the girl got up at once and drove the children before her into the cabin. In a little while Mrs Hermann had to leave us to quell what, from the sounds inside, must have been a dangerous mutiny. At this Hermann grumbled to himself. For half an hour longer Falk, left alone with us, fidgeted on his chair, sighed lightly, then at last, after drawing his hands down his face, got up, and as if renouncing the hope of making himself understood (he hadn't opened his mouth once) he said in English: "Well . . . Good-night, Captain Hermann." He stopped for a moment before my chair and looked down fixedly, I may even say he glared, and he went so far as to make a deep noise in his throat. All this was so marked that for the first time in our limited intercourse of nods and grunts he excited in me something like interest. But next moment he disappointed me – for he strode away hastily without a nod even.

His manner was usually odd it is true, and I certainly did not pay much attention to it; but that sort of obscure intention, which seemed to lurk in his nonchalance like a wary old carp in a pond, had never before come so near the surface. He had distinctly aroused my expectations. I would have been unable to say what it was I expected, but at all events I did not expect the absurd developments he sprung upon me no later than the break of the very next day.

I remember only that there was, on that evening, enough point in his behaviour to make me, after he had fled, wonder audibly what he might mean. To this Hermann, crossing his legs with a swing and settling himself viciously away from me in his chair, said: "That fellow don't know himself what he means."

There might have been some insight in such a remark. I said nothing, and, still averted, Hermann added: "When I was here last year he was just the same." An eruption of tobacco smoke enveloped his head as if his temper had exploded like gunpowder.

I had half a mind to ask him point blank whether he, at least, didn't know why Falk, a notoriously unsociable man, had taken to visiting his ship with such assiduity. After all, I reflected suddenly, it was a most remarkable thing. I wonder now what Hermann would have said. As it turned out – he didn't let me ask. Forgetting all about Falk apparently, he started a monologue on his plans for the future: the selling of the ship, the going home;

and falling into a reflective and calculating mood he mumbled between regular jets of smoke about the expense. The necessity of disbursing passage-money for all his tribe seemed to disturb him in a manner that was the more striking because otherwise he gave no signs of a miserly disposition. And yet he fussed over the prospect of that voyage home in a mail-boat like a sedentary grocer who has made up his mind to see the world. He was racially thrifty I suppose, and for him there must have been a great novelty in finding himself obliged to pay for travelling – for sea travelling which was the normal state of life for the family – from the very cradle for most of them. I could see he grudged prospectively every single shilling which must be spent so absurdly. It was rather funny. He would become doleful over it, and then again, with a fretful sigh, he would suppose there was nothing for it now but to take three second-class tickets – and there were the four children to pay for besides. A lot of money that to spend at once. A big lot of money.

I sat with him listening (not for the first time) to these heart-searchings till I grew thoroughly sleepy, and then I left him and turned in on board my ship. At daylight I was awakened by a yelping of shrill voices, accompanied by a great commotion in the water, and the short, bullying blasts of a steam-whistle. Falk with his tug had come for me.

I began to dress. It was remarkable that the answering noise on board my ship together with the patter of feet above my head ceased suddenly. But I heard more remote guttural cries which seemed to express surprise and annoyance. Then the voice of my mate reached me howling expostulations to somebody at a distance. Other voices joined, apparently indignant; a chorus of something that sounded like abuse replied. Now and then the steam-whistle screeched.

Altogether that unnecessary uproar was distracting, but down there in my cabin I took it calmly. In another moment, I thought, I should be going down that wretched river, and in another week at the most I should be totally quit of the odious place and all the odious people in it.

Greatly cheered by the idea, I seized the hair-brushes and looking at myself in the glass began to use them. Suddenly a hush fell upon the noise outside, and I heard (the ports of my cabin were thrown open) – I heard a deep calm voice, not on board my ship, however, hailing resolutely in English, but with a strong foreign twang, "Go ahead!"

There may be tides in the affairs of men which, taken at the flood . . . and so on. Personally I am still on the look-out for that important turn. I am, however, afraid that most of us are fated to flounder for ever in the dead water of a pool the shores of which are arid indeed. But I know that there are often in men's affairs unexpectedly – even irrationally – illuminating moments when an otherwise insignificant sound, perhaps only some perfectly commonplace gesture, suffices to reveal to us all the unreason, all the fatuous unreason, of our complacency. "Go ahead" are not particularly striking words even when pronounced with a foreign accent; yet they petrified me in the very act of smiling at myself in the glass. And then, refusing to believe my ears, but already boiling with indignation, I ran out of the cabin and up on deck.

It was incredibly true. It was perfectly true. I had no eyes for anything but the *Diana*. It was she that was being taken away. She was already out of her berth and shooting athwart the river. "The way this loonatic plucked that ship out is a caution," said the awed voice of my mate close to my ear. "Hey! Hallo! Falk! Hermann! What's this infernal trick?" I yelled in a fury.

Nobody heard me. Falk certainly could not hear me. His tug was turning at full speed away under the other bank. The wire hawser between her and the *Diana*, stretched as taut as a harpstring, vibrated alarmingly.

The high black craft careened over to the awful strain. A loud crack came out of her, followed by the tearing and splintering of wood. "There!" said the awed voice in my ear. "He's carried away their towing chock." And then, with enthusiasm, "Oh! Look! Look, sir! Look at them Dutchmen skipping out of the way on the forecastle. I hope to goodness he'll break a few of their shins before he's done with 'em."

I yelled my vain protests. The rays of the rising sun coursing level along the plain warmed my back, but I was hot enough with rage. I could not have believed that a simple towing operation could suggest so plainly the idea of abduction, of rape. Falk was simply running off with the *Diana*.

The white tug careered out into the middle of the river. The red floats of her paddle-wheels revolving with mad rapidity tore up the whole reach into foam. The *Diana* in mid-stream waltzed round with as much grace as an old barn, and flew after her ravisher. Through the ragged fog of smoke driving headlong upon the water I had a glimpse of Falk's square motionless shoulders under a white hat as big as a cart-wheel, of his red face, his yellow staring eyes, his great beard. Instead of keeping a look-out ahead, he was deliberately turning his back on the river to glare at his tow. The tall heavy craft, never so used before in her life, seemed to have lost her senses; she took a wild sheer against her helm, and for a moment came straight at us, menacing and clumsy, like a runaway mountain. She piled up a streaming, hissing, boiling wave halfway up her blunt stem, my crew let out one great howl, – and then we held our breaths. It was a near thing. But Falk had her! He had her in his clutch. I fancied I could hear the steel hawser ping as it surged across the *Diana's* forecastle, with the hands on board of her bolting away from it in all directions. It was a near thing. Hermann, with his hair rumpled, in a snuffy flannel shirt and a pair of mustard-coloured trousers, had rushed to help with the wheel. I saw his terrified round face; I saw his very teeth uncovered by a sort of ghastly fixed grin; and in a great leaping tumult of water between the two ships the *Diana* whisked past so close that I could have flung a hair-brush at his head, for, it seems, I had kept them in my hands all the time. Meanwhile Mrs Hermann sat placidly on the skylight, with a woollen shawl on her shoulders. The excellent woman in response to my indignant gesticulations fluttered a handkerchief, nodding and smiling in the kindest way imaginable. The boys, only half-dressed, were jumping about the poop in great glee, displaying their gaudy braces; and Lena in a short scarlet petticoat, with peaked elbows and thin bare arms, nursed the rag-doll with devotion. The whole family passed before my sight as if dragged across a scene of unparalleled violence. The last I saw was Hermann's niece with the baby Hermann in her arms standing apart from the others. Magnificent in her close-fitting print frock, she displayed something so commanding in the manifest perfection of her figure that the sun seemed to be rising for her alone. The flood of light brought the opulence of her form and the vigour of her youth in a glorifying way. She went by perfectly motionless and as if lost in meditation; only the hem of her skirt stirred in the draught; the sun rays broke on her sleek tawny hair; that bald-headed ruffian, Nicholas, was whacking her on the shoulder. I saw his tiny fat arm rise and fall in a workmanlike manner. And then the four cottage windows of the *Diana* came into view retreating swiftly down the river. The sashes were up, and one of the white calico curtains fluttered straight out like a streamer above the agitated water of the wake.

To be thus tricked out of one's turn was an unheard of occurrence. In my agent's office, where I went to complain at once, they protested with apologies they couldn't understand how the mistake arose: but Schomberg, when I dropped in later to get some tiffin, though surprised to see me, was perfectly ready with an explanation. I found him seated at the end of a long narrow table, facing his wife – a scraggy little woman, with long ringlets and a blue tooth, who smiled abroad stupidly and looked frightened when you spoke to her. Between them a waggling punkah fanned twenty vacant cane-bottomed chairs and two rows of shiny plates. Three Chinamen in white jackets loafed with napkins in their hands around that desolation. Schomberg's pet *table d'hôte* was not much of a success that day. He was feeding himself furiously and seemed to overflow with bitterness.

He began by ordering in a brutal voice the chops to be brought back for me, and turning in his chair: "Mistake they told you? Not a bit of it! Don't you believe it for a moment, captain! Falk isn't a man to make mistakes unless on purpose." His firm conviction was that Falk had been trying all along to curry favour on the cheap with Hermann. "On the cheap – mind you! It doesn't cost him a cent to put that insult upon you, and Captain Hermann gets in a day ahead of your ship. Time's money! Eh? You are very friendly with Captain Hermann I believe, but a man is bound to be pleased at any little advantage he may get. Captain Hermann is a good business man, and there's no such thing as a friend in business. Is there?" He leaned forward and began to cast stealthy glances as usual. "But Falk is, and always was, a miserable fellow. I would despise him."

I muttered, grumpily, that I had no particular respect for Falk.

"I would despise him," he insisted, with an appearance of anxiety which would have amused me if I had not been fathoms deep in discontent. To a young man fairly conscientious and as well-meaning as only the young be, the current ill-usage of life comes with a peculiar cruelty. Youth that is fresh enough to believe in guilt, in innocence, and in itself, will always doubt

whether it have not perchance deserved its fate. Sombre of mind
and without appetite, I struggled with the chop while Mrs
Schomberg sat with her everlasting stupid grin and Schomberg's
talk gathered way like a slide of rubbish.

"Let me tell you. It's all about that girl. I don't know what
Captain Hermann expects, but if he asked me I could tell him
something about Falk. He's a miserable fellow. That man is a
perfect slave. That's what I call him. A slave. Last year I started
this *table d'hôte*, and sent cards out – you know. You think he had
one meal in the house? Give the thing a trial? Not once. He has got
hold now of a Madras cook – a blamed fraud that I hunted out of
my cookhouse with a rattan. He was not fit to cook for white men.
No, not for the white men's dogs either; but see, any damned
native that can boil a pot of rice is good enough for Mr Falk. Rice
and a little fish he buys for a few cents from the fishing-boats
outside is what he lives on. You would hardly credit it – eh? A
white man, too . . ."

He wiped his lips, using the napkin with indignation, and
looking at me. It flashed through my mind in the midst of my
depression that if all the meat in the town was like these *table
d'hôte* chops, Falk wasn't so much to blame. I was on the point of
saying this, but Schomberg's stare was intimidating. "He's a
vegetarian, perhaps," I murmured instead.

"He's a miser. A miserable miser," affirmed the hotel-keeper
with great force. "The meat here is not so good as at home – of
course. And dear, too. But look at me. I only charge a dollar for
the tiffin, and one dollar and fifty cents for the dinner. Show me
anything cheaper. Why am I doing it? There's little profit in this
game. Falk wouldn't look at it. I do it for the sake of a lot of young
white fellows here that hadn't a place where they could get a
decent meal and eat it decently in good company. There's first-
rate company always at my table."

The convinced way he surveyed the empty chairs made me feel
as if I had intruded upon a tiffin of ghostly Presences.

"A white man should eat like a white man, dash it all," he burst
out impetuously. "Ought to eat meat, must eat meat. I manage to
get meat for my patrons all the year round. Don't I? I am not
catering for a dam' lot of coolies: Have another chop, captain . . .
No? You, boy – take away!"

He threw himself back and waited grimly for the curry. The

half-closed jalousies darkened the room pervaded by the smell of fresh whitewash; a swarm of flies buzzed and settled in turns, and poor Mrs Schomberg's smile seemed to express the quintessence of all the imbecility that had ever spoken, had ever breathed, had ever been fed on infamous buffalo meat within these bare walls. Schomberg did not open his lips till he was ready to thrust therein a spoonful of greasy rice. He rolled his eyes ridiculously before he swallowed the hot stuff, and only then broke out afresh.

"It is the most degrading thing. They take the dish up to the wheelhouse for him with a cover on it, and he shuts both the doors before he begins to eat. Fact! Must be ashamed of himself. Ask the engineer. He can't do without an engineer – don't you see – and as no respectable man can be expected to put up with such a table, he allows them fifteen dollars a month extra mess money. I assure you it is so! You just ask Mr Ferdinand da Costa. That's the engineer he has now. You may have seen him about my place, a delicate dark young man, with very fine eyes and a little moustache. He arrived here a year ago from Calcutta. Between you and me, I guess the money-lenders there must have been after him. He rushes here for a meal every chance he can get, for just please tell me what satisfaction is that for a well-educated young fellow to feed all alone in his cabin – like a wild beast? That's what Falk expects his engineers to put up with for fifteen dollars extra. And the rows on board every time a little smell of cooking gets about the deck! You wouldn't believe! The other day da Costa got the cook to fry a steak for him – a turtle steak it was, too, not beef at all – and the fat caught or something. Young da Costa himself was telling me of it here in this room. 'Mr Schomberg' – says he – 'if I had let a cylinder cover blow off through my negligence Captain Falk couldn't have been more savage. He frightened the cook so that he won't put anything on the fire for me now.' Poor da Costa had tears in his eyes. Only try to put yourself in his place, captain: a sensitive, gentlemanly young fellow. Is he expected to eat his food raw? But that's your Falk all over. Ask any one you like. I suppose the fifteen dollars extra he has to give keep on rankling – in there."

And Schomberg tapped his manly breast. I sat half stunned by his irrelevant babble. Suddenly he gripped my forearm in an impressive and cautious manner, as if to lead me into a very cavern of confidence.

"It's nothing but enviousness," he said in a lowered tone, which had a stimulating effect upon my wearied hearing. "I don't suppose there is one person in this town that he isn't envious of. I tell you he's dangerous. Even I myself am not safe from him. I know for certain he tried to poison . . ."

"Oh, come now," I cried, disgusted.

"But I know for certain. The people themselves came and told me of it. He went about saying everywhere I was a worse pest to this town than the cholera. He had been talking against me ever since I opened this hotel. And he poisoned Captain Hermann's mind, too. Last time the *Diana* was loading here Captain Hermann used to come in every day for a drink or a cigar. This time he hasn't been here twice in a week. How do you account for that?"

He squeezed my arm till he extorted from me some sort of mumble.

"Falk makes ten times the money I do. I've another hotel to fight against, and there is no other tug on the river. I am not in his way, am I? He wouldn't be fit to run an hotel if he tried. But that's just his nature. He can't bear to think I am making a living. I only hope it makes him properly wretched. He's like that in everything. He would like to keep a decent table well enough. But no – for the sake of a few cents. Can't do it. It's too much for him. That's what I call being a slave to it. But he's mean enough to kick up a row when his nose gets tickled a bit. See that? That just paints him. Miserly and envious. You can't account for it any other way. Can you? I have been studying him these three years."

He was anxious I should assent to his theory. And indeed on thinking it over it would have been plausible enough if there hadn't been always the essential falseness of irresponsibility in Schomberg's chatter. However, I was not disposed to investigate the psychology of Falk. I was engaged just then in eating despondently a piece of stale Dutch cheese, being too much crushed to care what I swallowed myself, let alone bothering my head about Falk's ideas of gastronomy. I could expect from their study no clue to his conduct in matters of business, which seemed to me totally unrestrained by morality or even by the commonest sort of decency. How insignificant and contemptible I must appear, for the fellow to dare treat me like this – I reflected suddenly, writhing in silent agony. And I consigned Falk and all his peculiarities to the devil with so much mental fervour as to forget Schomberg's existence, till he grabbed my arm urgently. "Well, you may think and think till every hair of your head falls off, captain; but you can't explain it in any other way."

For the sake of peace and quietness I admitted hurriedly that I couldn't; persuaded that now he would leave off. But the only result was to make his moist face shine with the pride of cunning. He removed his hand for a moment to scare a black mass of flies off the sugar-basin, and caught hold of my arm again.

"To be sure. And in the same way everybody is aware he would like to get married. Only he can't. Let me quote you an instance. Well, two years ago a Miss Vanlo, a very ladylike girl, came from home to keep house for her brother, Fred, who had an engineering shop for small repairs by the waterside. Suddenly Falk takes to going up to their bungalow after dinner and sitting for hours in the verandah saying nothing. The poor girl couldn't tell for the life of her what to do with such a man, so she would keep on playing the piano and singing to him evening after evening till she was ready to drop. And it wasn't as if she had been a strong young woman either. She was thirty, and the climate had been playing the deuce with her. Then – don't you see – Fred had to sit up with them for propriety, and during whole weeks on end never got a chance to get to bed before midnight. That was not pleasant for a tired man – was it? And besides Fred had worries then because his shop didn't pay and he was dropping money fast. He just longed to get away from here and try his luck somewhere else, but for the sake of his sister he hung on and on till he ran himself into debt over his ears – I can tell you. I, myself, could show a handful of his chits for meals and drinks in my drawer. I could never find out tho' where Fred found all the money at last. Can't be but he must have got something out of that brother of his, a coal merchant in Port Said. Anyhow he paid everybody before he left, but the girl nearly broke her heart. Disappointment, of course, and at her age, don't you know . . . Mrs Schomberg here was very friendly with her, and she could tell you. Awful despair. Fainting fits. It was a scandal. A notorious scandal. To that extent that old Mr Siegers – not your present charterer, but Mr Siegers, the father, the old gentleman who retired from business on a fortune and got buried at sea going home, *he* had to interview Falk in his private office. He was a man who could speak like a Dutch Uncle, and, besides, Messrs Siegers had been helping Falk with a good bit of money from the start. In fact, you may say they made him as far as that goes. It so happened that just at the time he turned up here, their firm was chartering a lot of sailing-ships every year, and it suited their business that there should be good towing facilities on the river. See? . . . Well – there's always an ear at the keyhole – isn't there? In fact," he lowered his tone confidentially, "in this case it was a good friend of mine; a man you can see here any evening; only they conversed rather low. Anyhow my friend's certain that Falk was trying to make all sorts of excuses, and old Mr Siegers was coughing a lot. And yet Falk wanted all the time to be married, too. Why! It's notorious the man has been longing for years to make a home for himself. Only he can't face the expense. When it comes to putting his hand in his pocket – it chokes him off. That's the truth and no other. I've always said so, and everybody agrees with me by this time. What do you think of that – eh?"

He appealed confidently to my indignation, but having a mind to annoy him I remarked, "that it seemed to me very pitiful – if true."

He bounced in his chair as if I had run a pin into him. I don't know what he might have said, only at that moment we heard through the half-open door of the billiard-room the footsteps of two men entering from the verandah, a murmur of two voices; at the sharp tapping of a coin on a table Mrs Schomberg half rose irresolutely. "Sit still," he hissed at her, and then, in an hospitable, jovial tone, contrasting amazingly with the angry glance that had made his wife sink in her chair, he cried very loud: "Tiffin still going on in here, gentlemen."

There was no answer, but the voices dropped suddenly. The head Chinaman went out. We heard the clink of ice in the glasses, pouring sounds, the shuffling of feet, the scraping of chairs. Schomberg, after wondering in a low mutter who the devil could be there at this time of the day, got up napkin in hand to peep through the doorway cautiously. He retreated rapidly on tip-toe, and whispering behind his hand informed me that it was Falk, Falk himself who was in there, and what's more, he had Captain Hermann with him.

The return of the tug from the outer Roads was unexpected but possible, for Falk had taken away the *Diana* at half-past five, and it was now two o'clock. Schomberg wished me to observe that neither of these men would spend a dollar on a tiffin, which they must have wanted. But by the time I was ready to leave the dining-room Falk had gone. I heard the last of his big boots on the planks of the verandah. Hermann was sitting quite alone in the large, wooden room with the two lifeless billiard tables shrouded in striped covers, mopping his face diligently. He wore his best go-ashore clothes, a stiff collar, black coat, large white waistcoat, grey trousers. A white cotton sunshade with a cane handle reposed between his legs, his side whiskers were neatly brushed, his chin had been freshly shaved; and he only distantly resembled the dishevelled and terrified man in a snuffy night-shirt and ignoble old trousers I had seen in the morning hanging on to the wheel of the *Diana*.

He gave a start at my entrance, and addressed me at once in some confusion, but with genuine eagerness. He was anxious to make it clear he had nothing to do with what he called the "tam pizness" of the morning. It was most inconvenient. He had reckoned upon another day up in town to settle his bills and sign certain papers. There were also some few stores to come, and sundry pieces of "my ironwork", as he called it quaintly, landed for repairs, had been left behind. Now he would have to hire a native boat to take all this out to the ship. It would cost five to six dollars perhaps. He had had no warning from Falk. Nothing . . . He hit the table with his dumpy fist . . . Der verfluchte Kerl came in the morning like a "tam' ropper", making a great noise, and took him away. His mate was not prepared, his ship was moored fast – he protested it was shameful to come upon a man in that way. Shameful! Yet such was the power Falk had on the river that when I suggested in a chilling tone that he might have simply refused to have his ship moved, Hermann was quite startled at the idea. I never realized so well before that this is an age of steam. The exclusive possession of a marine boiler had given Falk the whip hand of us all. Hermann, recovering, put it to me appealingly that I knew very well how unsafe it was to contradict that fellow. At this I only smiled distantly.

"Der Kerl!" he cried. He was sorry he had not refused. He was indeed. The damage! The damage! What for all that damage! There was no occasion for damage. Did I know how much damage he had done? It gave me a certain satisfaction to tell

him that I had heard his old waggon of a ship crack fore and aft
as she went by. "You passed close enough to me," I added,
significantly.

He threw both his hands up to heaven at the recollection. One
of them grasped by the middle the white parasol, and he
resembled curiously a caricature of a shopkeeping citizen in one
of his own German comic papers. "Ach! That was dangerous," he
cried. I was amused. But directly he added with an appearance of
simplicity, "The side of your iron ship would have been crushed in
like – like this matchbox."

"Would it?" I growled, much less amused now; but by the time
I had decided that this remark was not meant for a dig at me he
had worked himself into a high state of resentfulness against Falk.
The inconvenience, the damage, the expense! Gottferdam! Devil
take the fellow. Behind the bar Schomberg, with a cigar in his
teeth, pretended to be writing with a pencil on a large sheet of
paper; and as Hermann's excitement increased it made me
comfortingly aware of my own calmness and superiority. But it
occurred to me while I listened to his revilings, that after all the
good man had come up in the tug. There perhaps – since he must
come to town – he had no option. But evidently he had had a
drink with Falk, either accepted or offered. How was that? So I
checked him by saying loftily that I hoped he would make Falk
pay for every penny of the damage.

"That's it! That's it! Go for him," called out Schomberg from the
bar, flinging his pencil down and rubbing his hands.

We ignored his noise. But Hermann's excitement suddenly
went off the boil as when you remove a saucepan from the fire. I
urged on his consideration that he had done now with Falk and
Falk's confounded tug. He, Hermann, would not, perhaps, turn up
again in this part of the world for years to come, since he was
going to sell the *Diana* at the end of this very trip ("Go home
passenger in a mail-boat," he murmured mechanically). He was
therefore safe from Falk's malice. All he had to do was to race off
to his consignees and stop payment of the towage bill before Falk
had the time to get in and lift the money.

Nothing could have been less in the spirit of my advice than the
thoughtful way in which he set about to make his parasol stay
propped against the edge of the table.

While I watched his concentrated efforts with astonishment he threw at me one or two perplexed, half-shy glances. Then he sat down. "That's all very well," he said, reflectively.

It cannot be doubted that the man had been thrown off his balance by being hauled out of the harbour against his wish. His stolidity had been profoundly stirred, else he would never have made up his mind to ask me unexpectedly whether I had not remarked that Falk had been casting eyes upon his niece. "No more than myself," I answered with literal truth. The girl was of the sort one necessarily casts eyes at in a sense. She made no noise, but she filled most satisfactorily a good bit of space.

"But you, captain, are not the same kind of man," observed Hermann.

I was not, I am happy to say, in a position to deny this. "What about the lady?" I could not help asking. At this he gazed for a time into my face, earnestly, and made as if to change the subject. I heard him beginning to mutter something unexpected, about his children growing old enough to require schooling. He would have to leave them ashore with their grandmother when he took up that new command he expected to get in Germany.

This constant harping on his domestic arrangements was funny. I suppose it must have been like the prospect of a complete alteration in his life. An epoch. He was going, too, to part with the *Diana!* He had served in her for years. He had inherited her. From an uncle, if I remember rightly. And the future loomed big before him, occupying his thought exclusively with all its aspects as on the eve of a venturesome enterprise. He sat there frowning and biting his lip, and suddenly he began to fume and fret.

I discovered to my momentary amusement that he seemed to imagine I could, should or ought, have caused Falk in some way to declare himself. Such a hope was incomprehensible, but funny. Then the contact with all this foolishness irritated me. I said crossly that I had seen no symptoms, but if there were any – since he, Hermann, was so sure – then it was still worse. What pleasure Falk found in humbugging people in just that way I couldn't say. It was, however, my solemn duty to warn him. It had lately, I said, come to my knowledge that there was a man (not a very long time ago either) who had been taken in just like this.

All this passed in undertones, and at this point Schomberg, exasperated at our secrecy, went out of the room slamming the door with a crash that positively lifted us in our chairs. This, or else what I had said, huffed my Hermann. He supposed, with a contemptuous toss of his head towards the door which trembled yet, that I had got hold of some of that man's silly tales. It looked, indeed, as though his mind had been thoroughly poisoned against Schomberg. "His tales were – they were," he repeated, seeking for the word – "trash." They were trash, he reiterated and moreover I was young yet . . .

This horrid aspersion (I regret I am no longer exposed to that sort of insult) made me huffy, too. I felt ready in my own mind to back up every assertion of Schomberg's and on any subject. In a moment, devil only knows why, Hermann and I were looking at each other most inimically. He caught up his hat without more ado and I gave myself the pleasure of calling after him:

"Take my advice and make Falk pay for breaking up your ship. You aren't likely to get anything else out of him."

When I got on board my ship, the old mate, who was very full of the events of the morning, remarked:

"I saw the tug coming back from the outer Roads just before two P. M." (He never by any chance used the words morning or afternoon. Always P. M. or A. M., log-book style). "Smart work that. Man's always in a state of hurry. He's a regular chucker-out, ain't he, sir? There's a few pubs I know of in the East-End of London that would be all the better for one of his sort around the bar." He chuckled at his joke. "A regular chucker-out. Now he has fired out that Dutchman head over heels, I suppose our turn's coming to-morrow morning."

We were all on deck at break of day (even the sick – poor devils – had crawled out) ready to cast off in the twinkling of an eye. Nothing came. Falk did not come. At last, when I began to think that probably something had gone wrong in his engine-room, we perceived the tug going by, full pelt, down the river, as if we hadn't existed. For a moment I entertained the wild notion that he was going to turn round in the next reach. Afterwards, I watched his smoke appear above the plain, now here, now there, according to the windings of the river. It disappeared. Then without a word I went down to breakfast. I just simply went down to breakfast.

Not one of us uttered a sound till the mate, after imbibing – by means of suction out of a saucer – his second cup of tea, exclaimed: "Where the devil is the man gone to?"

"Courting!" I shouted, with such a fiendish laugh that the old chap didn't venture to open his lips any more.

I started to the office perfectly calm. Calm with excessive rage. Evidently they knew all about it already, and they treated me to a show of consternation. The manager, a soft-footed, obese man, breathing short, got up to meet me, while all round the room the young clerks, bending over their desks, cast glances in my direction. The fat man, without waiting for my complaint, wheezing heavily and in a tone as if he himself were incredulous, conveyed to me the news that Falk – Captain Falk – had declined – had absolutely declined – to tow my ship – to have anything to do with my ship – this day or any other day. Never!

I did my best to preserve a cool appearance, but, all the same, I must have shown how much taken aback I was. We were talking in the middle of the room. Suddenly, behind my back some ass blew his nose with a great noise and at the same time another quill-driver got up and went out on the landing hastily. It occurred to me I was cutting a foolish figure there. I demanded angrily to see the principal in his private room.

The skin of Mr Siegers' head showed dead white between the iron grey streaks of hair lying plastered cross-wise from ear to ear over the top of his skull in the manner of a bandage. His narrow sunken face was of a uniform and permanent terra-cotta colour, like a piece of pottery. He was sickly, thin, and short, with wrists like a boy of ten. But from that debile body there issued a bullying voice, tremendously loud, harsh and resonant, as if produced by some powerful mechanical contrivance in the nature of a fog-horn. I do not know what he did with it in the private life of his home, but in the larger sphere of business it presented the advantage of overcoming arguments without the slightest mental effort, by the mere volume of sound. We had had several passages of arms. It took me all I knew to guard the interest of my owners – whom, *nota bene*, I had never seen – while Siegers (who had made their acquaintance some years before, during a business tour in Australia) pretended to the knowledge of their innermost minds, and, in the character of "our very good friends", threw them perpetually at my head.

He looked at me with a jaundiced eye (there was no love lost between us), and declared at once that it was strange, very strange. His pronunciation of English was so extravagant that I can't even attempt to reproduce it. For instance, he said "Fferie strantch." Combined with the bellowing intonation it made the language of one's childhood sound weirdly startling, and even if considered purely as a kind of unmeaning noise it filled you with astonishment at first. "They had", he continued, "been acquainted with Captain Falk for very many years, and never had any reason . . ."

"That's why I come to you, of course," I interrupted. "I've the right to know the meaning of this infernal nonsense." In the half-light of the room, which was greenish, because of the tree-tops screening the window, I saw him writhe his meagre shoulders. It came into my head, as disconnected ideas will come at all sorts of times into one's head, that this, most likely, was the very room where, if the tale were true, Falk had been lectured by Mr Siegers, the father. Mr Siegers' (the son's) overwhelming voice, in brassy blasts, as though he had been trying to articulate words through a trumpet, was expressing his great regret at conduct characterized by a very marked want of discretion . . . As I lived I was being lectured, too! His deafening gibberish was difficult to follow, but it was *my* conduct – mine! – that . . . Damn! I wasn't going to stand this.

"What on earth are you driving at?" I asked in a passion. I put my hat on my head (he never offered a seat to anybody), and as he seemed for the moment struck dumb by my irreverence, I turned my back on him and marched out. His vocal arrangements blared after me a few threats of coming down on the ship for the demurrage of the lighters, and all the other expenses consequent upon the delays arising from my frivolity.

Once outside in the sunshine my head swam. It was no longer a question of mere delay. I perceived myself involved in hopeless and humiliating absurdities that were leading me to something very like a disaster. "Let us be calm," I muttered to myself, and ran into the shade of a leprous wall. From that short side-street I could see the broad main thoroughfare, ruinous and gay, running away, away between stretches of decaying masonry, bamboo fences, ranges of arcades of brick and plaster, hovels of lath and mud, lofty temple gates of carved timber, huts of rotten mats – an immensely wide thoroughfare, loosely packed as far as the eye could reach with a barefooted and brown multitude paddling ankle-deep in the dust. For a moment I felt myself about to go out of my mind with worry and desperation.

Some allowance must be made for the feelings of a young man new to responsibility. I thought of my crew. Half of them were ill, and I really began to think that some of them would end by dying on board if I couldn't get them out to sea soon. Obviously I should have to take my ship down the river, either working under canvas or dredging with the anchor down; operations which, in common with many modern sailors, I only knew theoretically. And I almost shrank from undertaking them shorthanded and without local knowledge of the river bed, which is so necessary for the confident handling of a ship. There were no pilots, no beacons, no buoys of any sort; but there was a very devil of a current for anybody to see, no end of shoal places, and at least two obviously awkward turns of the channel between me and the sea. But how dangerous these turns were I could not tell. I didn't even know what my ship was capable of! I had never handled her in my life. A misunderstanding between a man and his ship, in a difficult river with no room to make it up, is bound to end in trouble for the man. On the other hand, it must be owned I had not much reason to count upon a general run of good luck. And suppose I had the misfortune to pile her up high and dry on some beastly shoal? That would have been the final undoing of that voyage. It was plain that if Falk refused to tow me out he would also refuse to pull me off. This meant – what? A day lost at the very best; but more likely a whole fortnight of frizzling on some pestilential mudflat, of desperate work, of discharging cargo; more than likely it meant borrowing money at an exorbitant rate of interest – from the Siegers' gang, too, at that. They were a power in the port. And that elderly seaman of mine, Gambril, had looked pretty ghastly when I went forward to dose him with quinine that morning. *He* would certainly die – not to speak of two or three others that seemed nearly as bad, and of the rest of them just ready to catch any tropical disease going. Horror, ruin and everlasting remorse. And no help. None. I had fallen amongst a lot of unfriendly lunatics!

At any rate, if I must take my ship down myself it was my duty to procure if possible some local knowledge. But that was not easy. The only person I could think of for that service was a certain Johnson, formerly captain of a country ship, but now spliced to a country wife and gone utterly to the bad. I had only heard of him in the vaguest way, as living concealed in the thick of two hundred thousand natives, and only emerging into the light of day for the purpose of hunting up some brandy. I had a notion that if I could lay my hands on him I would sober him on board my ship and use him for a pilot. Better than nothing. Once a sailor always a sailor – and he had known the river for years. But in our Consulate (where I arrived dripping after a sharp walk) they could tell me nothing. The excellent young men on the staff, though willing to help me, belonged to a sphere of the white colony for which that sort of Johnson does not exist. Their suggestion was that I should hunt the man up myself with the help of the Consulate's constable – an ex-sergeant-major of a regiment of Hussars.

This man, whose usual duty apparently consisted in sitting behind a little table in an outer room of Consular offices, when ordered to assist me in my search for Johnson displayed lots of energy and a marvellous amount of local knowledge of a sort. But he did not conceal an immense and sceptical contempt for the whole business. We explored together on that afternoon an infinity of infamous grog shops, gambling dens, opium dens. We walked up narrow lanes where our gharry – a tiny box of a thing on wheels, attached to a jibbing Burmah pony – could by no means have passed. The constable seemed to be on terms of scornful intimacy with Maltese, with Eurasians, with Chinamen, with Klings, and with the sweepers belonging to a temple, with whom he talked at the gate. We interviewed also through a grating in a mud wall closing a blind alley an immensely corpulent Italian, who, the ex-sergeant-major remarked to me perfunctorily, had "killed another man last year". Thereupon he addressed him as "Antonio" and "Old Buck", though that bloated carcase, apparently more than half filling the sort of cell wherein it sat, recalled rather a fat pig in a stye. Familiar and never unbending, the sergeant chucked – absolutely chucked – under the chin a horribly wrinkled and shrivelled old hag propped on a stick, who had volunteered some sort of information: and with the same stolid face he kept up an animated conversation with the groups of swathed brown women, who sat smoking cheroots on the door-steps of a long range of clay hovels. We got out of the gharry and clambered into dwellings airy like packing crates, or descended into places sinister like cellars. We got in, we drove on, we got out again for the sole purpose, as it seemed, of looking behind a heap of rubble. The sun declined; my companion was curt and sardonic in his answers, but it appears we were just missing Johnson all along. At last our conveyance stopped once more with a jerk, and the driver, jumping down, opened the door.

A black mudhole blocked the lane. A mound of garbage crowned with the dead body of a dog arrested us not. An empty Australian beef tin bounded cheerily before the toe of my boot. Suddenly we clambered through a gap in a prickly fence . . .

It was a very clean native compound: and the big native woman, with bare brown legs as thick as bed-posts, pursuing on all fours a silver dollar that came rolling out from somewhere, was Mrs Johnson herself. "Your man's at home," said the ex-sergeant, and stepped aside in complete and marked indifference to anything that might follow. Johnson – at home – stood with his back to a native house built on posts and with its walls made of mats. In his left hand he held a banana. Out of the right he dealt another dollar into space. The woman captured this one on the wing, and there and then plumped down on the ground to look at us with greater comfort.

"My man" was sallow of face, grizzled, unshaven, muddy on elbows and back; where the seams of his serge coat yawned you could see his white nakedness. The vestiges of a paper collar encircled his neck. He looked at us with a grave, swaying surprise. "Where do you come from?" he asked. My heart sank. How could I have been stupid enough to waste energy and time for this?

But having already gone so far I approached a little nearer and declared the purpose of my visit. He would have to come at once with me, sleep on board my ship, and to-morrow, with the first of the ebb, he would give me his assistance in getting my ship down to the sea, without steam. A six-hundred-ton barque, drawing nine feet aft. I proposed to give him eighteen dollars for his local knowledge; and all the time I was speaking he kept on considering attentively the various aspects of the banana, holding first one side up to his eye, then the other.

"You've forgotten to apologize," he said at last with extreme precision. "Not being a gentleman yourself, you don't know apparently when you intrude upon a gentleman. I am one. I wish you to understand that when I am in funds I don't work, and now . . ."

I would have pronounced him perfectly sober had he not paused in great concern to try and brush a hole off the knee of his trousers.

"I have money – and friends. Every gentleman has. Perhaps you would like to know my friend? His name is Falk. You could borrow some money. Try to remember. F-A-L-K. Falk." Abruptly his tone changed. "A noble heart," he said, muzzily.

"Has Falk been giving you some money?" I asked, appalled by the detailed finish of the dark plot.

"Lent me, my good man, not given me," he corrected, suavely. "Met me taking the air last evening, and being as usual anxious to oblige— Hadn't you better go to the devil out of my compound?"

And upon this, without other warning, he let fly with the banana, which missed my head and took the constable just under the left eye. He rushed at the miserable Johnson, stammering with fury. They fell . . . But why dwell on the wretchedness, the breathlessness, the degradation, the senselessness, the weariness, the ridicule and humiliation and – and – the perspiration, of these moments? I dragged the ex-hussar off. He was like a wild beast. It seems he had been greatly annoyed at losing his free afternoon on my account. The garden of his bungalow required his personal attention, and at the slight blow of the banana the brute in him had broken loose. We left Johnson on his back still black in the face, but beginning to kick feebly. Meantime, the big woman had remained sitting on the ground, apparently paralyzed with extreme terror.

For half an hour we jolted inside our rolling box, side by side, in profound silence. The ex-sergeant was busy staunching the blood of a long scratch on his cheek. "I hope you're satisfied," he said, suddenly. "That's what comes of all that tomfool business. If you hadn't quarrelled with that tugboat skipper over some girl or other, all this wouldn't have happened."

"You heard *that* story?" I said.

"Of course I heard. And I shouldn't wonder if the Consul-General himself doesn't come to hear of it. How am I to go before him to-morrow with that thing on my cheek – I want to know. It's *you* who ought to have got this!"

After that, till the gharry stopped and he jumped out without leave-taking, he swore to himself steadily, horribly; muttering great, purposeful, trooper oaths, to which the worst a sailor can do is like the prattle of a child. For my part I had just the strength to crawl into Schomberg's coffee-room, where I wrote at a little table a note to the mate instructing him to get everything ready for dropping down the river next day. I couldn't face my ship. Well! she had a clever sort of skipper and no mistake – poor thing! What a horrid mess! I took my head between my hands. At times the obviousness of my innocence would reduce me to despair. What had I done? If I had done something to bring about the situation I should at least have learned not to do it again. But I felt guiltless to the point of imbecility. The room was empty yet; only Schomberg prowled round me goggle-eyed and with a sort of awed respectful curiosity. No doubt he had set the story going himself; but he was a good-hearted chap, and I am really persuaded he participated in all my troubles. He did what he could for me. He ranged aside the heavy matchstand, set a chair straight, pushed a spittoon slightly with his foot – as you show small attentions to a friend under a great sorrow – sighed, and at last, unable to hold his tongue:

"Well! I warned you, captain. That's what comes of running your head against Mr Falk. Man'll stick at nothing."

I sat without stirring, and after surveying me with a sort of commiseration in his eyes, he burst out in a hoarse whisper: "But for a fine lump of a girl, she's a fine lump of a girl." He made a loud smacking noise with his thick lips. "The finest lump of a girl that I ever . . ." he was going on with great unction, but for some reason or other broke off. I fancied myself throwing something at his head. "I don't blame you, captain. Hang me if I do," he said with a patronizing air.

"Thank you," I said, resignedly. It was no use fighting against this false fate. I don't know even if I was sure myself where the truth of the matter began. The conviction that it would end disastrously had been driven into me by all the successive shocks my sense of security had received. I began to ascribe an extraordinary potency to agents in themselves powerless. It was as if Schomberg's baseless gossip had the power to bring about the thing itself or the abstract enmity of Falk could put my ship ashore.

I have already explained how fatal this last would have been.

For my further action, my youth, my inexperience, my very real concern for the health of my crew must be my excuse. The action itself, when it came, was purely impulsive. It was set in movement quite undiplomatically and simply by Falk's appearance in the doorway of the coffee-room.

The room was full by then and buzzing with voices. I had been looked at with curiosity by everyone, but how am I to describe the sensation produced by the appearance of Falk himself blocking the doorway? The tension of expectation could be measured by the profundity of the silence that fell upon the very click of the billiard balls. As to Schomberg, he looked extremely frightened; he hated mortally any sort of row (*fracas* he called it) in his establishment. *Fracas* was bad for business, he affirmed; but in truth, this specimen of portly, middle-aged manhood was of a timid disposition. I don't know what, considering my presence in the place, they all hoped would come of it. A sort of stag fight, perhaps. Or they may have supposed Falk had come in only to annihilate me completely. As a matter of fact, Falk had come in because Hermann had asked him to inquire after the precious white cotton parasol which, in the worry and excitement of the previous day, he had forgotten at the table where we had held our little discussion.

It was this that gave me my opportunity. I don't think I would have gone to see Falk out. No. I don't think so. There are limits. But there was an opportunity and I seized it – I have already tried to explain why. Now I will merely state that, in my opinion, to get his sickly crew into the sea air and secure a quick despatch for his ship a skipper would be justified in going to any length, short of absolute crime. He should put his pride in his pocket; he may accept confidences; he must explain his innocence as if it were a sin; he may take advantage of misconceptions, of desires and of weaknesses; he ought to conceal his horror and other emotions, and, if the fate of a human being, and that human being a magnificent young girl, is strangely involved – why, he should contemplate that fate (whatever it might seem to be) without turning a hair. And all these things I have done; the explaining, the listening, the pretending – even to the discretion – and nobody, not even Hermann's niece, I believe, need throw stones at me now. Schomberg at all events needn't, since from first to last, I am happy to say there was not the slightest "*fracas*".

Overcoming a nervous contraction of the windpipe, I had managed to exclaim "Captain Falk!" His start of surprise was perfectly genuine, but afterwards he neither smiled nor scowled. He simply waited. Then, when I had said, "I must have a talk with you," and had pointed to a chair at my table, he moved up to me, though he didn't sit down. Schomberg, however, with a long tumbler in his hand, was making towards us prudently, and I discovered then the only sign of weakness in Falk. He had for Schomberg a repulsion resembling that sort of physical fear some people experience at the sight of a toad. Perhaps to a man so essentially and silently concentrated upon himself (though he could talk well enough, as I was to find out presently) the other's irrepressible loquacity, embracing every human being within range of the tongue, might have appeared unnatural, disgusting, and monstrous. He suddenly gave signs of restiveness – positively like a horse about to rear, and, muttering hurriedly as if in great pain, "No. I can't stand that fellow," seemed ready to bolt. This weakness of his gave me the advantage at the very start. "Verandah," I suggested, as if rendering him a service, and walked him out by the arm. We stumbled over a few chairs; we had the feeling of open space before us, and felt the fresh breath of the river – fresh, but tainted. The Chinese theatres across the water made, in the sparsely twinkling masses of gloom an Eastern town presents at night, blazing centres of light, and of a distant and howling uproar. I felt him become suddenly tractable again like an animal, like a good-tempered horse when the object that scares him is removed. Yes. I felt in the darkness there how tractable he was, without my conviction of his inflexibility – tenacity, rather, perhaps – being in the least weakened. His very arm abandoning itself to my grasp was as hard as marble – like a limb of iron. But I heard a tumultuous scuffling of boot-soles within. The unspeakable idiots inside were crowding to the windows, climbing over each other's backs behind the blinds, billiard cues and all. Somebody broke a window-pane, and with the sound of falling glass, so suggestive of riot and devastation, Schomberg reeled out after us in a state of funk which had prevented him from parting with his brandy and soda. He must have trembled like an aspen leaf. The piece of ice in the long tumbler he held in his hand tinkled with an effect of chattering teeth. "I beg you, gentlemen," he expostulated, thickly. "Come! Really, now, I must insist . . ."

How proud I am of my presence of mind! "Hallo," I said instantly in a loud and naïve tone, "somebody's breaking your windows, Schomberg. Would you please tell one of your boys to bring out here a pack of cards and a couple of lights? And two long drinks. Will you?"

To receive an order soothed him at once. It was business. "Certainly," he said in an immensely relieved tone. The night was rainy, with wandering gusts of wind, and while we waited for the candles Falk said, as if to justify his panic, "I don't interfere in anybody's business. I don't give any occasion for talk. I am a respectable man. But this fellow is always making out something wrong, and can never rest till he gets somebody to believe him."

This was the first of my knowledge of Falk. This desire of respectability, of being like everybody else, was the only recognition he vouchsafed to the organization of mankind. For the rest he might have been the member of a herd, not of a society. Self-preservation was his only concern. Not selfishness, but mere self-preservation. Selfishness presupposes consciousness, choice, the presence of other men; but his instinct acted as though he were the last of mankind nursing that law like the only spark of a sacred fire. I don't mean to say that living naked in a cavern would have satisfied him. Obviously he was the creature of the conditions to which he was born. No doubt self-preservation meant also the preservation of these conditions. But essentially it meant something much more simple, natural, and powerful. How shall I express it? It meant the preservation of the five senses of his body – let us say – taking it in its narrowest as well as in its widest meaning. I think you will admit before long the justice of this judgment. However, as we stood there together in the dark verandah I had judged nothing as yet – and I had no desire to judge – which is an idle practice anyhow. The light was long in coming.

"Of course," I said in a tone of mutual understanding, "it isn't exactly a game of cards I want with you."

I saw him draw his hands down his face – the vague stir of the passionate and meaningless gesture; but he waited in silent patience. It was only when the lights had been brought out that he opened his lips. I understood his mumble to mean that "he didn't know any card-games."

"Like this, Schomberg and all the other fools will have to keep off," I said, tearing open the pack. "Have you heard that we are universally supposed to be quarrelling about a girl? You know who – of course. I am really ashamed to ask, but is it possible that you do me the honour to think me dangerous?"

As I said these words I felt how absurd it was and also I felt flattered – for, really, what else could it be? His answer, spoken in his usual dispassionate undertone, made it clear that it was so, but not precisely as flattering as I supposed. He thought me dangerous with Hermann, more than with the girl herself; but, as to quarrelling, I saw at once how inappropriate the word was. We had no quarrel. Natural forces are not quarrelsome. You can't quarrel with the wind that inconveniences and humiliates you by blowing off your hat in a street full of people. He had no quarrel with me. Neither would a boulder, falling on my head, have had. He fell upon me in accordance with the law by which he was moved – not of gravitation, like a detached stone, but of self-preservation. Of course this is giving it a rather wide interpretation. Strictly speaking, he had existed and could have existed without being married. Yet he told me that he had found it more and more difficult to live alone. Yes. He told me this in his low, careless voice, to such a pitch of confidence had we arrived at the end of half an hour.

It took me just about that time to convince him that I had never dreamed of marrying Hermann's niece. Could any necessity have been more extravagant? And the difficulty was the greater because he was so hard hit himself that he couldn't imagine anybody else being able to remain in a state of indifference. Any man with eyes in his head, he seemed to think, could not help coveting so much bodily magnificence. This profound belief was conveyed by the manner he listened sitting sideways to the table and playing absently with a few cards I had dealt to him at random. And the more I saw into him the more I saw of him. The wind swayed the lights so that his sunburnt face, whiskered to the eyes, seemed to successively flicker crimson at me and to go out. I saw the extraordinary breadth of the high cheek-bones, the perpendicular style of the features, the massive forehead, steep like a cliff, denuded at the top, largely uncovered at the temples.

The fact is I had never before seen him without his hat; but now, as if my fervour had made him hot, he had taken it off and laid it gently on the floor. Something peculiar in the shape and setting of his yellow eyes gave them the provoking silent intensity which characterized his glance. But the face was thin, furrowed, worn; I discovered this through the bush of his hair, as you may detect the gnarled shape of a tree trunk in a dense undergrowth. These overgrown cheeks were sunken. It was an anchorite's bony head fitted with a Capuchin's beard and adjusted to a herculean body. I don't mean athletic. Hercules, I take it, was not an athlete. He was a strong man, susceptible to female charms, and not afraid of dirt. And thus with Falk, who was a strong man. He was extremely strong, just as the girl (since I must think of them together) was magnificently attractive by the masterful power of flesh and blood, expressed in shape, in size, in attitude – that is by a straight appeal to the senses. His mind meantime, preoccupied with respectability, quailed before Schomberg's tongue and seemed absolutely impervious to my protestations; and I went so far as to protest that I would just as soon think of marrying my mother's (dear old lady!) faithful female cook as Hermann's niece. Sooner, I protested, in my desperation, much sooner; but it did not appear that he saw anything outrageous in the proposition, and in his sceptical immobility he seemed to nurse the argument that at all events the cook was very, very far away. It must be said that, just before, I had gone wrong by appealing to the evidence of my manner whenever I called on board the *Diana*. I had never attempted to approach the girl, or to speak to her, or even to look at her in any marked way. Nothing could be clearer. But, as his own idea of – let us say – courting, seemed to consist precisely in sitting silently for hours in the vicinity of the beloved object, that line of argument inspired him with distrust. Staring down his extended legs he let out a grunt – as much as to say, "That's all very fine, but you can't throw dust in *my* eyes."

At last I was exasperated into saying, "Why don't you put the matter at rest by talking to Hermann?" and I added, sneeringly: "You don't expect me perhaps to speak for you?"

To this he said, very loud for him, "Would you?"

And for the first time he lifted his head to look at me with wonder and incredulity. He lifted his head so sharply that there could be no mistake. I had touched a spring. I saw the whole extent of my opportunity, and could hardly believe in it.

"Why! Speak to . . . Well, of course," I proceeded very slowly, watching him with great attention, for, on my word, I feared a joke. "Not, perhaps, to the young lady herself. I can't speak German, you know. But . . ."

He interrupted me with the earnest assurance that Hermann had the highest opinion of me; and at once I felt the need for the greatest possible diplomacy at this juncture. So I demurred just enough to draw him on. Falk sat up, but except for a very noticeable enlargement of the pupils, till the irises of his eyes were reduced to two narrow yellow rings, his face, I should judge, was incapable of expressing excitement. "Oh, yes! Hermann did have the greatest . . ."

"Take up your cards. Here's Schomberg peeping at us through the blind!" I said.

We went through the motions of what might have been a game of écarté. Presently the intolerable scandalmonger withdrew, probably to inform the people in the billiard-room that we two were gambling on the verandah like mad.

We were not gambling, but it was a game; a game in which I felt I held the winning cards. The stake, roughly speaking, was the success of the voyage – for me; and he, I apprehended, had nothing to lose. Our intimacy matured rapidly, and before many words had been exchanged I perceived that the excellent Hermann had been making use of me. That simple and astute Teuton had been, it seems, holding me up to Falk in the light of a rival. I was young enough to be shocked at so much duplicity. "Did he tell you that in so many words?" I asked with indignation.

Hermann had not. He had given hints only; and of course it had not taken very much to alarm Falk; but, instead of declaring himself, he had taken steps to remove the family from under my influence. He was perfectly straightforward about it – as straightforward as a tile falling on your head. There was no duplicity in that man; and when I congratulated him on the perfection of his arrangements – even to the bribing of the wretched Johnson against me – he had a genuine movement of protest. Never bribed. He knew the man wouldn't work as long as he had a few cents in his pocket to get drunk on, and, naturally (he said – *"naturally"*) he let him have a dollar or two. He was himself a sailor, he said, and anticipated the view another sailor, like myself, was bound to take. On the other hand, he was sure that I should have to come to grief. He hadn't been knocking about for the last seven years up and down that river for nothing. It would have been no disgrace to me – but he asserted confidently I would have had my ship very awkwardly ashore at a spot two miles below the Great Pagoda . . .

And with all that he had no ill-will. That was evident. This was a crisis in which his only object had been to gain time – I fancy. And presently he mentioned that he had written for some jewellery, real good jewellery – had written to Hong-Kong for it. It would arrive in a day or two.

"Well, then," I said, cheerily, "everything is all right. All you've got to do is to present it to the lady together with your heart, and live happy ever after."

Upon the whole he seemed to accept that view as far as the girl was concerned, but his eyelids drooped. There was still something in the way. For one thing Hermann disliked him so much. As to me, on the contrary, it seemed as though he could not praise me enough. Mrs Hermann, too. He didn't know why they disliked him so. It made everything most difficult.

I listened impassive, feeling more and more diplomatic. His speech was not transparently clear. He was one of those men who seem to live, feel, suffer in a sort of mental twilight. But as to being fascinated by the girl and possessed by the desire of home life with her – it was as clear as daylight. So much being at stake, he was afraid of putting it to the hazard of the declaration. Besides, there was something else. And with Hermann being so set against him . . .

"I see," I said, thoughtfully, while my heart beat fast with the excitement of my diplomacy. "I don't mind sounding Hermann. In fact, to show you how mistaken you were, I am ready to do all I can for you in that way."

A light sigh escaped him. He drew his hands down his face, and it emerged, bony, unchanged of expression, as if all the tissues had been ossified. All the passion was in those big brown hands. He was satisfied. Then there was that other matter. If there were anybody on earth it was I who could persuade Hermann to take a reasonable view! I had a knowledge of the world and lots of experience. Hermann admitted this himself. And then I was a

sailor, too. Falk thought that a sailor would be able to understand
certain things best . . .

He talked as if the Hermanns had been living all their life in a
rural hamlet, and I alone had been capable, with my practice in
life, of a large and indulgent view of certain occurrences. That
was what my diplomacy was leading me to. I began suddenly to
dislike it.

"I say, Falk," I asked quiet brusquely, "you haven't already a
wife put away somewhere?"

The pain and disgust of his denial were very striking. Couldn't I
understand that he was as respectable as any white man
hereabouts; earning his living honestly. He was suffering from
my suspicion, and the low undertone of his voice made his
protestations sound very pathetic. For a moment he shamed me,
but, my diplomacy notwithstanding, I seemed to develop a
conscience, as if in very truth it were in my power to decide the
success of this matrimonial enterprise. By pretending hard
enough we come to believe anything – anything to our advantage. And I had been pretending very hard, because I meant yet to
be towed safely down the river. But, through conscience or
stupidity, I couldn't help alluding to the Vanlo affair. "You acted
rather badly there. Didn't you?" was what I ventured actually to
say – for the logic of our conduct is always at the mercy of obscure
and unforeseen impulses.

His dilated pupils swerved from my face, glancing at the
window with a sort of scared fury. We heard behind the blinds
the continuous and sudden clicking of ivory, a jovial murmur of
many voices, and Schomberg's deep manly laugh.

"That confounded old woman of a hotel-keeper then would
never, never let it rest!" Falk exclaimed. Well, yes! It had
happened two years ago. When it came to the point he owned
he couldn't make up his mind to trust Fred Vanlo – no sailor, a bit
of a fool, too. He could not trust him, but, to stop his row, he had
lent him enough money to pay all his debts before he left. I was
greatly surprised to hear this. Then Falk could not be such a miser
after all. So much the better for the girl. For a time he sat silent;
then he picked up a card and while looking at it he said:

"You need not think of anything bad. It was an accident. I've
been unfortunate once."

"Then in heaven's name say nothing about it."

As soon as these words were out of my mouth I fancied I had said something immoral. He shook his head negatively. It had to be told. He considered it proper that the relations of the lady should know. No doubt – I thought to myself – had Miss Vanlo not been thirty and damaged by the climate he would have found it possible to entrust Fred Vanlo with this confidence. And then the figure of Hermann's niece appeared before my mind's eye, with the wealth of her opulent form, her rich youth, her lavish strength. With that powerful and immaculate vitality, her girlish form must have shouted aloud of life to that man, whereas poor Miss Vanlo could only sing sentimental songs to the strumming of a piano.

"And that Hermann hates me, I know it!" he cried in his undertone, with a sudden recrudescence of anxiety. "I must tell them. It is proper that they should know. You would say so yourself."

He then murmured an utterly mysterious allusion to the necessity for peculiar domestic arrangements. Though my curiosity was excited I did not want to hear any of his confidences. I feared he might give me a piece of information that would make my assumed *rôle* of match-maker odious – however unreal it was. I was aware that he could have the girl for the asking; and keeping down a desire to laugh in his face, I expressed a confident belief in my ability to argue away Hermann's dislike for him. "I am sure I can make it all right," I said. He looked very pleased.

And when we rose not a word had been said about towage! Not a word! The game was won and the honour was safe. Oh! blessed white cotton umbrella! We shook hands, and I was holding myself with difficulty from breaking into a dance of joy when he came back, striding all the length of the verandah, and said doubtfully:

"I say, captain, I have your word? You – you – won't turn round?"

Heavens! The fright he gave me. Behind his tone of doubt there was something desperate and menacing. The infatuated ass. But I was equal to the situation.

"My dear Falk," I said, beginning to lie with a glibness and effrontery that amazed me even at the time – "confidence for confidence." (He had made no confidences.) "I will tell you that I am already engaged to an extremely charming girl at home, and so you understand . . ."

He caught my hand and wrung it in a crushing grip.

"Pardon me. I feel it every day more difficult to live alone . . ."

"On rice and fish," I interrupted smartly, giggling with the sheer nervousness of escaped danger.

He dropped my hand as if it had become suddenly red hot. A moment of profound silence ensued, as though something extra-ordinary had happened.

"I promise you to obtain Hermann's consent," I faltered out at last, and it seemed to me that he could not help seeing through that humbugging promise. "If there's anything else to get over I shall endeavour to stand by you," I conceded further, feeling somehow defeated and overborne; "but you must do your best yourself."

"I have been unfortunate once," he muttered, unemotionally, and turning his back on me he went away, thumping slowly the plank floor as if his feet had been shod with iron.

Next morning, however, he was lively enough as man-boat, a combination of splashing and shouting; of the insolent commotion below with the steady overbearing glare of the silent head-piece above. He turned us out most unnecessarily at an ungodly hour, but it was nearly eleven in the morning before he brought me up a cable's length from Hermann's ship. And he did it very badly, too, in a hurry, and nearly contriving to miss altogether the patch of good holding ground, because, forsooth, he had caught sight of Hermann's niece on the poop. And so did I; and probably as soon as he had seen her himself. I saw the modest, sleek glory of the tawny head, and the full, grey shape of the girlish print frock she filled so perfectly, so satisfactorily, with the seduction of unfaltering curves – a very nymph of Diana the Huntress. And *Diana* the ship sat, high-walled and as solid as an institution, on the smooth level of the water, the most uninspiring and respectable craft upon the seas, useful and ugly, devoted to the support of domestic virtues like any grocer's shop on shore. At once Falk steamed away; for there was some work for him to do. He would return in the evening.

He ranged close by us, passing out dead slow, without a hail. The beat of the paddle-wheels reverberating amongst the stony islets, as if from the ruined walls of a vast arena, filled the anchorage confusedly with the clapping sounds as of a mighty and leisurely applause. Abreast of Hermann's ship Falk stopped the engines; and a profound silence reigned over the rocks, the shore and the sea, for the time it took him to raise his hat aloft before the nymph of the grey print frock. I had snatched up my binoculars, and I can answer for it she didn't stir a limb, standing by the rail shapely and erect, with one of her hands grasping a rope at the height of her head, while the way of the tug carried slowly past her the lingering and profound homage of the man. There was for me an enormous significance in the scene, the sense of having witnessed a solemn declaration. The die was cast. After such a manifestation he couldn't back out. And I reflected that it was nothing whatever to me now. With a rush of black smoke belching suddenly out of the funnel, and a mad swirl of paddle-wheels provoking a burst of weird and precipitated clapping, the tug shot out of the desolate arena. The rocky islets lay on the sea like the heaps of a cyclopean ruin on a plain; the centipedes and scorpions lurked under the stones; there was not a single blade of grass in sight anywhere, not a single lizard sunning himself on a boulder by the shore. When I looked again at Hermann's ship the girl had disappeared. I could not detect the smallest dot of a bird on the immense sky, and the flatness of the land continued the flatness of the sea to the naked line of the horizon.

This is the setting now inseparably connected with my knowledge of Falk's misfortune. My diplomacy had brought me there, and now I had only to wait the time for taking up the *rôle* of an ambassador. My diplomacy was a success; my ship was safe; old Gambril would probably live; a feeble sound of a tapping hammer came intermittently from the *Diana*. During the afternoon I looked at times at the old homely ship, the faithful nurse of Hermann's progeny, or yawned towards the distant temple of Buddha, like a lonely hillock on the plain, where shaven priests cherish the thoughts of that Annihilation which is the worthy reward of us all. Unfortunate! He had been unfortunate once. Well, that was not so bad as life goes. And what the devil could be the nature of that misfortune? I remembered that I had known a man before who had declared himself to have fallen, years ago, a victim to misfortune; but this misfortune, whose effects appeared permanent (he looked desperately hard up) when considered dispassionately, seemed indistinguishable from a breach of trust. Could it be something of that nature? Apart, however, from the utter improbability that he would offer to talk of it even to his future uncle-in-law I had a strange feeling that Falk's physique unfitted him for that sort of delinquency. As the person of Hermann's niece exhaled the profound physical charm of feminine form, so her adorer's big frame embodied to my senses the hard, straight masculinity that would conceivably kill but would not condescend to cheat. The thing was obvious. I might just as well have suspected the girl of a curvature of the spine. And I perceived that the sun was about to set.

The smoke of Falk's tug hove in sight, far away at the mouth of the river. It was time for me to assume the character of an ambassador, and the negotiation would not be difficult except in the matter of keeping my countenance. It was all too extravagantly nonsensical, and I conceived that it would be best to compose for myself a grave demeanour. I practised this in my boat as I went along, but the bashfulness that came secretly upon me the moment I stepped on the deck of the *Diana* is inexplicable. As soon as we had exchanged greetings Hermann asked me eagerly if I knew whether Falk had found his white parasol.

"He's going to bring it to you himself directly," I said with great solemnity. "Meantime, I am charged with an important message for which he begs your favourable consideration. He is in love with your niece . . ."

"*Ach so!*" he hissed with an animosity that made my assumed gravity change into the most genuine concern. What meant this tone? And I hurried on.

"He wishes, with your consent of course, to ask her to marry him at once – before you leave here, that is. He would speak to his Consul."

Hermann sat down and smoked violently. Five minutes passed in that furious meditation, and then, taking the long pipe out of his mouth, he burst into a hot diatribe against Falk – against his cupidity, his stupidity (a fellow that can hardly be got to say "yes" or "no" to the simplest question) – against his outrageous treatment of the shipping in port (because he saw they were at his mercy) – and against his manner of walking, which to his (Hermann's) mind showed a conceit positively unbearable. The damage to the old *Diana* was not forgotten, of course, and there was nothing of any nature said or done by Falk (even to the last offer of refreshment in the hotel) that did not seem to have been a cause of offence. "Had the cheek" to drag him (Hermann) into that coffee-room; as though a drink from him could make up for forty-seven dollars and fifty cents of damage in the cost of wood alone – not counting two days' work for the carpenter. Of course he would not stand in the girl's way. He was going home to Germany. There were plenty of poor girls walking about in Germany.

"He's very much in love," was all I found to say.

"Yes," he cried. "And it is time, too, after making himself and me talked about ashore the last voyage I was here, and then now again; coming on board every evening unsettling the girl's mind, and saying nothing. What sort of conduct is that?"

The seven thousand dollars the fellow was always talking about did not, in his opinion, justify such behaviour. Moreover, nobody had seen them. He (Hermann) seriously doubted if Falk possessed seven thousand cents, and the tug, no doubt, was mortgaged up to the top of the funnel to the firm of Siegers. But let that pass. He wouldn't stand in the girl's way. Her head was so turned that she had become no good to them of late. Quite unable even to put the children to bed without her aunt. It was bad for the children; they got unruly; and yesterday he actually had to give Gustav a thrashing.

For that, too, Falk was made responsible apparently. And looking at my Hermann's heavy, puffy, good-natured face, I knew he would not exert himself till greatly exasperated, and, therefore, would thrash very hard, and being fat would resent the necessity. How Falk had managed to turn the girl's head was more difficult to understand. I supposed Hermann would know. And then hadn't there been Miss Vanlo? It could not be his silvery tongue, or the subtle seduction of his manner; he had no more of what is called "manner" than an animal – which, however, on the other hand, is never, and can never be called vulgar. Therefore it must have been his bodily appearance, exhibiting a virility of nature as exaggerated as his beard, and resembling a sort of constant ruthlessness. It was seen in the very manner he lolled in the chair. He meant no offence, but his intercourse was characterized by that sort of frank disregard of susceptibilities a tall man, living in a world of dwarfs, would naturally assume, without in the least wishing to be unkind. But amongst men of his own stature, or nearly, this frank use of his advantages, in such matters as the awful towage bills for instance, caused much impotent gnashing

of teeth. When attentively considered it seemed appalling at times.
He was a strange beast. But maybe women liked it. Seen in that
light he was well worth taming, and I suppose every woman at
the bottom of her heart considers herself as a tamer of strange
beasts. But Hermann arose with precipitation to carry the news to
his wife. I had barely the time, as he made for the cabin door, to
grab him by the seat of his inexpressibles. I begged him to wait till
Falk in person had spoken with him. There remained some small
matter to talk over as I understood.

He sat down again at once, full of suspicion.

"What matter?" he said, surlily. "I have had enough of his
nonsense. There's no matter at all, as he knows very well; the girl
has nothing in the world. She came to us in one thin dress when
my brother died, and I have a growing family."

"It can't be anything of that kind," I opined. "He's desperately
enamoured of your niece. I don't know why he did not say so
before. Upon my word, I believe it is because he was afraid to lose,
perhaps, the felicity of sitting near her on your quarter-deck."

I intimated my conviction that Falk's love was so great as to be
in a sense cowardly. The effects of a great passion are unaccountable. It has been known to make a man timid. But Hermann
looked at me as if I had raved; and the twilight was dying out
rapidly.

"You don't believe in passion, do you, Hermann?" I continued,
cheerily. "The passion of fear will make a cornered rat coura-
geous. Falk's in a corner. He will take her off your hands in one
thin frock just as she came to you. And after ten years' service it
isn't a bad bargain," I added.

Far from taking offence, he resumed his air of civic virtue. The
sudden night came upon him while he stared placidly along the
deck, bringing in contact with his thick lips, and taking away
again after a jet of smoke, the curved mouthpiece fitted to the
stem of his pipe. The night came upon him and buried in haste his
whiskers, his globular eyes, his puffy pale face, his fat knees and
the vast flat slippers on his fatherly feet. Only his short arms in
respectable white shirt-sleeves remained very visible, propped up
like the flippers of seal reposing on the strand.

"Falk wouldn't settle anything about repairs. Told me to find
out first how much wood I should require and he would see," he
remarked; and after he had spat peacefully in the dusk we heard

over the water the beat of the tug's floats. There is, on a calm night, nothing more suggestive of fierce and headlong haste than the rapid sound made by the paddle-wheels of a boat threshing her way through a quiet sea; and the approach of Falk towards his fate seemed to be urged by an impatient and passionate desire. The engines must have been driven to the very utmost of their revolutions. We heard them slow down at last, and, vaguely, the white hull of the tug appeared moving against the black islets, whilst a slow and rhythmical clapping as of thousands of hands rose on all sides. It ceased all at once, just before Falk brought her up. A single brusque splash was followed by the long-drawn rumbling of iron links running through the hawse pipe. Then a solemn silence fell upon the Roadstead.

"He will soon be here," I murmured, and after that we waited for him without a word. Meantime, raising my eyes, I beheld the glitter of a lofty sky above the *Diana's* mastheads. The multitude of stars gathered into clusters, in rows, in lines, in masses, in groups, shone all together, unanimously – and the few isolated ones, blazing by themselves in the midst of dark patches, seemed to be of a superior kind and of an inextinguishable nature. But long striding footsteps were heard hastening along the deck; the high bulwarks of the *Diana* made a deeper darkness. We rose from our chairs quickly, and Falk, appearing before us, all in white, stood still.

Nobody spoke at first, as though we had been covered with confusion. His arrival was fiery, but his white bulk, of indefinite shape and without features, made him loom up like a man of snow.

"The captain here has been telling me . . ." Hermann began in a homely and amicable voice; and Falk gave a low, nervous laugh. His cool, negligent undertone had no inflexions, but the strength of a powerful emotion made him ramble in his speech. He had always desired a home. It was difficult to live alone, though he was not answerable. He was domestic; there had been difficulties; but since he had seen Hermann's niece he found that it had become at last impossible to live by himself. "I mean – impossible," he repeated with no sort of emphasis and only with the slightest of pauses, but the word fell into my mind with the force of a new idea.

"I have not said anything to her yet," Hermann observed,

quietly. And Falk dismissed this by a "That's all right. Certainly. Very proper." There was a necessity for perfect frankness – in marrying, especially. Hermann seemed attentive, but he seized the first opportunity to ask us into the cabin. "And by-the-by, Falk," he said, innocently, as we passed in, "the timber came to no less than forty-seven dollars and fifty cents."

Falk, uncovering his head, lingered in the passage. "Some other time," he said; and Hermann nudged me angrily – I don't know why. The girl alone in the cabin sat sewing at some distance from the table. Falk stopped short in the doorway. Without a word, without a sign, without the slightest inclination of his bony head, by the silent intensity of his look alone, he seemed to lay his herculean frame at her feet. Her hands sank slowly on her lap, and raising her clear eyes, she let her soft, beaming glance enfold him from head to foot like a slow and pale caress. He was very hot when he sat down; she, with bowed head, went on with her sewing; her neck was very white under the light of the lamp; but Falk, hiding his face in the palms of his hands, shuddered faintly. He drew them down, even to his beard, and his uncovered eyes astonished me by their tense and irrational expression – as though he had just swallowed a heavy gulp of alcohol. It passed away while he was binding us to secrecy. Not that he cared, but he did not like to be spoken about; and I looked at the girl's marvellous, at her wonderful, at her regal hair, plaited tight into that one astonishing and maidenly tress. Whenever she moved her well-shaped head it would stir stiffly to and fro on her back. The thin cotton sleeve fitted the irreproachable roundness of her arm like a skin; and her very dress, stretched on her bust, seemed to palpitate like a living tissue with the strength of vitality animating her body. How good her complexion was, the outline of her soft cheek and the small convoluted conch of her rosy ear! To pull her needle she kept the little finger apart from the others; it seemed a waste of power to see her sewing – eternally sewing – with that industrious and precise movement of her arm, going on eternally upon all the oceans, under all the skies, in innumerable harbours. And suddenly I heard Falk's voice declare that he could not marry a woman unless she knew of something in his life that had happened ten years ago. It was an accident. An unfortunate accident. It would affect the domestic arrangements of their home, but, once told, it need not be alluded to again for the rest of their lives. "I should want my wife to feel for me," he said. "It has made me unhappy." And how could he keep the knowledge of it to himself – he asked us – perhaps through years and years of companionship? What sort of companionship would that be? He had thought it over. A wife must know. Then why not at once? He counted on Hermann's kindness for presenting the affair in the best possible light. And Hermann's countenance, mystified before, became very sour. He stole an inquisitive glance at me. I shook my head blankly. Some people thought, Falk went on, that such an experience changed a man for the rest of his life. He couldn't say. It was hard, awful, and not to be forgotten, but he did not think himself a worse man than before. Only he talked in his sleep now, he believed . . . At last I began to think he had accidentally killed someone, perhaps a friend – his own father maybe; when he went on to say that probably we were aware he never touched meat. Throughout he spoke English, of course, on my account.

He swayed forward heavily.

The girl, with her hands raised before her pale eyes, was threading her needle. He glanced at her and his mighty trunk overshadowed the table, bringing nearer to us the breadth of his shoulders, the thickness of his neck, and that incongruous, anchorite head, burnt in the desert, hollowed and lean as if by excesses of vigils and fasting. His beard flowed imposingly downwards, out of sight, between the two brown hands gripping the edge of the table, and his persistent glance made sombre by the wide dilations of the pupils, fascinated.

"Imagine to yourselves," he said in his ordinary voice, "that I have eaten man."

I could only ejaculate a faint "Ah!" of complete enlightenment. But Hermann, dazed by the excessive shock, actually murmured, "Himmel! What for?"

"It was my terrible misfortune to do so," said Falk in a measured undertone. The girl, unconscious, sewed on. Mrs Hermann was absent in one of the staterooms, sitting up with Lena, who was feverish; but Hermann suddenly put both his hands up with a jerk. The embroidered calotte fell, and, in the twinkling of an eye, he had rumpled his hair all ends up in a most extravagant manner. In this state he strove to speak; with every effort his eyes seemed to start further out of their sockets; his head looked like a mop. He choked, gasped, swallowed, and managed to shriek out the one word, "Beast!"

From that moment till Falk went out of the cabin the girl, with her hands folded on the work lying in her lap, never took her eyes off him. His own, in the blindness of his heart, darted all over the cabin, only seeking to avoid the sight of Hermann's raving. It was ridiculous, and was made almost terrible by the stillness of every other person present. It was contemptible, and was made appalling by the man's overmastering horror of this awful sincerity, coming to him suddenly, with the confession of such a fact. He walked with great strides; he gasped. He wanted to know from Falk how dared he to come and tell him this? Did he think himself a proper person to be sitting in this cabin where his wife and children lived? Tell his niece! Expected him to tell his niece! His own brother's daughter! Shameless! Did I ever hear tell of such impudence? – he appealed to me. "This man here ought to have gone and hidden himself out of sight instead of . . ."

"But it's a great misfortune for me. But it's a great misfortune for me," Falk would ejaculate from time to time.

However, Hermann kept on running frequently against the corners of the table. At last he lost a slipper, and crossing his arms on his breast, walked up with one stocking foot very close to Falk, in order to ask him whether he did think there was anywhere on earth a woman abandoned enough to mate with such a monster. "Did he? Did he? Did he?" I tried to restrain him. He tore himself out of my hands; he found his slipper, and, endeavouring to put it on, stormed standing on one leg – and Falk, with a face unmoved and averted eyes, grasped all his mighty beard in one vast palm.

"Was it right then for me to die myself?" he asked, thoughtfully. I laid my hand on his shoulder.

"Go away," I whispered, imperiously, without any clear reason for this advice, except that I wished to put an end to Hermann's odious noise. "Go away."

He looked searchingly for a moment at Hermann before he made a move. I left the cabin, too, to see him out of the ship. But he hung about the quarter-deck.

"It is my misfortune," he said in a steady voice.

"You were stupid to blurt it out in such a manner. After all, we don't hear such confidences every day."

"What does the man mean?" he mused in deep undertones. "Somebody had to die – but why me?"

He remained still for a time in the dark – silent; almost invisible. All at once he pinned my elbows to my sides. I felt utterly powerless in his grip, and his voice, whispering in my ear, vibrated.

"It's worse than hunger. Captain, do you know what that means? And I could kill then – or be killed. I wish the crowbar had smashed my skull ten years ago. And I've got to live now. Without her. Do you understand? Perhaps many years. But how? What can be done? If I had allowed myself to look at her once I would have carried her off before that man in my hands – like this."

I felt myself snatched off the deck, then suddenly dropped – and I staggered backwards, feeling bewildered and bruised. What a man! All was still; he was gone. I heard Hermann's voice declaiming in the cabin, and went in.

I could not at first make out a single word, but Mrs Hermann, who, attracted by the noise, had come in some time before, with an expression of surprise and mild disapproval depicted broadly on her face, was giving now all the signs of profound, helpless agitation. Her husband shot a string of guttural words at her, and instantly putting out one hand to the bulkhead as if to save herself from falling, she clutched the loose bosom of her dress with the other. He harangued the two women extraordinarily, with much of his shirt hanging out of his waistbelt, stamping his foot, turning from one to the other, sometimes flinging both his arms straight up above his rumpled hair and keeping them in that position while he uttered a passage of loud denunciation; at others folding them tight across his breast – and then he hissed with indignation, elevating his shoulders and protruding his head. The girl was crying.

She had not changed her attitude. From her steady eyes that, following Falk in his retreat, had remained fixed wistfully on the cabin door, the tears fell rapid, thick, on her hands, on the work in her lap, warm and gentle like a shower in spring. She wept without grimacing, without noise – very touching, very quiet, with something more of pity than of pain in her face, as one weeps in compassion rather than grief – and Hermann, before her, declaimed. I caught several times the word "Mensch", man; and

also "Fressen", which last I looked up afterwards in my dictionary. It means "Devour". Hermann seemed to be requesting an
answer of some sort from her; his whole body swayed. She
remained mute and perfectly still; at last his agitation gained
her; she put the palms of her hands together, her full lips parted,
no sound came. His voice scolded shrilly, his arms went like a
windmill – suddenly he shook his thick fist at her. She burst out
into loud sobs. He seemed stupefied.

Mrs Hermann rushed forward babbling rapidly.

The two women fell on each other's necks, and, with an arm
round her niece's waist, she led her away. Her own eyes were
simply streaming, her face was flooded. She shook her head
back at me negatively, I wonder why to this day. The girl's
head dropped heavily on her shoulder. They disappeared
together.

Then Hermann sat down and stared at the cabin floor.

"We don't know all the circumstances," I ventured to break the
silence. He retorted tartly that he didn't want to know of any.
According to his ideas no circumstances could excuse a crime –
and certainly not such a crime. This was the opinion generally
received. The duty of a human being was to starve. Falk therefore
was a beast, an animal; base, low, vile, despicable, shameless, and
deceitful. He had been deceiving him since last year. He was,
however, inclined to think that Falk must have gone mad quite
recently; for no sane person, without necessity, uselessly, for no
earthly reason, and regardless of another's self-respect and peace
of mind, would own to having devoured human flesh. "Why
tell?" he cried. "Who was asking him?" It showed Falk's brutality
because after all he had selfishly caused him (Hermann) much
pain. He would have preferred not to know that such an unclean
creature had been in the habit of caressing his children. He hoped
I would say nothing of all this ashore, though. He wouldn't like it
to get about that he had been intimate with an eater of men – a
common cannibal. As to the scene he had made (which I judged
quite unnecessary) he was not going to inconvenience and
restrain himself for a fellow that went about courting and
upsetting girls' heads, while he knew all the time that no decent
housewifely girl would think of marrying him. At least he
(Hermann) could not conceive how any girl could. "Fancy
Lena! . . . No, it was impossible. The thoughts that would come

into their heads every time they sat down to a meal. Horrible!
Horrible!"

"You are too squeamish, Hermann," I said.

He seemed to think it was eminently proper to be squeamish if
the word meant disgust at Falk's conduct; and turning up his eyes
sentimentally he drew my attention to the horrible fate of the
victims – the victims of that Falk. I said that I knew nothing about
them. He seemed surprised. Could not anybody imagine without
knowing? He – for instance – felt he would like to avenge them.
But what if – said I – there had not been any? They might have
died as it were, naturally – of starvation. He shuddered. But to be
eaten – after death! To be devoured! He gave another deep
shudder, and asked suddenly, "Do you think it is true?"

His indignation and his personality together would have been
enough to spoil the reality of the most authentic thing. When I
looked at him I doubted the story – but the remembrance of Falk's
words, looks, gestures, invested it not only with an air of reality
but with the absolute truth of primitive passion.

"It is true just as much as you are able to make it; and exactly
in the way you like to make it. For my part, when I hear you
clamouring about it, I don't believe it is true at all."

And I left him pondering. The men in my gig lying at the foot of
the *Diana's* side-ladder, told me that the captain of the tug had
gone away in his boat some time ago.

I let my fellows pull an easy stroke; because of the heavy dew
the clear sparkle of the stars seemed to fall on me cold and
wetting. There was a sense of lurking gruesome horror somewhere in my mind, and it was mingled with clear and grotesque
images. Schomberg's gastronomic tittle-tattle was responsible for
these; and I half hoped I should never see Falk again. But the first
thing my anchor-watchman told me was that the captain of the
tug was on board. He had sent his boat away and was now
waiting for me in the cuddy.

He was lying full length on the stern settee, his face buried in
the cushions. I had expected to see it discomposed, contorted,
despairing. It was nothing of the kind; it was just as I had seen it
twenty times, steady and glaring from the bridge of the tug. It was
immovably set and hungry, dominated like the whole man by the
singleness of one instinct.

He wanted to live. He had always wanted to live. So we all do –

but in us the instinct serves a complex conception, and in him this instinct existed alone. There is in such simple development a gigantic force, and like the pathos of a child's naïve and uncontrolled desire. He wanted that girl, and the utmost that can be said for him was that he wanted that particular girl alone. I think I saw then the obscure beginning, the seed germinating in the soil of an unconscious need, the first shoot of that tree bearing now for a mature mankind the flower and the fruit, the infinite gradation in shades and in flavour of our discriminating love. He was a child. He was as frank as a child, too. He was hungry for the girl, terribly hungry, as he had been terribly hungry for food.

Don't be shocked if I declare that in my belief it was the same need, the same pain, the same torture. We are in his case allowed to contemplate the foundation of all the emotions – that one joy which is to live, and the one sadness at the root of the innumerable torments. It was made plain by the way he talked. He had never suffered so. It was gnawing, it was fire; it was there, like this! And after pointing below his breastbone, he made a hard wringing motion with his hands. And I assure you that, seen as I saw it with my bodily eyes, it was anything but laughable. And again, as he was presently to tell me (alluding to an early incident of the disastrous voyage when some damaged meat had been flung overboard), he said that a time soon came when his heart ached (that was the expression he used), and he was ready to tear his hair out at the thought of all that rotten beef thrown away.

I heard all this; I witnessed his physical struggles, seeing the working of the rack and hearing the true voice of pain. I witnessed it all patiently, because the moment I came into the cuddy he had called upon me to stand by him – and this, it seems, I had diplomatically promised.

His agitation was impressive and alarming in the little cabin, like the floundering of a great whale driven into a shallow cove in a coast. He stood up; he flung himself down headlong; he tried to tear the cushion with his teeth; and again hugging it fiercely to his face he let himself fall on the couch. The whole ship seemed to feel the shock of his despair; and I contemplated with wonder the lofty forehead, the noble touch of time on the uncovered temples, the unchanged hungry character of the face – so strangely ascetic and so incapable of portraying emotion.

What should he do? He had lived by being near her.

He had sat – in the evening – I knew? – all his life! She sewed. Her head was bent – so. Her head – like this – and her arms. Ah! Had I seen? Like this.

He dropped on a stool, bowed his powerful neck whose nape was red, and with his hands stitched the air, ludicrous, sublimely imbecile and comprehensible.

And now he couldn't have her? No! That was too much. After thinking, too, that . . . What had he done? What was my advice? Take her by force? No? Mustn't he? Who was there to stop him? For the first time I saw one of his features move; a fighting teeth-baring curl of the lip . . . "Not Hermann, perhaps." He lost himself in thought as though he had fallen out of the world.

I may note that the idea of suicide apparently did not enter his head for a single moment. It occurred to me to ask:

"Where was it that this shipwreck of yours took place?"

"Down south," he said, vaguely, with a start.

"You are not down south now," I said. "Violence won't do. They would take her away from you in no time. And what was the name of the ship?"

"*Borgmester Dahl*," he said. "It was no shipwreck."

He seemed to be waking up by degrees from that trance, and waking up calmed.

"Not a shipwreck? What was it?"

"Breakdown," he answered, looking more like himself every moment. By this only I learned that it was a steamer. I had till then supposed they had been starving in boats or on a raft – or perhaps on a barren rock.

"She did not sink then?" I asked in surprise. He nodded. "We sighted the southern ice," he pronounced, dreamily.

"And you alone survived?"

He sat down. "Yes. It was a terrible misfortune for me. Everything went wrong. All the men went wrong. I survived."

Remembering the things one reads of it was difficult to realize the true meaning of his answers. I ought to have seen at once – but I did not; so difficult is it for our minds, remembering so much, instructed so much, informed of so much, to get in touch with the real actuality at our elbow. And with my head full of preconceived notions as to how a case of "Cannibalism and suffering at sea" should be managed I said – "You were then so lucky in the drawing of lots?"

"Drawing of lots?" he said. "What lots? Do you think I would have allowed my life to go for the drawing of lots?"

Not if he could help it, I perceived, no matter what other life went.

"It was a great misfortune. Terrible. Awful," he said. "Many heads went wrong, but the best men would live."

"The toughest, you mean," I said. He considered the word. Perhaps it was strange to him, though his English was so good.

"Yes," he asserted at last. "The best. It was everybody for himself at last and the ship open to all."

Thus from question to question I got the whole story. I fancy it was the only way I could that night have stood by him. Outwardly at least he was himself again; the first sign of it was the return of that incongruous trick he had of drawing both his hands down his face – and it had its meaning now, with that slight shudder of the frame and the passionate anguish of these hands uncovering a hungry immovable face, the wide pupils of the intent, silent, fascinating eyes.

It was an iron steamer of a most respectable origin. The burgomaster of Falk's native town had built her. She was the first steamer ever launched there. The burgomaster's daughter had christened her. Country people drove in carts from miles around to see her. He told me all this. He got the berth as, what we would call, chief mate. He seemed to think it had been a feather in his cap; and, in his own corner of the world, this lover of life was of good parentage.

The burgomaster had advanced ideas in the ship-owning line. At that time not everyone would have known enough to think of despatching a cargo steamer to the Pacific. But he loaded her with pitch-pine deals and sent her off to hunt for her luck. Wellington was to be the first port, I fancy. It doesn't matter, because in latitude 44° south and somewhere halfway between Good Hope and New Zealand the tail-shaft broke and the propeller dropped off.

They were steaming then with a fresh gale on the quarter and all their canvas set, to help the engines. But by itself the sail power was not enough to keep way on her. When the propeller went the ship broached-to at once, and the masts got whipped overboard.

The disadvantage of being dismasted consisted in this, that they had nothing to hoist flags on to make themselves visible at a distance. In the course of the first few days several ships failed to sight them; and the gale was drifting them out of the usual track. The voyage had been, from the first, neither very successful nor very harmonious. There had been quarrels on board. The captain was a clever, melancholic man, who had no unusual grip on his crew. The ship had been amply provisioned for the passage, but, somehow or other, several barrels of meat were found spoiled on opening, and had been thrown overboard soon after leaving home, as a sanitary measure. Afterwards the crew of the *Borgmester Dahl* thought of that rotten carrion with tears of regret, covetousness and despair.

She drove south. To begin with, there had been an appearance of organization, but soon the bonds of discipline became relaxed. A sombre idleness succeeded. They looked with sullen eyes at the horizon. The gales increased, she lay in the trough and the seas made a clean breach over her. One frightful night, when they expected their hulk to turn over with them every moment, a heavy sea broke on board, deluged the store-rooms and spoiled the best part of the remaining provisions. It seems the hatch had not been properly secured. This instance of neglect is character-istic of utter discouragement. Falk tried to inspire some energy into his captain, but failed. From that time he retired more into himself, always trying to do his utmost in the situation. It grew worse. Gale succeeded gale, with black mountains of water hurling themselves on the *Borgmester Dahl*. Some of the men never left their bunks; many became quarrelsome. The chief-engineer, an old man, refused to speak at all to anybody. Others shut themselves up in their berths to cry. On calm days the inert steamer rolled on a leaden sea under a murky sky, or showed, in sunshine, the squalor of sea waifs, the dried white salt, the rust, the jagged broken places. Then the gales came again. They kept body and soul together on short rations. Once, an English ship, scudding in a storm, tried to stand by them, heaving-to pluckily under their lee. The seas swept her decks; the men in oilskins clinging to her rigging looked at them, and they made desperate signs over their shattered bulwarks. Suddenly her main-topsail went, yard and all, in a terrific squall; she had to bear up under bare poles and disappeared.

Other ships had spoken them before, but at first they had refused to be taken off, expecting the assistance of some steamer.

There were very few steamers in those latitudes then; and when they desired to leave this dead and drifting carcase, no ship came in sight. They had drifted south out of men's knowledge. They failed to attract the attention of a lonely whaler: and very soon the edge of the polar ice-cap rose from the sea and closed the southern horizon like a wall. One morning they were alarmed by finding themselves floating amongst detached pieces of ice. But the fear of sinking passed away like their vigour, like their hopes; the shocks of the floes knocking against the ship's side could not rouse them from their apathy: and the *Borgmester Dahl* drifted out again, unharmed, into open water. They hardly noticed the change.

The funnel had gone overboard in one of the heavy rolls; two of their three boats had disappeared, washed away in bad weather, and the davits swung to and fro, unsecured, with chafed rope's ends waggling to the roll. Nothing was done on board, and Falk told me how he had often listened to the water washing about the dark engine-room where the engines, stilled for ever, were decaying slowly into a mass of rust, as the stilled heart decays within the lifeless body. At first, after the loss of the motive power, the tiller had been thoroughly secured by lashings. But in course of time these had rotted, chafed, rusted, parting one by one; and the rudder, freed, banged heavily to and fro night and day, sending dull shocks through the whole frame of the vessel. This was dangerous. Nobody cared enough to lift a little finger. He told me that even now sometimes waking up at night, he fancied he could hear the dull vibrating thuds. The pintles carried away, and it dropped off at last.

The final catastrophe came with the sending off of their one remaining boat. It was Falk who had managed to preserve her intact, and now it was agreed that some of the hands should sail away into the track of the shipping to procure assistance. She was provisioned with all the food they could spare for the six who were to go. They waited for a fine day. It was long in coming. At last one morning they lowered her into the water.

Directly, in that demoralized crowd, trouble broke out. Two men who had no business there had jumped into the boat under the pretence of unhooking the tackles, while some sort of squabble arose on the deck amongst these weak, tottering spectres of a ship's company. The captain, who had been for days living secluded and unapproachable in the chart-room, came to the rail. He ordered the two men to come up on board and threatened them with his revolver. They pretended to obey, but suddenly cutting the boat's painter, gave a shove against the ship's side and made ready to hoist the sail.

"Shoot, sir! Shoot them down!" cried Falk – "and I will jump overboard to regain the boat." But the captain, after taking aim with an irresolute arm, turned suddenly away.

A howl of rage arose. Falk dashed into his cabin for his own pistol. When he returned it was too late. Two more men had leaped into the water, but the fellows in the boat beat them off with the oars, hoisted the boat's lug and sailed away. They were never heard of again.

Consternation and despair possessed the remaining ship's company, till the apathy of utter hopelessness reasserted its sway. That day a fireman committed suicide, running up on deck with his throat cut from ear to ear, to the horror of all hands. He was thrown overboard. The captain had locked himself in the chart-room, and Falk, knocking vainly for admittance, heard him reciting over and over again the names of his wife and children, not as if calling upon them or commending them to God, but in a mechanical voice like an exercise of memory. Next day the doors of the chart-room were swinging open to the roll of the ship, and the captain had disappeared. He must during the night have jumped into the sea. Falk locked both the doors and kept the keys.

The organized life of the ship had come to an end. The solidarity of the men had gone. They became indifferent to each other. It was Falk who took in hand the distribution of such food as remained. Sometimes whispers of hate were heard passing between the languid skeletons that drifted endlessly to and fro, north and south, east and west, upon that carcase of a ship.

And in this lies the grotesque horror of this sombre story. The last extremity of sailors, overtaking a small boat or a frail craft, seems easier to bear, because of the direct danger of the seas. The confined space, the close contact, the imminent menace of the waves, seem to draw men together, in spite of madness, suffering and despair. But there was a ship – safe, convenient, roomy: a ship with beds, bedding, knives, forks, comfortable cabins, glass and china, and a complete cook's galley, pervaded, ruled and possessed by the pitiless spectre of starvation. The lamp oil had been drunk, the wicks cut up for food, the candles eaten. At night she floated dark in all her recesses and full of fears. One day Falk came upon a man gnawing a splinter of pine wood. Suddenly he threw the piece of wood away, tottered to the rail, and fell over. Falk, too late to prevent the act, saw him claw the ship's side desperately before he went down. Next day another man did the same thing, after uttering horrible imprecations. But this one somehow managed to get hold of the broken rudder chains and hung on there, silently. Falk set about trying to save him, and all the time the man, holding with both hands, looked at him anxiously with his sunken eyes. Then, just as Falk was ready to put his hand on him, the man let go his hold and sank like a stone. Falk reflected on these sights. His heart revolted against the horror of death, and he said to himself that he would struggle for every precious minute of his life.

One afternoon – as the survivors lay about on the after-deck – the carpenter, a tall man with a black beard, spoke of the last sacrifice. There was nothing eatable left on board. Nobody said a word to this; but that company separated quickly, these listless feeble spectres slunk off one by one to hide in fear of each other. Falk and the carpenter remained on deck together. Falk liked the big carpenter. He had been the best man of the lot, helpful and ready as long as there was anything to do, the longest hopeful, and had preserved to the last some vigour and decision of mind.

They did not speak to each other. Henceforth no voices were to be heard conversing sadly on board that ship. After a time the carpenter tottered away forward; but later in the day Falk going to drink at the fresh-water pump, had the inspiration to turn his head. The carpenter had stolen upon him from behind, and, summoning all his strength, was aiming with a crowbar a blow at the back of his skull.

Dodging just in time, Falk made his escape and ran into his cabin. While he was loading his revolver there, he heard the sound of heavy blows struck upon the bridge. The locks of the chart-room doors were slight, they flew open, and the carpenter, possessing himself of the captain's revolver, fired a shot of defiance.

Falk was about to go on deck and have it out at once, when he remarked that one of the ports of his cabin commanded the approaches to the fresh-water pump. Instead of going out he stayed within and secured the door. "The best man shall survive," he said to himself – and the other, he reasoned, must at some time or other come there to drink. These starving men would drink often to cheat the pangs of their hunger. But the carpenter, too, must have noticed the position of the port. They were the two best men in the ship, and the game was with them. All the rest of the day Falk saw no one and heard no sound. At night he strained his eyes. It was dark – he heard a rustling noise once, but he was certain that no one could have come near the pump. It was to the left of his deck port, and he could not have failed to see a man, for the night was clear and starry. He saw nothing; towards morning another faint noise made him suspicious. Deliberately and quietly he unlocked his door. He had not slept, and had not given way to the horror of the situation. He wanted to live.

But during the night the carpenter, without even trying to approach the pump, had managed to creep quietly along the starboard bulwark, and, unseen, had crouched down right under Falk's deck port. When daylight came he rose up suddenly, looked in, and putting his arm through the round, brass-framed opening, fired at Falk within a foot. He missed – and Falk, instead of attempting to seize the arm holding the weapon, opened his door unexpectedly, and with the muzzle of his revolver nearly touching the other's side, shot him dead.

The best man had survived. Both of them had at the beginning just strength enough to stand on their feet, and both had displayed pitiless resolution, endurance, cunning and courage – all the qualities of classic heroism. At once Falk threw overboard the captain's revolver. He was a born monopolist. Then after the report of the two shots, followed by a profound silence, there crept out into the cold, cruel dawn of Antarctic regions, from various hiding-places, over the deck of that dismantled corpse of a ship floating on a grey sea ruled by iron necessity and with a heart of ice – there crept into view one by one, cautious, slow, eager, glaring, and unclean, a band of hungry and livid skeletons. Falk faced them, the possessor of the only fire-arm on board; and the second-best man – the carpenter – was lying dead between him and them.

"He was eaten, of course," I said.

Falk bent his head slowly, shuddered a little, drawing his hands over his face, and said, "I had never any quarrel with that man. But there were our lives between him and me."

Why continue the story of that ship, that story before which –
with its fresh-water pump like a spring of death, its man with the
weapon, the sea ruled by iron necessity, its spectral band swayed
by terror and hope, its mute and unhearing heaven – the fable of
the *Flying Dutchman* with its convention of crime and its
sentimental retribution fades like a graceful wreath, like a wisp
of white mist. What is there to say that everyone of us cannot
guess for himself? I believe Falk began by going through the ship,
revolver in hand, to annex all the matches. Those starving
wretches had plenty of matches! He had no mind to have the
ship set on fire under his feet, either from hate or from despair. He
lived in the open, camping on the bridge, commanding all the
after-deck and the only approach to the pump. He lived! Some of
the others lived, too – concealed, anxious, coming out one by one
from their hiding-places at the seductive sound of a shot. And he
was not selfish. They shared all alike. But only three of them all
remained alive when a whaler, returning from her cruising-
ground, nearly ran over the water-logged hull of the *Borgmester
Dahl*, which, it seems, in the end had in some way sprung a leak in
both her holds, but being loaded with deals could not sink.

"They all died," Falk said. "These three, too, afterwards. But I
would not die. All died, all! under this terrible misfortune. But was
I, too, to throw away my life? Could I? Tell me, captain? I was
alone there, quite alone, just like the others. Each man was alone.
Was I to give up my revolver? Who to? Or was I to throw it into
the sea? What would have been the good? Only the best man
would survive. It was a great, terrible, and cruel misfortune."

He had survived! I saw him before me as though preserved for a
witness to the mighty truth of an unerring and eternal principle.
Great beads of perspiration stood on his forehead. And suddenly it
struck the table with a heavy blow, as he fell forward throwing his
hands out.

"And this is worse," he cried. "This is a worse pain! This is
more terrible."

He made my heart thump with the profound conviction of his
cry. And after he had left me to go on board his ship I called up
before my mental eye the image of the girl weeping silently,
abundantly, patiently, and as if irresistibly. I thought of her tawny
hair. I thought how, if unplaited, it would have covered her all
round as low as the hips, like the hair of a siren. And she had

bewitched him. Fancy a man who would guard his own life with
the inflexibility of a pitiless and immovable fate, being brought to
lament that once a crowbar had missed his skull! The sirens sing
and lure to death, but this one had been weeping silently as if for
the pity of his life. She was the tender and voiceless siren of this
appalling navigator. He evidently wanted to live his whole
conception of life. Nothing else would do. And she, too, was a
servant of that life that, in the midst of death, cries aloud to our
senses. She was eminently fitted to interpret for him its feminine
side. And in her own way, and with her own profusion of
sensuous charms she also seemed to illustrate the eternal truth
of an unerring principle. I don't know though what sort of
principle Hermann illustrated when he turned up early on board
my ship with a most perplexed air. It struck me, however, that he,
too, would do his best to survive. He seemed greatly calmed on the
subject of Falk, but still very full of it.

"What is it you said I was last night? You know—" he asked
after some preliminary talk. "Too – too – I don't know. A very
funny word."

"Squeamish?" I suggested.

"Yes. What does it mean?"

"That you exaggerate things – to yourself. Without inquiry,
and so on."

He seemed to turn it over in his mind. We went on talking. This
Falk was the plague of his life. Upsetting everybody like this! Mrs
Hermann was unwell this morning. His niece was crying still.
There was nobody to look after the children. He struck his
umbrella on the deck. The girl would be like that for months.
Fancy carrying all the way home, second class, a perfectly useless
girl who is crying all the time. It was bad for Lena, too, he
observed; but on what grounds I could not guess. Perhaps of the
bad example. That child was already sorrowing and crying
enough over the rag doll. Nicholas was really the least sentimental person of the family.

"Why does your niece weep?" I asked.

"From pity," cried Hermann.

It was impossible to make out women. Mrs Hermann was the
only one he pretended to understand. She was very, very upset
and doubtful.

"Doubtful about what?" I asked.

He averted his eyes and did not answer this. It was impossible to make women out. For instance, his niece was weeping for Falk. Now he (Hermann) would like to wring his neck – but then . . . He supposed he had too tender a heart. "Frankly," he asked at last, "what do you think of what we heard last night, captain?"

"In all these tales," I observed, "there is always a good deal of exaggeration."

And not letting him recover from his surprise I assured him that I knew all the details. He begged me not to repeat them. His heart was too tender. They would make him feel unwell. Then, looking at his feet and speaking very slowly, he supposed that he need not see much of them after they were married. For, indeed, he could not bear the sight of Falk. On the other hand, it was ridiculous to take home a girl with her head turned. A girl that weeps all the time and is of no help to her aunt.

"Now you will be able to do with one cabin only on your passage home," I said.

"Yes, I had thought of that," he said brightly, almost. Yes! Himself, his wife, four children – one cabin might do. Whereas if his niece went . . .

"And what does Mrs Hermann say to it?" I inquired.

Mrs Hermann did not know whether a man of that sort could make a girl happy – she had been greatly deceived in Captain Falk. She had passed a very bad night.

Those good people did not seem to be able to retain an impression for a whole twelve hours. I assured him on my own personal knowledge that Falk possessed in himself all the qualities to make his niece's future prosperous. He said he was glad to hear this, and that he would tell his wife. Then the object of the visit came out. He wished me to help him to resume relations with Falk. His niece, he said, had expressed the hope I would do so in my kindness. He was evidently anxious that I should, for though he seemed to have forgotten nine-tenths of his last night's opinions and the whole of his indignation, yet he evidently feared to be sent to the right-about. "You told me he was very much in love," he concluded, slyly, and leered in a sort of bucolic way.

As soon as he had left my ship I called Falk on board by signal – the tug still lying at the anchorage. He took the news with calm gravity, as though he had all along trusted the stars to fight for him in their courses.

I saw them once more together, and only once – on the quarter-deck of the *Diana*. Hermann sat smoking with a shirt-sleeved elbow hooked over the back of his chair. Mrs Hermann was sewing alone. As Falk stepped over the gangway, Hermann's niece, with a slight swish of the skirt and a friendly nod to me, glided past my chair.

Those two met in sunshine abreast of the mainmast. He held her hands and looked down at them, and she looked up at him with her candid and unseeing glance. It seemed to me they had come together as if attracted, drawn and guided to each other by a mysterious influence. They were a complete couple. In her grey frock, palpitating with life, generous of form, olympian and simple, she was indeed the siren to fascinate that dark navigator, this ruthless lover of the five senses. From afar I seemed to feel the masculine strength with which he grasped those hands she had extended to him with a womanly swiftness. Lena, a little pale, nursing her beloved lump of dirty rags, ran towards her big friend; and then in the drowsy silence of the good old ship Mrs Hermann's voice rang out so changed that it made me spin round in my chair to see what was the matter.

"Lena, come here!" she screamed. And this good-natured matron gave me a wavering glance, dark and full of fearsome distrust. The child ran back, surprised, to her knee. But the two, standing before each other in sunlight with clasped hands, had heard nothing, had seen nothing and no one. Three feet away from them, in the shade, a seaman sat on a spar, very busy splicing a strop and dipping his fingers into a tar-pot, as if utterly unaware of their existence.

When I returned in command of another vessel some five years afterwards, Mr and Mrs Falk had left the place. I shouldn't wonder if Schomberg's tongue had succeeded at last in scaring Falk away for good; and, indubitably, there was some vague tale still going about the town of a certain Falk, owner of a tug, who had won his wife at cards from the captain of an English ship.

1901/1903

The Secret Sharer: An Episode from the Coast

On my right hand there were lines of fishing-stakes resembling a mysterious system of half-submerged bamboo fences, incomprehensible in its division of the domain of tropical fishes, and crazy of aspect as if abandoned for ever by some nomad tribe of fishermen now gone to the other end of the ocean; for there was no sign of human habitation as far as the eye could reach. To the left a group of barren islets, suggesting ruins of stone walls, towers, and blockhouses, had its foundations set in a blue sea that itself looked solid, so still and stable did it lie below my feet; even the track of light from the westering sun shone smoothly, without that animated glitter which tells of an imperceptible ripple. And when I turned my head to take a parting glance at the tug which had just left us anchored outside the bar, I saw the straight line of the flat shore joined to the stable sea, edge to edge, with a perfect and unmarked closeness, in one levelled floor half brown, half blue under the enormous dome of the sky. Corresponding in their insignificance to the islets of the sea, two small clumps of trees, one on each side of the only fault in the impeccable joint, marked the mouth of the river Meinam we had just left on the first preparatory stage of our homeward journey; and, far back on the inland level, a larger and loftier mass, the grove surrounding the great Paknam pagoda, was the only thing on which the eye could rest from the vain task of exploring the monotonous sweep of the horizon. Here and there gleams as of a few scattered pieces of silver marked the windings of the great river; and on the nearest of them, just within the bar, the tug steaming right into the land became lost to my sight, hull and funnel and masts, as though the impassive earth had swallowed her up without an effort, without a tremor. My eye followed the light cloud of her smoke, now here, now there, above the plain, according to the devious curves of the stream, but always fainter and farther away, till I lost it at last behind the mitre-shaped hill of the great pagoda. And then I was left alone with my ship, anchored at the head of the Gulf of Siam.

She floated at the starting-point of a long journey, very still in an immense stillness, the shadows of her spars flung far to the eastward by the setting sun. At that moment I was alone on her decks. There was not a sound in her – and around us nothing moved, nothing lived, not a canoe on the water, not a bird in the air, not a cloud in the sky. In this breathless pause at the threshold of a long passage we seemed to be measuring our fitness for a long and arduous enterprise, the appointed task of both our existences to be carried out, far from all human eyes, with only sky and sea for spectators and for judges.

There must have been some glare in the air to interfere with one's sight, because it was only just before the sun left us that my roaming eyes made out beyond the highest ridge of the principal islet of the group something which did away with the solemnity of perfect solitude. The tide of darkness flowed on swiftly; and with tropical suddenness a swarm of stars came out above the shadowy earth, while I lingered yet, my hand resting lightly on my ship's rail as if on the shoulder of a trusted friend. But, with all that multitude of celestial bodies staring down at one, the comfort of quiet communion with her was gone for good. And there were also disturbing sounds by this time – voices, footsteps forward; the steward flitted along the main deck, a busily ministering spirit; a hand-bell tinkled urgently under the poop-deck . . .

I found my two officers waiting for me near the supper table, in the lighted cuddy. We sat down at once, and as I helped the chief mate, I said:

"Are you aware that there is a ship anchored inside the islands? I saw her mastheads above the ridge as the sun went down."

He raised sharply his simple face, overcharged by a terrible growth of whisker, and emitted his usual ejaculations: "Bless my soul, sir! You don't say so!"

My second mate was a round-cheeked, silent young man, grave beyond his years, I thought; but as our eyes happened to meet I detected a slight quiver on his lips. I looked down at once. It was not my part to encourage sneering on board my ship. It must be said, too, that I knew very little of my officers. In consequence of certain events of no particular significance, except to myself, I had been appointed to the command only a fortnight before. Neither did I know much of the hands forward. All these people had been together for eighteen months or so, and my position was that of the only stranger on board. I mention this because it has some bearing on what is to follow. But what I felt most was my being a stranger to the ship; and if all the truth must be told, I was somewhat of a stranger to myself. The youngest man on board (barring the second mate), and untried as yet by a position of the fullest responsibility, I was willing to take the adequacy of the others for granted. They had simply to be equal to their tasks; but I wondered how far I should turn out faithful to that ideal conception of one's own personality every man sets up for himself secretly.

Meantime the chief mate, with an almost visible effect of collaboration on the part of his round eyes and frightful whiskers, was trying to evolve a theory of the anchored ship. His dominant trait was to take all things into earnest consideration. He was of a painstaking turn of mind. As he used to say, he "liked to account to himself" for practically everything that came in his way, down to a miserable scorpion he had found in his cabin a week before. The why and the wherefore of that scorpion – how it got on board and came to select his room rather than the pantry (which was a dark place and more what a scorpion would be partial to), and how on earth it managed to drown itself in the inkwell of his writing-desk – had exercised him infinitely. The ship within the islands was much more easily accounted for; and just as we were about to rise from table he made his pronouncement. She was, he doubted not, a ship from home lately arrived. Probably she drew too much water to cross the bar except at the top of spring tides. Therefore she went into that natural harbour to wait for a few days in preference to remaining in an open roadstead.

"That's so," confirmed the second mate, suddenly, in his slightly hoarse voice. "She draws over twenty feet. She's the Liverpool ship *Sephora* with a cargo of coal. Hundred and twenty-three days from Cardiff."

We looked at him in surprise.

"The tugboat skipper told me when he came on board for your letters, sir," explained the young man. "He expects to take her up the river the day after to-morrow."

After thus overwhelming us with the extent of his information he slipped out of the cabin. The mate observed regretfully that he "could not account for that young fellow's whims". What prevented him telling us all about it at once, he wanted to know.

I detained him as he was making a move. For the last two days the crew had had plenty of hard work, and the night before they had very little sleep. I felt painfully that I – a stranger – was doing something unusual when I directed him to let all hands turn in without setting an anchor-watch. I proposed to keep on deck myself till one o'clock or thereabouts. I would get the second mate to relieve me at that hour.

"He will turn out the cook and the steward at four," I concluded, "and then give you a call. Of course at the slightest sign of any sort of wind we'll have the hands up and make a start at once."

He concealed his astonishment. "Very well, sir." Outside the cuddy he put his head in the second mate's door to inform him of my unheard-of caprice to take a five hours' anchor-watch on myself. I heard the other raise his voice incredulously – "What? The Captain himself?" Then a few more murmurs, a door closed, then another. A few moments later I went on deck.

My strangeness, which had made me sleepless, had prompted that unconventional arrangement, as if I had expected in those solitary hours of the night to get on terms with the ship of which I knew nothing, manned by men of whom I knew very little more. Fast alongside a wharf, littered like any ship in port with a tangle of unrelated things, invaded by unrelated shore people, I had hardly seen her yet properly. Now, as she lay cleared for sea, the stretch of her main-deck seemed to me very fine under the stars. Very fine, very roomy for her size, and very inviting. I descended the poop and paced the waist, my mind picturing to myself the coming passage through the Malay Archipelago, down the Indian Ocean, and up the Atlantic. All its phases were familiar enough to me, every characteristic, all the alternatives which were likely to face me on the high seas – everything! . . . except the novel responsibility of command. But I took heart from the reasonable thought that the ship was like other ships, the men like other men, and that the sea was not likely to keep any special surprises expressly for my discomfiture.

Arrived at that comforting conclusion, I bethought myself of a cigar and went below to get it. All was still down there. Everybody at the after end of the ship was sleeping profoundly. I came out again on the quarter-deck, agreeably at ease in my sleeping-suit on that warm breathless night, barefooted, a glowing cigar in my teeth, and, going forward, I was met by the profound silence of the fore end of the ship. Only as I passed the door of the forecastle I heard a deep, quiet, trustful sigh of some sleeper inside. And suddenly I rejoiced in the great security of the sea as compared with the unrest of the land, in my choice of that untempted life presenting no disquieting problems, invested with an elementary moral beauty by the absolute straightforwardness of its appeal and by the singleness of its purpose.

The riding-light in the fore-rigging burned with a clear, untroubled, as if symbolic, flame, confident and bright in the mysterious shades of the night. Passing on my way aft along the other side of the ship, I observed that the rope side-ladder, put over, no doubt, for the master of the tug when he came to fetch away our letters, had not been hauled in as it should have been. I became annoyed at this, for exactitude in small matters is the very soul of discipline. Then I reflected that I had myself peremptorily dismissed my officers from duty, and by my own act had prevented the anchor-watch being formally set and things properly attended to. I asked myself whether it was wise ever to interfere with the established routine of duties even from the kindest of motives. My action might have made me appear eccentric. Goodness only knew how that absurdly whiskered mate would "account" for my conduct, and what the whole ship thought of that informality of their new captain. I was vexed with myself.

Not from compunction certainly, but, as it were mechanically, I proceeded to get the ladder in myself. Now a side-ladder of that sort is a light affair and comes in easily, yet my vigorous tug, which should have brought it flying on board, merely recoiled upon my body in a totally unexpected jerk. What the devil! . . . I was so astounded by the immovableness of that ladder that I remained stock-still, trying to account for it to myself like that imbecile mate of mine. In the end, of course, I put my head over the rail.

The side of the ship made an opaque belt of shadow on the darkling glassy shimmer of the sea. I saw at once something elongated and pale floating very close to the ladder. Before I could form a guess a faint flash of phosphorescent light, which seemed to issue suddenly from the naked body of a man, flickered in the sleeping water with the elusive, silent play of summer lightning in a night sky. With a gasp I saw revealed to my stare a pair of feet, the long legs, a broad livid back immersed right up to the neck in a greenish cadaverous glow. One hand, awash, clutched the bottom rung of the ladder. He was complete but for the head. A headless corpse! The cigar dropped out of my gaping mouth with a tiny plop and a short hiss quite audible in the absolute stillness of all things under heaven. At that I suppose he raised up his face, a dimly pale oval in the shadow of the ship's side. But even then I could only barely make out down there the shape of his black-haired head. However, it was enough for the horrid, frost-bound sensation which had gripped me about the chest to pass off. The moment of vain exclamations was past, too. I only climbed on the spare spar and leaned over the rail as far as I could, to bring my eyes nearer to that mystery floating alongside.

As he hung by the ladder, like a resting swimmer, the sea-lightning played about his limbs at every stir; and he appeared in it ghastly, silvery, fish-like. He remained as mute as a fish, too. He made no motion to get out of the water, either. It was inconceivable that he should not attempt to come on board, and strangely troubling to suspect that perhaps he did not want to. And my first words were prompted by just that troubled incertitude.

"What's the matter?" I asked in my ordinary tone, speaking down to the face upturned exactly under mine.

"Cramp," it answered, no louder. Then slightly anxious, "I say, no need to call any one."

"I was not going to," I said.

"Are you alone on deck?"

"Yes."

I had somehow the impression that he was on the point of letting go the ladder to swim away beyond my ken – mysterious as he came. But, for the moment, this being appearing as if he had risen from the bottom of the sea (it was certainly the nearest land to the ship) wanted only to know the time. I told him. And he, down there, tentatively:

"I suppose your captain's turned in?"

"I am sure he isn't," I said.

He seemed to struggle with himself, for I heard something like the low, bitter murmur of doubt. "What's the good?" His next words came out with a hesitating effort.

"Look here, my man. Could you call him out quietly?"

I thought the time had come to declare myself.

"*I* am the captain."

I heard a "By Jove!" whispered at the level of the water. The phosphorescence flashed in the swirl of the water all about his limbs, his other hand seized the ladder.

"My name's Leggatt."

The voice was calm and resolute. A good voice. The self-possession of that man had somehow induced a corresponding state in myself. It was very quietly that I remarked:

"You must be a good swimmer."

"Yes. I've been in the water practically since nine o'clock. The question for me now is whether I am to let go this ladder and go on swimming till I sink from exhaustion, or – to come on board here."

I felt this was no mere formula of desperate speech, but a real alternative in the view of a strong soul. I should have gathered from this that he was young; indeed, it is only the young who are ever confronted by such clear issues. But at the time it was pure intuition on my part. A mysterious communication was established already between us two – in the face of that silent, darkened tropical sea. I was young, too; young enough to make no comment. The man in the water began suddenly to climb up the ladder, and I hastened away from the rail to fetch some clothes.

Before entering the cabin I stood still, listening in the lobby at the foot of the stairs. A faint snore came through the closed door of the chief mate's room. The second mate's door was on the hook, but the darkness in there was absolutely soundless. He, too, was young and could sleep like a stone. Remained the steward, but he was not likely to wake up before he was called. I got a sleeping-suit out my room and, coming back on deck, saw the naked man from the sea sitting on the main-hatch, glimmering white in the darkness, his elbows on his knees and his head in his hands. In a moment he had concealed his damp body in a sleeping-suit of the same grey-stripe pattern as the one I was wearing and followed me like my double on the poop. Together we moved right aft, barefooted, silent.

"What is it?" I asked in a deadened voice, taking the lighted lamp out of the binnacle, and raising it to his face.

"An ugly business."

He had rather regular features; a good mouth; light eyes under somewhat heavy, dark eyebrows; a smooth, square forehead; no growth on his cheeks; a small, brown moustache, and a well-shaped, round chin. His expression was concentrated, meditative, under the inspecting light of the lamp I held up to his face; such as a man thinking hard in solitude might wear. My sleeping-suit was just right for his size. A well-knit young fellow of twenty-five at most. He caught his lower lip with the edge of white, even teeth.

"Yes," I said, replacing the lamp in the binnacle. The warm, heavy tropical night closed upon his head again.

"There's a ship over there," he murmured.

"Yes, I know. The *Sephora*. Did you know of us?"

"Hadn't the slightest idea. I am the mate of her—" He paused and corrected himself. "I should say I *was*."

"Aha! Something wrong?"

"Yes. Very wrong indeed. I've killed a man."

"What do you mean? Just now?"

"No, on the passage. Weeks ago. Thirty-nine south. When I say a man—"

"Fit of temper," I suggested, confidently.

The shadowy, dark head, like mine, seemed to nod impercept-ibly above the ghostly grey of my sleeping-suit. It was, in the night, as though I had been faced by my own reflection in the depths of a sombre and immense mirror.

"A pretty thing to have to own up to for a *Conway* boy," murmured my double, distinctly.

"You're a *Conway* boy?"

"I am," he said, as if startled. Then, slowly . . . "Perhaps you too—"

It was so; but being a couple of years older I had left before he joined. After a quick interchange of dates a silence fell; and I thought suddenly of my absurd mate with his terrific whiskers and the "Bless my soul – you don't say so" type of intellect. My double gave me an inkling of his thoughts by saying: "My father's a parson in Norfolk. Do you see me before a judge and jury on that charge? For myself I can't see the necessity. There are fellows that an angel from heaven – And I am not that. He was one of those creatures that are just simmering all the time with a silly sort of wickedness. Miserable devils that have no business to live at all. He wouldn't do his duty and wouldn't let anybody else do theirs.

But what's the good of talking! You know well enough the sort of ill-conditioned snarling cur—"

He appealed to me as if our experiences had been as identical as our clothes. And I knew well enough the pestiferous danger of such a character where there are no means of legal repression. And I knew well enough also that my double there was no homicidal ruffian. I did not think of asking him for details, and he told me the story roughly in brusque, disconnected sentences. I needed no more. I saw it all going on as though I were myself inside that other sleeping-suit.

"It happened while we were setting a reefed foresail, at dusk. Reefed foresail! You understand the sort of weather. The only sail we had left to keep the ship running; so you may guess what it had been like for days. Anxious sort of job, that. He gave me some of his cursed insolence at the sheet. I tell you I was overdone with this terrific weather that seemed to have no end to it. Terrific, I tell you – and a deep ship. I believe the fellow himself was half crazed with funk. It was no time for gentlemanly reproof, so I turned round and felled him like an ox. He up and at me. We closed just as an awful sea made for the ship. All hands saw it coming and took to the rigging, but I had him by the throat, and went on shaking him like a rat, the men above us yelling, 'Look out! Look out!' Then a crash as if the sky had fallen on my head. They say that for over ten minutes hardly anything was to be seen of the ship – just the three masts and a bit of the forecastle head and of the poop all awash driving along in a smother of foam. It was a miracle that they found us, jammed together behind the fore-bitts. It's clear that I meant business, because I was holding him by the throat still when they picked us up. He was black in the face. It was too much for them. It seemed they rushed us aft together, gripped as we were, screaming 'Murder!' like a lot of lunatics, and broke into the cuddy. And the ship running for her life, touch and go all the time, any minute her last in a sea fit to turn your hair grey only a-looking at it. I understand that the skipper, too, started raving like the rest of them. The man had been deprived of sleep for more than a week, and to have this sprung on him at the height of a furious gale nearly drove him out of his mind. I wonder they didn't fling me over-board after getting the carcass of their precious ship-mate out of my fingers. They had rather a job to separate us, I've been told. A sufficiently fierce story to make an old judge and a respectable jury sit up a bit. The first thing I heard when I came to myself was the maddening howling of that endless gale, and on that the voice of the old man. He was hanging on to my bunk, staring into my face out of his sou'wester.

" 'Mr Leggat, you have killed a man. You can act no longer as chief mate of this ship.' "

His care to subdue his voice made it sound monotonous. He rested a hand on the end of the skylight to steady himself with, and all that time did not stir a limb, so far as I could see. "Nice little tale for a quiet tea-party," he concluded in the same tone.

One of my hands, too, rested on the end of the skylight; neither did I stir a limb, so far as I knew. We stood less than a foot from each other. It occurred to me that if old "Bless my soul – you don't say so" were to put his head up the companion and catch sight of us, he would think he was seeing double, or imagine himself come upon a scene of weird witchcraft; the strange captain having a quiet confabulation by the wheel with his own grey ghost. I became very much concerned to prevent anything of the sort. I heard the other's soothing undertone.

"My father's a parson in Norfolk," it said. Evidently he had forgotten he had told me this important fact before. Truly a nice little tale.

"You had better slip down into my stateroom now," I said, moving off stealthily. My double followed my movements; our bare feet made no sound; I let him in, closed the door with care, and, after giving a call to the second mate, returned on deck for my relief.

"Not much sign of any wind yet," I remarked when he approached.

"No, sir. Not much," he assented, sleepily, in his hoarse voice, with just enough deference, no more, and barely suppressing a yawn.

"Well, that's all you have to look out for. You have got your orders."

"Yes, sir."

I paced a turn or two on the poop and saw him take up his position face forward with his elbow in the ratlines of the mizzen-rigging before I went below. The mate's faint snoring was still going on peacefully. The cuddy lamp was burning over the table on which stood a vase with flowers, a polite attention from the ship's provision merchant – the last flowers we should see for the next three months at the very least. Two bunches of bananas hung from the beam symmetrically, one on each side of the rudder-casing. Everything was as before in the ship – except that two of her captain's sleeping-suits were simultaneously in use, one motionless in the cuddy, the other keeping very still in the captain's stateroom.

It must be explained here that my cabin had the form of the capital letter L, the door being within the angle and opening into the short part of the letter. A couch was to the left, the bed-place to the right; my writing-desk and the chronometers' table faced the door. But anyone opening it, unless he stepped right inside, had no view of what I call the long (or vertical) part of the letter. It contained some lockers surmounted by a bookcase; and a few clothes, a thick jacket or two, caps, oilskin coat, and such like, hung on hooks. There was at the bottom of that part a door opening into my bath-room, which could be entered also directly from the saloon. But that way was never used.

The mysterious arrival had discovered the advantage of this particular shape. Entering my room, lighted strongly by a big bulkhead lamp swung on gimbals above my writing-desk, I did not see him anywhere till he stepped out quietly from behind the coats hung in the recessed part.

"I heard somebody moving about, and went in there at once," he whispered.

I, too, spoke under my breath.

"Nobody is likely to come in here without knocking and getting permission."

He nodded. His face was thin and the sunburn faded, as though he had been ill. And no wonder. He had been, I heard presently, kept under arrest in his cabin for nearly seven weeks. But there was nothing sickly in his eyes or in his expression. He was not a bit like me, really; yet, as we stood leaning over my bed-place, whispering side by side, with our dark heads together and our backs to the door, anybody bold enough to open it stealthily would have been treated to the uncanny sight of a double captain busy talking in whispers with his other self.

"But all this doesn't tell me how you came to hang on to our side-ladder," I inquired, in the hardly audible murmurs we used, after he had told me something more of the proceedings on board the *Sephora* once the bad weather was over.

"When we sighted Java Head I had had time to think all those matters out several times over. I had six weeks of doing nothing else, and with only an hour or so every evening for a tramp on the quarter-deck."

He whispered, his arms folded on the side of my bed-place, staring through the open port. And I could imagine perfectly the manner of this thinking out – a stubborn if not a steadfast operation; something of which I should have been perfectly incapable.

"I reckoned it would be dark before we closed with the land," he continued, so low that I had to strain my hearing, near as we were to each other, shoulder touching shoulder almost. "So I asked to speak to the old man. He always seemed very sick when he came to see me – as if he could not look me in the face. You know, that foresail saved the ship. She was too deep to have run long under bare poles. And it was I that managed to set it for him. Anyway, he came. When I had him in my cabin – he stood by the door looking at me as if I had the halter round my neck already – I asked him right away to leave my cabin door unlocked at night while the ship was going through Sunda Straits. There would be the Java coast within two or three miles, off Angier Point. I wanted nothing more. I've had a prize for swimming my second year in the *Conway*."

"I can believe it," I breathed out.

"God only knows why they locked me in every night. To see some of their faces you'd have thought they were afraid I'd go about at night strangling people. Am I a murdering brute? Do I look it? By Jove! if I had been he wouldn't have trusted himself like that into my room. You'll say I might have chucked him aside and bolted out, there and then – it was dark already. Well, no. And for the same reason I wouldn't think of trying to smash the door. There would have been a rush to stop me at the noise, and I did not mean to get into a confounded scrimmage. Somebody else might have got killed – for I would not have broken out only to get chucked back, and I did not want any more of that work. He refused, looking more sick than ever. He was afraid of the men, and also of that old second mate of his who had been sailing with him for years – a grey-headed old humbug; and his steward, too, had been with him devil knows how long – seventeen years or more – a dogmatic sort of loafer who hated me like poison, just because I was the chief mate. No chief mate ever made more than one voyage in the *Sephora*, you know. Those two old chaps ran the ship. Devil only knows what the skipper wasn't afraid of (all his nerve went to pieces altogether in that hellish spell of bad weather we had) – of what the law would do to him – of his wife, perhaps. Oh, yes! she's on board. Though I don't think she would have meddled. She would have been only too glad to have me out of the ship in any way. The 'brand of Cain' business, don't you see. That's all right. I was ready enough to go off wandering on the face of the earth – and that was price enough to pay for an Abel of that sort. Anyhow, he wouldn't listen to me. 'This thing must take its course. I represent the law here.' He was shaking like a leaf. 'So you won't?' 'No!' 'Then I hope you will be able to sleep on that,' I said, and turned my back on him. 'I wonder that *you* can,' cries he, and locks the door.

"Well, after that, I couldn't. Not very well. That was three weeks ago. We had had a slow passage through the Java Sea; drifted about Carimata for ten days. When we anchored here they thought, I suppose, it was all right. The nearest land (and that's five miles) is the ship's destination; the consul would soon set about catching me; and there would have been no object in bolting to these islets there. I don't suppose there's a drop of water on them. I don't know how it was, but to-night that steward, after bringing me my supper, went out to let me eat it, and left the door unlocked. And I ate it – all there was, too. After I had finished I strolled out on the quarter-deck. I don't know that I meant to do anything. A breath of fresh air was all I wanted, I believe. Then a sudden temptation came over me. I kicked off my slippers and was in the water before I had made up my mind fairly. Somebody heard the splash and they raised an awful hullabaloo. 'He's gone! Lower the boats! He's committed suicide! No, he's swimming.' Certainly I was swimming. It's not so easy for a swimmer like me to commit suicide by drowning. I landed on the nearest islet before the boat left the ship's side. I heard them pulling about in the dark, hailing, and so on, but after a bit they gave up. Everything quieted down and the anchorage became as still as death. I sat down on a stone and began to think. I felt certain they would start searching for me at daylight. There was no place to hide on those stony things – and if there had been, what would have been the good? But now I was clear of that ship, I was not going back. So after a while I took off all my clothes, tied them up in a bundle with a stone inside, and dropped them in the deep water on the outer side of that islet. That was suicide enough for me. Let them think what they liked, but I didn't mean to drown myself. I meant to swim till I sank – but that's not the same thing. I struck out for another of these little islands, and it was from that one that I first saw your riding-light. Something to swim for. I went on easily, and on the way I came upon a flat rock a foot or two above water. In the daytime, I dare say, you might make it out with a glass from your poop. I scrambled up on it and rested myself for a bit. Then I made another start. That last spell must have been over a mile."

His whisper was getting fainter and fainter, and all the time he stared straight out through the port-hole, in which there was not even a star to be seen. I had not interrupted him. There was something that made comment impossible in his narrative, or perhaps in himself; a sort of feeling, a quality, which I can't find a name for. And when he ceased, all I found was a futile whisper: "So you swam for our light?"

"Yes – straight for it. It was something to swim for. I couldn't see any stars low down because the coast was in the way, and I couldn't see the land, either. The water was like glass. One might have been swimming in a confounded thousand-feet deep cistern with no place for scrambling out anywhere; but what I didn't like was the notion of swimming round and round like a crazed bullock before I gave out; and as I didn't mean to go back . . . No. Do you see me being hauled back, stark naked, off one of these little islands by the scruff of the neck and fighting like a wild beast? Somebody would have got killed for certain, and I did not want any of that. So I went on. Then your ladder—"

"Why didn't you hail the ship?" I asked, a little louder.

He touched my shoulder lightly. Lazy footsteps came right over our heads and stopped. The second mate had crossed from the other side of the poop and might have been hanging over the rail, for all we knew.

"He couldn't hear us talking – could he?" My double breathed into my very ear, anxiously.

His anxiety was an answer, a sufficient answer, to the question

I had put to him. An answer containing all the difficulty of that situation. I closed the porthole quietly, to make sure. A louder word might have been overheard.

"Who's that?" he whispered then.

"My second mate. But I don't know much more of the fellow than you do."

And I told him a little about myself. I had been appointed to take charge while I least expected anything of the sort, not quite a fortnight ago. I didn't know either the ship or the people. Hadn't had the time in port to look about me or size anybody up. And as to the crew, all they knew was that I was appointed to take the ship home. For the rest, I was almost as much of a stranger on board as himself, I said. And at the moment I felt it most acutely. I felt that it would take very little to make me a suspect person in the eyes of the ship's company.

He had turned abut meantime; and we, the two strangers in the ship, faced each other in identical attitudes.

"Your ladder—" he murmured, after a silence. "Who'd have thought of finding a ladder hanging over at night in a ship anchored out here! I felt just then a very unpleasant faintness. After the life I've been leading for nine weeks, anybody would have got out of condition. I wasn't capable of swimming round as far as your rudder-chains. And, lo and behold! there was a ladder to get hold of. After I gripped it I said to myself, 'What's the good?' When I saw a man's head looking over I thought I would swim away presently and leave him shouting – in whatever language it was. I didn't mind being looked at. I – I liked it. And then you speaking to me so quietly –as if you had expected me –made me hold on a little longer. It had been a confounded lonely time – I don't mean while swimming. I was glad to talk a little to somebody that didn't belong to *Sephora*. As to asking for the captain, that was a mere impulse. It could have been no use, with all the ship knowing about me and the other people pretty certain to be round here in the morning. I don't know – I wanted to be seen, to talk with somebody, before I went on. I don't know what I would have said . . . 'Fine night, isn't it?' or something of the sort."

"Do you think they will be round here presently?" I asked with some incredulity.

"Quite likely," he said, faintly.

He looked extremely haggard all of a sudden. His head rolled on his shoulders.

"H'm. We shall see then. Meantime get into that bed," I whispered. "Want help? There."

It was a rather high bed-place with a set of drawers underneath. This amazing swimmer really needed the lift I gave him by seizing his leg. He tumbled in, rolled over on his back, and flung one arm across his eyes. And then, with his face nearly hidden, he must have looked exactly as I used to look in that bed. I gazed upon my other self for a while before drawing across carefully the two green serge curtains which ran on a brass rod. I thought for a moment of pinning them together for greater safety, but I sat down on the couch, and once there I felt unwilling to rise and hunt for a pin. I would do it in a moment. I was extremely tired, in a peculiarly intimate way, by the strain of stealthiness, by the effort of whispering and the general secrecy of this excitement. It was three o'clock by now and I had been on my feet since nine, but I was not sleepy; I could not have gone to sleep. I sat there, fagged out, looking at the curtains, trying to clear my mind of the confused sensation of being in two places at once, and greatly bothered by an exasperating knocking in my head. It was a relief to discover suddenly that it was not in my head at all, but on the outside of the door. Before I could collect myself the words "Come in" were out of my mouth, and the steward entered with a tray, bringing in my morning coffee. I had slept, after all, and I was so frightened that I shouted, "This way! I am here, steward," as though he had been miles away. He put down the tray on the table next to the couch and only then said, very quietly, "I can see you are here, sir." I felt him give me a keen look, but I dared not meet his eyes just then. He must have wondered why I had drawn the curtains of my bed before going to sleep on the couch. He went out, hooking the door open as usual.

I heard the crew washing decks above me. I knew I would have been told at once if there had been any wind. Calm, I thought, and I was doubly vexed. Indeed, I felt dual more than ever. The steward reappeared suddenly in the doorway. I jumped up from the couch so quickly that he gave a start.

"What do you want here?"

"Close your port, sir – they are washing decks."

"It is closed," I said, reddening.

"Very well, sir." But he did not move from the doorway and returned my stare in an extraordinary, equivocal manner for a time. Then his eyes wavered, all his expression changed, and in a voice unusually gentle, almost coaxingly:

"May I come in to take the empty cup away, sir?"

"Of course!" I turned my back on him while he popped in and out. Then I unhooked and closed the door and even pushed the bolt. This sort of thing could not go on very long. The cabin was as hot as an oven, too. I took a peep at my double, and discovered that he had not moved, his arm was still over his eyes; but his chest heaved; his hair was wet; his chin glistened with perspiration. I reached over him and opened the port.

"I must show myself on deck," I reflected.

Of course, theoretically, I could do what I liked, with no one to say nay to me within the whole circle of the horizon; but to lock my cabin door and take the key away I did not dare. Directly I put my head out of the companion I saw the group of my two officers, the second mate barefooted, the chief mate in long india-rubber boots, near the break of the poop, and the steward half-way down the poop-ladder talking to them eagerly. He happened to catch sight of me and dived, the second ran down on the main-deck shouting some order or other, and the chief mate came to meet me, touching his cap.

There was a sort of curiosity in his eye that I did not like. I don't know whether the steward had told them that I was "queer" only, or downright drunk, but I know the man meant to have a good look at me. I watched him coming with a smile which, as he got into point-blank range, took effect and froze his very whiskers. I did not give him time to open his lips.

"Square the yards by lifts and braces before the hands go to breakfast."

It was the first particular order I had given on board that ship; and I stayed on deck to see it executed, too. I had felt the need of asserting myself without loss of time. That sneering young cub got taken down a peg or two on that occasion, and I also seized the opportunity of having a good look at the face of every foremast man as they filed past me to go to the after braces. At breakfast time, eating nothing myself, I presided with such frigid dignity that the two mates were only too glad to escape from the cabin as soon as decency permitted; and all the time the dual working of my mind distracted me almost to the point of insanity. I was constantly watching myself, my secret self, as dependent on my actions as my own personality, sleeping in that bed, behind that door which faced me as I sat at the head of the table. It was very much like being mad, only it was worse because one was aware of it.

I had to shake him for a solid minute, but when at last he opened his eyes it was in the full possession of his senses, with an inquiring look.

"All's well so far," I whispered. "Now you must vanish into the bath-room."

He did so, as noiseless as a ghost, and then I rang for the steward, and facing him boldly, directed him to tidy up my state-room while I was having my bath – "and be quick about it". As my tone admitted of no excuses, he said, "Yes, sir," and ran off to fetch his dust-pan and brushes. I took a bath and did most of my dressing, splashing, and whistling softly for the steward's edification, while the secret sharer of my life stood drawn up bolt upright in that little space, his face looking very sunken in daylight, his eyelids lowered under the stern, dark line of his eyebrows drawn together by a slight frown.

When I left him there to go back to my room the steward was finishing dusting. I sent for the mate and engaged him in some insignificant conversation. It was, as it were, trifling with the terrific character of his whiskers; but my object was to give him an opportunity for a good look at my cabin. And then I could at last shut, with a clear conscience, the door of my stateroom and get my double back into the recessed part. There was nothing else for it. He had to sit still on a small folding stool, half smothered by the heavy coats hanging there. We listened to the steward going into the bath-room out of the saloon, filling the water-bottles there, scrubbing the bath, setting things to rights, whisk, bang, clatter – out again into the saloon – turn the key – click. Such was my scheme for keeping my second self invisible. Nothing better could be contrived under the circumstances. And there we sat; I at my writing-desk ready to appear busy with some papers, he behind me out of sight of the door. It would not have been prudent to talk in daytime; and I could not have stood the excitement of that queer sense of whispering to myself. Now and then, glancing over my shoulder, I saw him far back there, sitting rigidly on the low stool, his bare feet close together, his arms folded, his head hanging on his breast – and perfectly still. Anybody would have taken him for me.

I was fascinated by it myself. Every moment I had to glance over my shoulder. I was looking at him when a voice outside the door said:

"Beg pardon, sir."

"Well!" . . . I kept my eyes on him, and so when the voice outside the door announced, "There's a ship's boat coming our way, sir," I saw him give a start – the first movement he had made for hours. But he did not raise his bowed head.

"All right. Get the ladder over."

I hesitated. Should I whisper something to him? But what? His immobility seemed to have been never disturbed. What could I tell him he did not know already? . . . Finally I went on deck.

II

The skipper of the *Sephora* had a thin red whisker all round his face, and the sort of complexion that goes with hair of that colour; also the particular, rather smeary shade of blue in the eyes. He was not exactly a showy figure; his shoulders were high, his stature but middling – one leg slightly more bandy than the other. He shook hands, looking vaguely around. A spiritless tenacity was his main characteristic, I judged. I behaved with a politeness which seemed to disconcert him. Perhaps he was shy. He mumbled to me as if he were ashamed of what he was saying; gave his name (it was something like Archbold – but at this distance of years I hardly am sure), his ship's name, and a few other particulars of that sort, in the manner of a criminal making a reluctant and doleful confession. He had had terrible weather on the passage out – terrible – terrible – wife aboard, too.

By this time we were seated in the cabin and the steward brought in a tray with a bottle and glasses. "Thanks! No." Never took liquor. Would have some water, though. He drank two tumblerfuls. Terrible thirsty work. Ever since daylight had been exploring the islands round his ship.

"What was that for – fun?" I asked, with an appearance of polite interest.

"No!" He sighed. "Painful duty."

As he persisted in his mumbling and I wanted my double to hear every word, I hit upon the notion of informing him that I regretted to say I was hard of hearing.

"Such a young man, too!" he nodded, keeping his smeary blue, unintelligent eyes fastened upon me. "What was the cause of it – some disease?" he inquired, without the least sympathy and as if he thought that, if so, I'd got no more than I deserved.

"Yes; disease," I admitted in a cheerful tone which seemed to shock him. But my point was gained, because he had to raise his voice to give me his tale. It is not worth while to record that version. It was just over two months since all this had happened, and he had thought so much about it that he seemed completely muddled as to its bearings, but still immensely impressed.

"What would you think of such a thing happening on board your own ship? I've had the *Sephora* for these fifteen years. I am a well-known shipmaster."

He was densely distressed – and perhaps I should have sympathized with him if I had been able to detach my mental vision from the unsuspected sharer of my cabin as though he were my second self. There he was on the other side of the bulkhead, four or five feet from us, no more, as we sat in the saloon. I looked politely at Captain Archbold (if that was his name), but it was the other I saw, in a grey sleeping-suit, seated on a low stool, his bare feet close together, his arms folded, and every word said between us falling into the ears of his dark head bowed on his chest.

"I have been at sea now, man and boy, for seven-and-thirty years, and I've never heard of such a thing happening in an English ship. And that it should be my ship. Wife on board, too."

I was hardly listening to him.

"Don't you think," I said, "that the heavy sea which, you told me, came aboard just then might have killed the man? I have seen the sheer weight of a sea kill a man very neatly, by simply breaking his neck."

"Good God!" he uttered, impressively, fixing his smeary blue eyes on me. "The sea! No man killed by the sea ever looked like that." He seemed positively scandalized at my suggestion. And as I gazed at him, certainly not prepared for anything original on his part, he advanced his head close to mine and thrust his tongue out at me so suddenly that I couldn't help starting back.

After scoring over my calmness in this graphic way he nodded wisely. If I had seen the sight, he assured me, I would never forget it as long as I lived. The weather was too bad to give the corpse a proper sea burial. So next day at dawn they took it up on the poop, covering its face with a bit of bunting; he read a short prayer, and then, just as it was, in its oilskins and long boots, they launched it amongst those mountainous seas that seemed ready every moment to swallow up the ship herself and the terrified lives on board of her.

"That reefed foresail saved you," I threw in.

"Under God – it did," he exclaimed fervently. "It was by a special mercy, I firmly believe, that it stood some of those hurricane squalls."

"It was the setting of that sail which—" I began.

"God's own hand in it," he interrupted me. "Nothing less could have done it. I don't mind telling you that I hardly dared give the order. It seemed impossible that we could touch anything without losing it, and then our last hope would have been gone."

The terror of that gale was on him yet. I let him go on for a bit, then said, casually – as if returning to a minor subject:

"You were very anxious to give up your mate to the shore people, I believe?"

He was. To the law. His obscure tenacity on that point had in it something incomprehensible and a little awful; something, as it were, mystical, quite apart from his anxiety that he should not be suspected of "countenancing any doings of that sort". Seven-and-thirty virtuous years at sea, of which over twenty of immaculate command, and the last fifteen in the *Sephora*, seemed to have laid him under some pitiless obligation.

"And you know," he went on, groping shamefacedly amongst his feelings, "I did not engage that young fellow. His people had some interest with my owners. I was in a way forced to take him on. He looked very smart, very gentlemanly, and all that. But do you know – I never liked him, somehow. I am a plain man. You see, he wasn't exactly the sort for the chief mate of a ship like the *Sephora*."

I had become so connected in thoughts and impressions with the secret sharer of my cabin that I felt as if I, personally, were being given to understand that I, too, was not the sort that would have done for the chief mate of a ship like the *Sephora*. I had no doubt of it in my mind.

"Not at all the style of man. You understand," he insisted, superfluously, looking hard at me.

I smiled urbanely. He seemed at a loss for a while.

"I suppose I must report a suicide."

"Beg pardon?"

"Sui — cide! That's what I'll have to write to my owners directly I get in."

"Unless you manage to recover him before to-morrow," I assented, dispassionately . . . "I mean, alive."

He mumbled something which I really did not catch, and I turned my ear to him in a puzzled manner. He fairly bawled:

"The land — I say, the mainland is at least seven miles off my anchorage."

"About that."

My lack of excitement, of curiosity, of surprise, of any sort of pronounced interest, began to arouse his distrust. But except for the felicitous pretence of deafness I had not tried to pretend anything. I had felt utterly incapable of playing the part of ignorance properly, and therefore was afraid to try. It is also certain that he had brought some ready-made suspicions with him, and that he viewed my politeness as a strange and unnatural phenomenon. And yet how else could I have received him? Not heartily! That was impossible for psychological reasons, which I need not state here. My only object was to keep off his inquiries. Surlily? Yes, but surliness might have provoked a point-blank question. From its novelty to him and from its nature, punctilious courtesy was the manner best calculated to restrain the man. But there was the danger of his breaking through my defence bluntly. I could not, I think, have met him by a direct lie, also for psychological (not moral) reasons. If he had only known how afraid I was of his putting my feeling of identity with the other to the test! But, strangely enough — (I thought of it only afterwards) — I believe that he was not a little disconcerted by the reverse side of that weird situation, by something in me that reminded him of the man he was seeking — suggested a mysterious similitude to the young fellow he had distrusted and disliked from the first.

However that might have been, the silence was not very prolonged. He took another oblique step.

"I reckon I had no more than a two-mile pull to your ship. Not a bit more."

"And quite enough, too, in this awful heat," I said.

Another pause full of mistrust followed. Necessity, they say, is mother of invention, but fear, too, is not barren of ingenious suggestions. And I was afraid he would ask me point-blank for news of my other self.

"Nice little saloon, isn't it?" I remarked, as if noticing for the first time the way his eyes roamed from one closed door to the other. "And very well fitted out, too. Here, for instance," I continued, reaching over the back of my seat negligently and flinging the door open, "is my bath-room."

He made an eager movement, but hardly gave it a glance. I got up, shut the door of the bath-room, and invited him to have a look round, as if I were very proud of my accommodation. He had to rise and be shown round, but he went through the business without any raptures whatever.

"And now we'll have a look at my stateroom," I declared, in a voice as loud as I dared to make it, crossing the cabin to the starboard side with purposely heavy steps.

He followed me in and gazed around. My intelligent double had vanished. I played my part.

"Very convenient – isn't it?"

"Very nice. Very comf . . ." He didn't finish and went out brusquely as if to escape from some unrighteous wiles of mine. But it was not to be. I had been too frightened not to feel vengeful; I felt I had him on the run, and I meant to keep him on the run. My polite insistence must have had something menacing in it, because he gave in suddenly. And I did not let him off a single item; mate's room, pantry, store-rooms, the very sail-locker which was also under the poop – he had to look into them all. When at last I showed him out on the quarter-deck he drew a long, spiritless sigh, and mumbled dismally that he must really be going back to his ship now. I desired my mate, who had joined us, to see to the captain's boat.

The man of whiskers gave a blast on the whistle which he used to wear hanging round his neck, and yelled, "*Sephora's* away!" My double down there in my cabin must have heard, and certainly could not feel more relieved than I. Four fellows came running out from somewhere forward and went over the side, while my own men, appearing on deck too, lined the rail. I escorted my visitor to the gangway ceremoniously, and nearly overdid it. He was a tenacious beast. On the very ladder he lingered, and in that unique, guiltily conscientious manner of sticking to the point:

"I say . . . you . . . you don't think that—"

I covered his voice loudly:

"Certainly not . . . I am delighted. Good-bye."

I had an idea of what he meant to say, and just saved myself by the privilege of defective hearing. He was too shaken generally to insist, but my mate, close witness of that parting, looked mystified and his face took on a thoughtful cast. As I did not want to appear as if I wished to avoid all communication with my officers, he had the opportunity to address me.

"Seems a very nice man. His boat's crew told our chaps a very extraordinary story, if what I am told by the steward is true. I suppose you had it from the captain, sir?"

"Yes. I had a story from the captain."

"A very horrible affair – isn't it, sir?"

"It is."

"Beats all these tales we hear about murders in Yankee ships."

"I don't think it beats them. I don't think it resembles them in the least."

"Bless my soul – you don't say so! But of course I've no acquaintance whatever with American ships, not I, so I couldn't go against your knowledge. It's horrible enough for me . . . But the queerest part is that those fellows seemed to have some idea the man was hidden aboard here. They had really. Did you ever hear of such a thing?"

"Preposterous – isn't it?"

We were walking to and fro athwart the quarter-deck. No one of the crew forward could be seen (the day was Sunday), and the mate pursued:

"There was some little dispute about it. Our chaps took offence. 'As if we would harbour a thing like that,' they said. 'Wouldn't you like to look for him in our coal-hole?' Quite a tiff. But they made it up in the end. I suppose he did drown himself. Don't you, sir?"

"I don't suppose anything."

"You have no doubt in the matter, sir?"

"None whatever."

I left him suddenly. I felt I was producing a bad impression, but with my double down there it was most trying to be on deck. And it was almost as trying to be below. Altogether a nerve-trying situation. But on the whole I felt less torn in two when I was with him. There was no one in the whole ship whom I dared take into my confidence. Since the hands had got to know his story, it would have been impossible to pass him off for any one else, and an accidental discovery was to be dreaded now more than ever . . .

The steward being engaged in laying the table for dinner, we could talk only with our eyes when I first went down. Later in the afternoon we had a cautious try at whispering. The Sunday quietness of the ship was against us; the stillness of air and water around her was against us; the elements, the men were against us – everything was against us in our secret partnership; time itself – for this could not go on forever. The very trust in Providence was, I suppose, denied to his guilt. Shall I confess that this thought cast me down very much? And as to the chapter of accidents which counts for so much in the book of success, I could only hope that it was closed. For what favourable accident could be expected?

"Did you hear everything?" were my first words as soon as we took up our position side by side, leaning over my bed-place.

He had. And the proof of it was his earnest whisper, "The man told you he hardly dared to give the order."

I understood the reference to be to that saving foresail.

"Yes. He was afraid of it being lost in the setting."

"I assure you he never gave the order. He may think he did, but he never gave it. He stood there with me on the break of the poop after the maintopsail blew away, and whimpered about our last hope – positively whimpered about it and nothing else – and the night coming on! To hear one's skipper go on like that in such weather was enough to drive any fellow out of his mind. It worked me up into a sort of desperation. I just took it into my own hands and went away from him, boiling, and— But what's the use telling you? *You* know! . . . Do you think that if I had not been pretty fierce with them I should have got the men to do anything? Not it! The bo's'n perhaps? Perhaps! It wasn't a heavy sea – it was a sea gone mad! I suppose the end of the world will be something like that; and a man may have the heart to see it coming once and be done with it – but to have to face it day after day – I don't blame anybody. I was precious little better than the rest. Only – I was an officer of that old coal-wagon, anyhow—"

"I quite understand," I conveyed that sincere assurance into his ear. He was out of breath with whispering; I could hear him pant slightly. It was all very simple. The same strung-up force which had given twenty-four men a chance, at least, for their lives, had, in a sort of recoil, crushed an unworthy mutinous existence.

But I had no leisure to weigh the merits of the matter – footsteps in the saloon, a heavy knock. "There's enough wind to get under way with, sir." Here was the call of a new claim upon my thoughts and even upon my feelings.

"Turn the hands up," I cried through the door. "I'll be on deck directly."

I was going out to make the acquaintance of my ship. Before I left the cabin our eyes met – the eyes of the only two strangers on board. I pointed to the recessed part where the little camp-stool awaited him and laid my finger on my lips. He made a gesture – somewhat vague – a little mysterious, accompanied by a faint smile, as if of regret.

This is not the place to enlarge upon the sensations of a man who feels for the first time a ship move under his feet to his own independent word. In my case they were not unalloyed. I was not wholly alone with my command; for there was that stranger in my cabin. Or rather, I was not completely and wholly with her. Part of me was absent. That mental feeling of being in two places at once affected me physically as if the mood of secrecy had penetrated my very soul. Before an hour had elapsed since the ship had begun to move, having occasion to ask the mate (he stood by my side) to take a compass bearing of the Pagoda, I caught myself reaching up to his ear in whispers. I say I caught myself, but enough had escaped to startle the man. I can't describe it otherwise than by saying that he shied. A grave, preoccupied manner, as though he were in possession of some perplexing intelligence, did not leave him henceforth. A little later I moved away from the rail to look at the compass with such a stealthy gait that the helmsman noticed it – and I could not help noticing the unusual roundness of his eyes. These are trifling instances, though it's to no commander's advantage to be suspected of ludicrous eccentricities. But I was also more seriously affected. There are to a seaman certain words, gestures, that should in given conditions come as naturally, as instinctively as the winking of a menaced eye. A certain order should spring on to his lips without thinking; a certain sign should get itself made, so to speak, without reflection. But all unconscious alertness had abandoned me. I had to make an effort of will to recall myself back (from the cabin) to the conditions of the moment. I felt that I was appearing an irresolute commander to those people who were watching me more or less critically.

And, besides, there were the scares. On the second day out, for instance, coming off the deck in the afternoon (I had straw slippers on my bare feet) I stopped at the open pantry door and spoke to the steward. He was doing something there with his back to me. At the sound of my voice he nearly jumped out of his skin, as the saying is, and incidentally broke a cup.

"What on earth's the matter with you?" I asked, astonished.

He was extremely confused. "Beg your pardon, sir. I made sure you were in your cabin."

"You see I wasn't."

"No, sir. I could have sworn I had heard you moving in there not a moment ago. It's most extraordinary . . . very sorry, sir."

I passed on with an inward shudder. I was so identified with my secret double that I did not even mention the fact in those scanty, fearful whispers we exchanged. I suppose he had made some slight noise of some kind or other. It would have been miraculous if he hadn't at one time or another. And yet, haggard as he appeared, he looked always perfectly self-controlled, more than calm – almost invulnerable. On my suggestion he remained almost entirely in the bath-room, which, upon the whole, was the safest place. There could be really no shadow of an excuse for any one ever wanting to go in there, once the steward had done with it. It was a very tiny place. Sometimes he reclined on the floor, his legs bent, his head sustained on one elbow. At others I would find him on the camp-stool, sitting in his grey sleeping-suit and with his cropped dark hair like a patient, unmoved convict. At night I would smuggle him into my bed-place, and we would whisper together, with the regular footfalls of the officer of the watch passing and repassing over our heads. It was an infinitely miserable time. It was lucky that some tins of fine preserves were stowed in a locker in my stateroom; hard bread I could always get hold of; and so he lived on stewed chicken pâté de foie gras, asparagus, cooked oysters, sardines – on all sorts of abominable sham delicacies out of tins. My early morning coffee he always drank; and it was all I dared do for him in that respect.

Every day there was the horrible manœuvring to go through so that my room and then the bath-room should be done in the usual way. I came to hate the sight of the steward, to abhor the voice of that harmless man. I felt that it was he who would bring on the disaster of discovery. It hung like a sword over our heads.

The fourth day out, I think (we were then working down the east side of the Gulf of Siam, tack for tack, in light winds and smooth water) – the fourth day, I say, of this miserable juggling with the unavoidable, as we sat at our evening meal, that man, whose slightest movement I dreaded, after putting down the dishes ran up on deck busily. This could not be dangerous. Presently he came down again; and then it appeared that he had remembered a coat of mine which I had thrown over a rail to dry after having been wetted in a shower which had passed over the ship in the afternoon. Sitting stolidly at the head of the table I became terrified at the sight of the garment on his arm. Of course he made for my door. There was no time to lose.

"Steward," I thundered. My nerves were so shaken that I could not govern my voice and conceal my agitation. This was the sort of thing that made my terrifically whiskered mate tap his forehead with his forefinger. I had detected him using that gesture while talking on deck with a confidential air to the carpenter. It was too far to hear a word, but I had no doubt that this pantomime could only refer to the strange new captain.

"Yes, sir," the pale-faced steward turned resignedly to me. It was this maddening course of being shouted at, checked without rhyme or reason, arbitrarily chased out of my cabin, suddenly called into it, sent flying out of his pantry on incomprehensible errands, that accounted for the growing wretchedness of his expression.

"Where are you going with that coat?"

"To your room, sir."

"Is there another shower coming?"

"I'm sure I don't know, sir. Shall I go up again and see, sir?"

"No! never mind."

My object was attained, as of course my other self in there would have heard everything that passed. During this interlude my two officers never raised their eyes off their respective plates; but the lip of that confounded cub, the second mate, quivered visibly.

I expected the steward to hook my coat on and come out at once. He was very slow about it; but I dominated my nervousness sufficiently not to shout after him. Suddenly I became aware (it could be heard plainly enough) that the fellow for some reason or other was opening the door of the bath-room. It was the end. The place was literally not big enough to swing a cat in. My voice died in my throat and I went stony all over. I expected to hear a yell of surprise and terror, and made a movement, but had not the strength to get on my legs. Everything remained still. Had my second self taken the poor wretch by the throat? I don't know what I could have done next moment if I had not seen the steward come out of my room, close the door, and then stand quietly by the sideboard.

"Saved," I thought. "But, no! Lost! Gone! He was gone!"

I laid my knife and fork down and leaned back in my chair. My head swam. After a while, when sufficiently recovered to speak in a steady voice, I instructed my mate to put the ship round at eight o'clock himself.

"I won't come on deck," I went on. "I think I'll turn in, and unless the wind shifts I don't want to be disturbed before midnight. I feel a bit seedy."

"You did look middling bad a little while ago," the chief mate remarked without showing any great concern.

They both went out, and I stared at the steward clearing the table. There was nothing to be read on that wretched man's face. But why did he avoid my eyes, I asked myself. Then I thought I should like to hear the sound of his voice.

"Steward!"

"Sir!" Startled as usual.

"Where did you hang up that coat?"

"In the bath-room, sir." The usual anxious tone. "It's not quite dry yet, sir."

For some time longer I sat in the cuddy. Had my double vanished as he had come? But of his coming there was an explanation, whereas his disappearance would be inexplicable . . . I went slowly into my dark room, shut the door, lighted the lamp, and for a time dared not turn round. When at last I did I saw him standing bolt-upright in the narrow recessed part. It would not be true to say I had a shock, but an irresistible doubt of his bodily existence flitted through my mind. Can it be, I asked myself, that he is not visible to other eyes than mine? It was like being haunted. Motionless, with a grave face, he raised his hands slightly at me in a gesture which meant clearly, "Heavens! what a narrow escape!" Narrow indeed. I think I had come creeping quietly as near insanity as any man who has not actually gone over the border. That gesture restrained me, so to speak.

The mate with the terrific whiskers was now putting the ship on the other tack. In the moment of profound silence which follows upon the hands going to their stations I heard on the poop his raised voice: "Hard alee!" and the distant shout of the order repeated on the main-deck. The sails, in that light breeze, made but a faint fluttering noise. It ceased. The ship was coming round slowly; I held my breath in the renewed stillness of expectation; one wouldn't have thought that there was a single living soul on her decks. A sudden brisk shout, "Mainsail haul!" broke the spell, and in the noisy cries and rush overhead of the men running away with the main-brace we two, down in my cabin, came together in our usual position by the bed-place.

He did not wait for my question. "I heard him fumbling here and just managed to squat myself down in the bath," he whispered to me. "The fellow only opened the door and put his arm in to hang the coat up. All the same—"

"I never thought of that," I whispered back, even more appalled than before at the closeness of the shave, and marvelling at that something unyielding in his character which was carrying him through so finely. There was no agitation in his whisper. Whoever was being driven distracted, it was not he. He was sane. And the proof of his sanity was continued when he took up the whispering again.

"It would never do for me to come to life again."

It was something that a ghost might have said. But what he was alluding to was his old captain's reluctant admission of the theory of suicide. It would obviously serve his turn – if I had understood at all the view which seemed to govern the unalterable purpose of his action.

"You must maroon me as soon as ever you can get amongst these islands off the Cambodge shore," he went on.

"Maroon you! We are not living in a boy's adventure tale," I protested. His scornful whispering took me up.

"We aren't indeed! There's nothing of a boy's tale in this. But there's nothing else for it. I want no more. You don't suppose I am afraid of what can be done to me? Prison or gallows or whatever they may please. But you don't see me coming back to explain such things to an old fellow in a wig and twelve respectable tradesmen, do you? What can they know whether I am guilty or not – or of *what* I am guilty, either? That's my affair. What does the Bible say? 'Driven off the face of the earth.' Very well. I am off the face of the earth now. As I came at night so I shall go."

"Impossible!" I murmured. "You can't."

"Can't? . . . Not naked like a soul on the Day of Judgment. I shall freeze on to this sleeping-suit. The Last Day is not yet – and . . . you have understood thoroughly. Didn't you?"

I felt suddenly ashamed of myself. I may say truly that I understood – and my hesitation in letting that man swim away from my ship's side had been a mere sham sentiment, a sort of cowardice.

"It can't be done now till next night," I breathed out. "The ship is on the off-shore tack and the wind may fail us."

"As long as I know that you understand," he whispered. "But of course you do. It's a great satisfaction to have got somebody to understand. You seem to have been there on purpose." And in the same whisper, as if we two whenever we talked had to say things to each other which were not fit for the world to hear, he added, "It's very wonderful."

We remained side by side talking in our secret way – but sometimes silent or just exchanging a whispered word or two at long intervals. And as usual he stared through the port. A breath of wind came now and again into our faces. The ship might have been moored in dock, so gently and on an even keel she slipped through the water, that did not murmur even at our passage, shadowy and silent like a phantom sea.

At midnight I went on deck, and to my mate's great surprise put the ship round on the other tack. His terrible whiskers flitted round me in silent criticism. I certainly should not have done it if it had been only a question of getting out of that sleepy gulf as quickly as possible. I believe he told the second mate, who relieved him, that it was a great want of judgment. The other only yawned. That intolerable cub shuffled about so sleepily and lolled against the rails in such a slack, improper fashion that I came down on him sharply.

"Aren't you properly awake yet?"

"Yes, sir! I am awake."

"Well, then, be good enough to hold yourself as if you were. And keep a look-out. If there's any current we'll be closing with some islands before daylight."

The east side of the gulf is fringed with islands, some solitary, others in groups. On the blue background of the high coast they seem to float on silvery patches of calm water, arid and grey, or dark green and rounded like clumps of evergreen bushes, with the larger ones, a mile or two long, showing the outlines of ridges, ribs of grey rock under the dank mantle of matted leafage. Unknown to trade, to travel, almost to geography, the manner of life they harbour is an unsolved secret. There must be villages — settlements of fishermen at least — on the largest of them, and some communication with the world is probably kept up by native craft. But all that forenoon, as we headed for them, fanned along by the faintest of breezes, I saw no sign of man or canoe in the field of the telescope I kept on pointing at the scattered group.

At noon I gave no orders for a change of course, and the mate's whiskers became much concerned and seemed to be offering themselves unduly to my notice. At last I said:

"I am going to stand right in. Quite in — as far as I can take her."

The stare of extreme surprise imparted an air of ferocity also to his eyes, and he looked truly terrific for a moment.

"We're not doing well in the middle of the gulf," I continued, casually. "I am going to look for the land breezes to-night."

"Bless my soul! Do you mean, sir, in the dark amongst the lot of all them islands and reefs and shoals?"

"Well — if there are any regular land breezes at all on this coast one must get close inshore to find them, mustn't one?"

"Bless my soul!" he exclaimed again under his breath. All that afternoon he wore a dreamy, contemplative appearance which in him was a mark of perplexity. After dinner I went into my stateroom as if I meant to take some rest. There we two bent our dark heads over a half-unrolled chart lying on my bed.

"There," I said. "It's got to be Koh-ring. I've been looking at it ever since sunrise. It has got two hills and a low point. It must be inhabited. And on the coast opposite there is what looks like the mouth of a biggish river – with some town, no doubt, not far up. It's the best chance for you that I can see."

"Anything. Koh-ring let it be."

He looked thoughtfully at the chart as if surveying chances and distances from a lofty height – and following with his eyes his own figure wandering on the blank land of Cochin-China, and then passing off that piece of paper clean out of sight into uncharted regions. And it was as if the ship had two captains to plan her course for her. I had been so worried and restless running up and down that I had not had the patience to dress that day. I had remained in my sleeping-suit, with straw slippers and a soft floppy hat. The closeness of the heat in the gulf had been most oppressive, and the crew were used to see me wandering in that airy attire.

"She will clear the south point as she heads now," I whispered into his ear. "Goodness only knows when, though, but certainly after dark. I'll edge her in to half a mile, as far as I may be able to judge in the dark—"

"Be careful," he murmured, warningly – and I realised suddenly that all my future, the only future for which I was fit, would perhaps go irretrievably to pieces in any mishap to my first command.

I could not stop a moment longer in the room. I motioned him to get out of sight and made my way on the poop. That unplayful cub had the watch. I walked up and down for a while thinking things out, then beckoned him over.

"Send a couple of hands to open the two quarter-deck ports," I said, mildly.

He actually had the impudence, or else so forgot himself in his wonder at such an incomprehensible order, as to repeat:

"Open the quarter-deck ports! What for, sir?"

"The only reason you need concern yourself about is because I tell you to do so. Have them opened wide and fastened properly."

He reddened and went off, but I believe made some jeering remark to the carpenter as to the sensible practice of ventilating a ship's quarter-deck. I know he popped into the mate's cabin to impart the fact to him because the whiskers came on deck, as it were by chance, and stole glances at me from below – for signs of lunacy or drunkenness, I suppose.

A little before supper, feeling more restless than ever, I rejoined, for a moment, my second self. And to find him sitting so quietly was surprising, like something against nature, inhuman.

I developed my plan in a hurried whisper.

"I shall stand in as close as I dare and then put her round. I will presently find means to smuggle you out of here into the sail-locker, which communicates with the lobby. But there is an opening, a sort of square for hauling the sails out, which gives straight on the quarter-deck and which is never closed in fine weather, so as to give air to the sails. When the ship's way is deadened in stays and all the hands are aft at the main-braces you will have a clear road to slip out and get overboard through the open quarter-deck port. I've had them both fastened up. Use a rope's end to lower yourself into the water so as to avoid a splash – you know. It could be heard and cause some beastly complication."

He kept silent for a while, then whispered, "I understand."

"I won't be there to see you go," I began with an effort. "The rest . . . I only hope I have understood, too."

"You have. From first to last" – and for the first time there seemed to be a faltering, something strained in his whisper. He caught hold of my arm, but the ringing of the supper bell made me start. He didn't, though; he only released his grip.

After supper I didn't come below again till well past eight o'clock. The faint, steady breeze was loaded with dew; and the wet, darkened sails held all there was of propelling power in it. The night, clear and starry, sparkled darkly, and the opaque, lightless patches shifting slowly against the low stars were the drifting islets. On the port bow there was a big one more distant and shadowily imposing by the great space of sky it eclipsed.

On opening the door I had a back view of my very own self looking at a chart. He had come out of the recess and was standing near the table.

"Quite dark enough," I whispered.

He stepped back and leaned against my bed with a level, quiet glance. I sat on the couch. We had nothing to say to each other.

Over our heads the officer of the watch moved here and there. Then I heard him move quickly. I knew what that meant. He was making for the companion; and presently his voice was outside my door.

"We are drawing in pretty fast, sir. Land looks rather close."

"Very well," I answered. "I am coming on deck directly."

I waited till he was gone out of the cuddy, then rose. My double moved too. The time had come to exchange our last whispers, for neither of us was ever to hear each other's natural voice.

"Look here!" I opened a drawer and took out three sovereigns. "Take this anyhow. I've got six and I'd give you the lot, only I must keep a little money to buy some fruit and vegetables for the crew from native boats as we go through Sunda Straits."

He shook his head.

"Take it," I urged him, whispering desperately. "No one can tell what—"

He smiled and slapped meaningly the only pocket of the sleeping jacket. It was not safe, certainly. But I produced a large old silk handkerchief of mine, and tying the three pieces of gold in a corner, pressed it on him. He was touched, I suppose, because he took it at last and tied it quickly round his waist under the jacket, on his bare skin.

Our eyes met; several seconds elapsed, till, our glances still mingled, I extended my hand and turned the lamp out. Then I passed through the cuddy, leaving the door of my room wide open . . . "Steward!"

He was still lingering in the pantry in the greatness of his zeal, giving a rub-up to a plated cruet stand the last thing before going to bed. Being careful not to wake up the mate, whose room was opposite, I spoke in an undertone.

He looked round anxiously. "Sir!"

"Can you get me a little hot water from the galley?"

"I am afraid, sir, the galley fire's been out for some time now."

"Go and see."

He flew up the stairs.

"Now," I whispered, loudly, into the saloon – too loudly, perhaps, but I was afraid I couldn't make a sound. He was by my side in an instant – the double captain slipped past the stairs – through a tiny dark passage . . . a sliding door. We were in the sail-locker, scrambling on our knees over the sails. A sudden thought struck me. I saw myself wandering barefooted, bareheaded, the sun beating on my dark poll. I snatched off my floppy hat and tried hurriedly in the dark to ram it on my other self. He dodged and fended off silently. I wonder what he thought had come to me before he understood and suddenly desisted. Our hands met gropingly, lingered united in a steady, motionless clasp for a second . . . No word was breathed by either of us when they separated.

I was standing quietly by the pantry door when the steward returned.

"Sorry, sir. Kettle barely warm. Shall I light the spirit-lamp?"

"Never mind."

I came out on deck slowly. It was now a matter of conscience to shave the land as close as possible – for now he must go overboard whenever the ship was put in stays. Must! There could be no going back for him. After a moment I walked over to leeward and my heart flew into my mouth at the nearness of the land on the bow. Under any other circumstances I would not have held on a minute longer. The second mate had followed me anxiously.

I looked on till I felt I could command my voice.

"She will weather," I said then in a quiet tone.

"Are you going to try that, sir?" he stammered out incredulously.

I took no notice of him and raised my tone just enough to be heard by the helmsman.

"Keep her good full."

"Good full, sir."

The wind fanned my cheek, the sails slept, the world was silent. The strain of watching the dark loom of the land grow bigger and denser was too much for me. I had shut my eyes – because the ship must go closer. She must! The stillness was intolerable. Were we standing still?

When I opened my eyes the second view started my heart with a thump. The black southern hill of Koh-ring seemed to hang right over the ship like a towering fragment of the everlasting night. On that enormous mass of blackness there was not a gleam to be seen, not a sound to be heard. It was gliding irresistibly towards us and yet seemed already within reach of the hand. I saw the vague figures of the watch grouped in the waist, gazing in awed silence.

"Are you going on, sir?" inquired an unsteady voice at my elbow.

I ignored it. I had to go on.

"Keep her full. Don't check her way. That won't do now," I said, warningly.

"I can't see the sails very well," the helmsman answered me, in strange, quavering tones.

Was she close enough? Already she was, I won't say in the shadow of the land, but in the very blackness of it, already swallowed up as it were, gone too close to be recalled, gone from me altogether.

"Give the mate a call," I said to the young man who stood at my elbow as still as death. "And turn all hands up."

My tone had a borrowed loudness reverberated from the height of the land. several voices cried out together: "We are all on deck, sir."

Then stillness again, with the great shadow gliding closer, towering higher, without a light, without a sound. Such a hush had fallen on the ship that she might have been a bark of the dead floating in slowly under the very gate of Erebus.

"My God! Where are we?"

It was the mate moaning at my elbow. He was thunderstruck, and as it were deprived of the moral support of his whiskers. He clapped his hands and absolutely cried out, "Lost!"

"Be quiet," I said, sternly.

He lowered his tone, but I saw the shadowy gesture of his despair. "What are we doing here?"

"Looking for the land wind."

He made as if to tear his hair, and addressed me recklessly.

"She will never get out. You have done it, sir. I knew it'd end in something like this. She will never weather, and you are too close now to stay. She'll drift ashore before she's round. O my God!"

I caught his arm as he was raising it to batter his poor devoted head, and shook it violently.

"She's ashore already," he wailed, trying to tear himself away.

"Is she? . . . Keep good full there!"

"Good full, sir," cried the helmsman in a frightened, thin, childlike voice.

I hadn't let go of the mate's arm and went on shaking it.

"Ready about, do you hear? You go forward" – shake – "and stop there" – shake – "and hold your noise" – shake – "and see these head-sheets properly overhauled" – shake, shake – shake.

And all the time I dared not look towards the land lest my heart should fail me. I released my grip at last and he ran forward as if fleeing for dear life.

I wondered what my double there in the sail-locker thought of this commotion. He was able to hear everything – and perhaps he was able to understand why, on my conscience, it had to be thus close – no less. My first order "Hard alee!" re-echoed ominously under the towering shadow of Koh-ring as if I had shouted in a mountain gorge. And then I watched the land intently. In that smooth water and light wind it was impossible to feel the ship coming-to. No! I could not feel her. And my second self was making now ready to slip out and lower himself overboard. Perhaps he was gone already . . . ?

The great black mass brooding over our very mastheads began to pivot away from the ship's side silently. And now I forgot the secret stranger ready to depart, and remember only that I was a total stranger to the ship. I did not know her. Would she do it? How was she to be handled?

I swung the mainyard and waited helplessly. She was perhaps stopped, and her very fate hung in the balance, with the black mass of Koh-ring like the gate of the everlasting night towering over her taffrail. What would she do now? Had she way on her yet? I stepped to the side swiftly, and on the shadowy water I could see nothing except a faint phosphorescent flash revealing the glassy smoothness of the sleeping surface. It was impossible to tell – and I had not learned yet the feel of my ship. Was she moving? What I needed was something easily seen, a piece of paper, which I could throw overboard and watch. I had nothing on me. To run down for it I didn't dare. There was no time. All at once my strained, yearning stare distinguished a white object floating within a yard of the ship's side. White on the black water. A phosphorescent flash passed under it. What was that thing? . . . I recognised my own floppy hat. It must have fallen off his head . . . and he didn't bother. Now I had what I wanted – the saving mark for my eyes. But I hardly thought of my other self, now gone from the ship, to be hidden for ever from all friendly faces, to be a fugitive and a vagabond on the earth, with no brand of the curse on his sane forehead to stay a slaying hand . . . too proud to explain.

And I watched the hat – the expression of my sudden pity for his mere flesh. It had been meant to save his homeless head from the dangers of the sun. And now – behold – it was saving the ship, by serving me for a mark to help out the ignorance of my strangeness. Ha! it was drifting forward, warning me just in time that the ship had gathered sternway.

"Shift the helm," I said in a low voice to the seaman standing still like a statue.

The man's eyes glistened wildly in the binnacle light as he jumped round to the other side and spun round the wheel.

I walked to the break of the poop. On the overshadowed deck all hands stood by the forebraces waiting for my order. The stars ahead seemed to be gliding from right to left. And all was so still in the world that I heard the quiet remark, "She's round," passed in a tone of intense relief between two seamen.

"Let go and haul."

The foreyards ran round with a great noise, amidst cheery cries. And now the frightful whiskers made themselves heard giving various orders. Already the ship was drawing ahead. And I was alone with her. Nothing! no one in the world should stand now between us, throwing a shadow on the way of silent knowledge and mute affection, the perfect communion of a seaman with his first command.

Walking to the taffrail, I was in time to make out, on the very edge of a darkness thrown by a towering black mass like the very gateway of Erebus – yes, I was in time to catch an evanescent glimpse of my white hat left behind to mark the spot where the secret sharer of my cabin and of my thoughts, as though he were my second self, had lowered himself into the water to take his punishment: a free man, a proud swimmer striking out for a new destiny.

1908/1910